BABE'S BIBLE
LOVE LETTER

KAREN JONES

BABE'S BIBLE
The Women of The Book

DARTON · LONGMAN + TODD

Dedicated to Michael Wenham

First published in 2014 by
Darton, Longman and Todd Ltd
1 Spencer Court
140 – 142 Wandsworth High Street
London SW18 4JJ

ISBN: 978-0-232-53062-9

A catalogue record for this book is available from the British Library.

Designed and produced by Judy Linard
Printed and bound in Great Britain by Bell & Bain, Glasgow

CONTENTS

Also by Karen Jones

Gorgeous Grace: Babe's Bible I
Sister Acts: Babe's Bible II

Karen Jones is planning to lead a trip to Israel and Turkey in 2015 with McCabe Pilgrimages, following in the footsteps of the *Babe's Bible* trilogy.

Visit www.kejones.com or the *Babe's Bible* pages on www.darton-longman-todd.co.uk for more information.

ACKNOWLEDGEMENTS

Thank you Si for patiently helping me when my computer went crazy.

Thank you Sam for not complaining when there was no food in the house or when I asked you to do chores you don't normally do.

Thank you Keith and Mary Cotteral – you know why.

Thank you Barbara Hughes for reading and encouraging.

Thank you Sally Wheeler for mentoring me and praying with me during this time of writing.

Thank you Lin Button for your acceptance and love, your wise counsel and authoritative prayers for me.

1. BREATHTAKING

Ephesians 1:1–14

*When you believed, you were marked in him with a seal,
the promised Holy Spirit, who is a deposit
guaranteeing our inheritance.*

Mark's eyes followed Charmaine's slender leg as it wound itself around the stainless steel pole. Her glittering thong that nestled between perfectly sculpted cheeks almost disappeared into her flesh as she stretched her leg above her head, parallel with the pole. She caught his eye through the heat-haze of lust, but his gaze quickly slid to the small triangle of cloth between her legs, as his burning loins dictated to him, pulsing in time with the music.

As her act ended she bent to pick up a few stray notes that had fallen from the nest of her thong, her young breasts swinging freely and her long blonde hair tumbling forward. Mark knew exactly how he wanted to have her this time. He rose and followed her purposefully, as she swayed down the narrow catwalk to the stage curtain. The bouncer acknowledged him with a grunt and a nod as he made his way past him into the bowels of the club.

Sometime later he emerged from the neon-lit entrance onto the street, shrugging himself into his coat. Her shift would finish at 3.00 a.m. He couldn't wait for her tonight, he had a big presentation at work on Monday and needed the weekend to prepare for it, plus Josh was coming over for lunch to watch the game. It would take half an hour to get back to the flat by tube and he needed his sleep. Despite his reservations at leaving her to get a taxi home, he squared his shoulders against the cold and started walking towards the tube station. She was a survivor … she'd be okay.

He watched a group of Street Pastors on the other side of the road helping two drunken women up off the pavement. As he kept walking, he inwardly sneered at the stupidity of all concerned in the struggling cluster of humanity. *Why bother with drunken slags when they'll be out here again next weekend doing the same thing? Touchy-feely-heal-me-crap,* he smirked derisively, returning to thoughts of the pleasure he'd just enjoyed and reminding himself to put a Red Bull on the bedside cabinet for when she got home.

❀ ❀ ❀

Charmaine waited for her taxi outside the club. It was 3.15 a.m. A group of men stumbled out and stood near her, fumbling with their jackets. One of them sidled over, asking her for a light.

'I don't smoke,' she said, not taking her eyes off her phone screen and pressing the call button for the taxi again.

'You all alone?' he asked leaning in towards her.

She pulled away from him as the taxi service answered her call. She gave him a look of loathing, swearing at him and then spoke into the receiver, 'Where's my taxi?' she asked, keeping her voice as level as possible.

He reached out and grabbed her wrist. She instantly reacted twisting 360 degrees, breaking his grip. The sudden movement drew the other men's attention. As they crowded in behind him he reached for her again, but this time she was ready. She held a can of hairspray up from her bag, pointing it in his face.

'Look,' she said, 'I don't want to hurt you, you pathetic perv.'

Bawdy laughter oozed from them like a slow fart, 'But I'd like to hurt you,' he grinned and then spat.

Charmaine pressed the nozzle of the hairspray as he lunged for her. He let out a roar of pain.

'Is everything okay here?' a Street Pastor shouted as he and his team approached the group outside the gentlemen's club.

Charmaine's admirer had her up against the wall, his full weight pressed against her and one hand round her throat, while he furiously rubbed his eyes with the other. She took advantage of the distraction and pulled out of his grasp, gasping for breath, coughing, spewing obscenities at him and rubbing her neck.

A taxi pulled up to the kerb and Charmaine ran to it. Eyes streaming, the man lunged after her and caught her coat as she opened the passenger door. She struggled out of it, got in and slammed the door shut, leaving him with the fake fur dangling limply in his hands. She was laughing and holding up her middle finger at the window as the taxi pulled away into the night.

'That's that then lads. Best be getting home now, don't you think?' the leader of the Street Pastors team said amiably, only to be met with a barrage of verbal abuse.'Yeah, yeah …', he said,'go on home … it's cold out here … go sleep it off.'

※　　※　　※

Like a hummingbird's wings, Zack's thumbs moved across the keyboard of his Nintendo DS. Grace eyed the wobbly character apparently incapable of driving the car he was in. As he lurched over hilly graphics, capturing stars along his way, she couldn't help cringing every time he was thrown out of the car and crumpled in a heap on the primary coloured, digital background. Feeling irritated she got up and went to the magazine rack, pulling out a glossy. She idly began flipping through it as they waited for Zack's name to be called.

She came to an article entitled 'Your man's new top fantasy' and began reading, wondering whether it would give her insight into Peter. She felt even more irritated as she skipped down to the advice of the writer. Grace couldn't read any more. She looked at the back of Zack's bowed head, engrossed in his game. *How much do they pay these people to write such drivel?*

Closing the magazine she let it slide off her lap onto the seat beside her. Old memories scuttled across her mind of declining requests from clients for their darkest fantasies, often with some force. At least she had been allowed to decide what she would and wouldn't do. She now knew that trafficked women had no such privilege. She shivered involuntarily and tensed her pelvic floor muscles.

'Zack Hutchinson,' the receptionist called.

'Yes,' Grace replied and nudged Zack out of his digital world.

They both made their way out of the waiting room and down a corridor.

'Just a check-up, is it Zack?'

'Yes,' he replied as he settled himself in the dentist's chair and stared up into the light.

※　※　※

'I'll see you later … you happy to walk home after your voice lesson?'

'Yep,' Zack leaned over and kissed her on the cheek, smelling of the dentists, before getting out of the car. Grace wondered how much longer she could enjoy such a precious pleasure.

She drove the short distance back home, and then popped round to My Sister's House office to check on things with Melanie who was in charge that day.

After they'd made a cup of coffee and touched base on a few admin issues, the conversation turned to what she'd read in the magazine article at the dentists.

'Is that true?' she asked Melanie.

'Yeah … that's what Yusuf and Sony were trying to do that night you found me … that's why it got so violent … I fought them, even though I knew I didn't stand a chance … I'd have rather died fighting than give into that.'

Grace was silent.

'Most of my friends at uni tried everything,' Melanie continued, 'literally no holes barred, excuse the pun. That's what you do when you're head's full of porn, I guess,' she sighed. 'We're the digital generation. We've seen porn since we were young. I think the first time I saw it was on someone's phone sitting in the back of the school bus.'

Grace looked steadily at Melanie as she spoke. She looked down at her nails, then back at Melanie, changing the subject, 'How are the new girls?'

'One's only ten. She's from Ireland. Trafficked by her family. She's having an op to fix things tomorrow,' she gestured vaguely to her nether regions.

Grace nodded and grimaced, 'How's it going tracking the family down?'

'Oh, we already have. They're known by the Garda over there. When she's recovered from her op, we'll record her testimony if she'll let us. She's terrified of them. I think it'll take some time before she'll feel safe enough to talk.'

'Yep,' Grace held her breath and then let out a sigh. 'But they will be prosecuted in the end,' she paused, savouring the thought. 'How are you doing?'

'I'm okay – excited about the number of halfway houses we've got now. Rose is so great to work with and Val is fantastic at all the admin. Mum and me share the psychotherapy sessions pretty well …'

'But how are you ... you personally?'

'Oh,' Melanie laughed shyly, 'I'm not bad. I had a blip there recently with food. I think it was because of stuff that came up for me out of hearing one of the girls' stories. I've been working on it with my supervisor.'

'That's good,' Grace smiled encouragingly. 'Have you got a social life outside of here?' she pressed gently.

Melanie looked down at her computer keyboard and wiped an invisible speck of dust away, 'No ... not really ... me and Rose go to the cinema together some times. I'm not really interested in anything else at the minute.'

Grace studied her young face and decided not to push any further. 'Well, you sound like me! Peter's taking me out for our wedding anniversary tonight and I've realised I haven't got anything nice to wear that isn't at least ten years old. I'm going shopping now ... you don't fancy coming with me, do you? I could do with a second opinion.'

Melanie looked at Grace, trying to gauge whether the offer was genuine or out of pity.

'Honestly, Mel, I feel nervous about going clothes shopping. It's been so long – I'm really out of touch. Come with me, please?'

'Okay,' the 24-year-old smiled. 'I'll ring Gwen and see if she can cover me here.'

✳ ✳ ✳

Grace wore the cream linen dress and pale blue jacket Melanie had helped her choose that evening. She sat opposite Peter in a little French restaurant that had recently opened near their home. A candle glowed between them on the table. She reached over, squeezing his hand and said, 'Happy twentieth.' She smiled as with her other hand she pushed a small, black, velvet box across to him.

He looked surprised, his skin crinkling round his eyes with an affectionate smile. He pushed the lid up with his thumb to reveal a pair of gold cuff-links. He took one out and looked more closely at it. 'What does it say?' he asked, reaching for his glasses in his breast pocket.

Grace didn't reply. She watched him as she waited for him to read it for himself.

'Eph 1:13? What's that?' he looked up at her.

'Um ... let me see,' she smiled. 'Oh yes ... "You were marked in him with a seal, the promised Holy Spirit",' she quoted.

He smiled again and nodded, 'I'll memorise that.' He reached across and took hold of her hand, 'I love them ... thank you.'

'Can't believe we've been married this long! It doesn't feel like it, does it?' she asked caressing his palm with her thumb.

'No – it's gone far too quickly. I've loved every minute of it ... well except when you brought that prostitute home to stay,' he smiled ruefully remembering how angry he'd been with her.

Grace's expression became more serious as she thought of Anja ... what was it ... nearly five years ago? Old sadness rose within her, remembering how she had not been able to stop her friend from taking her own life.

Peter brought something out of his pocket. He turned his hand over, opening it as he did, revealing a ring with a red ribbon tied to it and a note attached.

Her smile returned slowly as she picked it up between finger and thumb. It was an eternity ring, a complete circle of diamonds. 'Oh Peter!' she gasped, reading the note, *Forever yours, all my love Peter.* 'You never said anything!'

Peter chuckled, enjoying the moment immensely, 'I know.'

She took off her engagement ring and slipped the eternity ring down her long, slender finger, admiring the stones as they sparkled in the candlelight. She put her other ring back on, enjoying them together at length. 'It's breathtaking,' she looked up, tucking thoughts of Anja away carefully.

'I know,' he laughed.

※   ※   ※

Despite Grace's efforts to hide it, Chloe saw it almost immediately. 'Wow! That is some collection of rocks,' she held Grace's hand up for good-natured inspection in the My Sister's House office. Rose, Gwen, Val, Mo and

Melanie crowded round to have a look. They'd gathered to have a meeting to discuss the presentation to clergy that they were planning for this year's Diocesan conference.

Grace felt embarrassed. 'I had no idea he was going to give it to me,' she said.

'What is it? Twenty?' Chloe looked up at Grace, who nodded. 'About time.' They shared a smile that was laced with sadness for the anniversaries that had not been for Chloe.

'What didya get him?' Mo asked, looking inquisitive.

'A pair of engraved cufflinks,' Grace smiled.

'Aw ... hope me and Sean still love each other in fifteen years' time like you two do,' Mo grinned.

'Love is an act of your will,' Gwen said emphatically.

'A daily choice,' Val added sagely, nodding her head.

'Yeah, yeah – I know all that – but romance, seduction, chemistry – don't that fade with time and familiarity?' Mo asked, watching Grace for any hint that it might be true.

'It comes and goes ... why?'

'I was just asking,' Mo's nonchalance wasn't fooling anyone.

'Love letters are good,' Val looked wistful, her plump cheeks turning slightly rosier than usual.

'If I wrote a love letter I'd 'ave him rollin' round the floor – an' not in a good way. I can't spell to save me life!' Mo laughed.

'What about love texts?' Melanie asked.

'Mmmmm,' Mo rocked her head from side to side ambivalently.

'I could write love letters for you,' Gwen offered. Everyone looked slightly surprised. 'What?' she challenged them. 'I read!' Her old-lady-neck wobbled in veined indignation.

'*Fifty Shades of Grey*?' Mo raised a knowing eyebrow.

'I have actually,' Gwen chuckled drily. 'I could do much better than that, my dear,' she shook her head disdainfully.

'Well ... you may 'ave got yourself a job, Gwen,' Mo sucked air through the gap in her front teeth, clicking her tongue with respect.

'Right girls, can we get back to the matter at hand. I know we've done two of these before, but we really need to be tight on this presentation. The Archbishop is going to be there.'

'Oooh!' Mo rolled her eyes sarcastically.

'If he gets the vision of what we're doing and proposing, he has the power to mobilise the national Church,' Grace quelled Mo's flippancy with a hard stare. 'Shall we start with you Val? Applying to trusts, putting together bids for charitable status and government funding ... Then you, Mo, on working with social services, case work and police connections?'

Mo nodded contritely.

※　※　※

Marie sat by James's bed, the Tuesday afternoon sunshine slanting through the dusty venetian blinds of his care home, making shadow-lines across his shrunken, shrouded frame. She chatted to him about their children's latest achievements, like she'd done every week of every month of every year since that horrendous day he'd left her and gone into another world.

Not many people understood why she kept doing it, but she was a woman of means, so as long as she was paying, the feeding tube stayed in and carers turned, changed and bathed him, massaged and manipulated his limbs daily. After the first year in hospital, the doctors had diagnosed him as being in a persistent vegetative state. Marie had agreed with their desire to release him but did not want to go to court for a decision to remove the feeding tube. That was when she'd found Crest House.

She wasn't even sure why she kept going or how much longer she could go on, but something compelled her. Maybe it was just that she couldn't let go? Or was too scared to admit that he'd gone? Maybe she liked having him here all safe and tidy ... not able to get himself into trouble? Here he was under control ... a vegetable ... not the crazy, impulsive, risk-taking, flawed man she'd loved and prayed for all those years.

She'd run out of trivia and couldn't help it as she began to speak her heart. 'I wish you'd come back ... I'm scared that the children are forgetting you ... the real you ... please James, can you hear me?' she whispered, allowing herself a moment of desperation. 'I'm scared I'm forgetting you ... Sometimes I really think you can hear me, but you can't be bothered to respond,' she touched his hand with a finger.

Why am I doing this to myself? I'm going to get emotional....

'It's so hard – this having you and not having you. It's like purgatory,' she was silent for a while watching his ribcage rise and fall rhythmically under the thin hospital blanket. 'I know my anxiety levels have come down ... the trauma of it all has eased ... I feel like I've come back to myself in the last year or so ... I know you'd laugh at this,' she smiled, 'but I've even been thinking about sex again ... a lot actually ... sex with you ... with anyone really,' she laughed at herself. 'Ironic isn't it? Now I really want it and you can't give it.'

She felt a muscle move under her finger. She dismissed it as a figment of her imagination. 'Anyway,' she continued, 'where was I?'

There it was again. She pressed her whole hand onto his hand. This time the muscle moved insistently.

'James? Can you hear me? If you can, do it again.'

He did.

'Do it again.'

He did.

'You can hear me?' she exploded. 'You can hear me!' she began shouting and pressing the call button she'd never had to use before.

※ ※ ※

Mark felt pleased with how his presentation had gone on Monday. He'd been basking in the glow of it all day. He looked at his phone, then back at his computer screen. *Just finish this analysis, then* ... he picked his phone up again and started texting, *See you in the Crown in an hour x.*

He glanced up to see his manager's secretary walking towards him. A rush of pride swelled his chest. His manager had a crazy schedule. It was rare for him to take time to send his secretary to congratulate anyone on a performance.

'Could you come into the office? Brian wants to see you now,' she smiled nervously. Mark couldn't tell if she was just a timid person or whether she was in awe of him.

'Sure,' he grinned magnanimously at her, pushing himself energetically out of his chair. He followed her into Brian's office. She closed the door behind her.

'Hi Mark ... come in ... come in ... have a seat,' Brian finished typing, only tearing his eyes from his computer screen as he finished speaking. Mark sat down, straightening his tie and folding his hands in his lap.

'Congratulations on yesterday,' Brian's serious face showed no emotion.

'Thank you,' Mark smiled.

'You're an excellent communicator. We've been lucky to have you,' he paused, then cleared his throat, looking straight at Mark.

'Thank you,' Mark said again. *We've been lucky to have you,* he thought as feelings of uncertainty began clambering over his nervous system like a spider.

'As you know the company is changing,' Brian kept solid eye contact.

'Yes,' Mark replied, his feelings turning to hope for that longed for, illusive promotion. He held his breath.

'The long term effects of the recession have meant that we have to cut jobs, even now ... and I'm afraid yours is one of them.' He watched to see if what he'd said had registered. Mark's face was blank. 'I'm sad to say that I have to let you go, Mark.'

'What?' Mark felt like he'd been winded.

'I'm afraid it's bad news for us ... hopefully our loss will be another's gain,' he tried to smile, but it looked more like a grimace.

'Bad news for you?' Mark's face contorted in disbelief.

'And for you, obviously,' Brian hurriedly added.

There followed a long interminable silence. His thoughts flew in a chaotic cyclone, like insects trying to escape the spiders' web.

Brian eventually placed his hands firmly on his desk and stood up. 'I hope you won't make this any more difficult for me than it already is, Mark. You know how this works. I need to escort you from the building now, so if you'll come with me,' he gestured to the door.

In a daze Mark rose, reaching the door as Brian turned the handle. 'You're a good man, Mark. If it's any consolation, I really didn't want to do this,' he placed his other hand on Mark's shoulder and squeezed.

'My things?' Mark said half-heartedly, knowing it was futile to ask, having seen it so many times before.

'My secretary will bring them down,' Brian said as he shepherded him through his secretary's office and out into the main corridor, which led to the foyer of the building's tenth floor. Mark didn't look at the secretary. He couldn't bear to see her pity.

As they rode the lift down, despair and rage vied for dominance within his aching chest. Neither spoke. Brian walked out of the building with him into the car park, giving the doorman a look loaded with meaning as he passed. He held his hand out to Mark, 'No hard feelings, Mark? I wish you all the best.'

Mark stared at the outstretched fleshy palm. He couldn't bring himself to respond.

'You'll get three months statutory severance pay, in line with your contract. That should give you some time at least to find another position in keeping with your skills and experience,' he cleared his throat again, his hand redundantly dropping to his side. 'On behalf of the company I'd like to thank you for all you've done.'

Mark hoped his eyes were boring holes into Brian's soul.

'If you'll be kind enough to wait here, the door man will ensure you get your personal belongings.' He made another attempt at a smile and then hurriedly retreated back into the building through the sliding glass doors that Mark knew would not open for him if he tried to follow.

❋   ❋   ❋

Marie and the children all cried when James's eyes opened for the first time in five years. He looked at them slowly one by one. He didn't speak, but tears trickled down his sunken cheeks and soaked his pillow. His right hand, the one Marie had felt move for the first time, was the only part of his body, other than his eyes, that seemed to be back in action.

Each one held it in turn and exclaimed in delight when they felt the faint movement of muscle as he responded to their questions with one flicker for no, and two for yes.

Yes, he'd been able to hear them for a long time. It was hard for Marie not knowing how long, but she felt euphoric that her visits had not been in vain. No, he wasn't in any pain. Yes, he was tired now. Yes, he wanted them to come tomorrow. They each kissed him goodbye.

Marie brought Grace and Trevor the next morning. Grace approached his bedside with trepidation. Would he remember? She prayed that God in his mercy would have wiped the memory of their last conversation from his brain.

'James – I've brought Trevor and Grace to see you,' Marie kissed him, speaking quietly into his ear.

Eventually James's eyes fluttered open. It took a while for him to focus on them, but when he did, Grace somehow knew that he had not forgotten.

'It's so good to see you again, James,' Trevor was saying.

'Hello, James,' Grace said quietly. 'Welcome back.'

He kept blinking tears away. Marie reached for a box of tissues and wiped his cheeks again and again.

'We won't stay,' Grace said, feeling hugely uncomfortable.

'No,' said Trevor. 'We'll come back soon ... we're so glad you're back James ... don't want to tire you too much.'

Grace hugged Marie, making her excuses and a quick escape. Once she was in her car she slumped back into the seat, exhausted. *Why couldn't you have taken those memories? Why? It wouldn't have been that hard for you, surely? ... Sorry ... thank you for the children getting their father back and for Marie getting her husband back ... sorry . . ..*

She texted Peter: *Just visited James Martin with Marie. Eyes open, crying, not speaking. Think his memory is intact.*

Peter phoned her immediately, 'Are you okay, babe?' he asked, ropes of concern took the strain in the sail of his voice.

'Yeah ... just feeling drained. It's so shocking after all this time in a coma. I'd really written him off.'

'I think we all had – except Marie of course.'

'He remembers ... I could see it in his eyes. Oh, Peter ... I don't want to have to talk about it with him. I don't know what to do.'

'Do you think he'll get his speech back?'

'Who knows. What time are you home tonight?' she asked, checking her watch pensively.

'I'll get away as soon as I can. Are you in tonight?'

'Yes. I'd set it aside for sermon prep.'

❊   ❊   ❊

When she got home she went to her desk, her half-written sermon still on the computer screen. It was the first in a series on Ephesians. She'd felt it was right to depart from the lectionary for a season: St Stephen's had hit a ceiling in terms of spiritual and numerical growth and she was aware that issues were bubbling beneath the surface that could potentially cause disunity and wanted to have a basis from which to address them.

Fear's voice had begun to be heard first among the old St Stephen's members over the possibility of losing their Anglo-Catholic heritage because of the influx of new converts fresh from the Alpha course. Then others, who had joined St Stephen's from mainly evangelical charismatic backgrounds, had begun making noises about issues of sexuality. There had been a meeting of the PCC where the agenda had been hijacked and a heated debate ensued. Grace was hard pressed to bring the meeting to order, managing to end with a rather ragged grace.

St Stephen's had grown to around the two-hundred mark. Many young families had joined them from the church school, through Grace's persistent involvement in assemblies, school fetes and working as one of the governors. She always carried Alpha invitations with her and as people were introduced to Christianity through the non-threatening medium of the course, many began attending Sunday services. She also always carried her diary with her, noting significant dates and events in the lives of those she met. Daily she prayed that God would give her His heart for the people in her parish, and it seemed her prayer was answered as more and more were drawn to her.

Grace had finally been able to convince the Diocese a year ago that they needed a children's worker, and had been able to get the ball rolling, advertising the job. The interviews had been held a couple of weeks ago. She had also asked for a curate.

Although these were all problems of a thriving, rather than a dwindling church, Grace was aware of the strain she had been under for some time. It underlay the tension she now felt over James Martin's recovery.

Reading through what she'd written calmed her to some degree. She went and made a cup of coffee and then returned to it feeling more in control.

She focused on reading the first fourteen verses of Ephesians again, shedding anxiety like layers of clothing. Each of St Paul's ideas warmed her. She scrutinised them, capturing momentary flashes of understanding.

'He chose us' ... *Didn't I choose him?*

'Before creation' ... *Outside of time?*

'*To be holy*' ... *Even James Martin?*

'*In love he adopted us*' ... *In love ... in love ... in love ...* She looked up at her Holman Hunt print, then she couldn't help looking down at her eternity ring, enjoying its flashes of fire and finally back at the text.

'*The mystery of his will*' ... *Why me? Why any of us?*

The shallow frown lines between her eyebrows that had developed over recent years and would not disappear no matter what product she applied to them, deepened as she struggled to get to grips with the text.

'*To bring all things together under one head.*' She mulled the thought over ... *All people who call on Your name ... whatever culture they have or tradition they treasure or things they've done ... Men, women, gentile, Jew ... gay, straight, confused ... sex worker, alcoholic, drug addict ... Anglo-Catholic, Pentecostal ... rich, poor ... James ... Mark ... Melanie ... Chloe ... me ... any who put their trust in Jesus.*

She returned to read, '*With a seal, the promised Holy Spirit, a deposit guaranteeing our inheritance.*' She thought of Peter and the cufflinks she'd given him. A sudden wave of thankfulness for him surged up and she prayed for a few moments in tongues.

'*To the praise of his glory*', she read and then continued in prayer.

It's like a love letter ... she thought back to Gwen's offer of writing for Mo ... *That's what people need. They need to be swept up, to catch their breath at the awesomeness of the love of God; to be consumed with a reciprocal love for Him and for each other.*

She opened her eyes and looked at her ring again, then lifted her mug to her lips and sipped her coffee. It occurred to her that she liked the smell of it more than the taste and fleetingly wondered what she would drink, if not coffee?

She pulled her mind back to task: *Paul under house arrest ... getting old ... future prospects grim ... writing to all those people who had come to know the love of God through him ... saints, he calls them ... holy ones ... set apart ... sending them a love letter ... his heart full of eternity, his body in chains ... a bit like James in his paralysed body ... Unable to go where he wished, unable to see them, uncertain of his future, waiting, waiting, waiting...*

She flicked to her documents and went to her writing folder. She found the document she'd entitled 'Sister Acts' and opened it, scrolling down to the end. *Been a while,* she smiled ruefully as she read, reconnecting with her old friends.

She'd left Mary and Lila as they walked away from Caesarea's prison where Junia, Mary's eldest daughter, was incarcerated with Paul. She opened a new document, putting her sermon to one side.

Now what was happening in Jerusalem around the time Paul wrote Ephesians? She went to her book on Israel's history. She heard Zack let himself in and call, 'Hello.' He came into her office and draped his arms round her neck.

'How was your lesson?'

'Good. She said I'm pretty much ready for the recital.'

'That's great darling,' she patted his hands resting on her shoulders.

'Can I make a cheese toasty?'

'Sure – just one though. I want you to still be hungry for dinner.'

'But, Mum, I'm starving now!'

'Another growth spurt? Okay two, but I still want you to eat dinner.'

'I will,' she could hear the triumphant smile in his voice as he made his way to the kitchen.

She returned to her reading and then turned to the newly opened document as fresh inspiration spilled over the rim of her mind through her fingers:

❁　❁　❁

AD 62

'Are you ready to meet with them?' Jair asked.

'Yes,' James replied quietly.

Jair never tired of looking at James's face. His mannerisms and expressions reminded him so much of his older step-brother. He smiled affectionately at him. 'They have confidence in you.'

'Yes ... perhaps I have played it too safely?'

'No, brother, you have lived as a devout Jew, as did your brother before you, who commanded us to be holy even as our Father in Heaven is holy. You have been the right leader for the Church for this season.'

'I have only ever wanted peace among our people. If only they had recognised Him when He came.'

'It is as He said, is it not?' Jair sighed.

'"Oh Jerusalem, Jerusalem,"' James quoted in a far-away voice, '"You who kill the prophets and stone those sent to you. How often I have longed to gather your children together, as a hen gathers her chicks under her wings, but you were not willing! Look, your house is left to you desolate. I tell you, you will not see me again until you say, "Blessed is he who comes in the name of the Lord."' James's voice caught on the last words and he covered his face with his hands, breathing hard.

Jair reached out and clasped James' shoulders. There was nothing to say. It had all been said. Besides there were no words for the foreboding they both felt.

James eventually drew his hands away from his face. 'Perhaps they will listen to me.'

'Perhaps,' Jair smiled a little.

They made their way towards the Temple, through the crowded streets of Jerusalem. Everything was as it had always been: shopkeepers and customers haggling over prices, children running, babies wailing, flies clustering over fruit and sweetmeats as women walked by carrying baskets on their hips. Jair walked behind James and the others who had joined them for this important meeting with the Scribes and Pharisees. They had agreed to rendezvous at the bottom of the Golden Gate steps. He marvelled at the normality of their surroundings – so at odds with the apprehension he felt.

Ahead he saw the group of Pharisees and Scribes, their prayer shawls in stark contrast to their black robes. There seemed to be a lot of other young men among them too; men with hard, cold eyes; men Jair had become aware of recently who seemed to inhabit the Temple courts, but were never seen in the sacred services. His anxiety escalated. He recognised others with whom he had discussed the scriptures over the years, hoping to convince them that the Messiah had indeed come. He stopped in his tracks when his eyes fell on one man: Aaron.

Everyone sat down on the steps as the Temple Governor gestured for them to be seated. He began the conversation by addressing James. 'On behalf of our people, welcome,' he said magnanimously.

Jair assembled the thoughts that had scattered at the sight of Aaron, and concentrated hard on James.

James inclined his head respectfully, 'Eleazer.'

'We have gathered together today to entreat you one last time to restrain the people from going astray after Jesus of Nazareth as if he were the Christ. We have confidence in you that you are a true Israelite and that you will see the wisdom of our request.'

There was a long pause, during which Jair could hear his pulse surging in his ears. So many memories flooded through his mind: of Lila dragged before Jesus in the Temple Courts; of Jesus himself, brought before the people only to hear them shout 'Crucify! Crucify!' and of Stephen. He looked at James's face and saw that he too was thinking similar thoughts. This was it.

'Why do you ask me concerning the Son of Man?' James used the term his brother had often used of himself. It was a term coined by the prophet Daniel, depicting the only man among men who could approach the Ancient of Days and enter into his presence. He alone was given authority, glory and power. It was he who the prophet foretold would be worshipped by people of every language and from every nation. His dominion would never pass away and his kingdom would never be destroyed.

Jair watched with resignation as the title James used of his brother offended his listeners. But even as he registered the emotion of despair, another emotion attended it. It was an inexplicable joy.

'He sits in Heaven at the right hand of the Ancient of Days and will soon return, coming upon the clouds of heaven,' James quoted the prophet Daniel.

'Hosanna,' Jair breathed, a bubble of joy burst on his lips, despite his apprehension. He heard another man near him utter, 'Hosanna to the son of David,' another term used to describe the longed for Messiah. Then another man on the far side of the crowd uttered the same phrase, then another. Jair looked past the outraged faces of the Pharisees to try to glimpse the men who had been surprised by joy. Instead his eyes fell on Aaron's face again. He saw confusion there.

'We are done with this!' declared Eleazer, leaping to his feet.

'Seize him!' he ordered as young men seeming to pre-empt the order, lunged across the space that divided the two groups.

It was all so quick.

No sooner had they grabbed James than they threw him down. One stamped his foot upon his neck, pinning him to the ground and brought his fist down simultaneously on his head. The sound of cracking bone and the explosion of blood splattering the stone steps, sent shock waves through the crowd. Jair watched stupidly as the young man raised his arm again high into the sky. Against the blue of heaven, he saw the jagged edge of a wet, crimson stone. As it arched viciously down again, other stones flew through the air past him.

Jair heard his name being shouted and felt someone pulling his arm. He looked round in a daze to see Aaron shouting in his face, 'Run, Jair! Run for your life!'

❋ ❋ ❋

'They have buried him right where he fell – by the Temple.'

Lila stared incredulously at her husband, her lips parted. 'As a warning?'

'Yes … I suppose,' Jair shook his head. 'I cannot stop seeing them striking his head. I see it again and again in my mind all the time. Why didn't I do something?'

'Didn't any soldiers see and try to intervene?'

'It was so quick … I heard soldiers running and shouting. Why didn't I stay with him – tell them what happened?'

Lila leaned across the table between them and clasped his hands, feeling the tremors that had not stopped running through them since yesterday. 'What would you have said, darling? Do you think they would have listened to you?'

He shook his head. 'I don't know … I should have stayed and said something!' anger constricted his throat. 'Instead I ran!' he pulled his hands from hers and buried his face in them.

'But if you had not, Jair, think what this day would be like for me?' she felt helpless.

'I lost him in the chaos ... Aaron ... Why did he help me?' he dragged his hands down his face as he spoke, muffling his words.

'I don't know ...' Lila didn't want to think about that. 'The important thing is to think about what we do now, Jair. All the other Church leaders are gathering. They need our support and clear thinking. We must prepare and go!'

With that Jair looked at her, the harrowing grief and trauma still molesting his eyes, 'You're right ... but I am not able ... please pray for me ... I can't stop shaking.'

Lila stood and came round the table to her husband's side. She laid her hands on his head and began to pray in tongues, knowing full well there was nothing she could have prayed intelligibly. Neither knew how long this went on for, but both knew later that during it, peace descended. The tremors ceased. Then suddenly Jair burst into tears, wailing out his grief until he was spent. She held his head against her chest and gently rocked him until he grew quiet and his breathing returned to normal. Slowly he wrapped his arms around her. They stayed like that for a long time.

'I hope when it is time, that we both go together,' he said looking up into her face.

She said nothing as she gazed down at him and stroked his hair back off his face. Eventually she spoke, 'I feel the Lord wishes me to go to the Temple to pray, Jair, while you attend the meeting. I will meet Mary there, as is our usual custom, and help her grasp the seriousness of our situation as gently as is possible. We will pray for the peace of Jerusalem and then meet you back here.'

'I don't want to be separated from you Lila. What if it is not safe for you?'

'Surely the Temple is still a safe place?'

'But they killed him right there – beside the Temple!'

'I know ... but women ... in the Temple?'

There was a pause, then, 'All right ... but don't stay long. Come straight back here and don't stop to talk to anyone.'

'We won't.'

❋   ❋   ❋

'I will speak with him, your Excellency,' Aaron's long, silver beard brushed against his black robes as he bowed low before the Roman Procurator's seat.

Albinus twisted a large signet ring on his left hand agitatedly, 'He who insults me, insults Caesar.'

'He is a foolish, bold youth,' Aaron responded as he slowly straightened up, gesturing dismissively with one hand. He was still a striking man, even in old age. His high cheekbones, intelligent eyes and deep, measured voice could still captivate those he set them upon.

Albinus looked at him sceptically, 'It was I who asked for this posting ... more fool me!' he glanced away in exasperation. 'Nero will not be pleased if I cannot control matters here. Judea has been a flea on Rome's back, biting the one that sustains it, with no thought of the consequences. And I assure you my friend, there will be consequences if things do not change. Nero is not a Caesar to be trifled with.'

'Restraint, your excellency, restraint,' Aaron gestured pleadingly with his elegant hands. 'The wise are those who wait and watch. The foolish rush in . . . .'

'If the High Priest admonishes me about my government of Jewish affairs one more time, I am afraid my restraint will run out. I have warned him, but I see that he views me as the flea on the back of Israel!' at this he let out a derisive snort. 'Me!'

'As I said, your Excellency, I will speak with him. His young mind is still malleable.' Aaron tried to dismiss the ominous dread that rose as he thought of Jonathan the High Priest and his friend Eleazer, the Temple Governor. The need to separate hand from glove was never more urgent.

The winds of change had been blowing through Jerusalem, winds he found more and more difficult to interpret. He had been shocked at the instant and vicious way James had been slaughtered. Those arrogant Zealots were everywhere – in the streets of Jerusalem and in the Temple courts. They had no regard for anyone, casting shadows of fear where ever they went. No one among his circle of influence, not even Josephus, knew where they were coming from. They showed an alarming lack of respect for tradition, for the Pharisees and Scribes and acted as if the Temple belonged to no one else but themselves.

'I hope you are right,' Albinus stood up as he spoke and began pacing up and down, clenching and unclenching his fists as he did, 'for your people's sake.' He stopped in front of him, his shrewd eyes meeting Aaron's, suspicious even of this most reliable of allies.

A cold shiver went through Aaron's body. He wasn't given to omens or intuitions, but he could not shake off the unfamiliar uncertainty that had been plaguing his waking hours ... and there had been many more of those of late.

Why hadn't *shalom* – peace – come to Israel? Hadn't he spent his life in service of the Law, the Temple and the people? Aaron shook his head and searched Albinus's face for an answer he knew he wouldn't find, 'We are living in changing times, but even so powerful men must be prudent and choose their battles carefully. I will speak with him,' he reiterated. 'God willing, he will listen to me.'

'Nero willing?' Albinus said with a sardonic smile.

Aaron responded with a well-practised polite smile.

※　※　※

On returning to the city, Aaron went straight to the Temple, despite the late hour. He shuddered involuntarily and moved as quickly as he could past the mound of earth and stones where James was buried.

He sought out Jonathan and found him deep in conversation with Eleazer in his chambers.

'What has that sly fox to say for himself then?' Jonathan asked as Aaron approached them.

'He wishes Israel well. He seeks peace.'

'Only so he can take more taxes from us and appear powerful in Nero's eyes. Fool!' Eleazer almost spat the last word with contempt.

'May I speak with you ... alone?' Aaron ignored the Temple Governor pointedly.

Jonathan nodded as he glanced at Eleazer. Aaron couldn't read the look they exchanged. Again uncertainty pulled at his mind like an irritating, needy child. He watched Eleazer sweep self-importantly from the room, and then turned to Jonathan.

'Haven't I taught you to keep your enemies close? You must cease your admonitions of the Procurator. In these times we must tread carefully.'

Jonathan sighed and looked bored.

Exasperated, Aaron gripped the younger mans' arm, 'Have I not advised you all these many years and enabled you to come to the position of power you hold? Listen to me now! You ... we are all in grave danger.'

Jonathan was staring at Aaron's hand on his arm. He raised his eyes slowly to Aaron's disdainfully, 'Remove your hand,' was all he said.

Aaron loosened his grip and let it fall to his side, bewildered. Where was the student he had taught? Where was the respectful tone in his voice and the affection in his eyes?

'I will not be requiring your advice any more Aaron. It is no longer useful to me. It belongs to a bygone era,' he stood as he spoke, brushing past Aaron, as he brushed their history aside. 'Why not find a place in the country to retire to? You are a wealthy man, and have served Israel well. Why not enjoy the fruits of your labours now in old age? Leave the distasteful world of politics to me and my generation.'

Aaron gazed at the High Priests back, silhouetted against the fading amber sky, which was framed by the arching window.

He was finished. The revelation, though shocking, didn't explode upon him. Rather, it rolled over and stared up at him with vacant eyes, like James's corpse. The needy child at the edge of his consciousness began wailing. Unfamiliar with the torment of failure, he rose slowly and left Jonathan without another word, all his strength gone.

'Mother please, let me,' Junia said.

'I can do it,' Mary retorted stubbornly.

'Why won't you let me help you?'

'You wait until you are old and then you'll know,' Mary responded as she tried for the third time to get her feet into her new sandals.

Junia stood and watched, quelling her impatience. Every time her mother went to put her foot into a sandal, she missed slightly, pushing it further and further away from her. Eventually she let out an exasperated sigh and gestured her defeat with a tremulous wave of her hand.

Junia knelt down and pulled the sandals close, gently lifting one foot and then the other, slipping the soft leather around them. 'We must oil your feet again. Your heels are a little cracked,' she observed.

'Later,' Mary said. 'I don't want to miss afternoon prayers.'

Junia nodded as she pushed herself up off the floor. She reached out and helped her mother to her feet. 'Will Lila be there?'

'Yes … always.'

Junia smiled, 'I will leave you with her. Do you think she could bring you back home? Andronicus has called me to an urgent meeting of apostles.'

'Of course my darling,' Mary smiled, tucking a stray strand of silver hair behind her ear and pulling her head scarf up over her head. 'You must tell me all about it on your return.'

The short journey from their shared home to the Temple was a slow one. Mary had to stop often for breath. Junia meekly held her energy in check, never once giving any hint to her mother that she was doing so. As she watched Mary struggle for breath she thought, as she often did, that life had taken far too great a toll on her.

Junia's own imprisonment had been one contributing factor and the other had been her father's illness. Those two years had been tortuous for her mother. Her already fragile emotional and mental state had fluctuated greatly, requiring much support and prayer from those close to her in the Church community. The night Philip had died, her mother's hair had gone completely white.

Junia had only been able to grieve from the distance of her

prison cell on the day they buried him. Paul and Andronicus were a great consolation, but she had longed to be with her family to say goodbye to her father and comfort her mother.

She and Andronicus had been inexplicably released from prison when Paul was sent to Rome in response to his appeal to Caesar. That had been in '59. Uncle Lazarus had died shortly after that, followed a few months later by Aunt Martha. Junia had been so grateful that she had been there to say goodbye to them and to be with her Mother. They both died peacefully in their sleep, not as the result of any sickness; it seemed as if they had both been called by name and had gone quietly in succession.

It wasn't long afterwards that they decided to return to Jerusalem from Caesarea. Lila and Jair had helped them move back to the city, finding a house not far from Junia and Andronicus for themselves. They met regularly with Mary to pray, either in their home, Junia's or in the Temple Courts. Junia and Andronicus had been able to resume their travels across Judea, giving oversight to the Churches they had planted.

As Junia waited and listened to her mother's laboured breathing she thanked God yet again for Lila.

'Come on then,' Mary interrupted her prayer.

'Sorry, Mama,' Junia grinned, sharing the joke over who was waiting for whom.

They covered the remaining distance to the temple without another rest.

On reaching the temple steps, they saw an incongruous mound of newly dug earth and stones over to one side. 'What is that?' Mary asked.

'I don't know,' Junia frowned. She didn't say so, but it looked like a shallow grave.

'Must be road works or drainage works for the washing facilities?' Mary mused. She gazed up to the top of the temple steps where she could see her friend shading her eyes against the afternoon sun. Her thudding heart lifted at the sight. She smiled and waved and with a surge of fresh energy climbed the steps.

Junia followed behind, shaking her head and marvelling at

the effect this friendship had on her mother. She watched as they embraced one another. 'Shalom, Lila,' she smiled, waiting her turn to kiss her affectionately. 'Is it all right if I leave mother with you? I am eager to get to the apostles gathering. I don't want to miss anything.'

'We will carry on the work God has called us to do here,' Lila agreed.

Mary began happily telling Lila about her new sandals as she lifted the hem of her garment to show them off. Junia kissed her lightly goodbye and with that turned to descend the temple steps. When she reached the bottom, she stood by the mound of earth, as a strange sensation crept upon her. She waited trying to discern what it was. She found herself bending over, unable to catch her breath for a time. Inexplicable silent tears streamed down her face as she gazed at the pile of earth and rocks. Somehow she knew someone very precious lay ignobly buried beneath.

※　※　※

'Thank you, Luke. What do you think?' Paul wiped his eyes slowly one at a time.

'I am at a loss for words, brother,' Luke's weather-beaten face glowed as he lowered his quill and rested it in its inkwell. 'Beautiful,' he said after a long pause, a tremor in his voice.

Paul let his hands drop to his sides. He suddenly felt exhausted. He didn't know how long he'd been standing, hands raised in prayer. The long chain that attached him to his guard rattled as he reached for the arm of his chair and lowered himself carefully into it, a sigh escaping his lips. He gazed across the room out the open window, past his guard who leaned out of it, chatting with two other soldiers. He wondered how they managed to keep standing out in the oven that Rome became at the height of summer. By the time the sun set, the paving and stonework of the huddled buildings radiated what heat they had absorbed during the day back into the dust-laden atmosphere.

It must be unbearable under those helmets and armour, Paul thought.

31

He was glad for Pudens, his guard, that he got to stay in the relative cool of the house that had been his prison for the past years. He was also glad that the shadow of a cypress tree stretched out over the course of the afternoon onto the front of the house where the other guards stood.

As he watched them he tuned into their conversation. It was hard to understand their rough Latin and he struggled to concentrate after the extreme spiritual focus he had just exercised.

'That's the word in our barracks,' one soldier was saying, as he leant over and spat into the gutter.

'Same story in ours,' added the other.

His guard shook his head, 'It doesn't bode well.'

'First his mother and now his wife ... Burrus dead and Seneca retired? Methinks the worst is yet to come,' the first soldier continued. 'Not good for us ... not good for Rome ... and those poor, deluded Christians?' he looked in through the window at Paul.

'Cannibals,' retorted the other soldier under his breath.

Pudens shifted his weight from one foot to the other, 'I don't think they are,' and shrugged his shoulders.

Paul gave thanks silently for the obvious discomfort this slander was having on his guard. He watched a trickle of sweat meander down his young neck.

'From what I know,' Pudens jerked his head in the direction of Paul seated not far behind him, 'that couldn't be further from the truth. He's a good man. I don't know why he's under house arrest.'

'You going soft?' laughed one of the soldiers.

'If you're not careful you'll end up as mad as Nero,' added the other with a derisive laugh.

Pudens swore at them, telling them where they could go.

So Nero has not only rid himself of Octavia, but had her killed also ... Paul felt familiar sadness swell his chest. *He is plunging deeper into the futility of darkness ...* he closed his eyes and turned his inner gaze heavenward again.

'He weds his mistress Poppaea this week. The celebration is expected to be city wide,' the soldier continued, ignoring Pudens' abuse.

'And all soldiers get extra rations,' said the other.

'I wonder how long she will last,' Pudens asked rhetorically.

There followed a short silence. Eyes still closed, Paul wondered what fearful thoughts lurked beneath their light conversation. Their fates were inextricably entwined with the madman who ruthlessly ruled the Roman Empire. Their lives were not their own.

Luke broke into his reverie, the familiar Aramaic a relief to Paul's concentration, 'Do you want to do any more work today?'

Paul opened his creased eyelids slowly and looked at Luke with a steady gaze, 'No ... I am spent. This old body is weak. It cannot sustain what it used to. My spirit yearns for resurrection life,' he smiled softly, his parchment skin crackling into craggy folds.

'You and me both,' Luke returned the smile through his silver beard. 'I will leave you now to rest. Joshua will bring you food before sunset. Is there anything you would specially like to eat today?'

'Grapes ... red grapes,' Paul smiled.

※　※　※

Joshua greeted Pudens in Latin, with a broad grin, 'How has the day been?'

'Hot,' said the soldier.

'How's our prisoner?'

'His body still chained, his mind free.'

'Luke read to me what he'd written today ... Did they translate it for you?'

'Paul did occasionally when he saw that I was listening.'

Joshua smiled, loving Paul for his passion to win Pudens' heart and mind. 'It's as if he is peering into eternities ... back before the foundations of the world and forward to what lies ahead.'

Pudens shrugged, attempting nonchalance.

Joshua smiled again, 'You and I both know you are as captivated as we are. You cannot hold out this pretence of disinterest for much longer.'

Pudens looked him in the eye, 'How do you know he is not mad?'

'Does madness lead to such exultant praise and ordered peace in the face of imprisonment, loneliness and impending death?'

Pudens chose not to reply, but led Joshua through the entrance hall into the room Paul inhabited, the long chain clanking from his wrist to Paul's with the rhythm of his gait.

'Besides,' Joshua continued as Pudens inspected the food he'd brought, 'he did not choose this life, this calling. It was not bestowed upon him by any earthly power. The authority in his teaching is not his own.'

Pudens nodded, indicating that he was satisfied there were no implements hidden in the food to enable Paul's escape. 'Nero too thinks he has divine authority.'

Joshua lifted the basket of food out of Pudens' hands and turned to Paul, resisting the temptation to argue.

Pudens returned to the pillared doorway, leaning himself against the warm, stonework. He stared out into the street where some children were chasing a cat. Over the year he had slowly learnt some of his prisoner's language, and despite himself he strained to listen to their conversation.

'Ah, Shua,' Paul's voice was soft and blurry from afternoon sleep, 'You are set apart for God, faithful and trustworthy.'

Joshua chuckled, 'How wonderful to be greeted like that. I've brought you grapes, as requested. They've just been picked.'

Pudens could hear the creak of the rope bed as Paul moved slowly to sit up. He heard the rasping brush of the cracked, dried soles of his feet on the stone floor, then the sound of water splashing on ceramic as Joshua washed the fruit.

Paul prayed for Pudens as he watched the afternoon sunlight catch in droplets of water that fell over the bowl's edges onto the dark wood of the table. *Oh the light ... the light ... it's so much brighter ... help me catch it and convey it like this ....*

Taking two smaller bowls, Joshua put grapes, pieces of bread and cakes of goats' cheese into them. He brought them over and sat down on the bed beside Paul, handing him his simple meal. They ate in silence.

Imagining them eating made Pudens' stomach rumble.

Joshua must have heard because a moment later he came into the hallway with a laden bowl. 'Here – share with us.'

Pudens often declined their offers of hospitality, trying to keep a professional boundary between them. But today he was particularly hungry. He accepted the gift with a slight smile, but did not join them in the room.

When Paul had finished he gave his bowl back to Joshua and stood to pray, his voice rising and falling in a hushed tone, 'Blessed are you, Lord our God, our Father, master of the universe, who nourishes the whole world with goodness, with grace, kindness and compassion.'

Joshua stood with him, joining in the prayer, 'Blessed are you Lord, who nourishes all,' their voices came together as they finished the traditional prayer.

Familiar with their ritual, Pudens put his head round the doorway, then came fully into the room with his empty bowl, 'Shall we go for our walk now?'

'That would be wonderful,' Paul beamed.

Joshua began collecting up the chain that hung from Paul's and Pudens' wrists so that it would not drag on the ground. He occasionally glimpsed the sores neither man complained of that lurked beneath the manacles. Luke treated them with his healing oils and changed the dressings regularly, but they never went away altogether. It wasn't right, Joshua thought as they made their way into the still heat of dusk.

As always Paul seemed unaffected by his circumstances, euphoric over the smallest things: birds swooping in an arching cloud overhead; the moon hanging low on the horizon urging the sun to relinquish its' glory. These things evoked rapt awe and wonder from the apostle. In between moments of worship he spoke softly to Pudens. 'You know, as I have told you many times, God is calling you to be his son. Before Jesus Christ came to us, I could never have said this to you. I praise Him that he found me and commissioned me to be an apostle to the Gentiles ... to bring His message to you. Jesus Christ sent me to find you, Pudens, to adopt you into his family.'

Pudens laughed, 'I thought you were sent here to stand trial for causing riots and disturbing the peace of the Empire.'

'If I had never been accused, I would not be with you now, would I?' Paul grinned and spread his hands, causing his chain to pull loose from Joshua's grasp. It fell, clanking against the cobbles, causing passers-by to gawp and stare. Joshua quickly pulled it up and hid it in the folds of his cloak.

'Your view of reality is more appealing than mine, but how true it is ... that I am still not sure of,' Pudens said as he led them through the narrow alley that took them down a slope to the western city wall.

As they went through the gate that led out onto the dark banks of the Tiber River, Paul stopped, closed his eyes and breathed in the smell of damp earth and moss. When he opened his eyes again, the sun was just touching earth, throwing burnt umber and scarlet across the undulating landscape and the smooth surface of the river. Swallows skimmed its golden skin, leaving fading arrow marks upon it.

Sensitive to his prisoner, Pudens waited for him.

'One day,' Paul turned his head and looked him in the eye, as Joshua watched and prayed, 'one day, God will accomplish everything He has purposed and planned. You've been chosen Pudens, now is your time to be adopted and one day we will celebrate together the unification of all things, of Jew and Gentile, of a redeemed humanity and a renewed creation. Can you not feel it? Does your heart not burn within you?'

Pudens stared out across the water to the glowing sun. 'I feel warmed when I am with you and your fellow believers. You know, I have a brother who speaks like you do. He has written to me several times telling me of this Jesus of yours.'

'What is his name – perhaps I know him?'

'Tychicus. He still lives in Asia. I haven't seen him for many years, not since we were boys.' As an afterthought he added, 'He is crippled down one side of his body.'

'Tychicus? Your brother? The Lord be praised! He is a faithful minister and fellow-servant in the Lord! The last time I saw him was in Troas, I think. Did you hear that Joshua?'

'Yes – how amazing!' Joshua exclaimed.

'Yes – Troas – that's where he is,' Pudens marvelled. 'What a small world!'

'Indeed,' Paul agreed. 'You know he used to pray for you and your whole family with such passion.'

'Did he?' Pudens was moved.

'Yes ... perhaps you being my guard is an answer to his prayers?' Paul said with a twinkle in his eye.

Pudens didn't respond, but looked out across the smooth surface of the river. In a low voice he said, 'But although I am warmed when I am with you, it is as though I am always a guest at your hearth.'

'It is you who keeps yourself a guest,' Paul replied. 'We welcome you to become part of our family. You've heard the story of Messiah. I know you believe it ... that you want to respond to His call. What keeps you?'

Pudens kicked a stone and watched it arc and fall, breaking the dark, smooth edge of the river into circles of reflected indigo and copper. 'As my brother told me, he is the good shepherd who knows his sheep by name ... and it's true, I do hear him calling me. But I am a Roman citizen, a soldier from Asia. I have sworn allegiance to the Emperor who has a divine claim to my life.'

Paul shook his head as they began walking again in silence for a time, the gathering dusk cloaking them in the flutter of batwings and chirruping frog-song. Joshua walked behind them by a pace or two, praying in the familiar tongue he'd always used but which was as yet still a mystery to him.

'We are called to live in two worlds ... to give respect to those in authority here, but to live for the praise of a higher power, from whom all authority comes,' Paul pointed heavenward. 'He is the one whose servant I am. He has commanded me and sent me to call people of every tribe and nation to Himself. Soon His family will outnumber the grains of sand on the seashore, as He promised our father Abraham,' Paul gazed at the deep red sinking sun as he spoke. 'Choose now Pudens ... choose to open your mind and soften your heart. Choose life and light, blessing and glory.'

Pudens looked at Paul's face bathed in sunset light. Somehow he knew his time had come. After all the time they'd shared together as guard and prisoner, they were about to become brothers. Right there on the banks of the river he suddenly knelt down, unable to hold the dam against love's current. Surprised, Joshua rushed to his side and together Paul and he lay there hands upon his head and prayed.

'Receive the Holy Spirit, Pudens,' Paul said, 'the promise, the seal and guarantee of what is to come.'

The dam burst; love flooded in; military training discarded; darkness fled and Pudens alternately wept and laughed like a child.

2. KNOWING

Ephesians 1:15–23

I keep asking that the God of our Lord Jesus Christ, the glorious Father, may give you the Spirit of wisdom and revelation, so that you may know him better.

By the time Charmaine arrived at the Crown, Mark had had several pints. She didn't notice at first as she regaled him with a story of the night's shift, pausing for breath only to order a double gin and tonic.

He didn't laugh when she'd finished the story, causing her to look at him properly, 'What's up, Markie?' she reached out and stroked his cheek with a tanned, red-nailed finger.

He pulled away from her slightly, causing the pint in his hand to slosh over onto the bar.

'How many have you had?' she asked. 'I thought you'd just finished work?'

Mark laughed cynically and raised his glass to his lips, drinking deeply.

With growing alarm, Charmaine pulled herself up on her high heels and turned to face him full on. 'What's wrong? Tell me now!' she demanded.

'I've been made redundant,' Mark looked up at her from his slouched position on the bar stool.

'What? I thought you were gonna be promoted?'

'Yeah,' his voice failed him.

Charmaine's mind started whirring, 'What did you get?'

'Three months ....'

'Did you know that was the deal?' she stared hard at him, the long painted nails of her right hand beginning to drum the wooden bar top.

'Yep,' he couldn't look at her again. 'It's the risk you take.'

She swore under her breath. 'What are we gonna do?' she asked.

'Don't know yet. Need to think about it.'

'Damn right,' she said, slugging back her drink in one go, leaving red lip gloss smeared across the rim. 'Right then …' she said agitatedly, 'Shall we go get some food to soak up the alcohol so you *can* begin thinking?'

Mark looked at her in surprise. He'd thought she'd be more compassionate – spend the evening helping him drown his sorrows in the pub. 'I don't want to eat,' he said flatly.

'So you're just gonna stay here and feel sorry for yourself?' she demanded.

'Yep – that sounds like a plan.'

She swore again, looking round the pub – specifically at the door.

'If you wanna go – just go,' he said.

She did.

※ ※ ※

Chloe,

I've been made redundant.

I've got three months' severance pay which won't go far.

Obviously I am looking for work, but I'm writing to ask you to be understanding if that takes time.

Hopefully I'll be employed again soon.

Mark.

Chloe read the rare email twice in the My Sister's House office. A sigh escaped her lips as she folded her arms over her muffin-top belly. Melanie and Grace looked across the office and asked in unison, 'What's wrong?'

'Your Dad's been made redundant.'

'Oh,' Melanie processed the information, slowly chewing a mouthful of her tuna sandwich.

'Yeah,' Chloe replied.

'Charmaine won't like that,' Melanie raised her eyebrows matter-of-factly.

'No,' Chloe looked back at her computer screen.

'Have you enough to live on without his contribution?' Grace asked.

'It would make life very tough,' Chloe frowned. 'Might help me lose this though,' she patted her midriff. 'Wouldn't be able to buy as much wine. But let's hope it doesn't come to that. I'm quite fond of it now,' she smiled self-deprecatingly as she stroked her tummy.

Grace and Melanie watched as she pressed reply and started to type.

Sorry to hear that Mark.
Happy job hunting.

Chloe.

❋   ❋   ❋

'Okay – so your head won't be in the shots, just from the neck down,' the photographer was saying as he flicked through images of Charmaine wearing provocative lingerie and in various poses.

She looked over his shoulder as she pulled her jeans on, 'I like the purple ones,' she said as she reached for her crisp white shirt.

'Mmmm …' he didn't look up, 'what do you want to be called?'

She was thoughtful as she did up her buttons, 'Lola,' she said at last, as she flashed him a flirtatious smile.

'Great,' his grin quickly dissolved into a business-like expression as he looked at her critically. 'So you clock on with us and once we get a booking the driver will pick you up at around nine at the latest with the other girls who're on tonight.'

'Tonight? That quick?'

'Yeah … when I press this button,' he pointed, 'you go live. There'll be a lot of interest in a newbie.'

'What are you doing now?' she looked at the paragraph he was writing.

'Oh just a profile about your personality.'

As she read she laughed and swore, 'You're good!'

'That's my job – *Whispers Agency* gives them what they want and they give us what we want. It's good business.'

'So someone just rings up and asks what you've got tonight?'

'Yeah, we ask them how long they want, they ask how much. Done.'

'So first hour is £120 and £100 for each hour after that? How much do I get?'

'Yeah, you get £40 and give us £60 per hour. Protection in this business is risky and expensive. It's the price you gotta pay,' he looked like he was prepared for an argument and seemed mildly surprised when she made no attempt to challenge him. He went on, 'Once a booking comes through, it's usually for one or two hours. You take the money first and ring the driver to tell him you've got it.'

'What if there's more than one guy there?'

'You leave. Rule is one client at a time otherwise it's not cost effective for us.'

Charmaine's expression remained business-like as she nodded.

'If they ask you to do extra stuff, you take the money first - fifty quid. And whatever you do, watch out for tricks to get condoms off. Half of them will try it. We don't want damaged goods,' he grinned again.

'I'm not doing anything extra,' she said emphatically.

'That's your call,' he shrugged. 'But *they* will want the extras. Oh, and watch out for phone blockers – this is what they look like,' he flipped to several images on his screen. 'You don't stay if you see one of these.'

'Okay,' she nodded.

'One last thing, a lot of them are on cocaine so be careful – they can get aggressive pretty quickly.'

She nodded again.

'Play the game, most of them just want to feel like they've impressed you ... you know,' he raised his eyebrows.

'Yeah,' she flashed another smile.

※　※　※

Mark placed two salmon fillets onto some tin foil. They were standing in their small kitchen, early evening spring sunshine poured through the window onto the granite work top between them.

They hadn't really spoken since he'd told her he'd been made redundant.

While Charmaine had gone to work at the club that afternoon, he'd eventually forced himself to shower and dress and then he'd dragged himself out to the shops. A reconciliatory dinner was in order.

He returned to find Charmaine leaning a hip against the kitchen units, still wearing her light mac and texting furiously.

'Hey,' Mark ventured. 'How was your shift?'

'Fine,' she didn't take her eyes off her phone.

'Thought I'd cook us dinner and then we could talk. Sorry about yesterday.'

'I can't. I've got a new job starting tonight.'

'Oh? Have you quit the club?' Mark's brow furrowed.

'No,' she continued to text.

Relieved he asked, 'What's the job?'

'It's with Whispers Agency,' she sniffed and looked up at him for the first time, eyes glittering like coal.

His sea-greens widened in alarm, 'What? As ... as what?'

'As one of their girls,' she stared belligerently at him.

He knew the agency; the colour drained from his face; his mouth hung open. 'Don't I have a say in this?'

'You didn't want to talk so I've sorted things out myself,' she snapped.

'Charmaine ... wait a minute ... I was in shock yesterday! Of course I want to talk and make plans with you. Why does everything have to be so immediate?'

'Why does everything have to be so slow?' she slammed her phone down on the work top.

'I've got three months leeway to get another job. We'll be fine,' he fought to control his voice.

'We're only just coming out of a recession, Mark. If you think it's going to be easy finding a job with the same level of pay you had before, then you better wake up and look around you. It's not gonna happen,' she picked her phone up again and stuffed it into her bag.

Mark knew she was right. He felt like he was facing another huge wave that was about to submerge him. Weak and paralysed by dread his shoulders sagged.

'Look I like sex ... and you know I'm good ... why shouldn't I get paid for it? For three nights a week I could be earning over a grand on top of what I already earn at the club. It's the one business a recession doesn't touch.'

Mark gazed at her helplessly. 'But it's not like stripping ....'

'No – it's better paid.'

'There's more to life than money ... don't do this, please. Just stay here tonight and we'll talk things through. We're clever together ... we'll come up with a plan ... you and I,' he reached through the bars of sunlight for her hand, but she withdrew it.

'Mark, you don't get it. You have no idea what poverty is like. I will do everything in my power to make sure I am never poor again. So save your breath. Nothing you say is going to change my mind,' she slung her bag over her shoulder. 'I'll see you tomorrow,' she said as she made for the door. 'Oh yeah, I got you a paper – happy job hunting.' She pulled the paper from her bag and threw it onto the work top.

'If you do this, we're finished!' he shouted desperately.

'Get over yourself,' she said casually over her shoulder, never wavering, swinging her hips down the hallway to the front door. She didn't look back.

I don't know her at all, he thought in a daze.

❆   ❆   ❆

Lord, I pray that the eyes of my heart may be enlightened in order that I may know the hope to which you have called me, the riches of your glorious inheritance in the saints and your incomparably great power for us who believe, Grace made Paul's prayer her own from Ephesians. She was kneeling in her study, bathed in early morning sunlight.

After a while she turned it into a prayer for the people at St Stephen's, then moved on using it as a prayer for My Sister's House team. She eventually settled on individuals: her mother, Peter, Zack, Chloe, Charlie, Josh, Melanie. Mark's face suddenly came vividly to mind ... *Haven't seen him for ages! Wonder how he's coping with his job loss? Mmmm ... Open the eyes of his heart so he'll know the hope to which you've called him, the rich inheritance that is his and your power that is available for him ...* she stayed with him for a while, blessing him again and again. Then she moved on, calling to mind the faces of the women and girls they'd rescued over the last few months.

❋ ❋ ❋

Chloe stepped out of the shower and quickly wrapped herself in a towel. She didn't like seeing her naked body. She pushed the bathroom window open a little more to diffuse the steam that was filling the room. She peered at her face in the mirror, but it was already misting. Wrapping her hair in another towel she waited for the cool air to clear the glass.

As she gazed at herself she knew she didn't really want to go out tonight. It was so much hard work: all that getting-to-know-you-conversation of first dates. It was exhausting.

She'd had two unsuccessful relationships over the years since her divorce. Both had lasted around a year, but had slowly lost momentum and petered out. Her recent exploration on a dating website had taken huge determination and resolve. But here she was again with *that* feeling.

What is the point? Why am I doing this to myself again?

Her mind drifted towards thoughts of Mark. She wondered how Charmaine had taken his redundancy; if he had applied for anything else yet; how he was coping with not going out to work. She raised a finger and thumb to her earlobe, squeezing it gently, wishing yet again that she had kept those diamond studs he'd given her for their tenth wedding anniversary. A sigh escaping her lips. Her fingers moved to the dark mole near her nose, feeling it's rounded, raised surface carefully. *Is it my imagination, or has it got bigger?*

She looked more closely, coming out of her reverie, glaring critically at herself. *Stop that! It's the same as it's always been. Now pull yourself together - you're going out with a very nice guy tonight. Maybe this time ...* but still Mark's blue-green eyes haunted her.

She hadn't prayed for many years, or gone to church for that matter, despite Melanie's continual invitations and Grace's unspoken ones. *Help him God,* she found herself praying. She was mildly surprised at herself. She had thought disillusionment had done its work and totally crushed any vestige of faith that might have survived the devastation of her life. She frowned.

God, I look old, she thought and turned away, dismissing the urge to pray as a trick of her mind to cope with the insecurity of another first date.

❋ ❋ ❋

'Can you raise your finger?' the physiotherapist asked. She was young and blonde, with a clear, rosy complexion. She watched James's forefinger resting in her palm. She could feel the muscle move, but not enough to lift the digit. 'That's good, James, really good. Your muscles are getting stronger. Do you want to do it again? Yes? Okay ... when you're ready.'

She could see the intense concentration in his eyes, although his face remained slack and lifeless. Again she felt the muscle move and this time his finger lifted a fraction off her palm. 'Hey ... you did it! You lifted it off my hand! Well done!' she beamed. 'Now try it one more time, and then I think we'll try your other hand.'

After a pause he did it again. She noted that he lifted it a little higher into the air. 'That's fantastic, James. Before you know it you'll be able to type! Imagine Marie's face when you type your first message to her,' she gently placed his hand back onto the bed.

There was no response in his left hand or either of his feet. She kept encouraging him nonetheless and by the time they had finished working together she knew he was exhausted from his efforts. 'You can have a little sleep now,' she smiled at him. He slowly closed his eyes. 'I'll be back tomorrow.'

✖ ✖ ✖

'We have a surprise for you,' the physiotherapist said to Marie.

It had been several weeks since James had opened his eyes. The first waves of euphoria had rolled over Marie, leaving in their wake a wash of uncertainty. She looked from the physiotherapist to James and then back again. Nothing had changed. She frowned, slightly bewildered.

The young woman placed a small laptop onto the bed near James's right hand, raising it at an angle on a pillow. Then she went and lifted James's head, arranging his pillows so that his head was at an angle where he could see the compact keyboard. She took his hand and gently placed it on the centre of the keyboard. It seemed it was touch sensitive as a suddenly stream of 'g's flew across the screen in a long ribbon.

But as Marie watched in amazement, he found the 'i' key and pressed it, then lifted and moved his forefinger painfully slowly to the 'L' key. It took a long time, maybe five minutes – Marie didn't know for sure, she was mesmerised. He had typed – *ILoveU*.

She cried.

❋ ❋ ❋

'Will he be able to move other parts of his body in time? Will he be able to speak?' Marie quizzed the consultant as they walked to the coffee machine down the corridor. He had been responsible for James over the last five years, on paper at least, but Marie had rarely seen him after that first year.

'We don't know. We're as amazed as you are,' he said hesitantly. 'As you know we've believed he was in a persistent vegetative state.'

He stopped beside the machine, shoving his hands deep into his pockets and rocking back on his heels. 'Marie, the chances of recovery are close to zero if the patient shows no signs of awareness one year after a traumatic brain injury such as James sustained. It's been five years!' he paused for effect.

'I know,' she replied not taking her eyes off his face, 'but we've seen that he is thinking coherently, that physiotherapy does work ... we know he's been able to hear us for a long time.'

'Yes ...' he smiled slightly, 'perhaps he has been in a minimally conscious state for some time without us recognizing it. If that is the case, then the chances of his recovery are greater.'

'So are you saying that he might recover speech and more movement?' Marie asked haltingly.

'In patients who recover from the vegetative state, the first signs of consciousness are often minimal and appear gradually, like James showed initially. He made a deliberate, non-reflexive movement. But in most cases of the minimally conscious state these movements are not accompanied by communication of thoughts and feelings so early on. So he is surprising in that sense.

'The state he's in now may be a transient condition on the way to further recovery of consciousness, or it may be chronic and permanent. So we will just have to wait and see,' he shrugged.

They stood facing each other in silence. Marie was the first to turn towards the machine and mechanically pull out a paper cup, punching the familiar buttons for her coffee of choice.

'There is one case – an American man called Terry Wallis – who had been in a minimally conscious state since a road accident in 1984. He started talking in 2003. Wallis also regained some ability to move his limbs, although he can't walk and still needs around-the-clock care.'

Her coffee cup filled, she raised her eyes to his face again. He could see the battle between hope and despair in them. 'But, Marie, remember, it's the only case I've heard of. I'm sorry not to be more helpful. I can't explain to you why this has happened or how long it will last. We're in uncharted waters here,' he sighed.

After he'd filled his cup, Marie said, 'I think I'll go and sit in the garden for a while.'

He nodded and watched her small frame diminish against the late afternoon sunlight that flooded through the double doors at the end of the hallway.

�֍ ✖ ✖

Later that evening Chloe leaned on the front door after she'd closed it and breathed, pressing her hand to her lips. She went into the study and watched in the anonymity of darkness as he got into his car and drove away. It had been a good first date, not as much of a strain as she had thought it might be. He had made it easy. But that kiss goodnight – she hadn't been prepared for that. It had begun on her cheek, lingering just long enough to seem innocent as it nudged towards her mouth.

She shook her head and smiled, *not as shy and retiring as you'd like me to think you are*. She went to the kitchen and turned a light on before half filling the kettle. As she waited for it to boil she found her mind wandering back to Mark again. She heard Melanie's key in the front door. 'Hi, love,' she called.

'Hi Mum, how was your date?' Melanie came in as she unbuttoned her coat.

'It was okay,' Chloe said. 'How was the movie?'

'Great! We went for a drink after – Rose wanted to talk to me about an idea she's had.'

'Oh?' Chloe stirred her drink and then lifted it to her lips, breathing in the warmth of it.

'She asked me if I'd be interested in moving into a flat with her.'

'Oh.' Chloe felt her stomach flip like a fish in a net.

'I said I'd talk to you about it first,' Melanie was watching her carefully for a reaction.

'Do you want a cup of tea?' Chloe asked evasively.

'Go on then,' Melanie pulled out a kitchen chair, hung her coat on the back of it and sat down patiently.

Chloe took her time, frantically gathering her thoughts together as she did. She eventually brought the steaming mugs over and sat down beside her daughter. 'As a parent you always know this day will come, but that doesn't prepare you for it,' she sipped her tea tentatively and tried to smile.

Melanie didn't say anything.

'Has she found a flat yet?'

'Yes ... it's actually not far from Dad's,' Melanie looked up at her mum.

'Oh ... when does she need to know?' Chloe's voice sounded hollow.

Melanie took a sip and swallowed, 'If I were up for it, we could put an offer in straight away.'

Silence.

'I think it would be great!' Chloe said eventually. 'I could sell this place and downsize a bit maybe.'

It was Melanie's turn to look surprised, 'But this is our home!'

'Yes ... but Josh has been talking about moving out and that would leave only Charlie and me when he finishes uni, and who knows how long it will be before he moves out? As far as I know, Dad still hasn't got another job, so if I were to sell, I could release some money up ... it would probably be good for everyone, wouldn't it?'

'I ... I guess so,' Melanie looked disconcerted. 'I do want to move out and build my own life, Mum, but part of me still wants everything to stay the same.'

'I know, love,' Chloe reached over and took hold of Melanie's hand. 'I feel the same ... but it might be the best thing ... a new beginning for all of us?'

Melanie squeezed her mum's small hand in hers as they looked for reassurance in each other's eyes.

�֎ ✖ ✖

Mark couldn't sleep. He texted her again, still with no reply and then picked up the paper and looked at the job vacancies page again. There had been nothing for weeks that was equivalent to his last position.

I should just take anything ... until something comes up ... casual work....

His eyes returned to an ad for a porter's job at the hospital again.

Maybe she'll stop if I get a job?

His stomach hadn't stopped churning thinking of what she was doing right now. He looked at his phone – still no reply; he texted her again.

Please come home.

He stared at the cursor at the end of the text blinking at him rhythmically, and then pressed 'send'.

God, please bring her back.

He frowned. What had possessed him to pray? Why on earth would God be interested in listening to him – if He existed? He reached for a pen and wrote down the contact details for the porter's job. He turned the TV on and surfed through several channels before settling on a nature program: killer whales attacking a mother and baby blue whale. He watched as the mother tried hopelessly to fend them off with her huge tail. The distraught underwater cries between baby and mother disturbed him so much, that he changed the channel to a twenty-four hour news show and turned the volume right down. But the whale-cries kept echoing in the cavernous void within him. He reached for his laptop ... for comfort ... for the one thing that blocked out the horror he felt ... even if it was for just a little while.

✖ ✖ ✖

Charmaine let herself in silently. It was 8 a.m. She wasn't surprised to see him asleep on the sofa, as had become his habit, the TV still on, his laptop beside him and his trousers undone. She headed for the shower.

When she came out, wrapped in her silk dressing gown, she went to the kitchen and turned the kettle on. As it boiled she heard Mark stirring. 'Charmaine?' he called.

'Yep,' she replied opening a cupboard and lifting out two mugs.

He came in rubbing his eyes. They gazed at each other wordlessly. Without asking him, she dumped a teaspoon of coffee granules into each mug and filled them from the kettle. She went to the fridge and got some milk.

'So how was it?' he asked.

She poured the milk, handed him his mug and just glared at him.

'That good huh?' he smirked.

'Probably better than your night,' she said scathingly.

'Don't talk to me like that!' he shouted, slamming his fist down on the worktop.

'I'll talk to you any way I like!' she shouted back. 'I'm the main breadwinner here, so you better get used to it,' her young, un-made-up face contorted.

Furious, Mark lunged at her, spilling his coffee everywhere. He grabbed at her dressing gown, but got her wet hair instead as she moved out of his reach. She screamed, whirling round and kicked him.

In pain he let go. She went to kick him again. This time he grabbed her foot, sending her sprawling onto the kitchen floor. Then he was on top of her pinning her down.

'If you put one mark on me, I swear to God I'll report you to the police,' she hissed, spitting in his face.

Mark's rage drained from him as fast as it had come. He stared down at her, wondering how it had come to this. He let her go and stood up, wiping the spittle from his cheek with his sleeve in bewilderment.

She got up off the floor, swearing obscenely, pushing past him.

Mark stayed in the kitchen until his heart had stopped racing. He slowly wiped up the spilled coffee and made himself another one. Eventually he went into the living room. She was watching a morning chat show, her knees pulled defensively up under her chin in a corner of the sofa.

He sat down at the other end uncertain of what to do next. Eventually she looked at him. 'What?' she asked rudely.

'Don't do this, Charmaine. I'm going to get another job – I swear. You don't need to ….'

She snorted derisively and looked back at the TV. 'You're going to magic up a job, are you?'

'I'm gonna take anything, until the right one comes up,' he said.

'I'll believe it when I see it,' she retorted, not looking at him.

Neither one apologised.

※　※　※

It was a dismal day. The heavy grey sky seemed to press down upon his head. He looked up as he neared the building at the patchwork of grey slabs and blind windows, trying to shake off the oppression he felt. He had thought he couldn't feel any worse, but his mood sunk lower still. Although it wasn't cold he zipped his jacket up further. He stopped and scrutinised the large map of the hospital site at the entrance and located the porters' unit. It took him twenty minutes of long corridors, stairs and lifts before he found it. A dishevelled man told him to sit in the hallway and wait to be called.

Mark obediently sat, pulling out his phone as he did. He checked to see if she'd texted him, but there was nothing. He felt so bleak he nearly texted Chloe, but quickly dismissed this as sentimental and pathetic. Then he thought of the kids. He texted them: *Hi, I'm about to have a job interview. Wish me luck.*

Charlie never replied to any of his texts or emails, so he didn't expect to hear back from him, but Josh and Melanie might. Josh replied first: *All the best Dad. What's it for?* J

Mark didn't want to tell him: *It's with the NHS,* was all he wrote.

Melanie's response came shortly afterwards: *That's good news Dad. Let me know how it goes x M.*

The comfort he felt from connecting to both children overwhelmed him so that his eyes blurred. Blinking he checked his phone again. She knew what time the interview was ... she was probably busy at the club.

He heard his name and jumped to his feet, dropping his phone into his jacket pocket and unzipping it as he walked towards the door where the dishevelled man stood guard. The interview didn't take long. He would start in the morning.

As he walked out he glanced at the man still standing in the corridor. 'It'll change your life,' the man said, his voice charred by years of smoking. Mark noticed that his teeth and fingers were stained the colour of wet straw.

'Cheers,' was all Mark could think of to say as he walked past him, trying to remember how to get back out again. *For the worse probably* - he thought. He pulled his phone out again and texted Charmaine, *I got the job – you can stop working for Whispers now.*

All the way home he kept checking his phone, but there was no response from her.

� ✻ ✻ ✻

'Could we pray together?' Grace lifted her head off Peter's chest.

'Sure, babe, what about?' Peter asked, closing his book and dropping it on top of the duvet.

'I can't get Mark out of my head – since Chloe got an email from him saying he'd been made redundant.' Grace propped herself up on her elbow, her head resting in her hand.

'Has it affected her yet?'

'No, but it will eventually ... so far he's kept up the agreed payments.'

'It's tough out there. They let all our illustrators go last week. London's being flooded with freelancers!'

'At least that's not his field and he doesn't have to compete with them,' Grace frowned. Another thought struck her. 'Are you in any danger?'

'No – don't think so. Graphic designers are a bit safer and anyway, I'm in charge,' Peter reached a hand up and ran it through his greying hair. Grace loved the sound his manicured nails made as they brushed through the coarse, thickness. 'But you never know ....'

'At least my job's safe,' Grace smiled.

Peter smiled back. 'Have you heard from Marie lately?'

Grace's smile disappeared. 'Yes, she phoned today.'

'Oh?'

'James has been able to type some words.'

'That's pretty incredible, isn't it?'

'Yes. He typed that he loved her. No one does that after five years of being in a coma!' She looked down and sighed, 'I'm torn – I'm glad for Marie, honestly, but then I feel sick.'

'Maybe we should pray about that as well then?' Peter reached over and curled his fingers between hers.

She didn't reply, but closed her eyes. She whispered, 'Could you pray?'

Peter surveyed his wife's face. She was still beautiful. The little lines that had formed around the edges of her mouth and between her eyebrows had added character to her Nordic features. Her skin was still smooth with only hints of shadows beneath the eyes. He tenderly ran a finger along the line of her jaw as he began to pray …

'Father, we lift Mark before you. Please give him the Spirit of wisdom and revelation, so that he could know you again. I pray that the eyes of his heart will be opened so that he'd know the hope to which he's called to, the inheritance that's his and the power that's there for him.

'I pray for James too that he'd know that he is in you and you are in him. Thank you for what he's been able to do, for your power working in his body. Please bring good out of this for everyone involved.

'And, Lord, please help Grace trust you that you know what you're doing.'

Grace smiled and said 'Amen,' as she opened her eyes. She leaned forward and kissed him, 'You've been reading Ephesians too!'

'Well I thought as you were doing a sermon series on it I should keep up.'

She kissed him again, then again.

A surge of desire swept through her as he pulled her into his arms, his hands sliding over the silk of her nightdress and dressing gown. She felt him hardening against her as he slowly pulled the silk up over her curves. Then he was kissing her neck, her chest, her breasts, running his tongue around a nipple and down to her belly button. She sighed, stretching out against the pillows as she ran her fingers through his hair, then gasped with pleasure as he went further down.

They fell asleep in each other's arms almost instantly afterwards. The next thing she knew, it was 5 a.m. She lay there for a while, hoping to drift back off to sleep again. But as the light grew so did her awareness. She slowly disentangled herself from Peter and their sheets. She'd been dreaming about Lila and Mary again. She sat up in bed, looking for her nightdress and dressing gown. She found them where they'd been thrown last night and pulled them on, pushing her curls back off her face. She lifted her laptop off the bedside table onto the duvet in front of her, found her story document and opened it. She read over several paragraphs and then began to write:

'James has been martyred!' Joshua looked up from reading Jair's letter that had arrived that morning, all colour draining from his face.

A stunned silence followed.

Eventually Luke asked, 'When?'

Joshua scanned the parchment again, turning it over to look at the seal. 'This was sent several months ago! Why has it taken so long to reach us?'

Paul lowered his head into his hands. As he began rocking back and forth, the rope bed on which he sat creaked rhythmically. Pudens, who was sitting next to him, reached over and placed his hand on Paul's shoulder, the manacled chain on his wrist rattling noisily.

'May I see?' Luke asked Joshua.

Joshua handed the letter to him, feeling the weight of revelation break upon him. Fear for his parents mounted with each breath he took. 'There must be trouble in Judaea for it to have taken so long to reach us?'

No one spoke. In the silence Joshua became aware of the noises from the street outside: the bleating of a goat in the foreground; wheels clattering over cobbles beyond that; women's voices, a backdrop of sound beyond that still, and the faint wail of a baby crying in the distance. All these sounds were like the introduction to a piece of music before the theme tune began.

It was Paul's voice that struck the first notes of lament. The others joined him, their grief rising like secondary instruments in harmony. Pudens had never experienced anything like it among his own people, and found he was caught up I this Middle Eastern expression of emotion. He didn't know who James was, but felt the injustice of his death as if he had been a dearly beloved brother. He found he was praying for the city of Jerusalem and for the Church there, as if it were his home and his people.

Luke began to quote the prophetic words Jesus had spoken before his death: 'Do you see this Temple? Truly I tell you, not one stone here will be left on another; everyone will be thrown down. You will be handed over to be persecuted and put to death, and you will be hated by all nations because of me. At that time many will turn away from the faith and will betray and hate each other, and many false prophets will appear and deceive many people. Because of the increase of wickedness, the love of most will grow cold, but the one who stands firm to the end will be saved. And this gospel of the kingdom will be preached in the whole world as a testimony to all nations, and then the end will come.'

The lament turned into intercession. The Holy Spirit bound them together as one in their cries for the Church in Jerusalem. They prayed for wisdom for those who were now leading, that they would have courage and boldness to keep proclaiming the Gospel of peace to their people, that many more would believe. They prayed for the Jewish leaders of the city, that they would seek God and not their own agendas. They prayed for comfort for James's surviving family who were still in the city. Then they turned to pray for the Roman procurator, that he would be humble and rule Judaea as one who would have to give an account.

Joshua fell to his knees and cried for his parents, begging God to preserve their lives. He felt uncomfortably conscious of the selfishness of his prayer, but Luke joined him in his request and then Paul and Pudens agreed it wholeheartedly. Together they prayed that Jair and Lila would soon be able to return to Ephesus, where Anna and Timothy were. Joshua brokenly pleaded for the opportunity to see his loved ones again. Luke knelt beside him, wrapping a strong arm around the younger man's shoulders.

It was only as they opened their eyes that they realised how long they had been in prayer. The room was dim, the afternoon sunlight faded to twilight.

❊ ❊ ❊

Pudens listened as Paul spoke and Luke wrote.

Paul had been kneeling by the window, hands in their customary raised position, for several hours.

When Joshua entered the room, bringing food and wine fresh from the market, he imagined it must have felt like this for the high priest of the Temple to enter the hushed Holy of Holies but once a year. He quietly laid his purchases on the table and squatted down on the floor, closing his eyes and leaning his head back against the wall.

The Spirit of wisdom and revelation … he pondered Paul's words … Come Holy Spirit … give us insight and understanding beyond our natural ability … to know you Lord God … to know your thoughts … your ways … they are not our ways.

As Joshua prayed his mind was filled with an image of an eagle sweeping down onto the Temple mount. As he watched, it seemed the eagle grew in size so that its wings totally engulfed the Temple, hiding it from view. An urge to cry out overtook him, so that he doubled over, gripping his stomach, trying to hold in the sound that barrelled up his windpipe. It escaped his lips as a throttled moan.

Paul turned from the window at the sound. Luke put down his quill and rested a hand on Joshua's shoulder. 'What is it brother?' he asked quietly.

Joshua tried to describe the image he had seen in his mind's eye, but each time he spoke, the urge to cry out overwhelmed him. Finally he managed to complete the description of what he'd seen.

'It is as the Lord told us,' Luke said eventually. 'The time must be near,' he looked over at Paul.

'Yes,' Paul slowly got to his feet and came away from the window towards them. 'When the curtain of the Holy of Holies was torn in two, not only were we able to enter into His presence, but He came among us, descending at Pentecost and came to dwell in all those who believed. This is the riches of his glorious inheritance in his holy people! He has departed from the Temple. One sacrifice has been made for all, for all time. *We* are now the Temple.'

Subdued, Joshua asked, 'Do you think it truly is the end … that the Temple will literally be destroyed?'

'I do,' Paul replied simply.

'And what of Jerusalem?' Joshua already knew the answer.

'I believe it will be lain waste,' Paul's voice was heavy with sadness.

'What you have seen and felt in your spirit, is as it will be,' Paul's voice faded to a whisper.

'Tell me about your Temple,' said Pudens. 'The only other great temple I know of is the temple to Artemis' in Ephesus. But I was a young boy, so my memory of it is faded.

The other three looked at one another and then together they described in detail the glories of the second Temple: the huge dressed stones; the sweeping, majestic steps; all the gates; Solomon's Colonnade; the Court of the Women; the Priests' Court; the Altar; the ornate curtain as thick as a man's fist; then the Holy of Holies all overlaid with beaten gold ... and the treasury. By the time they had completed their description, Pudens' eyes were wide.

❋ ❋ ❋

As they made their way through Caesarea's streets, Mary was inconsolable. She sat weeping beside Junia on the little wooden cart, pulled by a donkey. Andronicus held the reigns and occasionally had to exert some effort to direct the animal as it was waylaid by alluring fruit stalls. Ahead Lila walked beside Jair as he pulled a cart laden with luggage over the cobbled streets. Andronicus had taken it in turns with Jair, being younger and stronger, giving the reigns of the donkey to Junia, so that Lila had the chance to climb up beside Mary for some of the way from Jerusalem.

There had been a growing exodus of Christians from the city since James's death. Most had gone over the Jordan River to Pella. Beatings and confiscation of property had increased in recent months. No one was sure who the orders were coming from. They may have been coming from Eleazer, who held a powerful hold over the Temple and therefore all of Jerusalem. The Zealots, who'd grown in number and in organizing themselves, had also grown powerful. John of Gischala, their leader, was a close friend of Eleazer. Whoever it was, the message was clear – Jews who believed Jesus was the Messiah were no longer welcome among their own people.

Jair had sent a letter to Joshua in Rome and to Anna in Ephesus some months ago, telling them the sad news of James's death. He had no idea if it had even reached them, as lawlessness and corruption had burgeoned in Judaea. He had sent another to Anna before they left Jerusalem, informing them of their departure and plan to return to Ephesus, but again had little certainty it would reach her.

It had been hard to convince Mary to come with them. Junia assured her that she would gather all her sisters together and join them in Ephesus as soon as possible. Lila prayed that seeing her other daughters again at the harbour would not deter her from boarding the ship. She knew that if it were her, she would not want to leave them.

As they rounded a corner, a blast of sea air hit them, bringing back old memories for Lila of the day she realised she was pregnant with Joshua. A wave of longing to see him again engulfed her. She quickened her step. The noise and smells of harbour life grew stronger: creaking planks and ropes; gulls crying; men shouting; waves sloshing against ship-keels; briny seaweed; rotting fish; wet wood; sweating humanity. She covered her nose and mouth with her shawl.

The colossal temple to Caesar loomed ahead of them and beyond it, the sea. Lila wished they could be transported in the blink of an eye to Ephesus like Philip had been to Azotus. She did not relish the journey that lay ahead of them.

When Mary caught sight of her other daughters, she nearly fell out of the cart with excitement. Junia had to restrain her until Andronicus had brought them to a halt. No sooner had they stopped than she clambered down and moved faster than Junia had seen her move in a long time. She was soon swallowed up in a flurry of arms, shawls, tears and laughter.

That was a difficult parting. Leaving Junia to set up a new home all over again in Caesarea was hard enough, but leaving all four daughters behind was unbearable. As the ship pulled away from the harbour, Lila watched Mary forlornly wave her daughters goodbye. She fought the overwhelming foreboding that this would be the last time she would see them.

※ ※ ※

'What do you think?' Timothy asked Anna.

'It's pretty thorough,' she scanned the letter he'd written and was about to send to Paul.

'Is there anything I've missed?'

His meticulousness made her smile, 'I don't think so.'

'Have I been fair?' he frowned.

She paused as she weighed up her response, 'Yes, I think so. You haven't sided with either the Jewish or the Gentile believers. You've presented both points of view. You've shown how precious unity is to you and how you have worked hard to preserve it in the Church, teaching them to know the Lord, his will and what pleases him.'

Timothy sighed, raising his eyes to her face. They were so different to hers, sloping down at the corners so that they looked almost sleepy. His nose ran straight into his forehead, with no indent at the brow, in true Greek fashion. She loved how their children reflected both their ethnic backgrounds.

He smiled at her. 'Thank you,' he said simply.

She reached up and ran a finger along his eyebrow and down the slope of his eye to his left cheek, 'You symbolise the Church – Jew and Gentile mixed together as one.' She leaned towards him and kissed his full lips.

'Our children even more so!'

'Yes,' she nodded, lifting her shawl to see their youngest asleep cradled in the crook of her arm.

'I'd better take this down to the harbour.' He rolled up the parchment, tying it with a piece of twine. He lifted the sealing candle to melt it over the other candle that glowed steadily on his desk. He then smeared wax onto the parchment, pressing his signet ring into the hot stickiness. When it had hardened he slid it into the leather tubular encasing and buckled the top tightly.

'Could you ask at the harbour if there are any letters for us from Jerusalem? We haven't heard from Mama and Papa for some time. I'm getting a little anxious.'

'Yes. I will ask for news.'

※　※　※

On his return he found Anna in the kitchen, cutting vegetables with two of the oldest children, the baby strapped to her front with her shawl.

'Tell me,' she said as he came in.

He hesitated then stepped over to her and squatted down on the earthen floor beside her. 'Not good,' he frowned.

Anna held the knife and onion suspended in the air as she waited for Timothy to continue.

'The rumour is that war is about to break out in Israel.'

'No letter from Mama?' Anna asked.

'No – nothing. Just the hearsay of sailors,' he touched her arm affectionately.

At his touch she dropped it into her lap, the onion falling from her hand and rolling away. 'We must rally the Church to pray for peace. Can we send out a messenger? Is it too late?'

'My thoughts exactly,' he said. 'I've already dispatched two and I booked the lecture theatre on my way back from the harbour.'

Anna shook off her anxiety and reached for the onion that had escaped. She returned to preparations for dinner with an air of calmness which belied her internal fear.

As she put the finishing touches to the stew before pushing it further into the clay oven, she began to pray. *Lord God, preserve my mother and father. Please help them get out of Jerusalem. Please bring them here safely. I still need them ... please, Lord God.*

'Mama, why are you crying?' Sol asked.

'Am I? It must be the heat of the oven scalding my eyes. 'Come now, bath time,' she kept her voice light yet firm. 'Call the others.'

Sol ran out into the yard obediently, calling all five names in speedy succession.

✳ ✳ ✳

Anna was not there to meet them at the harbour. Neither was Timothy.

'My letter must not have got through,' Jair voiced everyone's disappointment.

Lila resolutely cheered herself with thoughts of surprising Anna at their home. As she stepped onto land, she prayed for strength. The journey had been exhausting.

They made slow progress past the 240 foot high marble temple to Artemis and the city's great library and amphitheatre, heading painfully slowly through the bustling streets for the suburbs. Jair was grateful that Mary stopped often, as pulling the cart uphill from the harbour was gruelling work. Lila knew that leaving her children behind was the true cause of Mary's exhaustion. She patiently stayed at her side, linking arms with her occasionally when the incline grew steep.

When they finally reached Anna's home all three of them were spent. Lila knocked on the outer door three times and waited, her heart hammering in her chest. Eventually the bolt rattled on the other side of the door as it was drawn back. Lila had intended to shout 'Surprise!', but instead she burst into tears at the sight of her daughter.

'Mama!' exclaimed Anna, 'What are you doing here?'

These last words were muffled in Lila's embrace.

❋ ❋ ❋

'We only gathered the Church last night to pray peace upon Israel … and I prayed for your safety and that the Lord would bring you back here,' Anna grinned broadly at her mother and father. They'd refreshed themselves and Anna had laid out a lunch of flat breads and hummus, olives, goats' cheese and grapes under the orange tree in their courtyard.

The children were losing their shyness and surreptitiously gravitating towards their grandparents and aunt. Anna held the baby in her lap, who was all gurgles and smiles whenever Jair looked at her.

'It is so good to be here!' exclaimed Lila, her arm around Sol's young shoulders. 'I can't believe how you have grown,' she patted his back. 'As we told you in our letters, it has become more and more difficult for the Church in Jerusalem.'

Mary nodded her head in agreement. 'My girls are following me here.'

An expression flashed across Lila's features. Anna knew, she just knew, that Mary's Lila didn't think the girls would ever come. She tore herself from that dark thought. 'But Mama, we have not heard from you in months. No letters have come. We were getting so worried.'

Jair's brow became one above his eyes, 'When you were not there at the harbour to greet us, I suspected as much. Lawlessness has grown in Israel. Albinus the Procurator is as corrupt as they come, taxing us ruthlessly to pay his bribes, but caring little for enforcing order within our borders. It was clear when James was martyred right by the Temple in broad daylight that the Romans were losing control of the province.'

'James ... martyred?' Timothy's mouth hung open.

Jair looked from Lila to Mary and then at his hands, 'Sorry ... I thought you at least knew this?'

'No,' Anna whispered, a quiver in her voice.

A stunned silence hung over the family. Even the youngest children didn't break it, but looked anxiously from one adult's face to another.

'What happened?' Timothy asked eventually.

Haltingly Jair told the story, the trauma of the memory revisiting him like delayed echoes of a thunderclap returning from a far-off mountain range. Lila held his hand as he spoke. Mary sighed several times and wiped her eyes with her scarf.

Timothy's face was ashen. It was he who eventually spoke when Jair had finished. 'We have much work to do in uniting Jew and Gentile here. But if Jewish believers are not welcome in their own home city, what hope have we of helping our Jewish brethren here to keep the bond of peace with Gentile believers within the Church?'

'Have there been struggles?' Jair asked, reining in his emotions with some effort.

Timothy and Anna exchanged glances before he replied. 'There has been a growing demand in the Church that all believers be circumcised and that the Law be upheld. As you can imagine, our Greek brothers have struggled with these concepts, as when they first heard the message they were not told they had to become Jews. Our Jewish brethren speak with a spirit of legalism which opposes the spirit of grace. They do not value the riches of his glorious inheritance in a joint holy people. No matter how much they hear the gospel preached, there are those who resist God's grace for his world. I have sent a letter to Paul regarding these matters.'

'If my letter about James did not reach you, I wonder if the one I sent Paul reached him.' Jair said almost to himself. 'We must write to him again.'

'Yes,' Timothy responded, 'come with me now. Let's word it together and take it to the harbour before sunset.'

A weary look crossed Jair's eyes, followed by a resolute expression. He ate the last bit of bread he'd been holding in his hand slowly and methodically before beginning to get to his feet.

'Papa ... no ... you are weary from your journey. Timothy – let him sleep. It can wait until tomorrow.'

❊ ❊ ❊

'Eleazer has rejected the new Procurator's gift for the Temple sacrifice.'

'What? Has Florus responded yet?' Aaron's head jerked up from the scroll he was reading. He glared at his household manager.

'Not as yet,' replied the servant. 'No one in the Temple is to allow gifts from the Procurator, or from any Gentile for that matter, to be brought into the Temple any longer.'

Aaron dropped the scroll and then very slowly lowered his head into his hands. After a long silence he looked up at the man who had been his servant for over thirty years. Speaking through his hands he said, 'I suppose the lawless men Eleazer has gathered to himself are standing guard at the Temple to enforce this new law?'

'Yes master.'

Aaron leaned back in his chair and breathed deeply, 'Prepare the household,' he said, running one hand down his beard, unable to rid himself of the horror that was descending upon him. 'We must make haste and leave Jerusalem as soon possible. We will need passage from

Caesarea – we will sail for Ephesus. I have relatives there.'

The servant barely concealed his shock, 'Ephesus?'

'We haven't much time. War is about to break in Israel. If we don't go now we may never escape,' he stood as he spoke, leaning heavily on his desk. 'I am not going to defect to Rome like Josephus has. So the only option left to me is to leave. Make haste. Time is of the essence.'

'Yes master,' the younger man bowed his head and withdrew obediently.

Aaron sat down again heavily. He rarely felt his age, but in that moment he felt as old as the hills. He gazed into space.

Slowly self-preservation began to recharge his brain. Knowing overwhelmed him; tears choked him; his life's work was going to be destroyed. He pulled out a clean piece of parchment, heavy resignation weighting his movements. He took up his quill and began to write.

3. CRAVING

Ephesians 2:1–10

All of us lived at one time, gratifying the cravings of our sinful nature and following it's desires and thoughts – but God in his great love for us, who is rich in mercy, has made us alive with Christ even when we were dead in transgressions – it is by grace you have been saved.

It took huge energy – putting on the uniform. The dull navy-grey of it sapped his strength from every place it touched his skin. He fought the desire to rip it off, avoided looking at himself in the mirror and left the flat without eating breakfast. Charmaine was still not back from her night shift.

He stood pressed against the window of the subway and didn't raise his eyes from his shoes. He'd worn his old trainers, the ones he used to play football in with Josh. He fished out his mobile phone and texted his son. *First day at new job. You fancy a drink somewhere after work?* He had never asked that before. Josh always came to his flat.

He slipped the phone back into the baggy pocket of his uniform as the doors jerked open ushering a surge of weary humanity into the already cramped compartment. No one spoke. Everyone shuffled feet and rustled papers, making themselves as small as possible.

He's probably still asleep, he comforted himself when there was no reply. *It's still early.* An irrational yearning for the days when the children were young jostled his practiced detachment. The train lurched at the same time, sending him into the back of the pin-striped suit standing in front of him.

'Sorry mate,' he muttered, crushing the jealousy that clutched round the edges of the void within his soul. He had similar suits hanging redundantly in his wardrobe.

'No problem,' came the clipped reply over the shoulder.

His was the next stop. As he stepped out onto the platform, the relief of being in an open space was short lived. It dawned on him, as he breathed in, that the unintentional bump with the suit was the most human contact he'd had in a while. Self-pity scratched the back of his throat.

As he approached the hospital entrance he slowed his step and squared his shoulders. *It's only for a while*, he repeated the mantra.

He was to accompany the shabby man he'd encountered at interview. As he followed him through endless, featureless corridors, over endless, featureless hours, the gaping hole inside him swirled like a vortex that threatened to pull him in on himself, obliterating the persona he'd strived so hard to build over the years.

They stopped for lunch in a drab cafeteria. Mark checked his phone. There was no reply from Josh and nothing from Charmaine – no reference points to throw a rope to. He stared at the dried out hamburger on his plate and the over-cooked fries, wondering why he had bought them. He swallowed hard.

His dishevelled companion was speaking. Mark forced himself to focus on what he was saying as well as to make himself eat something. 'The next guy we gotta move is interesting. Been in a coma for years and then one day just woke up. Brought him back here from whatever care home he's been mouldering away in, to do tests. He's, like, one of a kind, man. No one comes round after that many years.'

Mark looked at his guide and had a fleeting vision of him smoking pot in a tepee at Glastonbury. 'What happened to him?' he picked up the burger and braved a bite. It was as disappointing as it looked.

'Had his head kicked in five years ago, doing some crazy volunteer work outside nightclubs or something? Weird! Who'd do that?'

Mark shrugged and tried to take another bite as he swallowed the first with concerted effort.

'Some cult – Jesus freaks – can't remember what they're called. If pot were legal and alcohol was banned, we wouldn't have all the mess in our city centres on the weekends that we have to endure. Mad government policies. They could make as much on taxing drugs as they do drink and they'd save millions on treating alcohol-related illnesses.'

'I doubt it,' Mark retorted through the half eaten burger.

His guide, obviously onto his favourite subject, launched into a diatribe about government drugs policy. Mark switched off. By the end of lunch he had to throw most of his fries away.

He now knew his companion was called Shay (short for Seamus). Shay led him to their next appointment. Mark braced himself as they came to the open door. Shay knocked on the peeling painted doorframe.

'Oh good. Glad you're here. That was quick,' the doctor flicked a glance in both their directions without making eye contact. 'You know where to take him.'

It was a statement more than a question.

'Brain scan?' Shay slurred his words.

'That's right,' the doctor pushed his hands into his pockets. In a slightly louder voice he said, 'They're going to take you to the MRI scanner, James. I'll meet you there. Marie's probably already there with her coffee.'

Enough energy rose in Mark for his curiosity to climb over self-absorption. He raised his eyes from the floor and looked at the shrouded skeletal body on the bed. Beneath the sheet ribs and hip bones protruded. His eyes travelled up to the face. The profile looked vaguely familiar.

Shay went to the head of the bed pressing his foot on the bed's brake pad. 'You take that end. Press your foot on that pad – see – there?' he pointed down at the wheel. Mark obeyed. As he raised his eyes from the brake, having released it, he found himself looking into the face of the patient.

The eyes were sunken, the cheeks hollow, the forehead disfigured and misshapen, but he knew that he knew this man from somewhere. He could see a corresponding recognition in his eyes too. A muscle in the one hand that lay on top of the sheet began twitching slightly. The doctor was the first to spot it.

'Hang on a second ... what? Do you want the computer?' he placed his hand on the patient's hand. 'Yes? Okay,' he reached over to the bedside cabinet and lifted down a small compact laptop. He placed it beneath the patients hand so his fingers rested on the keyboard. They watched like boys burning an ant under a magnifying glass. One finger moved very slowly from key to key.

'Mark,' the doctor read. 'Who's Mark?'

'I'm Mark,' Mark said hesitantly not really wanting anyone to know who he was at that moment. 'Who are you?' he asked.

'This is James Martin,' the doctor answered for the patient.

'James? You came to my house once? God, a long time ago ... you gave me some CDs?' The memory flooded back. Mark leaned on the end of the bed and shook his head. 'I didn't know what had happened to you ... I left probably before ....'

James was working on the keyboard again, like a slug on gravel. *Gud2CU,* he wrote.

'Good to see you too,' Mark responded, smiling despite himself, after the doctor turned the laptop round for him to read. 'Who'd have thought you and I would meet again in a place like this?' Mark looked and saw, despite the slackness of the face, that there was mirth in the eyes. 'What a state!' he grinned shaking his head.

James slowly typed again, *UOrMe*

When the doctor showed him, Mark laughed, 'Me!' It was the best moment of his day – laughing at himself. It was liberating.

'We need to get a move on,' Shay interrupted. 'Hey, my name is the Irish for James, you know,' he said looking down on James as he began to move the bed towards the door. 'What are the chances?' he said in a voice that reminded Mark of Neil from *The Young Ones.*

※　※　※

Chloe woke early, the dream still vivid in her mind. She lay there for a while listening to the rain flinging itself against the window. She turned onto her side and curled herself up, enjoying the softness of her bed and the knowledge that she needn't get up for some time. She revelled in the spattering sound of fat rain on glass. She closed her eyes. *Please don't let it stop,* she prayed.

She was running through a wood, dodging slender tree trunks and leaping over bushes. The path wasn't always clear, but it didn't seem to hinder her. Ahead she could see a clearing where light filtered down through thick foliage, dappling the forest floor. She felt anticipation and exhilaration again as she recalled the dream, but couldn't grasp what happened next.

It was just beyond the periphery of her vision; like a diver trying to see something in murky water, it remained elusive. She pulled the duvet further up round her shoulder and sighed.

Her mind drifted to her recent date; to the goodnight kiss. She touched her lips with her fingers.

No, she thought, feeling mildly surprised at this revelation.

Mark. Her eyes opened.

She looked at her digital clock. 6.00 a.m.

Mark?

She felt irritated with herself and wondered where she was in her hormonal cycle. She closed her eyes again and started counting the days since her last period. Why did she think about him suddenly?

Stupid hormones, she thought dismissively.

She focused on the sound of the rain, wondering if it had abated slightly.

Mercy. The word just appeared and hung there in her consciousness like a Christmas bauble she couldn't remember putting on her tree.

What does it even mean?

She flung the duvet off in frustration and sat up. The rain sounded like it was renewing its efforts to claw its way through her window. She lifted the curtain a little and peered out at bulging, heavy, dark clouds.

Good old English summer. She shrugged herself into her dressing gown, tucking her hair behind her ears and looking for her slippers. She went downstairs and turned the kettle on, gazing out the window at the ruined watercolour that was the view of the back garden. When it had boiled she made herself a cup of tea, just dunking the tea bag in the water a couple of times. She didn't like it strong – it set her teeth on edge.

She wandered down the hall to her office – what had once been Mark's office – cradling the warmth of the mug to her chest. Sitting down at her desk and sipping her drink, she enjoyed the first sensation of hot liquid coursing down her throat. She reached over for the dictionary she always kept by the printer and thumbed through it until she found the word.

Kindness shown in not punishing a wrong-doer.

Chloe pondered this for a while. She wondered if it had a fuller meaning, maybe in Hebrew? She must ask Grace. But then the idea struck her that perhaps she'd find something on the internet. She opened her laptop and typed, 'Hebrew meaning of mercy' into her search engine. She clicked on an article entitled '*Distinctive Ideas of the Old Testament*,' by N.H. Snaith, London (1944).

'The Hebrew word "chesed" refers to God's love for his people Israel ... The nearest New Testament equivalent to "chesed" is "charis" (grace), as Luther realised ...

...The word is used only in cases where there is some recognised tie between the parties concerned. It is not used indiscriminately of kindness in general, haphazard, kindly deeds ... The theological importance of the word "chesed" is that it stands more than any other word for the attitude which both parties to a covenant ought to maintain towards each other ... the twin ideas of love and loyalty ... steadfastness and persistence of God's sure love ... all man's steadfastness is like the wild flowers, here today and gone tomorrow, whilst the Lord is steady and sure, firm and reliable.

... God's yearnings for the people of his choice are stronger still than his yearnings for justice. Here is the great dilemma of the prophets, and indeed the dilemma of us all to this day. Which comes first, mercy or justice?

...When we try to estimate the depth and the persistence of God's loving-kindness and mercy, we must first remember his passion for righteousness. It is so strong that he could not be more insistent in his demand for it, but God's persistent love for his people is more insistent still.

... The word stands for the wonder of his unfailing love ... the solving of the problem of the relation between his righteousness and his loving-kindness passes beyond human comprehension.'

'Well N.H Snaith, it's beyond my comprehension,' Chloe said out loud. The sound of her own voice in that room – the room where her clients came to unburden their souls, to be heard, to find compassion, to seek help to grow, to confess, to reconnect – brought her up short.

Don't I offer mercy here?

Silence.

So why can't I offer it to Mark?

Silence.

But I did ... and he abused it ... he was unfaithful to me again ... It had to be over.

She closed her eyes and waited, like Grace had taught her so long ago. She hadn't wanted to do this for years. It had felt too risky, but now something was drawing her like an undercurrent, and she found she wanted to give into it. Stillness settled upon her, despite the clattering of the rain outside.

Images formed on the screen of her imagination: of Mark on their wedding day in St Matt's, smiling down at her, a look of wonder and disbelief in his beautiful eyes; Mark holding Melanie and crying at the miracle of their first child; Mark playing football with Josh in the garden; Mark's patient kindness to her after her affair; making love on the kitchen table; renewing their vows in St Matt's; leaving his home, his family to live with Charmaine ... A hard lump choked her throat. *I can't do this,* she panicked.

We are divorced.

The coldness of the fact fluttered her eyes open. She looked at the computer screen, her eyes settling on the sentence: '*When we try to estimate the depth and the persistence of God's loving-kindness and mercy, we must first remember his passion for righteousness. It is so strong that he could not be more insistent in his demand for it, but God's persistent love for his people is more insistent still.*'

Well, God, I can't do this ... but you can. I can pray that you show him mercy ... but that's about it at the minute.

It's enough, came the thought instantly. She felt encouraged like a child.

Okay, Lord, show your mercy to Mark. Show him your kindness. Save him from himself – from the cravings that have caused a bit more of him to die every day. Bring him alive again – wake him up to all you have for him.

It occurred to her that she too needed waking. These last five years had been hard. She'd had to keep going. She'd held everything together for the kids. She'd set up her own counselling practice so as to keep the house and she'd run My Sister's House. She'd faced each day resolutely and ended them in the comfort of wine – self-medication – but it had done the job. She'd survived, but only like a post-operative patient on morphine.

What have you got for me? Is there more ... or is this it?

She looked at the drawer where she kept her old journal and Study Bible. She hadn't opened it in a long time. Slowly she reached for the handle and pulled it. She lifted the Bible onto her desk and the journal that Grace had given her for Christmas 2012. She opened it to the last entry and read:

I found him again, but this time I think it was live.

I think he knew her.

Old feelings rushed back like a tsunami. She inhaled sharply, pressing her hand on her chest, before reading on.

I can't bear to have him near me.
    It's over.
    It's got to be over.
    I can't do this again ... after all we've been through, so publicly too.
    If he doesn't end it soon, I will.
    And where are you?
    Do you even care?
    Didn't you make vows with us ... weren't you there when we renewed them?
    You're the third strand in this cord that isn't supposed to be easily broken.
    Do you even exist?
    It's broken.

She rubbed her chest, soothing the pounding of her heart. She flipped the page back to see what her Bible reading had been that day. Would she even have recorded it?

She had.

It was Psalm 66: 1-12.

She'd underlined verse twelve.

' ... *we went through fire and water, but you brought us to a place of abundance.*'

Slowly she picked up a pen and scrawled the date a few lines below the last entry. Then she wrote:

Hello God — it's me again.
    It's been a long time — five years!
    I'm sorry.
    I guess I've been going through what you call fire and water?
    You know.
    I woke this morning thinking of Mark and mercy.
    I can't — .
    However, you can. I've prayed you would.

I don't know what's going on in his life.
Perhaps you've prompted me to pray?
Psalm 66:10 says that 'you refined us like silver'.
Is that what you've been doing?
I feel like I've been semi-conscious, not fully awake or asleep.
But today something is changing — like I want to wake up.
And what about this place of abundance?
What is that?

❊ ❊ ❊

'What do you fancy?' Chloe asked Grace as they leaned against the bar of their favourite pub, scanning the specials board.

'I don't really know,' Grace absently twisted a white-blonde ringlet round her finger.

'I'm going for a chicken Caesar,' Chloe made up her mind.

'Really?' Grace eyed her friend in surprise.

'Yeah! I'm turning over a new leaf ... or something,' Chloe's gaze was level.

The barman left the till and came towards them, 'What'll it be ladies?' he asked.

'A diet coke and?' Chloe looked to Grace.

'No wine?'

'No.'

'Oh ... um ... I'll have a white wine spritzer with soda and ice please.' She turned to Chloe, 'You're full of surprises today!'

Chloe replied with a smile, tucking her glossy hair behind her ears.

'What's brought all this on?' Grace wanted to know.

'I know you're going to be really glad about this, but if you can restrain yourself a little, that would be great!' Chloe began, grinning broadly. 'I started praying again and I think God is speaking to me ... at least, I mean, I'm reading the Bible. So I thought I'd get healthy too ... you know drink less, eat more fruit and veg?'

Grace obediently restrained the huge emotions that swelled her chest and threatened to burst it. Her eyes watered and through a wobbly smile she said, 'That's so great Chloe.'

The barman slid their drinks across the polished wood and took their food order: two chicken Caesar salads in the end. As they made their way to their alcove looking out on the pub garden, Grace wrapped an arm round Chloe's neck and couldn't resist giving her a big kiss on the cheek.

'Oh stop it,' Chloe said pushing her away.

Grace sat down, wiping her eyes. 'Sorry ... I knew you'd come back some day ... just didn't know when.'

'I didn't think I would. But then I woke the other morning thinking about Mark and about mercy. That's what sent me back to reading the Bible.'

'Really?' Grace's blue eyes blurred again. She wiped them with the backs of her hands and laughed, 'That's so fantastic!'

They sat smiling affectionately at each other for a while.

'I looked up the Hebrew meaning of the word mercy. It was really helpful.'

'*Chesed*,' Grace smiled and nodded. 'It's unique. The idea of stepping into someone else's shoes and thinking with their thoughts and feeling with their feelings ... it's quite revolutionary.'

Chloe frowned, 'I didn't read that, but that's interesting.'

Grace went on, 'It's what Jesus did for us. He stepped into our shoes, became like us. God in skin, so that God's mercy would triumph over his judgement.'

Chloe's eyes widened slightly. 'That's what it said ... about God's demand for mercy being even greater than his demand for justice.'

'It's mind blowing, isn't it?'

'Yep ... I've begun praying for mercy for Mark.'

Grace said, 'I've been praying for Mark recently too ' ... without stopping she blurted out the thought that next struck her, 'Hey, maybe he'll come back if you're coming back?'

'To me?' Chloe was shaking her head. 'I don't want him back,' she frowned and sipped her drink. 'To God maybe, or even just to his kids would be good,' she sighed.

'Elizabeth Taylor and Richard Burton did it,' Grace was like a dog with a bone.

Chloe pursed her lips. 'No.' she shook her head, a long lock of chestnut silk fell over her face, obscuring one eye and the dark mole near her nose.

A waitress brought two large salad bowls over, giving Chloe the chance to think.

'It would never work ….'

Grace thoughtfully chewed some of her salad. When she'd finished she quoted, 'If you live by the Spirit so that you won't gratify the desires of your sinful nature, maybe it would be possible?'

Chloe rolled her eyes.

※　※　※

Josh hadn't texted back by the end of the day, so Mark made his weary way home thinking of Charmaine. He half-hoped she would be there and half-hoped she wouldn't. A sludge of emotions oozed within him as he turned the key in the lock. The first thing to hit him was the smell of perfume and hairspray. He passed the empty living room and went to the bedroom, taking off the shirt of his offending uniform. Charmaine walked out of the bathroom, freshly showered and dressed in tracksuit bottoms and a sleeveless T-shirt.

They stared at each other across the double bed.

'Hi,' she said.

'Hi,' he replied.

'Nice outfit,' she quipped.

Mark didn't reply.

'So how was your first day?' She sat down on the edge of the bed, flinging her freshly dried blonde tresses over her shoulder.

'How was your night?' he retorted pointedly.

'Is this how it's gonna be?' she demanded irritably, turning her face away from him.

'It doesn't have to be,' Mark parried.

Charmaine swore. Then, 'What do you want me to say? It was terrible? I hated it?'

'You don't have to say anything! Just stop it! Quit! I'm working now,' he raised his voice.

She laughed cynically, shaking her head.

'What? Being a porter isn't good enough?' he shouted shaking the grey-blue shirt in his fist.

The scathing look in her eyes said it all.

Mark dropped his arm to his side, fiddling with the label on the inside of the collar. He felt lost. He started to smile, 'So being a hooker is fine ... but a porter?'

'I earned £400 last night. How much did you earn today?'

'There's more to life than money,' he said fixing his gaze on her.

'I agree,' she nodded.

Mark felt momentarily hopeful, but then she said, 'There's sex and power too ... and I want all three.'

Strangely a memory of a Year 10 school play came vividly to Mark's mind. He'd landed the lead role for the first time in his life and had loved the adulation he'd received from girls who'd previously never given him a second glance. It was the last performance and the last scene, when one of the backdrops began sagging and then falling during his most significant monologue. The horror of seeing the painted fabric fluttering to the floor, revealing the ugly, blacked out backstage and gawping stage hands, was too much and Mark had forgotten his lines in a frozen daze. He'd never acted again.

He gazed at Charmaine now, wondering how he could have been so deceived.

'What?' she asked rudely.

His mind was blank.

'You look pathetic Mark, like a rabbit in headlights,' she sneered.

He turned from her to the wardrobe, fished out a clean shirt and slipped it on, slowly buttoning it up. When he got to the fourth button he looked at her. 'I want you out of here,' he said quietly.

'Suit yourself,' she retorted. 'I'll sleep on the sofa.'

'No ... I mean out of my flat.'

It was her turn to stare. 'Get over yourself, Markie,' she quipped, looking at her nails.

'I'm serious, Charmaine. If you won't give this up, I want you out. I'm not sharing you with other men, not for money, not for anything.'

'But you didn't mind sharing me with other men as a stripper. You knew what you were getting with me. Why the drama now? Nothing's really changed.'

'Everything's changed.'

'You can't afford to keep this place and pay child support,' she changed tack.

Mark marvelled at her calculating nature, shaking his head, 'You are something else ... why have I not seen it before?'

'Because you had your eyes on my ass like every other man,' she snapped, jumping to her feet in a sudden rage.

The final length of backdrop fluttered to the floor between them.

'I'm going out. When I come back I want you and all your stuff gone,' he said calmly.

'Where am I supposed to go?' she demanded.

'I don't know ... maybe to one of your clients or your pimp?'

As he walked out the bedroom door, a bottle of perfume sailed past his head and smashed on the hallway wall. He didn't hesitate, even though he realised he was still wearing his uniform trousers and old trainers. He grabbed his jacket and left.

※　※　※

He tried calling Josh several times, with no joy. Then he tried Melanie. She answered after three rings, 'Hi, Dad, you okay?'

'Yeah ... yeah ... Are you busy tonight? Could we meet up?'

'Oh ... um ... no, I'm not busy. What do you want to do?' she asked.

'Could we meet for a drink and a chat?' Mark forced his voice to stay light.

Melanie agreed to meet him in half an hour.

He waited for her over a pint of ale at the quiet bar. Several other men stood alone with their drinks. *Is this what I've become?*

He noted their eyes following Melanie as she walked towards him. He knew what they were thinking.

'Hi, Dad. This is a surprise. What's up?'

'Does something have to be up for me to want to see you?'

'No ... but you haven't wanted to much, in the past,' she said candidly.

Mark took it. 'You're right. I'm sorry. I've been a crap dad.'

Melanie didn't say anything to soften the confession.

In the pause that yawned between them, Mark glanced at her profile several times, realizing how like her mother she was. A pang of regret caught him off guard, that he'd missed all those little growing up moments over the past five years. 'What do you want to drink?' he asked eventually.

'I'll have half a cider and blackcurrant,' she said, still not looking at him.

Mark ordered and paid for the drink and then came back to stand beside her perched on her bar stool. 'So how's life?' he asked lamely.

She looked frustrated. 'Is this really why you wanted to see me? To shoot the breeze?'

Mark hadn't counted on her being so defended. Flustered, he took a large gulp from his glass. When he'd swallowed, he wiped his mouth nervously with the back of his hand, 'I'm just warming up ... you know ... like people do?' he hoped she'd play ball.

'Dad,' Melanie turned her gaze on him.

'Well,' Mark stumbled, 'I've been missing all of you recently and wanting to get back in touch. Losing my job has been a bit of a wake-up call.'

'Oh,' Melanie said. She eyed him over her glass. 'But you've got a new job now haven't you?'

'Yes.'

'What is it?'

'I'm working for the NHS.'

'Doing what?'

'HR,' the lie came easily.

'That's a bit of a change for you? Or are you doing any analysis for them as well?'

'Not so much of that. More logistics.'

"Mmmm,' she nodded and sipped her drink scrutinizing him.

'So how are you?'

'I'm okay. I'm moving out. Actually it's a flat near you. I'm sharing with a friend.'

'That's great!' Mark's mood lifted momentarily. 'Can I help you move in?'

'That would be nice. We might need a few things doing.'

'How's your work going? Are you still with My Sister's House?'

'Yeah – I oversee all the halfway houses as well as working with Mo on case work.'

'You love it don't you?'

'I do,' she smiled shyly, 'it's very rewarding. I'll keep doing it as long as we can get the funding.'

How different from Charmaine, he thought. 'What about your social life? What do you like doing?'

She shrugged a little, 'I like a good film now and then ... a good book.'

'Anybody special in your life?'

She looked hurt. 'No – I haven't got time for that. What do you care anyway Dad? Why the sudden interest?'

'I've never stopped caring ... I ... I just couldn't be there ... mum didn't ....'

'Don't blame mum!' Melanie interrupted him acidly.

'Sorry ... I wasn't ... I mean ....' This was proving more difficult than he had imagined.

'I don't rate leaving your wife and kids for a girl not much older than your daughter as caring,' Melanie said coldly.

Mark couldn't look at her. He bit his lip. 'You're right,' he said eventually. 'I screwed up big time.'

Melanie wondered as she scanned his profile: 'Something else has happened hasn't it, Dad? What's going on?'

Mark felt like he was the child. He shook his head and forced himself to look at her and smile, 'No, no ... I'm fine, really, I just miss you guys. I want to make amends – if I can.'

'You can't go back and change things. This is how it is now,' she said emphatically. Then in a softer voice, 'It's nice that you wanted to meet up. More of this wouldn't go amiss.'

'So, could we meet again soon?' he asked hopefully.

'Okay, I'd like that.' She gave him a guarded smile.

❊ ❊ ❊

Grace sat at her desk waiting for inspiration. She rubbed her chin and felt an offending bristle. She jumped out of her chair and went to the hall mirror. Sure enough – there it was again! She ran up the stairs to find her tweezers.

After successfully removing the affront to her femininity she checked her face for anything else she'd not noticed. Lines under the eyes – yes; round the mouth – yes; between the eyebrows – yes. Nothing else? No new white, wiry hairs amongst her curls – no. *I am procrastinating!*

She returned downstairs and forced herself to type the sermon title and date onto the blank screen. As she gazed at it, her mind wandered to a conversation she'd had with Melanie. *Something is definitely going on with Mark. She didn't say, but she knew it too. Lord, get him! Bring him back! Save him from himself – from his cravings ....*

Her mind ranged over a variety of things: the food shopping she needed to do some time in the next two days, the ironing pile that looked like it had spawned a litter of baby ironing piles, the gay couple who were coming to see her later on that evening and then – Lila and Mary – and Aaron. The yearning to be in their world overtook her. She flicked to her documents and her writing file and opened her story to read through the last chapter.

Before she knew it, she was gone. She opened her Bible and read Ephesians 2:1-10. Life's demands could wait – she started writing:

Aaron stood with his feet planted firmly apart on the deck of the ship as it tipped and rolled. Shading his eyes he searched the coastline for the harbour they had all been longing for. 'There it is!' he shouted to his servant, the wind ripping the words from his lips.

It had been too long, too rough and too exhausting a journey. He never wanted to set foot on another ship. He picked his way between the other passengers towards the bow, looking down at the bulkhead as it sliced its way through the Mediterranean. Safe-harbour could not come soon enough.

His servant was busy organizing the rest of his household in preparation for landing. Sounds of the commotion behind him were thrown with each gust of wind. He tore his eyes from the waves as a thought struck him, 'Where are the scrolls?' he barked at his servant.

'Here master, with me,' the servant pointed to a large trunk beside him.

'Good,' Aaron clapped him on the shoulder. 'We will disembark first; the captain has given me his word.'

The servant nodded knowing a bribe had changed hands. He gave instructions for everyone to move close to the starboard side where the gangplank would be lowered. There were six in their party with all their worldly possessions with them. It would be a slow process unloading when they docked. The servant dreaded the task of procuring transportation. Haggling was something he hated and he was afraid his language skills would fail him. His master had been in foul temper throughout the journey and he wanted nothing less than to arouse his anger.

❋ ❋ ❋

'Ruth, how good to see you! The years haven't changed you,' Aaron's relief at being on land added greater enthusiasm to his charm than he genuinely felt as he kissed his sister on both cheeks.

'Nor you brother,' she returned his kisses. 'You must be exhausted after your long journey? Where is Leah? Oh there she is!' she exclaimed exuberantly not waiting for Aaron to reply and reaching past him to embrace his wife.

'Darling, this is my brother Aaron and his lovely wife Leah,' she stepped back to draw her husband in to greet them both. 'Aaron, let me introduce you to Onesiphorus.' He was a tall Greek with broad shoulders and sturdy limbs. His hair was dark with only a few silver traces around his ears.

'It is good to meet you at last Aaron. I have heard so much about you,' he bowed his head respectfully towards them both. Leah in turn bowed hers, smiling demurely. 'How was the journey?' he asked her.

'It was terrible!' Aaron exhaled, speaking for Leah. 'We have never been so glad to have our feet on solid ground.'

'A warm welcome awaits you at our home,' Onesiphorus smiled at Leah and then turned to Aaron, 'May I introduce my steward to yours? Between them they can arrange everything and follow on behind us.'

'Yes certainly,' Aaron replied.

Introductions were made and the two stewards began the tedious logistics. Ruth took Leah's arm and began leading her ahead of the men away from the harbour. Irritated by this Aaron followed, quickening his pace to overtake the women.

Onesiphorus was surprised to be momentarily left behind.

'So, you have been married to my sister for how long now?' Aaron asked over his shoulder as he overtook the women and settled into a pace in front of them.

Onesiphorus leaned forward to hear him as he almost ran to keep up with him. 'Rueben died four years ago ... so it must be nearly two years, I think.'

'Did you know my previous brother-in-law? He was a dear friend of mine.'

'Yes. I met him through the synagogue. He was a good teacher.'

'He was a good student,' Aaron confirmed.

'You taught him?'

'Yes.'

'Well, you did a fine job there! Sadly his health deteriorated rapidly over the time I knew him, but he didn't let it stop him teaching the scriptures. His passing was a great loss and sadness to our community.'

Aaron nodded. 'Brother, tell me how our people fare in this great city? Are there many synagogues?' Aaron asked.

'The Jewish community does very well here. There are synagogues and Churches scattered throughout the city.'

'Churches?' Aaron turned his sharp eyes upon him.

'Many have become followers of the Way,' Onesiphorus explained. 'Paul of Tarsus began preaching here some years ago, first in the synagogue and then in the lecture hall of Tyrannus. Have you heard of him?'

Aaron laughed, 'Heard of him? He was one of my protégés, a Pharisee among Pharisees.'

'So do you too believe that Jesus of Nazareth is the Christ?' Onesiphorus's face was alight with interest.

'I wouldn't say I have quite reached that conclusion as yet,' Aaron parried diplomatically, 'however I know much about the movement ... it has grown exponentially in Judaea.'

'We've heard tell – even in these troubled times.'

'Indeed.' Determined to steer the conversation away from

anything to do with Christianity Aaron said, 'War is immanent. Jerusalem is in factions. Any house divided against itself is sure to fall,' he concluded.

'When we heard about the death of the apostle James our hearts were broken. We have been fasting and praying for the leaders of the Jerusalem Church. Your letter added fuel to the foreboding we sense for Israel.'

Well-practiced in the art of denial, Aaron skimmed over his memory of James's brutal death. 'So you and Ruth are followers of the Way?' he asked drawing his hand down his silver beard, soothing the agitation he felt.

'Indeed we are. A large gathering of the Church meets in our home on the Lord's Day.'

'On the first day of the week?'

'That's right.'

'I hope Ruth still observes the Sabbath?' Aaron barely hid his alarm, skirting round an elderly woman moving slowly under the weight of a large basket of fruit.

'Certainly – we all do. I don't know if you realise this, but I was a convert to Judaism through Ruben. When Paul preached here I went on to become a follower of Jesus, along with Ruben and Ruth and many others in the synagogue. It was actually Paul who presided at our wedding,' Onesiphorus grinned proudly.

Aaron nodded, 'Mmmm.' He was trying to sound interested.

'We have continued to observe Jewish custom; after all, our Lord said he had come to fulfil the whole law and the prophets. Being a follower of Jesus has brought the scriptures more alive to us.'

Aaron's eyes were inscrutable as he clawed his emotions back behind a polite mask. 'How fascinating,' was all he could say. They stopped to let a donkey and cart pass by.

They walked in silence for a while, then Onesiphorus said, 'We are approaching one of the seven wonders of the world! Aphrodite's Temple, one of the tallest buildings of its kind.' Both men knew he was filling the stilted silence with trivia as he gestured to the huge marble columns that soared ahead of them above all the surrounding buildings.

Aaron gave the architecture a contemptuous glance. 'It is nothing compared to the Temple in Jerusalem.'

'I'm sure you're right,' Onesiphorus realised his new relative was going to need to be handled carefully. He looked over his shoulder and willed Ruth and Leah to catch up with them. Then a thought occurred to him, 'Let's wait for the women here under the shade of this tree. These old legs aren't what they used to be,' he grinned congenially.

Aaron gratefully agreed, even though he knew the younger man had ample strength. He was tired. Their conversation had drained all his reserves. He wished only to lie down and sleep. When he was rested he would be more able to think clearly. He knew if he said much more he would expose his true feelings towards their so-called Messiah. He didn't know how long he was going to have to rely upon his sister's hospitality. It would never do to argue with them at this early stage. He leaned against the trunk of the tree and gratefully accepted the goat-skin of water that Onesiphorus handed him.

❋　❋　❋

The Church gathered in the large courtyard of Ruth's home. The servants had stretched awnings across the space in the early hours of the morning, tying them to the trees that overhung the walls. They had a table set at one end with bread and wine, cold meats, fruits and cheeses. Against his better judgement, Aaron had agreed to address the people, bringing news of Jerusalem.

As he watched the people enter, it was easy to spot the Gentiles. He wondered how his sister could bear to defile her home in this way. He made sure he kept his distance from them and was glad he had made Leah stay in seclusion. He grudgingly gave his sister the benefit of the doubt and thought that perhaps they had all been circumcised. How else could she allow them over her threshold?

'Jerusalem is under great threat,' he began when the infernal singing had ceased. Such long, repetitive songs praising the various alleged attributes of the Christ. He'd almost lost the will to live. But as he'd watched and listened to them, keeping his face devoid of emotion, a plan had begun to form in his mind. What if he were to become part of the Church, become one of their teachers? Fighting, challenging and persecuting them had not worked in Jerusalem, perhaps subterfuge would work in this new world order? He could ensure that they adhered to Moses, the law and prophets.

He told them of the ruthless Florus, the Roman governor, and corrupt Albinus before him, who had increased taxes year on year, paying bribes, lining his own pockets and releasing robbers from prison if the price was right. He spoke of the growing factions among the powerful in Jerusalem – John of Gischala, who'd been a general in the Jewish army, now leading the Zealots; Simon Bar Gioras leading several thousand who had degenerated into a band of looters; and Eleazer Bar Simon, the Temple Captain, who sought to restore religious practice of Judaism to the nation.

'A house divided against itself will not stand!' Aaron declared the mantra that had played in his head since he'd tried to speak to Jonathan the High Priest. 'For many years a regular sacrifice was offered in the Temple on behalf of the Roman Emperor. When Eleazer ordered that these sacrifices be stopped and Jonathan, the High Priest colluded with him, I knew it was over. It was then that I believed God had work for me to do elsewhere – here in the new world. I wish to help you establish the honour of his Name and to be a blessing in this place and to many nations,' he paused for effect.

'Thank you for welcoming me and my household into your community. Our grief at leaving our homeland is softened by your warm fellowship,' he spread his elegant hands magnanimously in a gesture of gratitude.

Ruth stood and thanked him for what he'd said. She led a time of prayer for Jerusalem, which again seemed to go on for an interminably long time. Prayers were said in different languages and then interpreted. Aaron was appalled that his sister led. He knew she spoke Greek, Hebrew and Aramaic, but not the strange tongue she spoke in when she prayed. He had heard of the phenomenon said to accompany the alleged giving of the Spirit of God to followers of Jesus. He listened sceptically as she babbled and then someone across the courtyard interpreted.

Then the leader of the Church, a man named Timothy, who Ruth had pointed out to him earlier along with an elderly couple called Priscilla and Aquilla, stood at the table and led them in the strange ritual of bread and wine that had caused many to suspect that the Christians were cannibals. Timothy's wife stood beside him, a striking Jewess. Together they distributed the bread and wine to the people as they came forward. They ended the ritual with a celebratory song and then the meal began in earnest.

Aaron watched in horror as Jew and Gentile ate together. In order to survive this new way of life he must bend – he must give the benefit of the doubt – but before he could think further the leader's wife had brought him a plate of food and was asking him, 'Where is Leah? I have food for her too,' she smiled up into his face.

Aaron felt momentarily foolish. Her eyes ... He blinked.

'Where is your wife?' she repeated, raising her voice above the babble of conversation.

'Sorry,' he recovered, 'she is resting. I will take it to her. Thank you,' he forced a smile.

'I'm Anna,' she said, 'I'm married to Timothy. Together we lead the Church here in Ephesus with the help of Priscilla, Aquilla, Onesiphorus and your lovely sister.'

He took the plates of food she held out to him, 'Thank you,' he said again, asking casually, 'So have you always lived in Ephesus?'

'Oh no, I am from Jerusalem. It is terrible to hear what is happening there. I pray daily for our home.'

'Who are your parents? Perhaps I know them?' his pulse quickened.

'I doubt it. They travelled for many years with the apostle Paul and have only returned here recently for much the same reasons as you.'

'They are here? Tell me – I may know them,' Aaron held anticipation in check.

'My father is Jair Bar Jonas and my mother's name is Lila,' Anna smiled. 'You will meet them soon enough. They are not here today as my father has been ill.'

Aaron's mouth filled with saliva. He swallowed. His heart hammered against his ribs.

Those eyes...

As he skirted round the crowded courtyard, trying not to let anyone touch the plates of food he carried in his hands, his nervous system was charged with energy. He felt vital, young again. This woman was the fruit of his and Lila's union – his daughter! His mind raced as he entered the guest chamber where Leah waited for him. He gave her the food and sat in silence to eat his.

'Can I come out soon?' she asked.

'No, there are Gentiles present.'

'But are Anna and Ruth there?'

Angrily Aaron replied, 'Yes, they are defiling themselves by eating and drinking with Gentiles. Do you wish to defile yourself in such a way?'

'No, but I just wanted to see what was going on. The singing sounded so beautiful.'

'Beautiful?' he said scathingly. 'If you like turgid repetition!'

Leah glanced longingly at the shuttered window.

'Eat your food and give thanks that you are not like them,' he commanded.

They ate the remainder of their meal in silence. After Aaron said the traditional prayers of thanksgiving he took her plate and stood up. 'I will return shortly.'

Leah's gaze drifted sadly towards the window again.

❋ ❋ ❋

'I would love to meet your wife,' Anna was saying.

'Would that be acceptable to you Timothy?' Aaron asked deferentially.

'If Anna wishes it,' Timothy smiled at his wife, 'She knows the Lord's voice well, Aaron. I trust and rely on her discernment.' Seeing the look of surprise on Aaron's face he jumped at the opportunity to teach, 'You see, Aaron, Jesus has taught us a new way of relating to one another. We are to submit to each other out of reverence for

Him. We men are to love our wives as He loves the Church and gave Himself up for her. In Him there is no male nor female, no Jew nor Gentile, no slave nor freed men. We are all one in Christ. The good news we preach is that of reconciliation of male and female, of all people and all things under one head – our Lord Jesus Christ.'

'Yes,' Aaron nodded, 'how fascinating.' The smile on his lips did not reach his eyes. He turned to Anna eager to escape. 'Shall we find Leah?'

'Yes – let's,' Anna took his arm.

Timothy watched them as they walked away. It struck him fleetingly how alike they were.

❋ ❋ ❋

That evening as Aaron lay down to sleep, Leah said, 'She is very like you.'

'Who?' Aaron asked innocently.

'Anna – it's something about her eyes.'

Aaron did not look her way, but rolled over, turning his back to her and blowing out the night light. 'Perhaps we have some distant relative in common,' he muttered, closing his eyes and willing his wife to cease.

'She is very beautiful,' Leah went on in the darkness.

'Mmmm ....'

'But she is too young for you – she could be your daughter.'

Aaron's eyes flew open – his temper a touch paper, 'Be quiet woman!' he barked.

She knew she shouldn't, but she couldn't help herself. She had seen the way he looked at the younger woman, how there had been a connection between them. Disregarding her own safety, she said, 'I am not blind. I can see.'

The blow came quicker than she'd expected, knocking the wind out of her. She gagged and retched.

'You talk putrid rubbish as usual,' she felt the words in spittle and garlic-laced breath on her face as he grabbed her throat. She managed to drag in some air as she cowered against the wall. 'Do not speak of this to me again,' he hissed, his grip tightening around her neck.

As quickly as his rage had fired, it died. He let go and she could hear him breathing hard as his head fell back on the pillow. He turned away and she heard him mutter, 'Why must you make me so angry? I don't wish to hurt you.'

She lay frozen still for a long time until she heard his first snore. Then her body began to tremble.

※ ※ ※

Lila watched Jair's chest rise and fall in shallow breaths. Occasionally she leaned forward, lifted the cloth from the bowl of water, wrung it out and dabbed his thin face and neck. She had sent a letter to Joshua in Rome last week asking him to come. The illness had gone on too long.

She heard a tap at the door and looked up. It was Mary. 'Anna wants to see you. Shall I take over for a while?'

Lila's heart lifted. She nodded and pushed herself slowly off the carved wooden chair. She felt slightly light-headed as she stood. She closed her eyes and waited for her vision to clear. She felt Mary's touch on her arm, 'Are you all right?'

'I might need to eat something,' Lila said to her old friend, 'I forgot breakfast this morning.'

'Lila,' Mary scolded, 'you must eat. We cannot have both of you laid low.'

'I know, I know,' Lila agreed. She moved towards the door as she gave Mary a little smile.

Touching the walls for support, she made her way down the hallway to the large living room where she knew she would find Anna with several children. 'Shalom my darlings,' she said as she entered.

'How is Papa?' Anna asked looking up from the downy head of her youngest at her breast.

'The same,' Lila sighed as she settled into the couch opposite her daughter and gathered two of her grandchildren to her. 'Give Grandma a kiss,' she leaned in to one then the other as they happily obeyed. 'That's better … I feel almost happy again,' she smiled affectionately down at their upturned faces.

'You look faint, Mama,' Anna said.

'I forgot to eat this morning,' Lila explained.

'I'll get you something in a moment. Some yogurt and fruit?'

'That would be lovely,' Lila replied. As she watched her daughter finish nursing her baby, her heart swelled with emotion. 'I remember feeding you.'

Anna looked up and smiled.

'I could hardly believe you were real or that it was possible to love someone so much.'

Anna looked back down, 'I know. You never seem to run out of love for them, do you?'

'You were such a miracle, such a blessing. I thought I would only ever have you, but then I had Joshua too. So precious.'

'Why was I such a miracle?' Anna asked again. She'd often wondered but never got a proper answer from her mother.

Whether it was because Lila's blood sugar was low or because her mind was affected by anxiety for Jair, or both, her usual guard was down when it came to the facts surrounding Anna's origin. 'We couldn't have children. A Seer had told Papa that he would survive a fatal childhood illness, but would not be able to father children as a result. She said the curse would only be broken when he met a mysterious stranger,' Lila's voice was soft and dreamy.

'So he was healed when he met Jesus? You conceived me after you both met Jesus?' Anna asked, trying to get the whole story straight in her mind.

Lila looked at her daughter, her eyes focusing slowly. Her mouth opened then shut. She swallowed. 'I need something to eat Anna, and drink too. Would you be so kind as to get them for me?'

'Of course, Mama,' Anna said, feeling slightly frustrated. 'Here, take her for me,' she stood up and gently lowered the sated baby into Lila's lap.

'She looks so like you,' Lila smiled touching chubby fingers curled in a loose fist resting against her pink cheek. 'And like your father,' she added in almost a whisper.

'I can't see Papa in her at all,' Anna said as she went to the kitchen. 'In fact I can't see Papa in any of them!' she laughed.

Lila gazed after her.

❋ ❋ ❋

'I'm not sure,' said Onesiphorus.

'What's not to be sure of?' Ruth asked.

'Again – I'm not sure. Granted he is eloquent and schooled in the art of rhetoric. Over the last few weeks, despite buying a property and moving into it, his engagement with the young men has been admirable. His knowledge and passion for the scriptures is second perhaps only to Paul's.'

'He taught Paul, you know,' Ruth said.

'So I gather,' her husband nodded. 'He is a very good teacher. However there is something that bothers me – like a mosquito that I can't see, but can only hear buzzing somewhere behind me in the dark.'

'Oni,' Ruth laughed, 'you are funny! He's my brother. We need not be suspicious of him. His motives are pure – the honour of the Lord's name. You heard him yourself!'

'I know,' he shook his big, dark head and then rubbed his eyes. 'I do like him,' he assured her, reaching over and cupping her chin in his hand. 'All I can say is that I have a check in my spirit every time you've suggested he teach the whole Church. What have Priscilla and Aquilla said? Do you know what Timothy and Anna think?'

'They respect his knowledge of the scriptures greatly too – Anna especially.'

'Perhaps we should gather to seek the Lord together on the matter?' Onesiphorus suggested.

'Yes, that would be good.'

'I think it's that I'm not sure of his love for our Lord Jesus Christ.'

'But he told me yesterday he would like to be baptised.'

'Really?' Onesiphorus's eyebrows disappeared into his curly hairline. 'Well, that is good to hear!'

'See! You worry too much,' she leant forward and kissed him.

�֎ ✖ ✖

'I repent of my sins,' Aaron repeated after Aquilla as they stood side by side in the Cayster River. 'I turn to Christ,' he said obediently.

Ruth wiped her eyes; Oni scrutinised the scene through narrowed eyes; Anna felt overwhelming affection for this man who had come to mean so much to her in so short a time; and Timothy quietly reserved judgement. Priscilla was the only woman who Aaron had not been able to charm. She shared Onesiphorus's forebodings, unfounded as they apparently were. She had held her peace. As Aquilla submerged Aaron in the lapis-green waters, she prayed he would truly believe and be saved.

Lila and Mary were not present. Jair was still ill, despite the elders gathering to anoint him with oil and pray for his healing the previous night.

Anna had left the children at home with their Grandma. It was wonderful to be free to focus and pray without distraction.

When Aaron waded to shore, Leah and the servants went next. Anna handed him a towel and as she did, he leant in and kissed her on the cheek.

'Thank you, Anna,' he smiled down at her affectionately.

She threw her arms around his neck, surprising herself as well as him.

Timothy watched wondering how this bond between them had grown so quickly. He felt uncomfortable about it, but couldn't put his finger on why. He trusted Anna completely, she would never be unfaithful to him – she loved the Lord too much for such trivialities and he was confident of her devotion to him and the children. He noticed Oni looking sceptically at them as well and made a mental note to discuss his misgivings with him later.

4. PEACEMAKING

Ephesians 2:11–22

You who once were far away have been brought near ...
For he himself is our peace, who has made the two one and
has destroyed the barrier, the dividing wall of hostility.

IvSeenHim.

Marie read it slowly, then searched her husband's eyes. 'Who?' she asked hesitantly.

Jesus.

She blinked several times, 'What was he like?' she whispered eventually.

ShorterThanMe.

Marie laughed, 'Well I guess he would be ... he's from the Middle East. They are generally shorter than Europeans.'

IWishICudTellU.

'I'm in no rush honey. We have all the time in the world. Type it.'

Aaaaaaaaaaaaa.

'Oh love ....'

HeSaidItWudBeHard.

She waited.

ThisIsHell.

'I know ... I know.' She stroked his limp hand.

IWantToHoldU. Tears rolled from his eyes.

'I know,' was all Marie could say in an anguished whisper. She leaned down and kissed his hand, then rose to her feet and kissed his slack mouth and cheek.

She stroked his hair back off his misshapen forehead.

When she sat down again he started typing: *ThankU.WillHave2Do.*

Marie covered her face with her small hands.

DontCry.WontBeLong.

She read it through tears, 'What do you mean?'

HeSaidWasOnly4AWhile.

'Does that mean you're going to recover?' her eyebrows rose, creasing her forehead.

Dunno.

She thought for a while and decided not to pursue the matter, then asked again, 'What was he like?'

WonderfulShiningAmazing.

Marie sat in silence weighing up whether she believed he really had seen Jesus or whether it was some chemical trick of his comatose brain. She opted for a fifty-one per cent belief in the former, eventually saying, 'There aren't enough words are there?'

No.

'Where were you when you were with him?'

NotHeavenButVeryGreen.

'A bit like here?'

LordsPimsBetter.

Marie laughed, 'No wonder you stayed so long!'

CanYouTurnMe.

'Sure, honey,' she stood and easily moved him. He was so light now, a shadow of his former self. She spent some time manipulating his legs and feet, one at a time. Then she began massaging his calves, wasted as they were.

Higher, he typed.

She looked and smiled, moving her hands up to his thighs.

Higher, he typed again.

'You're just frustrating yourself,' she said gently as she looked up after some fruitless labour.

Again a tear escaped as he closed his eyes.

'James.'

He kept his eyes shut.

'James!' Marie insisted.

Not looking at her, he opened them only to type, *IWantToDie,* then closed them again.

Marie sat down heavily beside his bed. Despair crept upon her. How long was this going to go on for and why would he be sent back if it was just going to be for this? She listened to the ticking of the wall clock opposite his bed, the sounds of nurses chatting out in the corridor and her own heartbeat.

James was typing again, *Sorry.*

When she read it she took hold of his hand and kissed it tenderly.

❊ ❊ ❊

The phone rang. Grace reached across her Parochial Church Council minutes which were spread across her desk and grabbed the receiver. 'Hello?'

'Hello, is that Grace?'

'Yes … Bishop Duncan?' she smiled. She'd know his voice anywhere.

'Yes … how are you Grace? You all set for your presentation at the Diocesan Conference?'

'Just about. One or two things still to tie up, but other than that ….'

'Good, good,' he paused. 'I was wondering if you would come and see me. I have something I wish to discuss with you.'

'Oh? Can you give me an idea what it's about?' she frowned opening her diary and flicking through several full weeks.

'I'd rather not talk with you about it on the phone. Could you come to my office tomorrow any time?'

She flicked back to the present week and looked at her next day's schedule. What could she drop? Morning Prayer? Staff meeting with the new children's worker? Home communion with Joan before lunch? Deanery chapter meeting over lunch? Prep time for the PCC meeting in the evening about the refurbishment plans? Zack's music recital? Family dinner and then the PCC? It would have to be prep time.

'I could make a 3.00 p.m. meeting for half an hour. Would that work for you?' she bit the end of her pen.

'I'll get Julia to move things around. That will be fine. I'll see you then.'

❊ ❊ ❊

Parking her car, Grace sat outside the Bishop's house. She finished making a few notes on the St Stephen's refurbishment papers before folding them in half and slipping them into her cavernous bag, which she then dragged out behind her and slammed the car door shut. She checked her watch again. She was one minute off 3.00 p.m.

'Hi, Julia,' she smiled at the secretary who opened the door.

'Hi, Grace, go right on in, the Bishop is expecting you,' she indicated his office door with her hand. 'Tea or coffee?' she asked as Grace walked by.

'Just some hot water please. I've started drinking green tea. It's supposed to help your metabolism. Got my own.'

'Really?' Julia asked pressing her hands on her hips. 'That's what Bishop Duncan says too. Maybe I should try it!'

'I've had a lot more energy since I've been drinking it,' Grace smiled as she knocked once.

'Grace,' he threw it open instantly. 'Come in. Has Julia sorted you out with a drink?'

'Yes, thanks,' she said as she walked past him, catching the scent of lavender and leather on his skin. Her hand rose involuntarily to her neck and through her hair. She sat down.

Bishop Duncan went to the easy chair opposite her, a low coffee table between them. As he settled himself he asked after Peter and Zack and she in turn enquired after Wendy and their ever-expanding number of grandchildren. The feeling like she was about to start a race slowly ebbed as she relaxed into his company. It had been a long time since they'd last been alone together. She was mildly surprised at her reaction even after all this time.

Julia brought in their cups and quietly closed the door behind her. Grace fished out her green tea bags and put one into her cup, stirring it gently.

'Green tea? I drink that too, but only first thing in the morning and last thing at night' he smiled.

'Yes – it's given me a lot more energy.'

'I know, it's wonderful stuff isn't it? So ...' Bishop Duncan lifted his coffee to his lips and sipped carefully. There was no hiding the pleasure in his eyes. 'How are you? It's been a long time.'

'I'm well. Busy, happy, a bit tired,' she touched her neck again and pulled at a golden ringlet.

'I'm not surprised! Goodness, St Stephen's has outstripped all of the churches in the Diocese in numerical growth.'

'Really? I wasn't aware of that.' Despite herself, Grace blushed.

Bishop Duncan chuckled, 'No one can believe that an Anglo-Catholic church is thriving like yours is, and under the leadership of a woman. I love it!' he declared. 'There are some perks to my job!' he grinned and sipped his coffee again.

'I – I knew we were the largest church in the Deanery, but not the Diocese?' she said, a hint of disbelief still in her voice.

'Well you are! And it's not just about your church's size; it's also about the rate of growth. You and your team are doing an outstanding job, Grace.'

'Thank you,' she smiled, quite overwhelmed by his praise. 'They are a great bunch!'

He nodded his head in agreement, 'They certainly are.' He folded his hands and then fixed her with a purposeful look. 'We haven't got much time, so I'll get right to what I wanted to discuss with you,' he drew breath and then launched in. 'I would like you to go and meet Caroline Boddington, the Archbishop's appointment secretary. I have submitted your name for the preferment list, so the next step is for you to meet with her.'

'Preferment for what?' Grace asked stupidly.

'For the roles of Archdeacon or Bishop,' Bishop Duncan held her gaze evenly.

'But I don't want to be an Archdeacon or a Bishop,' Grace replied. She watched his face fall and then added hurriedly, 'I'm really flattered and grateful, but honestly, I'm not ambitious – well not in that way.'

'But you would be an outstanding candidate!'

Grace looked down at her hands, feeling her stomach flip over again. 'I haven't the heart for middle management, Bishop Duncan. No offence!' she looked up at him through her ringlets.

'None taken,' he smiled, humour sparkling in his eyes.

'I love what I'm doing now at the coal face of parish ministry and with My Sister's House. I would hate to get stuck in management. I know this might appear to be a lack of ambition for the cause of women, but I'm not sure becoming one of the first women bishops in Britain will change that much on the ground for the average woman. I feel like what I'm doing now is the best use of my time, skills and energy. I'm a community leader; I'm empowering women and enabling men to realise the benefits of their emancipation. And I'm playing a small part in the fight against human trafficking in this country and on a global scale too. I don't want to give any of that up.'

Silence hung between them like a suspension bridge. Across it came a truckload of chemistry. 'That is exactly why you must go and meet with her,' Bishop Duncan leaned forward intently, his grey eyes piercing her blues.

Grace stared back, at a loss for words. Then quietly, 'Really, Bishop Duncan, I don't want to.'

He leaned back into his chair and sighed, running his hands over his thin, silver hair. 'Grace, as your Father in God, I am asking you to prayerfully consider this.'

Grace felt shocked at his use of the traditional term and the inferred authority that went with it. Then suddenly she began to smile.

'What?' he asked, a corresponding smile played round his mouth.

'Sorry ... it was just you saying "Father in God" ... sorry,' she reiterated and laughed.

He chuckled, 'I know, but how else am I going to get you to think seriously about this, you stubborn woman?'

'I'm so sorry. You're right. I *am* being stubborn. I *will* do as you have asked. But I can't guarantee you'll get the answer you want.'

'That will have to do then,' he smiled. 'Now, I want an answer from you sooner than later.'

'Okay,' she said, nodding her head, her curls bouncing gently against her cheeks. 'I'll let you know next week, if that's okay with you?'

She rose to go, putting her nearly empty cup down on the low table. He stood as she straightened up so that they came face to face. Grace's breath caught in the back of her throat as their eyes met. It was probably only a split-second, but it felt like an age. She broke it with a little nervous cough and said, 'Right then, I'll speak to you soon,' and turned to go.

'Grace,' Bishop Duncan said.

She turned.

'It's good to see you.' His eyes said more.

'Yes,' she replied, biting her lip.

❋   ❋   ❋

She lay awake beside a snoring Peter. It was 3.00 a.m. She turned onto her side and punched her pillow a few times. When she laid her head down again the pain at the base of her skull was still there. She pressed into it with her fingertips, resisting doing the sensible thing of getting up to find painkillers.

It had gone to her head like champagne – his praise of her – the preferment list – the look in his eyes. Her mind kept circling round and round the pleasure of it. *But I don't want to be a bishop! Idiot! And we've been through all this before …*

Eventually she did get up and took something for the pain.

✖ ✖ ✖

'How you doing?' Mark looked down at James as he wheeled his bed down the corridor.

The compact laptop was now strapped to his hand and bolstered by a pillow that had been unceremoniously taped to the back of it so James could always see the screen. He slowly typed: *Crap.*

'Join the club mate,' Mark responded.

As they waited for a lift, James typed: *Wot?*

'Ah you don't want to hear my woes. You've got enough of your own. Just wanted you to know you're not alone.'

Cheers.ButTellMe.

The lift doors opened slowly and Mark wheeled the bed in carefully. It took a long time for the doors to close again. 'You know me and Chloe got divorced?'

No.

'Yeah, well. Let's put it this way, I wish I'd listened to you when you came round that time with those CDs. Wish I'd gone on that course with you.'

WotHappened?

'Do you remember what you gave me?'

Yes.

'Well, I carried on doing what I was doing – you know?' he paused lamely, and then continued. 'Anyway, one day Chloe found me. That was it. I left, moved in with Charmaine. Life seemed good for a while; well, she was good.'

A string of *a*'s appeared across the screen. Mark smiled. 'God, it must be tough for you like this? Not being able to … have you any … you know?

Have got any feeling?'

Nooooooooooooooo.

The lift doors opened and they were faced with a large group of Somalis. Mark had to repeatedly ask them to move out of the way before he could wheel James past them.

'Oh, mate – I'm sorry! Mind you, I'm not getting any action either these days.'

HowCome?

Mark snorted derisively, 'She was so good, she's doing it for a job now. I couldn't take it. Kicked her out. She wouldn't stop. Says she wants it all – money, sex and power.'

GoodLuckWithThat.

Mark looked grim. They'd arrived at the reception desk. He handed over James's file and was told to take a seat in the waiting area.

SoWasItWorthIt?

'What? Losing the love of my life; my job; my home exchanged for a poky flat; not seeing my kids, especially Charlie? No, don't think so.'

SoundsLikeYourWorseOffThanMe.

Mark didn't reply as the familiar gloom tightened its grip round his head.

'James Martin?' the receptionist called.

Mark stood and began pushing James's bed forward.

❋ ❋ ❋

Everything was gone: the flat-screen TV, laptop, iPod dock, kettle, rugs, microwave, hairdryer, duvet and pillows. Mark wandered from room to room in a disbelieving daze. All his aftershaves had been smashed on the bathroom floor, as was the mirror. In the kitchen the cutlery was thrown everywhere.

Very slowly he began to pick things up, but then realised the time. He left the flat only to go to Ikea for a new duvet, pillows, mirror and kettle before they closed. When he returned he went to his task with renewed vigour and by midnight the place was straight.

As he laid his head down on his new pillow his last thought was of Chloe and the children, before exhaustion mercifully took him.

❋ ❋ ❋

Charlie lay on the bed watching Jules try on his new jeans and T-shirt. He was slender – willowy was the word that always sprung to Charlie's mind when he watched him. Jules turned from side to side, his hipbones jutting out above the jeans. 'What do you think?'

'You look gorgeous, as ever,' Charlie grinned.

'No really – be honest, what do you think?'

'That's what I really think! Why don't you believe me when I tell you how hot you are? Every man in the club will want you tonight.'

Jules looked up from adjusting the jeans lower onto his hips. He smiled. Charlie's heart skipped a beat.

'What are you wearing?' Jules swivelled round to see if his designer underwear was showing enough above the jeans. He pushed them down a little more and surveyed his handiwork with some satisfaction.

'I've been meaning to say – Melanie called me earlier today. She wants to meet up with me and Josh about something – said it was important.'

'You're not coming out with me?' Jules swept his silky hair back off his forehead, a look of alarm in his eyes.

'You don't mind really do you? I mean you're a party all on your own, Jules, and it's not like my family normally interfere in my life and make me change our plans.'

Jules, hands on hips, looked like he was going to speak several times, but kept changing his mind. Eventually he came and sat down on the bed beside Charlie.

'What if I pull? I mean – I don't trust myself!' his big brown eyes peered through his hair.

'One night? Just one night? Come on, Jules – you can practice a modicum of self-control surely for one evening without me there?' Charlie said irritably.

'I just know what I'm like, Charlie. I'm not hiding anything from you. I'm just being honest.'

Charlie frowned. Jules reached over and stroked the furrow between Charlie's eyebrows with two fingers. Charlie turned his head away.

'It's not like we're married or anything,' Jules sulked.

'Yeah, but we've been together since we were teenagers. You're the only one for me!' Charlie glared at him.

'And you're the only one for me too. I'm just not good with temptation – you know that.'

Charlie's expression softened, 'What if I join you at the club later, after I've met with Mel and Josh?'

Jules's face lit up. 'If I knew you were coming, I'd be fine. What time do you think you'd be able to get away?'

'Maybe midnight? Depends what my sister wants to talk about. I'll text you when we're nearly done.'

'Okay,' Jules leaned forward and kissed his mouth.

❋   ❋   ❋

'When is term over?' Melanie asked.

'In two weeks,' Charlie replied, stirring his drink with a straw.

'Yeah, same for me,' Josh added.

'So are you both going home?'

'Yep,' the brothers said in unison.

'Last time for me, I think,' Josh said.

'Oh?' Melanie asked, scooping salsa onto a nacho.

'Yeah – me and Lorraine are moving in together when I finish my masters. Her dad's helping us with the deposit and that.'

'That's great!' Charlie smiled at his brother, hoping it was believable.

'Have you told Mum yet?'

'I've mentioned it a few times, just to warm her up to the idea, but I need to have a proper talk with her about it.'

'Cuz you know, I'm moving out?' Mel wiped her fingers on her paper napkin.

'Where are you going?' Charlie frowned.

'Oh – I'm flat sharing with a friend. It's near Dad's actually. You've met Rose, haven't you?'

Both brothers nodded diffidently. Both knew she used to be a hooker and neither knew exactly how they should feel about that.

There was a pause between the siblings as they took stock.

'So,' Charlie said, 'it's going to be me and Mum.'

'Well, that's one of the things I wanted to tell you. She's talking about selling up and buying something smaller and cheaper.'

'What?' Josh exclaimed.

'But that's our home!' said Charlie.

'Yeah, well, Dad's lost his job and although he's got a new one, I don't think it's anywhere near as well paid. She wants to alleviate the financial pressure on both of them, and free up some money for herself too.'

'Don't know why she's worried about him?' Charlie grunted into his drink. 'It's not like he ever worried about her.'

Neither of the others responded.

'So what's he doing now?' Charlie asked eventually.

'Something for the NHS,' Melanie shrugged.

Josh added, 'Yeah I got that text. Don't you get texts from him?' he looked at Charlie.

'I changed my number. I haven't had any contact with him for years now.'

'Really?' Josh looked surprised.

'Don't look like that, Josh; you know he thought the sun shone out of your ass. I may as well have not existed. Anyway, I'll never forgive him for what he did to Mum.' As Charlie said it he saw a look cross his brother's features that read *mummy's boy*. He swallowed the anger that burned acidly in the back of his throat. He lifted his drink and took several gulps.

'Anyway,' Melanie grabbed the moment to defuse the mounting tension, 'the other thing I wanted to talk to you guys about was Dad himself. I am worried about him. I accept how you feel Charlie, but when I saw him recently, I have to say I actually felt sorry for him. He admitted to me that he knows he's screwed up big time and that he's been a crap dad.'

'To you guys, maybe, but he was fine with me,' Josh interjected.

'Whatever!' Melanie rolled her eyes. 'It shouldn't matter what he's done; he's still our dad. I think there's a whole lot he's not saying. I could see it in his eyes.'

'What do you expect us to do?' Charlie asked defensively.

'I don't know yet,' Melanie faltered. 'Give him a second chance?'

Charlie stared at her.

Their meals arrived and for a while they preoccupied themselves with their plates.

'Would you consider meeting up with him? With me and Josh?' Melanie asked, after several mouthfuls of chilli con carne and rice.

Charlie shook his head. 'What would be the point?'

'Look, I still haven't forgiven him either for what he did, but he's our Dad. He's a human being. He's made crap decisions, sure, but don't we all?'

Both brothers stared at their sister.

'Some of us do,' Josh quipped.

Charlie gazed at his brother, marvelling at his arrogance. 'Yeah – we all make mistakes,' his eyes slid past his brother's smug face. 'But there's no way I'm ready to see him or talk to him at the minute.'

'Well, will you at least think about it?' she pleaded.

'Okay – not promising much, but I will. While I'm doing that, you two can support him in whatever he's going through and I'll help Mum sell and move.'

❋ ❋ ❋

'I don't know,' Chloe said into the receiver. She listened and then shook her head. 'I don't think I can.'

She paused.

'Can I let you know? Okay, thanks. Look, I've got to go now. I'll text you later. Okay, bye,' she hung up with a sigh of relief.

No – don't want it to go any further. She touched her lips remembering the stealth of that goodnight kiss. She shrugged the memory off like it was a wet raincoat, letting it drop to the tiled floor. She went to the kitchen sink to clear away the dishes that had collected on the draining board over the last couple of days. Then she turned to wipe the glass table down. As she leaned over it, images of Mark on top of her on their old wooden table flooded her mind. She stopped still as a shiver went through her body. She smiled. *Can still arouse me, all these years later!* She raised her eyebrows and shook her head, marvelling as she returned to tidying to the kitchen.

The estate agent had booked three viewings for the day. She could hear Charlie moving around upstairs going from room to room doing the last bits and bobs. He was a perfectionist; she knew he would make it immaculate. She turned and scanned the kitchen with a critical eye, worrying that when he came downstairs he would fuss over some minor detail she had missed.

'Mum?' Charlie shouted down the stairs.

'Yes?' Chloe called back, moving towards the kitchen door into the hallway.

'Jules needs another towel for his hair and there isn't one in the airing cupboard.'

'Oh, right – there's a pile of fresh towels in the laundry room. I'll just get them.'

Charlie met her at the bottom of the stairs on her return and took the folded towels out of her arms, 'Thanks, Mum,' he grinned.

She smiled back affectionately, pushing down the niggling anxieties she had for him. He was happy, that was the main thing.

'How much more time have we got before the first viewing?' he said turning and walking up the stairs.

'Around forty minutes,' she looked at her watch.

'Jules will be ready in about ten. Can you put the kettle on?'

'Sure,' she headed for the kitchen again.

A waft of fragrance preceded them as they entered the kitchen holding hands. 'What would you like for breakfast?' Chloe asked. 'Bacon and eggs or cereal and toast?'

'Can I just have some fruit, Chloe?' Jules swept his silky hair off his forehead with a practiced swoop of his hand.

'Sure, I've actually got some tropical fruit mix in the fridge. Would that do?'

'Lovely,' he smiled, his dark, doe-eyes crinkling slightly at the edges.

'I'll just have cereal,' Charlie added.

'Fine,' Chloe lifted several boxes out onto the worktop.

While they busied themselves with breakfast they chatted airily about the houses they were going to look at later that day. Chloe wondered how Mark would have coped with Jules and Charlie living together under his roof. She was glad she didn't have to deal with that particular can of worms.

Before they knew it the doorbell was ringing and so began the carnival, which is the process of selling and buying houses in England. Little did they know it would go on for weeks, taking up nearly all of the boys' summer holiday.

※　※　※

'Are you sure you don't want me to come with you, Charlie?' Jules asked, his brow furrowing with concern.

'Yep. It's gonna be hard enough seeing him after all this time without adding you into the mix. I'll be okay,' Charlie grinned cheerfully. 'What's the worst he can do to me?'

'Treat you like he's always done?' Jules ventured.

Charlie shrugged, 'Yeah! I can deal with that. Here give me a hug and wish me luck,' he spread his arms.

Jules got up from where he sat on the bed and wrapped himself around Charlie. They stood entwined for several minutes and then as they drew apart Jules said, 'Keep eye contact – don't let him pull you down.'

'Thanks.' Charlie grabbed his leather jacket hanging on the back of a bedroom chair and headed for the door. 'Enjoy your evening with Mum.'

'Oh I will! We're watching *Moulin Rouge* and ordering take-away,' Jules followed him downstairs to the front door. Charlie kissed him and then turned resolutely to do one of the hardest things he'd done in his young life.

※　※　※

Mark gulped down the shot of whisky, grimacing as he did. He stared at his reflection in the new bathroom mirror, 'Get your act together!' he growled.

He stood gripping the edge of the sink, his knuckles whitening. He breathed deeply, squared his shoulders and turned to go, but then came back, reached for the whisky bottle and poured himself another shot, downing it in one. He shook his head viciously, gave himself one last glare in the mirror and then headed for the door.

It was a warm summer evening. As he made his way through the crowded bar out into the pub garden, he steeled himself. There they were, all three of them. He held his breath and watched them for a moment until Melanie looked up, saw him and waved. He made his legs obey and crossed the short distance of daisy-strewn grass to the round table they occupied. Charlie had his back to him and didn't turn round as the other two watched him approach.

'Hi Mel, Josh,' his voice sounded strange in his own ears. He clapped Josh on the back and then came round to give Melanie a kiss on the cheek. He felt heat flame up his neck, conscious of Charlie's eyes upon him. When he straightened up he couldn't put the moment off any longer. Their eyes met and a charge went through him. It was like looking in the mirror, only twenty years ago. 'Hello, Charlie,' he said, the table a safety buffer between them. 'Been a long time.'

'Hi, Dad, it's good to see you.'

Mark heard the strain in his youngest son's voice. It suddenly dawned on him that this might be harder for Charlie than it was for him. A surge of empathy rose within him. 'Good to see you too – you look great!'

'Thanks.' There was a pause, which Melanie broke nervously.

'Shall we order our food – get it out of the way?'

'What are you all drinking?' Mark asked as he lifted a menu.

They gave him their drink orders and then when he was about to walk away he realised, 'Give me your food orders too – sorry – should have asked that already!' He grinned sheepishly.

They all chose.

When he returned the three of them were leaning in on the table, their heads close together in conversation. *Well at least we did something right for the three of them to still be speaking to each other,* he mused. He pulled out his chair and sat down, his eyes drawn to Charlie's face like a magnet. *God, he's good looking* he thought. *Was I that good looking?* His hand rose involuntarily, rubbing his jaw, feeling the end of the day stubble. Charlie was talking about his university course, something about his dissertation. *God, he's nearly finished uni!*

He was happy to wait and watch as they talked. He noticed how Josh occasionally patronised Charlie and how his youngest son would look away. He saw Melanie trying to defuse the tension between them when it arose, like a soldier traversing a minefield. It occurred to him that she was old beyond her years. *It's all that bloody psychology she's studied,* he thought. *She needs to get a life.*

'So, Dad, what's your new job like? You enjoying it?' Josh asked.

'I wouldn't say that,' Mark grimaced, 'but it'll do for now.'

'What are you doing?' Charlie asked, his blue-green eyes piercing Marks.

'Logistics for the NHS,' he found he couldn't hold Charlie's gaze and flicked a glance at Josh for comfort. This son admired him, believed he could do anything.

'What does that mean?' asked Charlie pointedly. Mark felt the disdain hit him like cold water in the face. He blinked several times.

'Moving equipment and materials to where they're needed; making sure supply and demand match up – you know,' he shrugged, desperately trying to hide his shame.

'You mean you're a porter?' Charlie asked incredulously.

'Charlie!' Josh glared at his brother.

'It's okay Josh,' Mark touched his older son's arm, brushing his discomfort aside. He tried to smile at Charlie. 'Actually – yeah – I am a porter.' There it was – his cards on the table – what a relief! It reminded him of laughing at himself with James Martin.

'What?' Josh's mouth gaped open.

'Yeah,' Mark sighed. He might as well tell them everything. 'I got made redundant a few months ago. Had to leave the office the same day and with only three months' severance pay.'

'Dad, I'm so sorry!' Melanie said.

'It's okay, didn't want to worry you. Anyway – Charmaine freaked out and, well, the long and the short of it is, we've split up.' He looked at his folded hands on the table. When he raised his eyes it was Charlie he looked at first. He saw a gloating pleasure in his face. It went straight to his heart in a sharp, jagged pain.

'That's too bad,' Josh was saying.

'I knew something was going on with you, Dad – I didn't realise things were this tough,' Melanie added. 'Does Mum know?'

'Only that I lost my job and was looking for a new one. I've managed to keep up my payments to her, which is good.'

'That is good,' Charlie said pointedly.

Josh turned on his younger brother and glared at him, 'Kick a man when he's down, why don't you!' he growled.

Charlie didn't look at him, but kept boring holes into Mark. 'Well, maybe now he knows what it feels like,' Charlie's expression remained calm.

Mark lifted a hand to rub his face again, noticing the tremor in it. 'It's all right, Josh. I deserve it. He's right – let him express himself.'

It was Charlie's turn to look surprised. He raised his eyebrows questioningly, 'You mean that? You really want to hear it all? Cuz I've got a whole lot more where that came from,' the rage pricked through his voice like a thistle hidden in lush grass.

'I would like to hear it all, Charlie. I'm so glad you agreed to meet me after all this time today – but maybe here's not the best place?' he drew a deep breath. 'Do you think we could just keep it light tonight? It's a start isn't it?' As he was speaking a waiter brought two laden plates to the table followed closely by a waitress carrying the other two orders.

Charlie looked nonplussed, waiting for all the plates to be put down. When they were alone again, Melanie reached over and took Charlie's hand. 'I know it feels weird, but give it a chance,' she tried to smile.

'Okay – for you,' he smiled back at her, tucking his huge sense of injustice away for now.

'Thank God for that,' Josh said out of the side of his mouth.

'Thanks, Charlie,' Mark said. He hoped his son believed him. He picked up his knife and fork, forcing his stomach to prepare to receive what he was about to put into it. The others followed suit and as they began to eat the conversation slowly began again, skimming over minor details of all their lives.

※　※　※

'Charlie's gone with them,' Chloe said into the receiver. 'Yeah, first time he's seen Mark in five years!'

'That's so great, Chloe. It's an answer to your prayers, don't you think?' Grace asked.

'I know, it is so amazing! Do you think it really has got something to do with what I've been praying?'

'No doubt in my mind – you've begun to make a way to peace. That's what praying mercy does.'

'It could just be coincidence?'

'Yeah – but isn't it amazing how many more coincidences happen when you pray?'

Chloe laughed, despite herself. 'You're good!'

'Trust me, I'm a vicar!' Grace quipped.

After she put the phone down, Grace stared at her computer screen. She'd felt the urge to write but had deleted several attempts before Chloe had phoned her. Now she knew what it was she wanted to write. She smiled thinking fondly of Charlie. 'You'll get there, sweetie,' she said to him as if he were there. 'I must stop talking to myself,' she countered 'It's the first sign of madness!' she shook her curly head as she began to type with fresh enthusiasm. 'The dividing wall of hostility! Oh yes,' she grinned.

Joshua leaned into the spray that came in bursts over the helm of the ship as they approached Ephesus harbour. He willed the ship to go faster, as he had done every waking hour of their journey. He turned to Luke, sitting a few feet behind him, his eyes half closed against the brilliant sunshine. 'Nearly there!' he declared.

Luke raised a hand to shield his eyes as he squinted up. He got to his feet carefully and came to stand beside him. He clasped an arm around his shoulders, 'Not long now,' he looked at Joshua who continued to stare towards the harbour as if his life depended upon it. Luke's chest constricted, as he offered up another prayer to preserve Jair's life at least until they arrived.

When they docked Joshua was the first onto dry land. He turned urgently to help Luke disembark and then together they ploughed their way through the crowds of sailors, hawkers, beggars and fellow travellers. They hurried through the busy streets of Ephesus out into the suburbs.

It was Anna who opened the door to them and who promptly dissolved into tears on sight of her brother. They wasted no time on ceremony as Anna led Joshua by the hand, crying as she did.

Lila looked up from Jair's pallid face, brightness stealing into her tired eyes as she focused on her son. 'Shua!' she exclaimed. He moved to her before she could stand, falling on his knees and burying his head in her lap. All the emotion he had held down came flooding out in sobs that wracked his body. Lila held him as he convulsed with each one, her face glistening wet. 'Oh Shua,' she whispered again and again. 'You came!'

Luke had gone to the other side of the bed and held Jair's wrist expertly between thumb and fingers. He then lowered his head to rest on Jair's chest to listen for a while. Then began a long series of questions directed at Lila and Anna, all of which they found difficult to answer.

How long had he felt unwell? When did the fever start? Had he complained of particular pains anywhere? When was the last time he had been fully conscious? How much did he eat each day? And drink?

Joshua stayed kneeling beside his mother, staring alternately at his father's face and then at Luke's. Anna stood pensively behind him, her hands resting on her brother's shoulders.

Eventually Luke straightened up, his face wearing an expression that only Joshua could read. 'He's dying?' Joshua asked in a whisper.

'I can't be sure, but his heart rate is very slow and his breathing shallow. You've said he hasn't eaten for days and has had very little water. Not once has the fever broken?' He struggled to hide the distress in his voice beneath his practiced bedside manner.

Lila shook her head slowly.

'I can't believe he has lasted as long as you say. He must be exhausted. What did he say to you the last time he was conscious?'

'He asked for Joshua.' Anna squeezed her brother's shoulders.

'Perhaps he has been waiting for you,' Luke said to Joshua. 'I don't think it will be long now that you are here.'

'Is there nothing we can do?' Joshua asked, the anguish palpable in his voice.

'I think your mother and sister have done everything that could be done. Look at them, they have not rested, but nursed him day and night.'

Joshua looked up into his mother's face, the tears choking him.

Lila wiped his cheeks with her thumbs and then pressed them to her lips.

They fell silent around Jair, as each processed the reality of facing life without him.

Joshua shuffled closer on his knees towards the bed and took his father's limp hand in his. He pressed it to his face, kissing it. 'Papa, I'm here. I've come to see you. Can you hear me? You asked for me and here I am,' he sniffed.

The silence drew out around them, broken only by Jair's shallow breaths.

Lila studied her son's face tenderly, brushing a curl back off his forehead and running her fingers down through the rest of his tangled locks. 'You must be hungry and thirsty. Can I get you something?' she asked quietly.

Joshua shook his head, not taking his eyes off his father's face.

Lila understood. He would fast now until the end. She glanced up at Luke, who nodded in the affirmative. She rose slowly to her feet, leaving her seat for Joshua, who gladly took it, stretching his legs out in front of him and wiggling his toes, which had gone numb.

Luke followed Lila from the room and down the long corridor, through the lounge to the kitchen at the back of the house. Only when she was sure they were out of earshot did she turn and cling to Luke, sobbing out her exhausted grief. He held her, gently rocking her like a mother would. Lila wondered, as she often had, at his strange ability to connect in such a feminine way. She understood that his medical experience had revealed things to him about women that most men knew nothing about. The comfort he gave those he cared for was magnified by his ability to step into their shoes. Many times while watching Luke practice his medicine she had been reminded of the way Jesus had been with women.

'What do you want us to pray?' Luke asked.

She lifted her head from his shoulder, her eyelashes sticking wetly together, her expression puzzled. Luke marveled at her beauty. Age had not stolen it from her. In fact the tiny creases around her eyes and mouth had added rather than detracted from her appearance. What made her even lovelier was how unaware she was of her power. He smiled down at her, 'Shall we pray for healing or shall we pray he goes soon?'

'We have all prayed for healing. Even the elders came and anointed him with oil and prayed, as Paul instructed, but his condition has only worsened. You think he is dying, don't you? So perhaps we should let him go – give him permission to go. Maybe he's lasted this long because I was not willing ....' A look of horror filled her eyes. 'Have I caused him to suffer more?' her hand flew to her mouth as fresh tears surged down her cheeks.

'No, Lila, no.' Luke shook his head reassuringly. 'I think he's been waiting for Joshua. Besides, remember the Lord taught us that we cannot even do the little thing of adding an hour to our lives by worrying. All our days are written in his book before one of them comes to be.'

Lila nodded unable to speak for a moment.

'It's our job to pray and the Lord's to heal if he so wills it. We need to agree how we are going to pray from now on.'

She breathed deeply, wiped her eyes and then replied, 'I'd like him to become conscious before he goes – so he can see Joshua one last time. I would love the last memory he takes with him to be of all our faces around him.'

And so they prayed.

On returning to the room with refreshments, they found Mary and Timothy sitting on the floor with their backs against the wall and children climbing all over them. Anna had settled herself beside her husband, leaning her head against his shoulder and feeding the baby. Joshua still sat at his father's side, a gentle smile on his lips as he watched his nephews and nieces use their papa as a climbing frame.

Lila put her tray down on the mosaic bedside table. She poured water into Jair's cup and then sat down on the bed, lifting his head carefully off his pillow and putting the rim of the ceramic cup to his cracked lips. 'Jair my love, drink a little. It will refresh you. Jair, can you hear me darling?'

The children stopped whispering and giggling. They were all on Timothy by this stage, hanging round his neck like little monkeys, their wide eyes fixed on the unfolding drama. The only sound that broke the silence was that of the baby suckling at her mother's breast.

'Jair – have a little water my love,' Lila coaxed again. She tipped the cup and a trickle of water ran between his lips and down his chin. It caused him to sputter and cough weakly. Lila persisted, pressing the cup against his lips. 'That's it darling, have a little more.'

This time his Adam's apple bobbed, indicating he had actually swallowed some liquid. 'That's good,' said Luke encouragingly.

Late afternoon sunlight slanted through the wooden shutters, which fended off the worst of the Mediterranean heat. The bars of light that fell across the foot of the bed had slowly been growing longer as they watched Jair's life ebb away. It was Luke who moved to the window and thrust the shutters wide, flooding the room with that unique, warm, golden light that comes at the end of the day. When he turned back into the room his eyes fixed on Joshua, with deep affection.

Surprised by the sudden movement and burst of light, Joshua looked up. He had been unaware of the passing of time or the darkening of the room. Momentarily distracted from his grief, he rose and went to stand beside his friend, looking out the window at the view beyond. The city basked in vibrant warmth as swallows swooped on hot air currents, chasing tiny insects and calling to one another. Joshua let a fresh flow of tears course silently down his face and into his beard as Luke gripped his hand, which rested on the window sill.

'Jair – shalom my love – shalom,' Lila's voice was thick with emotion.

As Mary got awkwardly to her feet and made her way to stand beside Lila, Joshua spun around and covered the space between the window and the bed in one bound, nearly knocking her over, 'Papa?' he cried.

Jair's lips moved but no sound came from them.

Joshua fell to his knees and bent forward to hear what his father was trying to say. 'Say it again, Papa, I couldn't hear you,' he said urgently.

'Shua.' Jair managed a whisper.

'Yes, Papa, I'm here.'

Jair gazed at his son lovingly. Then his eyes swivelled interminably slowly to Lila's. 'Lila,' he whispered. Then 'Anna?' It was barely audible but everyone heard the question in it.

'I'm here, Papa,' Anna gave the contented baby to Timothy. 'I've been here all the time.'

It took a while for Jair to turn his head and focus upon her face. He drank her in as she knelt beside her brother and kissed his hand. Then his eyes slid past her to Timothy surrounded by their children. A smile tugged at the edges of his thin lips. His eyelids closed, then opened again with huge effort. Despite his weakness, affection glowed in his eyes.

Timothy and the children got to their feet, all except the youngest one who clung to his neck. He carried her with him to the bedside while the others clustered round him, reaching out little hands to touch Jair's parchment skin.

Jair's eyes returned to Joshua's face. 'When did you come?' He had so little breath he mouthed the words.

'Today – this morning.' Joshua said, leaning down and kissing his father's cheek.

'I knew you'd come,' Jair whispered, trying to swallow and closing his eyes with the effort. No one spoke as they listened to his shallow breathing. Eventually Jair said, 'It's my time.'

'Oh, Jair, my love, I so hoped we'd go together,' Lila cried, stroking his cheek tenderly.

He opened his eyes and tried to focus on her face, but failed. His lids began to close again as his breathing became fainter.

'Papa, we love you so much,' Anna wept.

Joshua rested his forehead on his father's chest, his shoulders shook.

The grandchildren looked on, not fully comprehending, but weeping with the adults.

Lila kissed his cheek, then his lips, 'I won't be far behind you,' she said. 'Wait for me,' she kissed them again. When she drew back she knew he had gone. There were no more breaths, only slackness in the muscles around his mouth. She gently lifted his chin with her finger until his lips met. Then she broke down and cried as their souls were torn apart.

In a broken voice Joshua began to recite a prayer haltingly, 'May the Lord remember the soul of my father, my teacher, who has gone on to His world, may his soul be bound in the Bond of Life, together with the souls of Abraham, Isaac, and Jacob; Sarah, Rebecca, Rachel, and Leah; and together with the other righteous men and women in the Garden of Eden. Amen.'

Anna tried to join him, but couldn't get past 'my teacher'. The children clung to her, comforting her with soft, cooing noises and with their gentle hands. Timothy knelt behind her, wrapping his arms around her waist and holding her to him.

The sun sank into the sea beyond the city. It threw its dying rays into the room, one of which reached Jair's face. As they all watched, it illuminated his features so that it seemed as if the Lord Himself was bending down to kiss him. Then the light faded as quickly as it had come, leaving Jair looking paler than any of them could remember.

They lingered round the bed, talking in subdued voices, comforting one another as twilight fell. Eventually Lila reached for the edge of the sheet that covered his wasted body. She began to pull it up until his face was hidden from sight. Then she rose to her feet and everyone else followed, filing out of the room quietly behind her. Luke brought up the rear. He whispered a final blessing and then closed the door softly behind him.

❋   ❋   ❋

The first time Lila saw Aaron was after Jair's funeral. In her grief-stricken state, she thought she was seeing things, but there was no mistaking him on her second furtive glance.

'What's the matter, Mama?' Anna asked at her side.

Lila tore her eyes from Aaron, who was deep in conversation with a group of young men, to look into her daughter's face. 'Why is he here?'

'Who?' Anna asked.

'Him,' Lila indicated with her chin, averting her eyes, not daring to look directly at him.

Anna searched the crowded courtyard, 'Do you mean Aaron?'

'How do you know his name?' Lila was shocked.

'He is Ruth's brother – Onesiphorus's brother-in-law. He came to Ephesus around the time Papa became ill. That's probably why you've not met him yet. He joined the Church and was baptised a few weeks ago – he and his whole household. He's a great teacher. You know he actually taught brother Paul in Jerusalem?' she went on, but as the words came out of her mouth she began to realise that something was very wrong with her mother, 'I know you don't know him, but it's kind of him to come and pay his respects, don't you think?'

Lila lowered her head, 'Where's Mary?' she asked in a strained voice. 'Can you get her for me?' she pulled her headscarf further down over her face as she spoke.

'She's in the kitchen, I think.' Anna's brow furrowed with concern at her mother's agitation. She looked over her shoulder and turning, reached for Timothy. He was talking with Onesiphorus and quickly responded, going in search of Mary.

When Mary came, Lila took her by the arm and together they made their way in the opposite direction to where Aaron stood, heads close together. Anna stared after them, bemused.

'What was wrong?' Timothy asked.

'I don't know,' Anna replied. 'She seemed almost afraid. It was very strange. I hope Mary can calm her down.'

Timothy gazed after the older women, a puzzled expression on his face. 'What triggered it off?' he asked.

'She asked me why Aaron was here and who he was.'

'Oh?' Timothy scratched his beard thoughtfully.

❋   ❋   ❋

'Did he see you?' Mary asked.

'No – I don't think so – but he must know I'm here – he must know it is Jair who has died and that this is *his* Anna! Oh no!' Lila exclaimed as the thought exploded in her mind.

'Surely not?' Mary soothed.

'But he'll have put two and two together. Anna's father has died – surely he'll know his name – surely he'll be looking for me now?'

'After all these years – really – you think so?'

'Why else is he here?'

'Anna said he'd joined the Church – got baptised – he and his whole family. Maybe he has really changed?'

'Mary,' Lila was exasperated, 'does a leopard change its spots?'

Mary shrugged uncertainly. 'Paul did … you did.'

Lila had no reply to that. They fell into a thoughtful silence together, while Lila fiddled agitatedly with the tassels that edged her shawl. 'I can't cope with this, not now … what am I going to do? Jair has gone and I … I … I am lost,' her eyes welled up.

Mary wrapped an arm around her. 'You are not lost, Lila,' she said firmly, 'the Lord is still in charge ... he will lead you. You must lean hard upon him now.'

Lila focused on what Mary was saying. She spoke with the quiet authority of one who had known many losses. Lila clasped her hand. 'Pray for me Mary ... I am so afraid ... I can't think clearly ... I need time ... oh Lord, help me,' she wept.

Mary joined her in a prayer that came from the depths of her soul. It struck her as she poured it out that nothing was wasted, not even the experiences of life that seemed so pointless: her loss of Stephen; of her own mind for a time; then of Phillip; and now the daily longing for her daughters. She knew the terrain of loss. That knowledge would prove invaluable now. She would walk with Lila all the way and help her navigate it. But the added turmoil of Aaron entering their lives again was the unknown element. Mary prayed for wisdom and discernment.

'Can we go now? I don't need to stay, do I?' Lila asked shakily.

'No ... I'm sure people will understand ... come,' Mary took her by the arm and helped her up. As they returned through the courtyard towards Anna, Lila saw Aaron bearing down purposefully upon them. Why had she thought she could avoid the inevitable? Her heart thudded against her ribs; her legs felt they would give way. She gripped Mary's arm frantically.

'What?' Mary asked, but before Lila could answer Aaron was beside them.

'Shalom, Lila. Shalom, Mary. It is terrible that we meet again under such sad circumstances, but it does my heart good to see your faces again,' his smile lit up his entire face.

Lila cowered into Mary. Her whole body trembled. 'Shalom, Aaron,' Mary replied calmly. 'How kind of you to pay your respects today.'

'Jair was one of my oldest friends,' Aaron said sincerely. 'When I learned that you too had come to Ephesus, I had hoped we would be reconciled. But that was not to be. My deepest condolences,' he directed this last sentence towards Lila with a slight bow of his head.

Lila acknowledged it only by pressing further into Mary's side.

'It's been a long day,' Mary said politely. 'We are going to retire.'

'Of course you must,' Aaron replied. 'You will be in my prayers.'

Lila stole an incredulous glance at his face. She didn't believe the look of contrition and concern she saw there. She tore her eyes away from him, looking over her shoulder for Anna. He knew ... she knew he knew ... there was no point pretending or hiding. 'Anna,' she called.

Anna turned from her conversation with Joshua and Timothy, 'Yes, Mama?'

'I need to rest now. Mary is taking me.'

Her face full of compassion, her daughter smiled, 'It's been a long day. You must be exhausted.' She leaned in and kissed Lila's cheek as Aaron looked on. 'I'll come and check on you in a little while.'

Lila managed a little smile in return as Mary began to lead her towards the bedrooms that lined the far side of the courtyard. 'He knows ... he knows she is his,' she muttered to Mary.

'Yes ... they look so alike!' Mary couldn't help exclaiming.

'Do you think Anna has realised?'

'No – not in a million years!' Mary comforted.

'What about others? Do you think Timothy sees the resemblance? Not only in her, but also in his children? Oh dear Lord ... hide my sin ... hide me,' she began to weep again as they entered through the low doorway into the cool shade of the hallway. 'It's as though, with Jair gone, I am left undefended. My sins laid out in plain sight for all to see. When Anna discovers the truth, how will she react?' Lila fell on her bed, sobbing.

Mary sat down beside her, rubbing her back gently. 'Now Lila, stop this ... you are giving in to fear. We have not been given a spirit of fear, but of love, power and a sound mind. Bring your thoughts captive to Christ. Trust him ... he is still in control, even now, even of this.'

Lila continued crying and shaking.

'Come now sister, you are overwrought. Come,' she coaxed, 'turn over and rest. I'll stay with you. Everything is going to be all right. All will be well ... shalom, sweetheart, shalom.'

Slowly Lila lifted her head and turned over. Mary moved round to lie beside her, cradling her head against her arm. Softly she began to sing a lullaby that they had both sung for Anna when she was a baby. Lila's breathing grew calmer. Eventually she closed her eyes in exhausted sleep.

❋   ❋   ❋

Anna turned to Aaron, 'I don't know how she will recover from this,' she confided, 'Papa meant everything to her. They were so close.'

'I know,' replied Aaron.

Anna looked up in surprise, 'Pardon?'

'I knew your father and mother well,' he said simply.

'But you never said?'

'Forgive me ... I wanted to be sure. Your father was one of my oldest friends. When you told me his name, I hoped to be reunited with him, but sadly it was not to be.'

Anna looked quizzically at him, 'If you had told me, I would have brought you to his bedside.'

'I had no idea death was at his door, my dear. If I had known I would have come to visit him, believe me,' he sighed.

Anna scrutinised his face. 'Why did Mama react so strangely to you?'

'I don't know,' the lie came easily. 'She is in deep grief. We are not ourselves when sorrow overwhelms us.'

'I suppose not,' Anna admitted. After a pause she said, 'No wonder I have felt such affection for you – it must run in my blood!' she smiled. She could not read the expression in his eyes.

5. REVEALING

Ephesians 3:1–13

In reading this you will be able to understand …
the mystery of Christ, which has now been revealed by the Spirit …
This mystery is that through the gospel the Gentiles are heirs
together with Israel, members together of one body, and sharers
together in the promise in Christ Jesus.

'I don't like the word "Gentile",' Zack said, his mouth full of Sunday roast dinner.

'Wait until your mouth is empty,' Peter chided.

'Sorry,' Zack muttered and swallowed.

'Come again?' Peter encouraged with an indulgent smile.

'Mum kept calling us "Gentiles" in her sermon today … I didn't like it,' Zack repeated, looking pointedly at Grace.

Grace's mother was sitting next to him playing with her food. Light sparkled off her bejewelled fingers as she toyed with a piece of broccoli. 'Only Jewish people use that word to differentiate between themselves and the rest of the human race, Zack. We don't use labels like that,' she frowned across the table at her daughter.

'Well, *we* do,' Grace stood her ground. She quickly turned her energy from the temptation to argue with her mother, to trying to explain to her son. 'Gran's right … it is a term used by God's chosen people to define those who are not His people. I don't blame you for not liking it Zack … I don't either.'

'So why did you go on about it in your sermon?' Zack pressed as he speared another roast potato with his fork.

'I only used it to make the point that now, because of Jesus, there need not be such a term. All people can be called and chosen to be God's people. Before Jesus came, that wasn't possible.'

'Oh I wasn't really listening – I just heard you use it several times and didn't like it,' Zack grinned.

Peter chuckled, 'I have to admit it was one of your longer sermons, babe.'

'Cheers,' Grace said defensively and looked down at her plate.

'Oh Grace can go on a bit when she wants to – it's the journalist in her,' her mother said to no one in particular. 'Sounds like it was a good thing I missed this one?' she leaned into Zack and nudged him playfully.

'Yeah – it *was* boring. Mum, when can I stop coming to church? I mean, there's hardly anyone there my age and it isn't aimed at someone like me, is it?'

Grace's defensiveness increased, but she tried to hide it behind humour, 'I suppose you hear enough of me at home?' her smile barely made it to her eyes.

Zack rolled his eyes, 'Yeah!'

'Poor Zackie,' his grandmother tousled his hair affectionately, oblivious to her daughter's discomfort.

Peter said, 'I suppose you can decide for yourself after your confirmation next month.'

Grace looked at her husband. 'Getting confirmed isn't meant to be the ending of church involvement, it's meant to be a renewed continuation – a declaration of intent,' she couldn't help the strangled sound of her voice, feeling more and more unhappy with the direction the conversation was going.

'That's true, but most kids seem to drift away from church around their mid-teens. What Zack's saying isn't a reflection on you personally, it's just the way it is.' Peter tried to win her with an affectionate smile.

Grace put a forkful of food into her mouth to stop herself saying anything more. She nodded and adopted a nonchalant expression, hoping the conversation would now move on.

'Yeah, it's not you Mum,' Zack grinned at her again.

She swallowed and smiled, 'I know.' Then she distracted them by saying, 'Peter, Mum's glass is empty.'

'Oh sorry ... here,' Peter filled his mother-in-law's glass.

'Thank you, dear,' she gave him a warm look as she elegantly lifted the wine to her lips. 'That is a lovely one. Where's it from?'

'Brazil, I think,' Peter said looking at the label on the bottle. 'Yep!' he confirmed, 'it's a good one.'

Grace's mother started talking animatedly about her forthcoming trip to Brazil with two friends from her tennis club. Inwardly Grace breathed a sigh of relief as the lure of Rio took over the conversation.

Later when Peter had taken her mother into the living room and Zack was helping stack the dishwasher, she said, 'You don't *have* to come to church, Zack. You don't *have* to do anything. I didn't know you felt like that.'

'Didn't want to upset you,' he said sheepishly.

'I understand,' she patted his hand. 'Here, can you take the coffee in to them?' she kept her voice light.

'Sure,' he said picking up the cafetiere. She followed him with a tray of mugs, sugar and milk, bracing herself for an afternoon of trivia.

※ ※ ※

'What's wrong?' Peter asked later that evening.

'Nothing,' Grace responded as she slipped her nightgown over her head, letting it slip down over her skin in smoky, purple ripples. She turned to the mirror on her dresser and lifted a pot of face cream, unscrewing the lid. She expertly applied dots round her eyes, between her eyebrows and around her mouth, then down her neck and across her chest. In slow circular motions she lightly rubbed it in until she was satisfied her job was done.

Peter watched her from the bed. 'I know you – you're annoyed with me, aren't you?'

'No, I'm not,' she looked at him in the mirror, not wanting to talk about it.

'Do you fancy some angry sex?' he grinned.

'No thanks,' she replied, 'because I'm not angry.'

'Okay, how about some plain old horny sex?' he patted her side of the bed.

She weighed up her response, eyeing him in the mirror, deciding to roll with it. 'Okay! How do you want me?' she turned and faced him, sliding a hand down one leg playfully.

'Oh now that's a difficult one. I'd like to have you in so many ways – narrowing it down to one is tough!' he laughed, 'Come here.'

Catlike, she climbed onto the bed. When she reached him, she kissed him slowly, biting his lower lip a little.

'Ouch! You are angry!' he said pulling away enough to look into her eyes.

'Do you want sex or not?' she asked, feeling her irritation threatening to override her control.

'Well – if you insist,' he grinned pulling one of her shoulder straps off. It fell down her arm, causing her neckline to hang low. 'Oh – hello,' Peter smiled at her breast.

Good, she thought. *That's him sorted.*

Later – much later – Grace lay awake listening to his deep breathing. She regretted the sex, not that she hadn't enjoyed it, but she felt even more irritable with him now, although she still didn't fully understand why. She stared at the chink of light on the ceiling that came through where the curtains hadn't been properly closed. She thought over the day: the morning service; her sermon; lunch; Zack and Peter's comments; her mother – God, her mother! And then suddenly there was Bishop Duncan, the candid pleasure in his grey eyes. Warmth flooded her as she thought of his words of praise and the preferment list. As she turned onto her side, she thought she could smell lavender and leather. It comforted her.

※　※　※

'Whatever you decide you want to do,' Grace was saying as she poured tea into each of their mugs, 'I want you to remember that you are always *in* and even if you opt out, you still belong to God.'

Zack grunted through a mouthful of toast and marmalade, rolling his eyes.

'Is this a continuation of yesterday's conversation?' Peter asked.

'Sorry,' she took a gulp of tea. 'I know it's a bit heavy this time of the morning ... but I wanted to say it yesterday and didn't get the chance.'

'I know, Mum.' Zack's smile was longsuffering. 'You worry too much.'

Peter gave her a look as if to say, *I told you so.* Swiftly he changed the subject as he saw the flash of anger in her eyes again. 'Have you heard if Chloe's had any offers on her house yet?'

'She's had one,' she replied, looking at Zack, wanting to pursue the church issue. 'She hopes to exchange contracts sometime this week. It's a bit less than the asking price, but not by much. So she should be able to go ahead and buy the little house she and Charlie and Jules have seen out near Virginia Water.'

'Nice location,' Peter mused. 'Be good to get moved before the boys go back to uni.'

'Mmmm,' Grace nodded. 'Have you got everything, my love,' she asked, returning her focus to Zack as he stood and slung his school bag over his shoulder.

'Yep ... see you later,' he leaned down and planted a kiss on her cheek.

'Bye, love – have a good day – learn something.' She noticed as she watched him affectionately that his trousers were a little short for him.

Goodness, they're only just new – when will he stop growing?

Peter gave him a high-five as he passed him, 'All the best for the start of term.'

'It's not fair that uni students don't go back for ages yet!' Zack moaned over his shoulder as he headed for the door. 'Charlie and Jules are go-carting today. I want to go.'

'Well you can't!' said Peter, more to himself than his son who was halfway down the hall by this time. 'But I do agree about it not being fair – nine grand for thirty weeks of the year, and if you're lucky you might see a tutor a couple of times a term?' he shook his head in disgust.

'Grumpy old man,' Grace quipped.

'I know,' Peter laughed, 'can't help it! Right – I'd better go.' He gulped down the remains of his tea as he stood up. He pulled his suit jacket off the back of his chair and slung it on one arm and then the other, shrugging his shoulders into it. He came round the table to Grace and bent down, 'That was fun last night,' he grinned, kissing the end of her nose.

She didn't look him in the eye.

'What *is* wrong Grace?' he asked.

'I don't know. If I did I would have told you by now.'

'Well, when you do, call me,' he kissed her forehead and straightened up.

'Bye,' she said in a small voice.

After he'd gone, she cleared the breakfast things away and went to her desk. She had half an hour before Morning Prayer. She sat down and closed her eyes, turning her palms upwards in her lap.

What is it?

She waited.

Don't feel valued ... my priesthood....

She pondered the revelation for a moment.

Daughter, mother, wife ... but not priest ...A prophet is never welcome in their own home...

Hurt soared like a bird let out of a cage.

That's it ... Zack's rejection of the Church ... feels like he's rejecting my priesthood ... and Peter didn't defend the Church ... didn't defend me ... and Mum ... well Mum can't help herself!

She opened her eyes and looked at her blue and gold icon of Jesus hanging above her desk. His gaze gently worked upon her.

Am I wrong to connect my identity so much with the Church? Isn't being a priest my true identity? Isn't this my calling? Shouldn't my nearest and dearest understand and honour that?

She closed her eyes again and waited. Nothing more came. She became aware of the clock in the hall ticking time away. She sighed, opened her eyes and reached for her Book of Common Prayer and her Bible as she stood to go.

'Hi, Anne,' she smiled as she entered the church at one of the women who faithfully attended the daily parish ritual. 'Would you do the readings?'

'Sure,' Anne grinned. 'What are they?'

Grace told her and as they looked them up, Gwen came in, then Val, Mo, Melanie, Chloe and Rose followed shortly behind her, along with the two church administrators, the children's worker and the two Church Wardens.

'How was Street Pastoring on the weekend?' Grace asked Anne as they waited for any last minute stragglers.

'A bit hairy ... nearly got punched, but managed to dodge it!' she curled a silvery-white strand of hair behind her ear and pointed at her cheek, 'Otherwise I'd have a good old bruise here.'

'You are amazing ... don't know how you do it,' Grace said admiringly.

'I guess you do impossible things when you know you're called to them,' Anne replied matter-of-factly. Grace nodded, thinking about the hurt she felt. At that Marie came through the church door and sat down beside her, 'Hi everyone, sorry I'm a bit late.'

'Hi, Marie, you're not late – just bang on time,' Grace said with a welcoming smile. She noted the dark circles under the delicate, pale skin around her eyes and the weary expression.

'How's the invalid?' Anne asked.

'The same,' Marie replied.

'He's a right pain, isn't he? I've told him several times to get better immediately, but he keeps lying there like a stubborn old mule! We need him back on the Street Pastors Team. Honestly the lengths some people will go to to shirk their responsibilities,' Anne joked.

Marie smiled half-heartedly. 'He's always been stubborn ... it's what's got him through life,' her lower lip quivered.

Anne immediately realised that Marie was not her usual pragmatic self and that her stoic dam of self-control was about to crumble. 'Sorry Marie, I didn't mean to upset you.'

Marie wiped away a tear, 'It's okay Anne ... I'm just not in a good way today.'

Grace interjected, 'What can we pray for Marie?'

Marie breathed in deeply, then exhaled slowly, her petite frame seemingly diminishing as she did. 'Oh I don't know ... it's hard, this not knowing. Is he going to get better or is he going to get worse? Or even more terrible still ... is he going to stay like this indefinitely?'

In the silence that followed a collective compassion exuded from the group. No one spoke, but their love for her was palpable in the air. As she cried softly, her small shoulders shook and Grace began the liturgy for Morning Prayer. One of the readings was from Psalm 23. When they came to: 'Even though I walk through the valley of the shadow of death, I will fear no evil,' they all paused as one before going on to the next sentence, 'for you are with me, your rod and your staff they comfort me.'

Marie sat with her eyes closed as they read the Scriptures over her. Grace could see the peace descending upon her as the group ministered tenderly. She felt a surge of pleasure as the people of St Stephen's confidently loved one another.

I love ministry! She thought, joy exploding in her soul. In the same instant she had a mental picture of kneeling in the cathedral, a bishop's mitre being placed on her head.

Prayers were over.

People were putting books away and moving chairs back into place. Grace couldn't move. She felt shocked. She didn't want to be a bishop. She wanted to keep doing this. Why had she had that picture?

'Are you okay?' Chloe asked, touching her shoulder.

Grace looked up in a daze, 'Yes ... sorry ... just had a weird thought,' she shook her head and got to her feet.

✳   ✳   ✳

Mark sat by James's bedside, reading the *Telegraph* to him. It had become his habit to spend his free time there. He had found a kindred spirit trapped in this paralysed body. Although able bodied, Mark identified with his paralysis in the very depths of his being. He would read to him, listen to Radio 4 with him and carry on the stilted conversations that the laptop allowed. He never felt tense, bored or restless when he was with him. In fact he felt more relaxed in his company than he did anywhere else. Mark hadn't given much thought to why this might be. He simply looked forward to the next visit.

Mark.

'Yes?'

NeedToAskUSomething.

'Oh? What?'

ThinkItsTheRightTimeNow.

'What do you mean?' intrigued, he put the paper down.

DoUKnowWhoUR?

Mark laughed dryly, 'Oh you're not gonna get all philosophical on me now are you?'

Maybe.

'What's brought this on?' Mark asked hesitantly.

DoUKnowWhoUR? – came the question again.

'Shit,' Mark looked at the ceiling and then down at James's face. He started folding the paper up noisily and looked like he was about to stand up, when it seemed he had second thoughts. He sat back in his chair and crossed his arms over his chest defensively, 'I used to think I did, but now I'm not so sure.'

WhatChanged?

As he stared at James, so helpless, a shadow of his former self, Mark's defenses didn't last long. 'I've done things I didn't know I was capable of; hurt people I thought I loved,' he hesitated.

GoOn.

Mark gazed at the cursor blinking at him on the computer screen, 'I used to think I was a good guy – not perfect – but, you know – good. I kind of expected the promotions I got at work, thinking I deserved them. Even after Chloe found out about me and Charmaine I still thought that somehow life owed me ... that I deserved everything I wanted.

'Well, I wanted Charmaine and I got her; I wanted my freedom – I got it; I wanted promotion – I got it – although I had less money because of the divorce – still I thought it would all pan out in my favour in the end. Having Charlie against me hurt, sure, but I thought he'd come round soon enough. And Melanie ... well naturally she'd feel for her mother, being female. But I knew she'd always love me. But now, here I am ... I know I'm no good,' he spread his hands; letting them drop to his lap, 'No good and here with you!' he laughed shakily. 'So do you know who you are?'

Yes.

'Are you gonna tell me?'

OnlyIfUReallyWantToKnow.

'You've got my attention James ... stop messing me about!' Mark grinned.

ImASonOfGod.

Mark sighed, 'Thought you might say something like that.'

ButImNotGood.

'Well you must be to be a son of God?'

IvDoneThingsImAshamedOf.

Mark stared at the screen, his hands limp in his lap.

DontKnowHowMariePutUpWithMe.

Mark smiled sadly, 'Well Chloe didn't put up with me.'

WiseWoman.

Mark's half-laugh was mirthless. 'So what kind of things have you done?'

LiedCheatedUsedLotsOfWomenViolentAbusive.

Mark quietly digested this information, a surprised look on his face. 'So how are you so sure God wants you for a son?'

ItsIncredibleRight?GoFigure!

'Aren't you just getting religious 'cuz you can't do any of those things anymore? What if you got mobility back?'

ThisIsTheRealDealMark.

'I thought that once ... but I just couldn't be good ... I tried, I really did ... but couldn't do it.'

ThatsTheWholePoint.

'What is?'

WeCantBeGood.ThatsWhyWeNeedASaviour.

Mark frowned, 'What's the point of believing in a Saviour, if it doesn't change the way you live your life ... if you still keep on sinning?'

LifesTough.OvercomingEvilWithGoodIsNeverEasy.JCHelpsUsInOurWeakness.

'JC? – Oh you mean Jesus? But I prayed I wouldn't give into temptation. God, I prayed ... but ... well you know ... you've been there, done that, by the sounds of it. It didn't work. I couldn't resist. He didn't help me in my weakness ... and besides, I guess I didn't really want him to help me. That's the trouble with temptation – you don't want to be saved from it. Ah!' Mark suddenly exclaimed and stood up, running his hands through his hair in frustration. In short, staccato sentences he added, 'I can't do this right now, James. You're doing my head in. Sorry. Look, I'm gonna have to go, mate. I'll come see you tomorrow. No hard feelings?'

OfcourseNot.Praying4U.GotNothingElseToDo.

Mark read his response, patted his limp hand in an apologetic manner and left the room faster than a frightened rabbit.

❋ ❋ ❋

'Mum?'

'Yes?' Chloe replied.

'I saw Dad for the first time the other day ... with Mel and Josh.'

'I know,' she smiled across the glass kitchen table.

'Oh ... I didn't know you knew,' Charlie looked anxious.

'It's okay ... I'm glad you saw him.'

'I'm not sure I am,' he replied.

'How did you feel at first?' she asked, her head to one side.

'Well ... I had this overwhelming desire to run into his arms and hug him. But then when he started to talk the feelings changed. I got angrier and angrier. I could have punched him in his smug face.'

Chloe frowned, 'Oh Charlie ... that's not good ... not good for you. Did you say anything about how you felt?'

'Yeah ... I think so ... it's a bit of blur now ... he asked to have a fresh start,' he looked down at his hands folded on the clear table top.

'And?' she asked encouragingly.

'I don't know. I hate him for what he did to you ... to us. How can he expect to be forgiven just like that?' his handsome features contorted with emotion.

'Maybe he doesn't ... maybe he's just hopeful that with time and relationship, healing could happen?' Chloe desperately hoped her counselling skills were masking her own feelings convincingly.

'Is that what you really think, Mum?' Charlie wasn't fooled.

'This isn't about me!' she parried. 'This is about you Charlie ... do you really want to go through life carrying all this unresolved anger and hurt? It's not good for you, sweetie, not good at all. I worry about you.'

He searched her face, his blue-green eyes reminding her so much of Mark's.

'I worry about you,' he said back.

She reached over and rested her hand on his, 'Please don't ... really ... that's not your job ... you're not the parent in this relationship.'

'Parents don't have a monopoly on caring,' he retorted.

'No ... but I don't want you carrying my stuff. I'm dealing with it myself. You know I've begun praying mercy for him?'

The shutters came down in his eyes at this. He pulled his hands from under hers. 'I thought you didn't believe in all that crap anymore?' he said looking away.

'I haven't, not for years, but I woke up the other morning thinking about your Dad, with the word mercy in my head. I didn't know what it meant, so I went and looked it up. Then I opened my old journal. As I read the last entry and the Bible verses for that day ... what was it? Five years ago?'

He nodded.

'Well I found myself talking to God again ... almost despite myself. It was so weird.'

Charlie said nothing, just watched her warily.

'I admit I'm not at the place yet where I personally want to be merciful, but I've begun asking God to be merciful towards him. I guess that's sort of the same thing as allowing your Dad the possibility of a fresh start.'

At least Charlie was listening, she thought. As she watched him it dawned on her that she was the one with the power to effect change. She'd always felt powerless in the storms of her life. She'd thought of Charmaine as being the powerful one. A verse of scripture long forgotten floated to the surface of her mind, *'What you bind on earth will be bound in heaven, what you loose on earth will be loosed in heaven.'*

Surprised, she made a mental note to look it up later.

'Jules thinks I'll get hurt all over again ... that he'll just treat me the way he always has. A leopard doesn't change its spots and all that.'

'Maybe ... but you'll never know unless you give him a chance,' Chloe smiled at herself as she said the words. It was like she was preaching to herself. 'You know Charlie, we have a choice: every time we get hurt, we can choose to build up our defences in order to protect ourselves or we can take the risk of remaining vulnerable and open and being hurt again. I'm realizing that I've chosen defence over the years and it's not been good. So much of my life has been shut down, boarded up, locked away. I've been safe from hurt, but so limited. I'm sorry I've modelled that way of being to you.' Surprising herself, she sat back in her chair to review what she'd just said.

'You've got nothing to apologise for! You've done nothing wrong. It's Dad who's got a lot to make up for,' anger sparked his eyes. Restlessly he picked up the estate agent's profile of the house in Virginia Water. 'Anyway ... what time are we meeting the estate agent?'

That was that: end of conversation. But despite their abrupt return to the matter at hand, Chloe knew Charlie would come back to the deep places they had dived to. He needed time to process. A surge of love for him swept over her, so she stood up and came behind him, wrapping her arms round his neck and kissing the top of his head. 'Two. Is Jules coming?'

'Yep. Wouldn't miss it!'

'What do you want for lunch? Pizza? Soup and bread? Caesar salad?'

'We're both off carbs at the minute, so salad please. I'll text him.'

'But he's just upstairs!' Chloe laughed.

'I know,' Charlie grinned at her as she went to the fridge and opened its door. 'But if I go up there, I know I'll only be tempted to go back to bed. Let me help you get lunch ready. I'll make the dressing.'

❋ ❋ ❋

Grace dialled his number and listened to it ringing at the other end of the line.

'Bishop Duncan's office,' came Julia's voice. 'How can I help you?'

'Hi, Julia, it's Grace Hutchinson. Is Bishop Duncan around? Could I have a quick word?' she noticed her heart beat thudding faster and louder in her chest.

'He was hoping you'd call today. He's in a meeting at the minute, but asked me to interrupt it if you called. Can you hold on a moment?'

'Sure,' the pleasure Grace felt at hearing this information washed through her entire body in warm waves. She held her breath.

'Hello, Grace! I hope you have good news for me?' Bishop Duncan's voice was warm with affection.

'Well, that depends on your point of view,' Grace laughed.

'Yes?' he encouraged her.

'My answer is yes ... okay ... I'd be honoured.'

'Fantastic! My prayers have been heard! Ha! So tell me how you came to this change of mind – I'm fascinated!' she visualised his grey eyes dancing with laughter.

'I ... I ...' she faltered, 'I don't know really ... I think it was around thoughts of my calling ... my identity as a priest. I'm not sure ... but I said I'd give you an answer this week, so there it is.'

'Fantastic! I'll get Julia on to the Archbishop's office immediately. Thank you Grace. Wonderful stuff! Right I better get back to my meeting. Could Julia pin you down for another meeting in a week or two?'

'Certainly,' she smiled.

'What was Peter's reaction?'

'I haven't told him yet,' a pang of guilt cut through her pleasure.

'Oh,' there was a pause. 'Shouldn't you have discussed it with him before this phone call?' she could hear other questions in his voice.

'I wanted to tell you first,' she said in a small voice. 'I guess I was scared that he might try and put me off ... and it wouldn't take much ... anyway it's about me – my calling – my identity. I just wanted you to be the first to know. I'll speak to him this evening.'

'Okay ... Thank you Grace,' his tone was deep velvet.

'Thank you,' she responded almost in a whisper, fully aware that they had both said a lot more.

After hanging up she stared into space, images of kissing him playing on the screen of her imagination.

The phone rang breaking her reverie, 'Hello, Reverend Hutchinson speaking,' she said guiltily.

'Hi babe,' the sound of Peter's voice increased her guilt.

'Oh hi,' she replied uncertainly.

'So any idea what's nettled you yet?'

'Yes ... I'll tell you when I see you.'

'Tell me now. I hate this.'

'Oh, Peter,' she hesitated.

'I'll just keep ringing you until you tell me,' he retorted stubbornly.

She knew he meant it and sighed, 'Oh all right. Yesterday I felt hurt by you, Zack and Mum, but especially you.'

'Yeah, I got that. Just not sure why though?'

Grace bit her lip in frustration, 'You see ... that's it ... you don't get how important my calling is to me. I think you think ministry is just like any old job, but it isn't. I'm a priest, Peter. It's my calling; it's who I am – my identity. It felt like none of you value who I am, not really. I can accept that from Mum – she doesn't know any better – and Zack is just being a teenager, I guess – but you ... I hoped you would have defended me or backed me up or something!'

'I was only trying to help Zack. It can't be easy having a vicar as his Mum. Your calling isn't necessarily his calling.'

'I agree, but still ... that's what I've been feeling. You wanted to know.'

There was silence on the other end of the line as Peter took stock. Then, 'Well I'm sorry you felt like that Grace, but it wasn't my intention that you would feel undermined. I love you and the way you live out your calling. I support you a hundred percent. But Zack may never love the Church in the same way as you do. That doesn't make him bad.'

'I know that!' Grace retorted angrily.

'Don't you realise how powerful you are? That you have the ability, as

Zack's Mum, to put guilt on him over something he has no need to feel guilty about?'

It was Grace's turn to fall silent. Then she said, 'I just want the best for him.'

'I know you do – we both do. But he's growing up and making his own decisions. Perhaps he will make some that we don't think will be the best for him, but we've got to let him make them. It's his life.'

'I know,' she replied, her voice softer and more vulnerable. 'I know I took it personally when it wasn't meant that way.'

'He loves you and so do I ... and so does your Mum ... in her own kind of way.'

Grace laughed, 'Tell me about it!' Then in a rush she added, 'Look, Peter, the Bishop's asked me if he can put my name forward for the preferment list. That means I might be able to apply or be called to interview for Archdeacons' or Bishops' jobs.'

'Wow! When was this?'

'Last week.'

'Why didn't you tell me sooner?' she heard the hurt in his voice.

'I don't know really,' she went on in a rush, 'I think at first I thought I was going to say no. But as I've gone on, I've realised how much my priestly identity means to me. Maybe I was scared you'd laugh or belittle it. It's such an honour!'

'Grace, how can you say that? I think it's amazing! I'm your biggest fan!'

Bishop Duncan's euphoric response to her 'yes' echoed in her mind as she thought, *No, you're not.*

'Sorry,' she said contritely, 'just feeling vulnerable.'

'You really are, aren't you? So when are you going to give him your answer?'

'I just have,' she held her breath.

'Before telling me?' again she heard the amazed hurt in his voice.

'I'm sorry ... I should have discussed it with you ... I was going to, but then I got defensive yesterday ... I don't know what else to say, but sorry.'

'Right,' he said clipping the 't' sharply. 'Well, we can talk more this evening. I have to say I'm a bit hurt, Grace. I can't pretend I understand.'

'I'm out tonight. It'll have to wait. I told you I didn't want to do this on the phone, but you wouldn't listen.'

'Okay – I've got to go now. I'll try and get away early so we can have at least some time before dinner to talk.'

'Okay – bye,' she said, relieved.

'Bye,' he sounded angry.

She sat back exhausted, surveying the piles of paperwork on her desk. The last thing she wanted to do now was work. She clicked on the Word document that was always open on her desktop. Up came her story.

What's being revealed to you, Lila? Escapism took over as she began reading over her last chapter. Soon she was lost in her characters and their relationships, happily burying the unresolved issues with Peter.

'I'm having a small gathering at my home tomorrow evening. I hope you and Timothy will be able to attend?'

'May I ask what it is for?' Anna enquired as they ate their meal under the shade of the orange tree in her courtyard. Members of the Church sat in clusters where there was shade, sharing their communal lunch together. It had been a wonderful celebration of the Lord's Day. Timothy had taught from one of Paul's letters, his quiet confidence adding weight to every word he spoke. He was much loved by the community, not just for his gentleness and youthfulness, but also because of his faithfulness in visiting every member, Jew or Gentile, slave or free, any who were in difficulty or sickness. He knew them each by name and taught all the elders to do likewise, so that their fellowship was rich and warm.

In the wake of her father's passing she had noted that Timothy had grown in authority. It seemed he had taken on not only Paul's mantle, but her father's also. His love for scripture had always matched her father's, but now when he taught it, it seemed to become a living, breathing thing; an arrow that went straight to his hearers' hearts. Anna wondered, now that Papa was re-united with the Lord, whether he had been interceding for his son-in-law. The idea made her smile.

'It is our way of saying thank you to all of you for your kind welcome – only a small social gathering,' Aaron was saying.

Unknowingly Anna smiled an almost mirror-image smile of his as she responded, 'That is so thoughtful and kind! I'm sure we will be able to come. I don't think there are any other meetings happening tomorrow night. I will check with Timothy.'

As she spoke a young Greek convert came to sit with them, 'May I join you?' he asked respectfully.

'Of course, Neo, come sit,' Anna patted the stone floor beside her, half cast in shadow. 'You know Aaron, don't you?'

'We have not spoken as yet. I've been eager to make your acquaintance, Aaron – I have heard so many good things about you from the other young men. On my return from Thessalonica I've heard little else but your name.'

Aaron nodded, 'Ah, the great Neo returns!' he brushed a fly away from his plate with a laconic sweep of his hand. 'They have told me all about you. How did you fare in that great city?'

'We led many to Christ and helped them establish a Church in one of their homes. It was incredible how joyfully the people received our message. It truly is good news, indeed it is,' he nodded animatedly.

'Neo is one of our evangelists,' Anna informed Aaron.

'That is evident,' Aaron replied.

Lila turned to Neo. 'Tell Aaron how you came to faith. It is such an inspiring story.'

Neo hesitated as he looked at Aaron. He wasn't sure Aaron was that interested, but obediently began, 'Well ... I grew up here in Ephesus, the son of a priestess.'

Aaron cleared his throat and ran his hand down his silver beard. His discomfort was not lost on Neo as he continued, 'My mother was a devout woman and taught me what she understood of divine love. However as I grew older I began to see that her devotion to Artemis did not result in blessings, but rather much suffering. The men who used her for sacred intercourse were often not as pious they appeared.

'When she became ill and could no longer carry out her duties at the temple I nursed her until she died. I was sixteen. Not once did the High Priest come to visit her. Not one offering was made for her recovery. When they realised her sickness was fatal they stopped her meagre wage. Not only did she live out her last days in pain, but also in poverty. When she breathed her last, I swore I would never worship the goddess again because the love she embodied was a lie.

'It was not long after, I heard about Paul who was teaching in the lecture hall of Tyrranus. Like many of my friends I was curious about his teachings: he performed many miracles, you know. One of my friends whose tongue had been cut off as a child in order that he might earn a living as a beggar discovered that during one of Paul's lectures it had grown back. For the first time he spoke clearly, praising God at the top of his voice.

'If only I had known about Paul before my mother died. I would have brought her to him.' He paused as sadness shadowed his features.

'I went to see him at the lecture hall. Then I asked to see him privately. He spent many days with me talking and praying, opening the scriptures to me. I had never had a father before. Paul became my father in God,' Neo ended with a sigh. 'I hope to go and visit him in Rome soon,' he said, a hopeful smile playing about his mouth.

'At what stage did he circumcise you?' Aaron asked coolly.

Anna looked at him in surprise, as did Neo. 'He didn't,' replied the young man.

The discomfort that Neo had detected in the older man, turned distinctly into something more like hostility. 'You are not circumcised?' Aaron asked.

'No,' said Neo. 'I am not a Jew. I am a follower of Christ. Paul did not instruct me in this matter and neither has Timothy, Priscilla, Aquilla or Jair. None of us Greek believers have been circumcised.'

'Yet all of them - barring the woman Priscilla of course - including Jesus himself, were circumcised,' Aaron's eyes pierced Neo's. 'Even Timothy who is half-Greek was purified by Paul himself. Is this not so?' Aaron turned to Anna.

Embarrassed and bewildered Anna could do nothing more than nod her head at first. Her mind was racing. Then suddenly she said, 'But he didn't do it as a means of purification or for his salvation.

That only comes through faith in Jesus Christ.'

Aaron smiled at her indulgently, 'My dear child, you speak of things beyond your understanding.'

She felt affronted, but then quickly chastised herself for being so outspoken with so great a teacher. After all he had taught Paul. And the way he called her his *dear child* ... there was a softness in his voice that confused and bewildered her. She felt the hot prickle of tears and blinked furiously. Her grief suddenly threatened to overwhelm her. She panicked and struggled to her feet, dropping her ceramic plate on the stone courtyard floor. It shattered into hundreds of tiny pieces. 'Sorry,' she said, 'Excuse me,' and ran from them into the house.

'Whatever has happened?' Mary asked as Anna almost fell over her in the kitchen.

Anna was sobbing uncontrollably. Mary gripped her by the arms and gently drew her into an embrace. 'There, there my love. It's going to be all right. Tell me what has happened?'

Eventually Anna lifted her head and tried to speak between stuttering gasps and sobs, 'Aaron was ... was ... was ... saying ... I didn't understand ... I ... I ... I ... tried to ... but Neo ... wasn't ... wasn't ....'

'Wasn't what, my dear,' Mary asked patiently.

'Cir ... cir ... cumcised.'

'What?'

'Then ... then ... he called me his ... his ... dear child and I ... I ... thought of Papa. I ... I ... couldn't ... stop ....' she ended in a fresh flood of tears.

'Oh, Anna, you are overwrought with grief! We shouldn't have celebrated the Lord's Day in your home today. We should have asked Ruth and Onesiphorus or Priscilla and Aquilla. Come now, come and lie down. Let me get you settled and then I'll bring Timothy to you. Sweet love, come,' she gently led Anna through the house to her bedroom.

※ ※ ※

'It wasn't terribly clear what had made her so upset,' Mary was saying to Timothy and Lila, 'but whatever it was, it was something to do with a conversation between Aaron and Neo.'

'I'll speak with them first before I go to her,' Timothy said gravely. 'Perhaps we were foolhardy to have the Lord's Day celebration in our home so soon after Jair's passing?'

'Yes ... I think perhaps so,' Lila frowned. 'We needn't grieve like those who have no hope, yet still the parting of death is so painful for us who are left behind.'

Timothy looked at his mother-in-law speculatively. 'Is there anything you want to tell me, Lila – anything I need to know?'

Her eyes widened in surprise, 'Why do you ask?'

'I don't know,' he said, 'it was just a feeling ... never mind,' he patted her hand, dismissing the sense that she was keeping some secret from him. *We're all exhausted. We must rest and wait upon the Lord, or we will all come undone.*

He made his way through the courtyard where the few remaining Church members lingered. Aaron was still in conversation with Neo under the orange tree.

'Brothers,' Timothy greeted them, 'sorry to interrupt your conversation, but I wanted to check with you before I go to Anna, as to what happened to trigger her emotional reaction? She was not very coherent.'

Aaron spread his arms as he stood up. Timothy respectfully responded and embraced the older man, 'Come sit with us a while, Timothy,' Aaron indicated with a sweeping gesture. Timothy sat down between them.

'So what happened?' he asked.

'I think perhaps it was my fault, Timothy. I called her "my dear child". I should have known better than to stir up her filial emotions so soon after Jair's passing. It was a slight of speech – I hope you – and she will forgive me?'

Timothy's mouth hung slightly open as he stared at Aaron, revelation dawning upon him in one turbulent cresting wave. He quickly shut his mouth and turned to Neo, hoping Aaron would not see what he now understood. 'Is that how it seemed to you?' he asked the younger man.

'Well, we were having a discussion about whether us Gentile believers should keep Jewish laws ... I think it stirred up some emotional response in Anna before her grief overtook her.'

'Oh?' Timothy turned his head questioningly back to Aaron.

'It was nothing really,' Aaron ran his hand over his beard. 'We were exploring the ways in which we are called to live holy lives. I believe it was too much theology for her ... at this difficult time.'

Neo opened his mouth to speak, but took warning from Aaron's glance, and closed it again.

'Anna loves theology. She is a capable thinker ... but as you say ... this is a difficult time ... for all of us,' Timothy could not shake off the alarm he felt. He studied Aaron momentarily and then decided to smile, 'Thank you brothers – I'm sorry to have disturbed you. I must go to her now. I'm sure rest will restore her to good humour.'

Both men nodded, expressing their hope that Anna would indeed quickly recover her equilibrium. As Timothy walked away, his mind was in a whirl. *He is her father! That's why they have bonded so closely! That's why they look so alike! That's what Lila was hiding! That's why Anna is so upset ... even if she does not consciously know it yet. Dear Lord, help me know what to do* ... he prayed. *And this theological issue ... is there more to it than Aaron is letting on?* He shook his head, his jaw muscles tightening. There was trouble ahead, for certain.

He slowly opened their bedroom door and peered into the gloom. Mary had closed the shutters. Anna lay curled in a foetal position shrouded by a thin linen sheet. He came in closing the door softly behind him and padded to her side. He knelt down and gently took her hand in his, stroking her smooth skin lightly with his thumb.

Her swollen eyelids half opened, and fresh tears trickled from them on seeing him. Her lower lip quivered.

'Don't speak my love – rest – it's all right – all will be well,' he soothed.

She closed her eyes again as her shoulders shook.

※　※　※

'May I ask you something,' Timothy's gaze did not waver.

Lila nervously tucked a strand of hair behind her ear as she looked up from her chopping board. The pomegranate she'd cut in half lay displaying its crimson fleshy seeds wrapped in pale pink pith. She returned to one half, holding it firmly in hand and taking a spoon to scoop out the jewel-like seeds. 'Of coarse Timothy, you may ask me anything. Whether I can answer it or not is another matter,' she smiled and scooped the seeds into a bowl.

Leaning in close and in a low voice he asked, 'Was Jair Anna's father?'

Lila continued scooping out the pomegranate. When she eventually raised her eyes to his face they were lit by an internal flame. 'In every way – yes he was her father.' She put the spoon down decisively and turned to face him. 'But not by blood.'

'Do you know who her blood-father is?' he persisted.

'Yes I do,' she lifted her perfectly shaped head, looking more dignified than Timothy had ever seen her look before. He waited. 'As you know, the Apostle John has come to live in Ephesus with Mary, Jesus' mother. When they first arrived we spent much time with them ... we are old friends ... that was before Jair became ill. Did you know John is writing his account of the Gospel?'

'Yes ... yes I did,' Timothy's was perplexed as he wondered where she was going with this.

'We spent much time talking with him about the things we experienced as we travelled with the Lord. He was particularly interested in how I first came to meet Him.'

'Oh?' Timothy's curiosity was aroused.

Lila took a deep breath, 'The Pharisees were looking for a basis on which to accuse Jesus. One of the Pharisees had a mistress. He used her, arranged to be caught in the act of adultery with her, and together with a mob of angry men, dragged her before the Lord one morning as he taught in the Temple courts.

'They threw her before him, abused, beaten and bleeding, her clothes torn, her hair undone. It was the perfect trap: if he judged her according to the Law of Moses, he would have had to have her stoned to death – but then he would have lost favour with the people – the sinners whom he so loved to spend his time with. The Pharisees and teachers of the Law would be vindicated.

'But if he did not judge her according to the Law of Moses, He would show himself to be the charlatan they said he was – not the Son of God – not the Messiah or even a prophet or a good man – for God and His laws cannot change.'

Timothy was mesmerised, 'What did he do?'

'He bent down and began writing on the ground with his finger.'

'What did he write?' Timothy leaned forward in anticipation.

'No one knows,' she replied, a smile playing on her lips.

Timothy looked deflated.

'The same finger that wrote the commandments on stone tablets, was writing again on the stone paving of the Temple courts. He alone defined sin and He alone could forgive it. He could have rightly sat in judgment, yet he chose to bend down to write a new commandment in the dust she was covered in. They kept on questioning him until he finally straightened up and said to them, "If any one of you is without sin, let him be the first to throw a stone at her".'

Timothy's eyebrows rose in wonder.

Lila laughed softly, 'Then he stooped down again and continued writing on the ground with his finger, as if he were reiterating that He was the first and the final Word, that all the Law was fulfilled in Him. He had come because none of us could fulfil it; we needed forgiveness; a way out; a saviour.'

She paused and sighed. 'One by one they began to go away, the oldest ones first, until only Jesus was left with the woman still standing there.

'Finally he straightened up and asked her, "Where are they? Has no one condemned you?"

"No one, sir," she replied.

"Then neither do I condemn you. Go now and leave your life of sin".'

Lila's face was aglow. The telling of the story never ceased to work its magic upon her. She revelled in it, all her shame and anxiety slipping away, like dust washed away with clear water.

Timothy was looking at her with new eyes, 'This woman – this woman was you?' he asked.

She nodded.

'And the Pharisee?'

'Yes ... it was Aaron, Jair's childhood friend.'

Timothy's covered his mouth with his hand.

'I was carrying Anna in my womb, although Aaron did not know. I have often wondered whether knowing would have made him change his plans. Jesus saved both my life and Anna's that day. And then ...' she paused for effect, 'Jair was there. He took me back home. He washed my wounds and bandaged them. He nursed me back to health. When I told him of the baby he welcomed her as his own.'

Timothy blinked back tears.

When she spoke again Lila's voice was soft and small, 'Once you experience such grace and mercy you are forever changed. We could not return to our old lives. We chose to follow Jesus wherever he went after that.'

'And Anna knows nothing of this?' Timothy queried.

'She knows that Jair had been cursed, that we were childless. I have let her believe that she came into being because we encountered Jesus – which is true. She would never have breathed if it were not for Him. The Lord did heal Jair because we soon conceived Joshua ... our second little miracle,' she smiled.

'What about Aaron? Does he know that Anna is his?' Timothy's brow furrowed.

'When he found out, it was around the time of the first persecution of the Church. He kidnapped her, but Jair risked his life to get our daughter back.'

'What age was she? Did she understand what was happening at the time?'

Lila shook her head, 'No she was only little. She was very traumatised, but we continued to pray peace and healing upon her. She is the strong woman she is today because of all she has been through.'

Timothy accepted this truth with a nod of his head and a smile,

'Although she does not consciously know or understand, perhaps she is being re-traumatised all over again by Aaron's relationship with her?' he mused.

Lila digested this silently.

'I have been baffled by how quickly and how deeply they have bonded. Now that I know your story, it is as clear as day to me,' he smiled. 'Thank you for trusting me with it.'

Lila bowed her head and studied her fingers, 'I don't know whether it would be good to tell Anna or not? What are your thoughts?'

'I need to wait upon the Lord and pray for wisdom. What I do know now is that when Aaron called her his "dear child", I believe that was the trigger for her tears. It seems to me the issue of upholding the Law may also be connected to her emotional upheaval, seeing as she is the fruit of an unlawful act, even though she doesn't consciously know it.'

'Goodness ... do you really think that is possible?'

'I don't know ... anything's possible. And what about Aaron? What do you think? Has he an agenda? Did he come to Ephesus with the aim of seeking you and Anna out? Is his conversion to The Way genuine? I know he has received baptism, he and his whole household; that he is a great teacher of the scriptures, with a deep love for Jerusalem and the Temple. I know he is broken-hearted over what is happening there. But has he truly changed?'

'This is what has terrified me,' Lila said. 'But Mary pointed out that Paul changed from being a persecutor of the Church. She also reminded me that I had changed from living a life of sin to ... to ... becoming a follower of Jesus.'

'Yes ... but not all those who cry "Lord, Lord" truly know Him,' Timothy pulled at his earlobe thoughtfully.

'No ....' Lila could think of nothing more to say.

※ ※ ※

'"Dear Paul, my father in God, my friend and teacher.
Greetings, from the Church here in Ephesus.

I hope this finds you well and rejoicing in God, despite your chains?

I write first to inform you of the sad news that our brother Jair has gone to be with the Lord. He was much loved and is greatly missed. His clear grasp of the whole council of God in scripture is a great loss to the Church here.

Joshua and Luke arrived in time to see him before he left us. It was a precious re-union, if brief. I believe Joshua wishes to stay for some time to comfort his mother and sister in their grief. Your loss of them has been our gain."'

Paul translated as he read aloud for Pudens. He raised his head from squinting down at the letter in his hands. 'Dear Jair – such a good man. What joy for him that he is now with the Lord,' he sounded almost envious, 'but what sorrow for Joshua, Anna and Lila. Thank God Joshua got there in time to say goodbye,' Paul smiled. 'I wonder how long Joshua and Luke plan to stay?' he mused, rubbing his eyes irritably in preparation to read on. He raised the parchment close to his face and squinted as he continued,

"'I am also writing to ask for your wisdom on another matter. I don't know if you have heard, but an old friend of yours has joined the Church here. His name is Aaron. He says he taught you at one time. He certainly has a deep love for the Law and for the scriptures. However I am unsure as to whether he has grasped the Gospel of Grace. I fear that he may encourage those of the circumcision group and that because he is a gifted orator, disunity will grow among us because of his persuasiveness. I would greatly value your insights into this matter."'

'Aaron!' he exclaimed. 'How I had hoped to convince him all those years ago!'

'Who is he?' Pudens asked as he cut a section of apple with a short knife and deftly flicked it into his mouth.

'He was one of the Sanhedrin, the ruling party, in Jerusalem – a man of great influence. If I had been able to win him for Christ back then, perhaps all of Jerusalem would have believed and history would be different,' he looked back down at Timothy's letter and frowned. 'So he has left his beloved Temple city. Things must be very bad.

'And how, I wonder, did he become part of the Church? It was he who funded my efforts to put a stop to it. With his patronage I did unspeakable things to my brothers and sisters, in the name of Moses, the Law and the prophets.

'After my conversion I went to see him in hopes that I could win him, but he would not listen. He severed our friendship and swore an oath to stop me at every turn.'

'Praise the Lord, if the truth has really been revealed to him!' Pudens crunched down on a fresh piece of apple.

'But has it? I wonder ...' Paul said thoughtfully. 'He was a very shrewd man, a powerful politician. We must pray for him, for Timothy and the other leaders of the Church. We must seek the Lord's mind on this matter Pudens. Will you assist me?'

'Certainly, brother Paul. You know I take great pleasure in participating in God's will being done. I love raising my voice to heaven in prayer.'

Paul's face cracked into a broad smile, 'You have been so easy to teach Pudens. You have taken to intercession like a ship to the sea.'

'I believe I was made for it,' Pudens' eyes were bright, 'since that evening by the Tiber, my life has truly changed.'

'Let's kneel before the Father and pray that out of his glorious riches he may strengthen Aaron with power through the Holy Spirit so that Christ may truly dwell in his heart by faith.'

6. DEEPENING

Ephesians 3:14–21

I pray that you, being rooted and established in love, may have power, together with all the Lord's people, to grasp how wide and long and high and deep is the love of Christ, and to know this love that surpasses knowledge—that you may be filled to the measure of all the fullness of God.

Peter hadn't made it home early after all on the day they'd argued. It was a whole week before they spoke properly to each other again.

Zack tiptoed round them and watched with bated breath for the breakthrough. It came on Saturday morning when they were all in their pyjamas and dressing gowns, eating toast and marmalade in front of the TV. The news was on – a piece about women bishops and the appalling discrimination some had suffered. Grace sighed; Peter stopped chewing his food and Zack furtively glanced at them both.

'If someone treated you like that, I'd bloody punch their lights out,' Peter swallowed the remainder of his half-chewed toast.

Surprised Grace looked at him directly, probably for the first time in a week. 'Really? I thought you might join them?'

'How can you say that, Grace?' Peter swivelled in his chair to face her. 'I love you so much!'

Grace's eyes welled up, 'You do? Even though I didn't discuss it with you first?'

'Of course you idiot! I was annoyed for a bit ... but you must have had your reasons ....'

'What didn't you discuss with him?' Zack interjected.

They both turned and looked at him. Grace started laughing through her tears. Peter got up, crossed the living room and flopped down beside her on the sofa, wrapping his arms around her.

'You crazy woman! I love everything about you! You should know that by now,' Peter's words were muffled in her hair.

'I'm so sorry I didn't tell you first ... or ask you what you thought ... I think it went to my head.' She kissed his cheek several times and then his mouth.

Zack watched them with a grimace on his face, relieved that the tension was broken. 'Thank God I don't have to walk round on eggshells any more ... and can you stop that ... it's disgusting!'

'Sorry,' Grace turned to him and smiled.

'We'll get a room,' Peter laughed.

'Don't make me vomit!' Zack retorted grabbing his chance at taking control of the TV remote and changing the programme to *The Big Bang Theory*.

Make-up sex in the shower later that morning was wonderful. As she towel dried her curls, thoughts of Bishop Duncan seemed less appealing. It was very strange, she mused, this 'thing' she had for him.

※　※　※

Marie sat beside James, reading the paper to him. As usual she had begun at the back with the sports pages. Occasionally he interrupted her with a typed question or exclamation, so when he started typing she put the paper down and looked at the computer screen.

CanYouSeeThem?

'See who?' Marie asked, looking back down and scanning the broadsheet for what he was referring to.

TheAngels.

Marie looked first at James and then around the room slowly. 'No ... sorry, love ... I can only see you.'

LookByTheDoor.TwoOfThem.

Marie obeyed, screwing her eyes up. 'No ... can't see them. What do they look like?'

ShiningBlueWhiteGoldFire.

'Wow ... wish I could see them,' Marie reached her hand out and pressed it on James's forehead. It was cool.

ImNotHallucinating.TheyAreReal.

'How does it feel seeing them?' she peered over her shoulder tentatively.

AwesomeTerrifyingExciting.

'Why do you think they're here? And why are they only letting you see them? Can you ask them to let me see them?' she dropped her voice and squinted her eyes again hoping she might glimpse something.

IDontKnow.IWillAsk.

After a minute Marie whispered, 'What did they say?'

DidntSayWhyUCantSeeThem.JustSaidTheKingdomWasComing.

Alarmed Marie grabbed his free hand, 'What does that mean? Have they come to get you?'

TheyDontSeemToBeInterestedInMe.TheyAreWaitingFor...

'For what? Who?' Marie's curiosity overtook her anxiety.

For ...

At that moment Mark came through the door, 'Hi, Marie! How's the patient today? Not giving you too much grief, I hope?' he grinned and came over to her, kissing her on the cheek.

'Hi, Mark,' she replied as she glanced at the computer screen again.

James typed: *Him.*

'You've got perfect timing!' she smiled. 'I was just about to go.'

'Oh don't leave on my account – I can come back some other time,' he said apologetically.

'No – really – I need to run a couple of errands. I was getting bored reading the sports section anyway – you can take over – much more your thing than mine.'

Mark relaxed. 'Hello mate, how are you today?' he turned his attention on James as Marie bent to kiss him goodbye. When she'd gone he sat down in her chair and picked up the paper, 'So where did she get to?'

DontReadThat.IWasGettingBoredToo.

'Oh?' Mark let the paper drop from his hands onto the bed. 'So what do you want to talk about?'

CanWeCarryOnOurConversationFromTheOtherDay?

'Do we have to?' Mark frowned uncomfortably, shifting in his seat.

WhatDidUThinkAfterULeft?

'I didn't! I went to the pub and had a few pints, like normal people do.'

JesusSentMeBackForU.

IDidntWantToComeBackToThisButIDidItForU.

'What are you talking about? You feeling all right mate? Shall I call a nurse?' Mark looked concerned.

ImFine.ItsUWhoNeedsHelpNotMe.

'I'm feeling distinctly uncomfortable here James ... can we change the subject ... or I'm going to have to go,' Mark summoned whatever authority he thought he might have into his voice.

LookIHaveBeenWithJesus.

SeenHim.

TalkedToHim.

ItsBeenAmazing.

ComingBackIsTheHardestThingIvEverDone.

HeSaidItWouldOnlyBeForALittleWhile.

SoTheSoonerUGetUrselfSortedOutWithGodTheSoonerICanGo.

Mark stared at the blinking cursor on the computer screen, his mouth slightly ajar. Then he slowly swivelled his eyes to James's. 'Are you for real? You're not getting all religious on me?'

IfUdKnownMeBeforeUdKnowIDontDoReligious.

'So ...,' Mark faltered, 'You've seen Jesus?'

Yep.

'Can you see him now?'

No.ButThereAreTwoBigFuckOffAngelsBehindU.

Mark's head snapped round to look behind him. Then he laughed, 'Stop messing with me!'

ImNot.TheyvBeenThereForAgesWaitingForU.

'I don't believe you – how come I can't see them?'

IDontKnow.

'Have they said anything to you?'

Yep.TheySaidTheKingdomWasComing.

'And ... what does that mean?'

LetsWaitAndSeeShallWe.

Mark gazed at James's wasted face. He was torn as to whether to take him seriously or not. He wasn't quite sure what to say next, so he didn't say anything.

In the silence he tried to see if he could sense the angels James said were there. He closed his eyes momentarily, but opened them again when he heard James slowly typing.

JCToldMeToBringUHome.HeToldMeToTellUHeMissesU.

'Bring me home? To Chloe and the family? To the Church? To Heaven – does he want me to die? I don't understand. What does "bring me home" mean?'

ToHim.FriendshipWithHim.

'Oh ….' Mark digested this, then muttered, 'Why would he want to be friends with someone like me?'

NoIdea.Lol.

Mark laughed.

TheyAreStandingEitherSideOfYouNow.

Mark stole a glance to his left and then his right. He might as well play along with James, if it made him happy. 'What are they doing?'

LovingYou.

Despite himself, Mark felt a lump in his throat.

TheyAreSingingNow ... TheLoveOfGod ... TheLoveOfGod ...

Mark tried to clear his throat. He felt very warm and heavy. The next thing he knew he was sliding off the chair and onto the floor. He couldn't seem to command his body to do anything. As he lay on the floor, looking up at the underside of James's bed it occurred to him that this must be what it was like for James. The thought had no sooner crossed his mind when a desire to cry overtook him. He was powerless to stop it. Deep guttural sobs surged up from his soul.

How long he lay there crying like a baby, he didn't know ... or care. Eventually he was spent. He lay still wondering what it had all been about. He noticed how light – how happy he felt. He couldn't remember the last time he'd experienced such carefreeness – maybe as a boy? He rolled onto his side to sit up, but couldn't. It was as though he had become part of the floor, as if he were made of the same substance. He tried again, but to no avail. He opened his mouth to speak, but his stupid lips and tongue would not obey him. He wondered then if perhaps he was having a stroke. But surely it would have been painful? He tried to speak again and this time laughter gurgled up from within him. He laughed until his sides hurt and his chest ached.

He was making so much noise that a nurse came in to see what was going on. Laughter was not a common sound in hospital. Alarmed she ran to Mark, kneeling down beside him. 'What happened? Are you okay?' she asked urgently.

All he could do was go off into another peal of laughter. She ran to get help and soon there were four nurses around him, preparing to lift him off the floor. Weak and utterly elated, Mark co-operated with them as best he could. Slowly the power of speech returned to him as they worked to get him into a sitting position and then hoisted him to his feet.

'Thank you ... thank you ...' was all he could say.

'What happened?' asked the senior nurse.

'Not sure,' he replied with a weak laugh. 'I'm okay though ... you don't need to worry. I'll be fine.' He sighed deeply, chuckling some more.

Looks were exchanged and then the nurses left him slumped in the chair beside James. James typed, *SoTheKingdomCame.*

'If that's the Kingdom, let it come!' Mark laughed, wiping his eyes with shaky hands. As he spoke he happened to look at the wall clock up above James's bed. 'Two hours? Have I been gone for two hours?'

Yep.

'Oh my God! I can't believe that! Really? Is that clock right?'

Yep, came James's reply.

'Hope I don't get the sack now I've missed two appointments.'

DontWorry.ThisWasMoreImportant.

'I don't understand though ... what was going on? What's the point of crying and laughing?'

NoIdea,ButSureUWillKnowSoonEnough.

'I better get back to work ... that is if I still have a job!' Mark stood up, swaying on his feet. 'God, I feel like I'm drunk.'

Pentecost, James typed.

Mark leaned down and wrapped an arm around James's skinny shoulders, 'I love you mate,' he was surprised at the strength of emotion he felt, 'I'll see you later.' As he straightened up he looked into James's eyes. They were dancing with laughter, incongruous with his pallid, frozen face. 'Don't remember the last time I told a bloke I loved him!' Mark grinned, 'I think I've gone completely nuts!'

James watched him as he made his way gingerly to the door. He even walked like he was drunk. *ThatWasGreat*, he thought towards the two glorious beings beside his bed. They smiled down at him as they began fading from sight. James closed his eyes, wishing he could go with them into that other world, that more solid, substantial dimension. *ItsOnlyForALittleWhile*, he comforted himself as he imagined flying free.

✳ ✳ ✳

Chloe rummaged through the hanging dresses. *No, no, no,* she thought in frustration. *Where is it?* She moved to the next rack of garments in the second-hand shop and began the whole process again. *Why can't you find a little black number when you want one?* she fumed.

Suddenly the door of the shop was flung open and a young girl stumbled in, wild eyed and agitated. 'Anne,' she shouted, 'Anne!'

The woman behind the counter stood up in surprise and said, 'Can I help you?'

'I want Anne. Doesn't she work here? I thought she worked here,' the girl said as she stalked towards the counter, flicking her long blond hair over her shoulder as she passed Chloe, a strand of it whipping her cheek. Despite herself, Chloe turned to watch the drama unfold.

'Anne does volunteer here a couple of days a week, but not today, luv. Can I help you?'

'No, I need Anne. When will she next be in?' the girl demanded.

'Tomorrow morning,' the shop assistant did not look at all happy with how the conversation was developing.

The girl swore and flicked her hair again, 'Tomorrow's too late. I need her today. Is there any way I can contact her? Can you give me her mobile phone number?'

'I'm afraid I can't do that, luv.'

'Well could you ring her and give her my number and ask her to call me ASAP?' the girl was persistent.

'I – I guess there would be no harm in that,' the assistant looked uncertain.

'Great – okay – tell her Charmaine came in today and needs to speak to her urgently. This is my number. Please can you call her now. I really need to speak with her today.'

'I'll try,' said the woman, looking anxiously round the shop. There was no one else there other than Chloe. She opened the door behind her, which led into the storeroom, shouting, 'George – can you come and take over for me? I need to make a phone call.'

George appeared moments later, his skinny frame clad in denim from head to toe. 'Alright?' he said through yellowed teeth, eyeing Charmaine up through a pair of smudged spectacles. The woman ducked past him and went into the privacy of the storeroom to make her call.

Charmaine drummed long painted nails on the counter impatiently and Chloe quickly turned back to her search, batting away the thought that this might be Mark's Charmaine. She was now in the jeans section, even though jeans were not what she'd come for.

The woman returned, surprise in her voice, 'Anne's on her way down here now. She says to wait for her.'

'Great – thanks,' said the girl. 'Can I sit down in one of the changing rooms? I'm not feeling great.'

'Um ... sure ... just leave the curtain open so we can see you.'

'So I won't nick anything?' the girls tone was caustic.

'No – in case you faint or something,' replied the assistant. George watched her, his eyes huge and unblinking behind the murky surface of his glasses.

There was no way Chloe was leaving now. She had to see the drama to its conclusion. She decided to try a pair of jeans on and a shirt. As she went into the cubicle next to Charmaine's she could hear the girl's erratic breathing. *I think she's high on something,* she thought.

'Hello,' came a familiar voice. Chloe stuck her head out of the curtain to see Anne from church walk into the shop.

'Hi Anne!' she exclaimed. 'Fancy meeting you here!'

'I volunteer here,' Anne grinned.

'Oh Anne,' Charmaine had leapt from the changing cubicle before Chloe could respond and had a hold of one of Anne's arms in both hands. 'Thanks for coming down. I really need your help. Can we go and talk somewhere?'

'Sure,' Anne said pragmatically. 'The coffee shop over the road?' she looked over her shoulder in the direction of the street.

'Okay,' Charmaine said moving instantly towards the door.

'Wait, wait, wait a minute,' Anne said, untangling herself from Charmaine's grip. She made to go towards Chloe, but Charmaine caught her arm again.

'Haven't got time for socializing Anne – this is urgent!' Charmaine insisted.

'Okay, okay ... but do you mind if I invite Chloe along too? She might be able to help you too, you know.'

The girl looked in Chloe's direction sceptically. 'Doubt it,' she muttered.

Not wanting to miss any of this, Chloe quickly returned the items she'd tried on at the counter and smiled apologetically, 'Didn't fit – thanks.' She hurried to follow the other two out the door.

Once they were seated in the tiny café and had ordered coffees, Charmaine began to talk manically. *She's definitely on crack or something,* Chloe thought as she watched her.

'You know me, Anne, we've been friends for a while now ... I wouldn't lie to you.'

'Couldn't,' Anne corrected. 'I'd know straight away.'

'Yep – well the thing is I need a place to stay.'

'What happened to lover boy who I met the other night at the club? He seemed all right,' Anne asked.

'He was my pimp!' Charmaine laughed coldly.

'Oh right,' Anne pushed her glasses up her nose. 'I wouldn't have thought that. He seemed a nice young man.'

'Yeah, sure he is when he wants to be. That doesn't matter now though, cuz the police raided the flat this morning. I got out the bathroom window. Can't go back there now.'

'Right – did they take him into custody?'

'Don't know. Probably. I didn't hang about to find out.'

'No, of course you didn't,' Anne nodded sagely.

'So do you know if there's somewhere I could stay for a bit, you know, until I get myself straight?' Charmaine rubbed the end of her nose with the back of her hand, chewing the insides of her cheeks.

Anne looked at Chloe.

Although she was uncertain, Chloe said, 'Charmaine, I'm Chloe – Anne and I go to the same church. I run a rescue centre for sex-traffic victims. There are a couple of beds free at the minute, but we have quite strict rules for residents.'

'Wow! How about that? What a coincidence!' Charmaine looked at

Chloe properly for the first time, her blue eyes darting over Chloe's face.

'Are you high on something at the minute?' Chloe asked candidly.

'Woah! Are you the police?' exclaimed Charmaine.

'No, but you can't take drugs if you're going to stay with us. We'll search you thoroughly before we let you in and we'll keep on checking you every day. You can smoke, but only in the gardens under supervision. We'll keep your cigarettes and lighters – you can't have anything that you might use to self-harm. We'll need to take your phone too so you can't contact suppliers or so your pimp or traffickers can't call or trace you.'

'Sounds like prison!' Charmaine said caustically.

'Hey,' Chloe felt annoyed, 'you're the one needing a place to stay. It's up to you.'

'Charming,' the girl said and rolled her eyes at Anne.

'It's all we've got,' Anne replied firmly. 'Take it or leave it.'

'Haven't got much choice, have I?' Charmaine said.

'And you can't work while you stay with us – not as a hooker. We'll help retrain you, help you find other work if you want.' Chloe smiled, despite her growing feelings of dislike for the girl.

'Well – maybe I could stay for a couple of days – just until my head clears and I can make my own plans – that would be great,' she smiled a brittle smile. It was as close to gratitude as she could get.

'Let me make a few calls first,' Chloe said getting up from their table and heading for the door.

❋ ❋ ❋

Melanie's mouth dropped open when Anne and her mother came into My Sister's House with the girl in tow. She quickly shut it, her eyes darting to her mother's to see if she'd noticed her reaction. It appeared she had not. Melanie scrabbled her scattered thoughts together and composed herself as best she could. She wondered if Charmaine would remember her. They had met only once in the early days. If she did, she didn't show it.

They went through all the paperwork and procedure of induction into My Sister's House. Melanie could tell Charmaine was coming down fast from a high. By the time they took her phone off her and searched her bag and clothing for anything she might use to harm herself or others, her irritability had turned to outright nastiness.

Gwen arrived in time to take her up to her room. She was to have the only single room in the house. It was up in the eaves. 'Follow me dear – it's quite a climb,' they heard Gwen say as she disappeared up the first flight of stairs followed by the girl, swinging her hips.

'She is some piece of work,' Chloe exhaled, tucking her dark hair behind her ears.

'Oh yes,' agreed Anne. 'She's a character all right.'

Melanie said nothing, just filed Charmaine's papers away carefully.

'Hope she doesn't want counselling ... don't know if I could do it!' Chloe laughed. 'That's the first time I've not felt an ounce of sympathy for one of them.'

Melanie frowned, trying to decide whether to say something now or not. She decided not to.

'Mmmm ... I think that's the way she likes it,' Anne replied. 'She doesn't want anyone feeling sorry for her. She's incredibly well defended. Reminds me of me. I was so damaged – I couldn't let anyone be kind to me or love me, in case I'd fall apart. Kept everyone at arm's length. It was me against the world.'

'But you changed,' Chloe said thoughtfully.

'Yes ... slowly. It takes a long time to trust when you've survived abuse.'

'You think that's what's happened to her?' Chloe leant her chin on her hand.

'Maybe – she's never said – but we've got a connection – an affinity. I wouldn't be surprised if, in many ways, her story's not that different from mine.'

Chloe's phone rang, making everyone jump.

'Hi, Charlie, how's your day been? What? On your own? With Jules? Oh my God, really? Okay – well maybe I'll go out for dinner then – see if anyone's free for a girls' night out! Okay – bye love – hope it goes well.' She hung up looking amazed. 'That was Charlie – your Dad's asked him to go for a drink this evening and Charlie's taking Jules!'

Melanie shook her head in disbelief. What was happening in her family?

※　※　※

'Thanks for coming,' Marie greeted Grace as she entered James's hospital room. They kissed each other on the cheek.

'Hello, James,' Grace said as warmly as she could.

'Have a seat,' Marie indicated the blue plastic chair on the far side of James's bed. Grace went and sat on its edge, balancing her floppy, huge tan leather bag on her knees. It was small comfort in the way of defence, but she felt less vulnerable with it between her and the inert body shrouded in a frayed NHS sheet.

James was typing, *HiGrace.LongTimeNoSee.*

Grace fielded a pang of guilt, quickly followed by a flash of anger, and in her most professional pastoral voice she said, 'So tell me what's been happening? Marie says you've been seeing angels?'

OYesAndMore.

'Well Mark came in this afternoon ... oh sorry James ... do you want to tell it?' Marie reached out and squeezed his hand.

UTell.Quicker.

She smiled at him and then proceeded to tell Grace all about what had happened that afternoon, from what James had typed and what the nurses had told her.

Despite herself, Grace felt excitement growing within her, 'How funny!' she smiled. 'Crying and laughing for two hours non-stop?'

'I know! Have you ever heard of anything like it?' Marie looked quizzically at Grace.

'Yes – it sounds just like James said – the Kingdom coming – the Love of God being revealed to Mark.'

'But I don't think he understood what was happening to him, did he James?'

DoesntMatter.

Grace waited for him to finish typing before she said anything. 'I agree – the intellectual understanding will come. It's first been revealed to his emotions – the place of his deepest pain.'

ILikeIt.

Marie nodded slowly, 'I see. So you really think there were angels here to minister to Mark – to help the Kingdom come in his life?'

Grace looked at James, 'If James said he saw them, then I believe him. He's not the sort of person that's given to that kind of thing, is he?'

'No,' Marie laughed.

No, echoed James.

'I'm going to get a cup of coffee. Do you want one Grace?' Marie asked.

'Um ... I can't stay long ... but okay, I'll have a small black coffee,' she put her hand in her bag to fish for her purse.

'No, no,' Marie said, 'it's on me!'

After she'd gone Grace sat uncomfortably beside James. 'So …' she began. She watched him type slowly with growing horror.

ImGladWeAreAlone.IWantedToAskYouToForgiveMe.IKnow.

At first she wanted to say, 'I have no idea what you're talking about,' and to dismiss the whole thing out of hand. But as she went on in the silence, she knew the time had come. There was no need to pretend any more. 'I'd hoped you wouldn't remember our last conversation.'

RememberEverything.

Grace shuddered.

BeenWithJesus.MetOurDaughterRebecca.

Grace couldn't breathe. Her chest hurt. She clutched at it in a panic.

ShesBeautiful.HairLikeYours.

'How did you know that name?' she whispered.

ImGoingBackThere.NotLongNow.HereForMark.

Grace's head was spinning, she couldn't understand what he had written. She read it again, and again, trying to get her thoughts to calm down. She wanted to cry, but didn't. She turned her eyes from the computer screen to James's face. For the first time – the first time ever – they looked steadily into each other's eyes.

Then he was typing again. She pulled her gaze from his to read.

ImSoSorryForWhatIDidToYou.

She turned back to face him. There were no words – none at all. For such an articulate woman, it was shocking to feel so utterly speechless.

Marie returned carrying two paper cups of coffee. Grace leaned back in her chair, relieved. Marie seemed to sense the atmosphere and said very little as she handed Grace her cup and then went to sit down. For a time they sat in silence. Then James began typing again.

AngelsHereAgain.

Both women looked about them, then at each other. Marie was the first to smile, then Grace as she closed her eyes. *Oh God, oh God, oh God* ... she prayed, spilling into silent tongues.

'I'd like you to apply for the post,' Bishop Duncan said quietly.

Grace pressed the phone harder to her ear, 'But I've only just gone onto the preferment list. Isn't there some sort of waiting time to prove your mettle or something?' Grace frowned as she wrestled her ego.

His voice had that gravelly quality that Grace found so hard to resist. 'You've already proved yourself. That's why you're on the list!'

'But if I applied and got the job – I'd have to leave St Stephen's and My Sister's House. When would it be? In the New Year?'

'Yes – probably in March of next year.'

'Can I come back to you after I've had a think about it?'

'Of course ... and talk to Peter before giving me your answer.'

She smiled, 'Yes – I will. Thank you, Bishop Duncan.'

'I'll get Julia to send the details through to you.'

'Thank you.'

After she hung up she stared at her hands. *Archdeacon! Wow! Who'd have thought it possible? But do I want it? Of course I do! But I don't want to let go of everything else.* She smiled, knowing what Peter would say. She was about to reach for the phone again to call him when it rang.

'Hello? Hi, Chloe. Tonight? Can I call you back? I need to check something with Peter first. Okay.' She hung up and dialled Peter's number.

'Hi, darling, have you got a minute?'

'Sure,' he said easily, 'always for you.'

She grinned, 'Well, the Bishop's asked me to apply for the job of Archdeacon. It doesn't mean I'll get it – there'll be other applicants – but what do you think? Should I?'

'Are you joking, babe? That's amazing! I'm so pleased for you! Of course you should apply! If you got it, when would it start?' his voice was full of warmth and pleasure.

'Probably March ... I feel quite shocked, even though I knew it might be coming at some stage. It's all happening really quickly.'

'Ah, Grace – fantastic! Have you seen a job spec yet?'

'No, not yet, but it should come through by this evening. We can go through it together. Oh, Chloe wants me to go for a girls night out tonight – will you be okay to cook dinner for you and Zack when you get home?'

'No problem! Go celebrate!'

'Oh I won't tell her – won't tell anyone – not until I've got the job – if I get it.'

❋   ❋   ❋

After Chloe told her about Mark meeting up with the boys that evening, Grace swirled the light, golden wine around the bowl of her glass and gazed at it intently. 'Wonderful,' she said quietly.

'It is, isn't it?' Chloe replied leaning her chin on one hand and raising her glass to her lips with the other.

'And it all started with you praying for mercy,' Grace mused.

'Do you think?'

'Yes. Are you still praying that?'

'It's changed a bit. I'm actually praying *mercifully* now. I mean, I'm stepping into his shoes in a way I've never done before, never wanted to before!'

'Don't blame you. But wow! Look at what's happening – you know what happened to Mark today when he visited James?'

'No?'

So Grace told her.

'Two hours … crying and laughing?'

'Yep.'

'Well …' Chloe flopped back in her seat astounded, her wine glass abandoned on the table. Then a thought suddenly struck her, 'Oh, you know there's a new girl in the house – oddly enough her name's Charmaine. She's a pretty cool customer, high as a kite on crack or something this afternoon.'

'Oh? How did she come to us?'

'She came looking for Anne when I was in the second-hand shop. We brought her. Think she'll only stay as long as it suits her purposes. I didn't like her much.'

Grace raised her eyebrows and lifted her wine glass. She was beginning to feel tired. She emptied her glass in one gulp, 'Do you mind if we call it a night, Chloe? I'm suddenly feeling shattered.'

'No, not at all,' Chloe replied reaching to finish her drink. 'Maybe the boys are back by now. I wonder how it went.'

'Mmmm,' Grace stretched. 'Come on, girl, let's go,' she grabbed her bag.

When she got home she sat down at her desk, checked her emails first before heading into the living room to cuddle up to Peter and Zack. As she sat there scrolling through them, knowing she wasn't going to read any of them properly tonight, James Martin's words came back to her:

BeenWithJesus.MetOurDaughterRebecca.

ShesBeautiful.HairLikeYours.

Her eyes wandered helplessly over the papers strewn across her desk. They fell on her open Bible and the verses from Ephesians she had underlined earlier that week in red pen:

'I pray that you, being rooted and established in love, may have power, together with all the Lord's people, to grasp how wide and long and high and deep is the love of Christ, and to know this love that surpasses knowledge—that you may be filled to the measure of all the fullness of God.'

'... this love that surpasses knowledge,' she said out loud. She went back to her computer and clicked on her story document. She read through what she had last written. The exhaustion evaporated. Suddenly alert and clear-headed, she began to write.

She heard Zack pad into her study behind her, but didn't turn from the screen. Not even when he wrapped his arms round her neck and kissed her cheek goodnight.

'Night,' she said, her fingers never wavering as they tapped out the inspiration that was flooding through her.

'That was a wonderful evening Aaron hosted the other night, wasn't it?' Mary asked.

'Mmmm,' came Anna's reply, muffled by the pillows in which her face was buried.

'How many events has he held at his home now?'

'Don't know ... five ... six? Why?'

Mary methodically kneaded a knot near Anna's right shoulder blade, 'I don't know if you or Timothy have noticed, but I think he only invites the Jewish members of the Church to his home?' Mary reached over to the bedside cabinet for her scented oil. She poured a little into the palm of her hand, replaced the bottle and then rubbed the oil gently into Anna's smooth skin in circular motions.

'Mmmm ... can't say I've noticed. Been busy enjoying them!' Anna's voice sounded slightly irritated.

'Maybe it's just my imagination,' Mary decided to say no more on the matter. She worked on in silence for a while until Anna abruptly sat up.

'Why did you say that?'

'I was just thinking aloud ... sorry,' the older woman smiled, knowing Anna as well as she did, she knew the matter would not be dropped until she had come to a conclusion.

'But you've got me thinking now,' Anna frowned.

'Careful,' Mary teased.

Anna laughed.

'Lie down again – I haven't finished yet,' Mary ordered.

Obediently Anna lay down.

'I must say you are much more peaceful now. Most of the tautness has gone from your shoulders. There are just two problem areas remaining either side of your spine, here,' she placed her forefingers on both spots.

'I know. I feel better. Not so overwhelmed.'

'That's good,' Mary's fingers cascaded down either side of Anna's spine in a running motion.

'I love it when you do that – always have,' Anna said.

'I know,' smiled Mary remembering how she'd held her plump baby limbs so easily in her hands all those years ago; how she'd taught her simple massage techniques when she was no more than three and watched her practice on Jair and Lila. A wave of sadness swept through her at the mental image of Jair laughing in their sun-drenched courtyard; of that first tiny house in Jerusalem. They had been such happy times. He had been the father and brother to her she'd never known ... not until Jesus had re-united her with Lazarus.

She eventually finished the massage in silence. 'Now stay here for a little while – sleep. I'll come and wake you. Mama and I have the children in hand.'

'Mmmm,' Anna replied gratefully.

❋ ❋ ❋

Mary shielded her eyes as she came out into daylight. It took a moment to adjust her vision, but when she did, she saw Lila, Joshua and Luke sitting in the shade of the orange tree surrounded by all the children. They were eating a picnic of flat breads, hummus, grapes and dates.

The baby lay asleep in Lila's lap covered with her headscarf to ward off insects.

It was clear to Mary how much Joshua's presence had comforted Lila in the aftermath of Jair's death. Mother and son – kindred spirits. Luke was not exactly excluded when he was with them, but as Mary watched them, she could see how he held himself back; kept a respectful distance; allowed them to enjoy each other without the hindrance of having to involve him in every little nuance of conversation. She smiled as she approached them.

'Shalom everyone,' she spread her arms in greeting.

'Aunty Mary!' the children cried, getting to their feet, two of them running to her. 'You smell lovely,' said one.

'I know – I've been massaging Mama.' Mary tucked longing for her own daughters firmly away in her heart.

'Can you massage me?'

'No, me.'

'Me too,' the childish chorus grew in volume.

'Let Aunty Mary sit down and eat something children or she will faint!' Lila scolded good-naturedly, subduing them into giggles as they all tried to sit as close to Mary as possible.

'How is she today?' Joshua asked.

'She is much, much better. These weeks of quiet and rest have done her the world of good. She is more herself, I think.' Mary dipped a piece of bread into the hummus and tore a couple of grapes from the cluster at the centre of the little group.

'Massage is so good for anxiety,' Luke agreed.

'Aunty Mary is the best,' Sol grinned. 'She taught all of us.'

'She did indeed,' Lila smiled sadly thinking of how she had practiced all Mary had taught her on Jair.

'Speaking of anxiety,' Luke said, 'I had one of the young Greek Church leaders come to see me the other day – Neo? Do you know him?'

Lila answered, 'Yes – he was there with Aaron when Anna became so distraught.'

'I see,' Luke nodded thoughtfully.

'What is he anxious about?' Lila asked.

'Not fulfilling all the laws of Moses. He wanted to know about circumcision.'

'Oh no!' exclaimed Lila, 'Why is he worrying about that?'

'That's what Aaron was talking to him about with Anna,' Mary interjected.

'But under the new covenant that Jesus inaugurated we become children of God through faith in him, not through circumcision or because we obey the law,' Joshua said using his hands excessively.

'What did you say to him, Luke?' Lila asked.

'From a medical point of view we discussed the hygiene benefits of such an operation. We also discussed the lengthy healing process and the amount of pain he would have to endure. Finally because we are brothers in Christ, we discussed the root of his anxiety, which was spiritual. I assured him that he did not need to do this to please God or to make himself "spiritually clean".'

'Good,' Lila and Mary chorused together.

'Let's hope that's the end of it,' Lila added.

'I'm not sure if it will be,' Mary mused. 'Have you noticed that at all of Aaron's dinners, only the Jewish members of the Church have been invited?'

Joshua looked at Luke and then back at Mary. 'We don't know everyone so we wouldn't have been able to tell for certain.'

'I haven't been, so I wouldn't know,' Lila added.

'We must raise it with Timothy,' Joshua said.

'Yes,' Mary replied, 'but a gentle warning: Anna has grown very fond of Aaron. She will not hear a bad word said against him, and I'm sure that means Timothy will be cautious.'

Luke frowned, 'Well, I will talk with him. Paul would challenge such things immediately.'

Mary and Lila looked at each other and smiled, 'Yes he would,' Mary's grin broadened thinking of the apostle.

❄ ❄ ❄

'Can I come in?' Timothy asked hesitantly standing at the door of a small house in one of the poorer parts of Ephesus, 'I've heard you are not well, Neo?'

'Just a minute,' came the reply. He heard some movement and then a stifled groan of pain.

'Neo, I'm coming in – you sound like you need help,' Timothy pushed the flimsy wooden door to one side and entered the shadowed interior. There was only one room. As his eyes adjusted to the gloom he noted several pots and pans on a shelf, the ashes of a small fire near the door and a large clay water pot against one wall, which most people filled at the local well early in the mornings, before it got too hot. He moved to it and lifted the lid, rocking it slightly. As he thought, there was hardly any water left in it.

He looked across the room to what made for a bed – a rush mat on the clay floor, with a single blanket covering a very pale young man. His skin was glistening with sweat and his face was ashen. 'Neo, what is wrong?' he crossed the room in two strides and knelt down beside the boy.

'I'm fine, really I am,' Neo protested. 'I'll be back to normal in a day or two.'

Timothy reached out and touched his forehead. 'You have a fever, Neo. Is there no one here to look after you?'

'Not since mother died. Anyway it was I who looked after her. I'm used to caring for myself. The Lord will help me too,' he tried to smile, but winced instead.

'Tell me where the pain is. How long have you had it? Do you want me to call Doctor Luke?' Timothy persisted.

'No, no – really I'm fine. Brother Aaron said he would visit me soon, so please don't bother Doctor Luke.'

Timothy eyed him discerningly. 'Neo – you and I have been friends since Paul led you to Christ. We have no secrets, surely? Let me help you. You don't know when Aaron will come ... how many days has it been since you've been ill? Two? How do you know he won't leave it for another two days?'

Neo looked anxiously down at his torso under the thin, dirty blanket, then back at Timothy's concerned face. 'Please understand – I want to do everything to please God.'

'I have no doubt you do, Neo ... you are a good man, a great evangelist.'

A smile briefly broke through pain, only to disappear as quickly. Slowly he lowered the blanket until Timothy could see the infected part of his body. Despite himself Timothy gasped, 'Oh, Neo, what have you done?'

'I wanted to fulfil all the law. I spoke to Doctor Luke about it, but he tried to dissuade me. So I did it myself.'

'Oh ... dear Lord,' Timothy whispered remembering his own circumcision at Paul's hands and the excruciating pain he had gone through. 'Neo, I am going to get Doctor Luke. He will know what to do to help you and to ease your pain. Please don't worry – he will not be angry – he will just want to make sure you are as safe as he can make you.' With that Timothy got to his feet and turned to go.

'You're not angry with me?' Neo asked hesitantly.

'I'm angry, but not with you. I'll bring Luke back with me.' With that he was gone.

※　※　※

'I couldn't believe it!' Timothy was saying as they walked as quickly as they could through the crowded afternoon streets of Ephesus. 'Doing it himself? I don't know how he could? The pain!' he exclaimed shying from the thought.

'I should have followed him up. I thought our conversation was reassurance enough for him.'

'Obviously not!' Timothy's anger had continued to boil on both the journey to find and to bring back Doctor Luke.

'I told him he needn't worry about circumcision – that we had a new covenant now. I thought he was listening to me.'

'Maybe he was, but then someone else got to him later on?' Timothy stepped back into the gutter to let a heavily laden donkey pass with its owner.

It defecated as it went by, dung splattering over his sandaled toes. He looked down in frustration, 'That reminds me, I must go and collect water for him as soon as we get there. Who knows how long it's been since he's had fresh water to drink or wash with?'

Luke smiled to himself, admiring this man for his servant leadership. He thought of Jesus washing his disciple's feet – unafraid of doing women's work. *The least – the greatest – the servant of all,* he thought as his smile broadened.

When they reached the hovel that was Neo's home, Timothy briskly picked up the water jar and headed for the well without saying a word, leaving Luke alone with the lad.

'Shalom, Neo,' he knelt down beside him. 'Now let me have a look at you,' his voice was kind.

Neo didn't stop him pulling back the blanket.

'Well I must say, it's not too bad a job … for a novice,' he smiled.

Neo's defences were slowly coming down. 'Aren't you angry with me? You told me I didn't need it, that I shouldn't do it.'

'I'm angry with myself Neo. I should have followed you up to make sure you were clear in your mind. Maybe this would never have happened if I'd done my job properly. Well, son, you're going to need to wash it and apply this ointment every time you urinate. I'm going to give you something for the fever too and something for the pain. Here, drink this,' he lifted a small brown bottle out of his leather bag, uncorking it as he spoke.

'What is it?' Neo asked as he lifted it to his lips.

'It will ease the pain for a while,' Luke smiled as he watched him gulp it down. 'Take this for the fever,' he unfolded a small package, revealing a creamy powder. 'It doesn't taste good, but it will help.' Neo grimaced as he shook it into his mouth obediently.

When Timothy returned with water, Luke showed Neo how to clean the wound and how to apply the ointment. Then both Timothy and Luke laid hands upon the young man's head and prayed that the infection would heal up quickly and that recovery would be swift.

'We will return tomorrow to see how you are. Now keep that blanket off it. In fact, can I take it home and wash it for you? It could do with a clean,' Timothy took hold of the offending blanket.

Timothy brought Anna with him the next day so that she could cast her eye over Neo's accommodation and decide what things needed doing. When they arrived they found he had another visitor – Aaron.

'Shalom,' Aaron rose from his crouched position on the floor as they entered the hovel.

'Shalom, Aaron,' Anna said warmly. 'It's so good of you to visit the sick,' she said affectionately.

'It is nothing,' he said.

'Shalom, Brother Aaron,' Timothy said with more reserve. 'How is our patient today?'

'He seems well,' Aaron turned to Neo, returning to his knees beside the lad.

'I'm so much better than I was yesterday,' Neo beamed at Timothy.

'Glad we helped,' Timothy smiled.

'The pain has eased and I don't think I have a fever any more. Feel,' he raised his head for Timothy, who placed his palm gently upon the smooth brow.

'You are right. You look much better! Now I've brought Anna with me so we can make a list of things that need doing here. I hope you won't object?'

'Oh ... um ... I'm fine, really I am,' grinned the invalid.

'Would it be okay with you if I made a list and you checked it before I go? Just some basic things that will make life that little bit more bearable, especially when you are ill,' Anna felt maternal affection for him.

When she'd made her list and Neo had agreed on it, Aaron took her arm and gently drew her to one side, whispering, 'I will pay for whatever he needs.'

Anna looked up in surprised pleasure, 'Thank you Aaron. That is most kind.'

On their return walk home Anna said, 'Aaron is so generous – he is paying for everything on Neo's list.'

'Is he?' Timothy asked, one sloped eyebrow raised.

'Yes. We are so blessed to have him among us. He's such a gifted teacher and so compassionate. I'm sure Brother Paul would be thrilled to know Aaron is working to advance the Gospel.'

Timothy said nothing. He hadn't told Anna what was wrong with Neo, nor had he mentioned his suspicions about why Neo had damaged himself as he had. He hoped Paul would reply soon to his letter. He needed his authority before he grasped this particular nettle, as he suspected many other Jewish believers were secretly rallying to Aaron. It had not passed his notice how the Jewish members of the Church had flocked to Aaron's parties and how eager they were to socialise amongst themselves exclusively. It was galling to watch them pay close attention to every word spoken by leaders of pure Jewish descent and not to him, although Paul had given him oversight of the Church.

※　※　※

'Neo, my son,' Aaron spoke reassuringly, 'what you have done required much courage and zeal for God's Law. It will surely not go unrewarded in this world and the next. You truly are one of the chosen, set apart for God. If there is anything I can do to assist you, anything at all, do not hesitate to ask.'

'Thank you, Aaron, you are kindness itself,' Neo's chest swelled with pride. 'I knew I was doing the right thing, despite what Doctor Luke and Timothy said. I don't know what I would have done without your guidance and support in the face of their opposition.'

'I'm sure they are not opposed to God's Law, Neo. Both men are circumcised themselves you know.'

'Then why have they not taught us this from the beginning? Why keep us Gentiles from receiving the full blessings of truly being part of the chosen race?'

'I'm sure that was not their intent,' Aaron sounded magnanimous. 'We must cover over their omission with love, mustn't we?'

'You're so wise,' Neo replied, looking up in awe at Aaron's distinguished face. 'We must pray that the Lord shows them their error.'

'Indeed,' Aaron smiled benignly upon his young ward. 'Now, this meeting tonight of the young men – are you sure you are up to it? Wouldn't you rather rest a while longer before teaching them?'

'Really, I'm fine. The pain has all but gone and I have no more fever. The sooner I can teach them, the better. Anyway – we will be doing it together, so if I do suddenly weaken, you can take over.'

'All right, but you will accept the litter I am sending so you will not have to walk?'

'Thank you, yes.'

With that Aaron stood to leave, 'Good. I will see you later.'

❋ ❋ ❋

'Thank you for coming tonight brothers,' Aaron greeted the gathering of young men in the lecture hall. 'You have all been brought to faith in the One True God by this great disciple,' he turned to Neo, honouring him with a slight bow of his head, 'and I know you will agree with me when I say, he is an example to us all.' A chorus of approval rose from them, causing Neo's face to glow. 'Neo – the floor is yours,' Aaron stepped back and sat down.

Neo began teaching his listeners, who were all Gentile converts, about his convictions regarding circumcision. It was met with a mixed reception, but Aaron had prepared him for this. He had advised him to simply see it as an introduction, a *making-them-aware-session*, enabling them to begin thinking about the matter. He advised him not to be dogmatic or directive, but simply to tell them his process of thought leading up to his actions.

'I will support you, Neo. Don't worry, my son, they will follow you,' Aaron had said.

❋ ❋ ❋

'That's four lads from the Church who've come and asked me about it!' Luke exclaimed. 'Something is going on and I don't like it.'

Priscilla sat opposite him. She frowned turning to Aquilla, 'In all our time in teaching here it's never been an issue. I wonder why it suddenly is.'

Aquilla scratched his beard thoughtfully. 'I'm trying to think if I've ever had a conversation about it with any of the men?'

'I've written to Paul for his wisdom on the matter,' Timothy said. 'I hope I get his reply soon.'

Anna sat quietly beside him, lost in thought with Joshua on her other side. 'Wasn't Aaron talking to you and Neo about it on the Lord's Day when you ....'

Anna's head snapped round to face her brother, 'He was only explaining Jewish thought on the subject. I don't think he was advising it,' she felt heat rise up her neck.

'Do you think your brother might be behind the present interest?' Timothy asked Ruth who was leaning her head on Oni's shoulder.

Anna looked at Timothy, 'Didn't you hear what I just said?' she asked him.

'I did my dear, but Ruth knows him better than any of us. I think it's worth hearing what she might think.'

Anna looked away irritably.

'I hardly think I know him better than the rest of you ... it's been years since we shared a family home. All I *do* know is he's a political animal – always has been. Religion and politics featured highly in his life from an early age.'

Lila watched Anna's face and knew she was in trouble. *Oh my baby, my sweet love ... what can I do? If I tell you ... if I don't tell you ... I can't win. But he would have had us both killed all those years ago ...* she twisted her hands together anxiously. Mary gently touched her arm to calm her, exchanging a meaningful look.

'I have to say,' said Oni, 'that I have been uncertain of his true beliefs all along.'

'But that's the nature of a politician,' Ruth laughed, 'you never know what they really think.'

'True,' Oni smiled. 'If you like, I will talk to him,' he looked to Timothy.

'I want to pick our battles carefully, Oni. The unity of the Church is at stake here. Let's wait until we have Paul's reply before we proceed. That way we have more solid ground to stand on.'

※ ※ ※

Pudens opened the door with a broad smile, 'Tychicus!' he exclaimed, stepping down into the street and catching the other man up in a bear hug. 'It's so good to see you!'

'Good to see you too, brother,' he laughed, his staff falling onto the cobbles with a clatter.

'Let me,' Pudens bent down to retrieve it. 'Lean on me,' he instructed as he straightened up, putting a strong hand under his brother's withered arm. The cripple stepped up to the door with his good leg, leaning hard on Pudens and dragging his left behind him. He reached for the doorframe with his good hand and with a push from his brother, pulled himself up onto the step and through the door.

Pudens handed him his staff and together they made their way slowly down the hallway, the long chain attaching him to Paul clanking all the way. 'Do you have to wear that all the time?' his brother asked.

'All the time I'm on duty.'

'You might as well be a prisoner!' Tychicus rolled his one good eye.

'Ah – there are no prisoners in here. We are freer than anyone out there.'

'True, but look at your wrist,' he'd taken hold of his brothers arm and was peering under the manacle at the scabs and sores beneath it.

Pudens grinned, 'Oh, I have missed you,' he hugged him again. 'What news do you bring from home?'

'Can't a man rest before he has to give an account?'

'Of course, of course ... come,' he opened the door that led into Paul's chamber.

'Tychicus!' Paul greeted him, arms wide, eyes blazing with affection.

Tychicus raised his single-eyed gaze from the floor in front of him through the doorway to the old man bent over a Spartan desk, quill in hand. The energy with which he rose to his feet was incongruous with the white hair and the lines on his face.

'Paul, how good it is to see you again,' he replied.

'Please come and rest yourself. How was your journey?' Paul

indicated the chair he had just vacated. Pudens gently assisted him as he lowered himself into it.

Before he knew it Paul was on his knees with a bowl of water and was removing one sandal and then the other from his dusty feet. He watched the older man wash first his good foot and then his withered one. He then lifted them carefully into his lap and dried them one at a time with a towel.

'How was the sea and the river? The tides must be strong and the river swollen at this time of year? And the bird life - oh all the herons and storks – what a sight they must have been?'

'It was fine – yes, quite fine – yes, there was always something to be looking at as we neared the shores. It's been several years since my last trip. I'd forgotten how beautiful it is at this time of year.'

'Was the last time we were together in Troas?'

'Yes ... we sailed ahead of you and waited for you and Luke there.'

'That's right,' Paul smiled. 'And I talked too much.'

Tychicus laughed, 'All night, if I recall ... Poor Eutychus ... one minute dozing comfortably in our meeting and the next falling from the third story window!'

'What?' Pudens' eyes widened.

'That's right – when they picked him up he was dead – no heartbeat,' Paul recalled.

'Then you threw yourself on him, wrapping your arms around him and he breathed again.'

'That's right ... I remember,' Paul nodded. 'God still had things for that young man to do. It was not his time.'

Tychicus smiled. 'He and his wife lead a Church in their home now. He never did recover the full use of his memory, but his wife reminds him daily. Somehow it works and they are such a blessing.'

'Good ... good,' Paul smiled and sighed.

'So the fall affected his memory?' Pudens asked.

'Yes. He can remember things from a long time ago, but not from the day before. Strange ...' Tychicus mused.

Pudens placed a goblet of wine and a plate of fruit beside his brother on the desk. 'You must be thirsty?'

'Yes, thank you,' Tychicus twisted round and reached for the wine with his good hand. He drank deeply while the other two men settled themselves on the rope-bed.

'So ... tell us more news,' Pudens demanded.

The time flew by. Dusk settled over the city and still they talked on. Pudens lit candles and brought out bread, cheeses and cold meat. They drank wine and talked late into the night. Before Pudens took his brother home and locked Paul in for the night, they laid hands upon Tychicus and blessed him.

Anyone looking on would have surmised that they were two drunken men returning from a night of merriment, one more inebriated than the other. Pudens had to practically carry his brother back to the barracks.

❇ ❇ ❇

'I want to send you to Ephesus.' Paul said it like he was sending Tychicus on an errand to the local market.

'Oh?' Tychicus looked surprised.

'I want you to deliver this letter personally to Timothy and to encourage him with news of how I am doing here. He is very dear to me, as are you. I can think of no better gift than for the two of you to strengthen one another. Would you do this for me?'

'I've only been here a few weeks and already you are sending me on a mission! Of course I will gladly go. But let me stay a few more days – it is so precious being with Pudens again.

'I wish I could go with you,' Pudens said, envy in his voice. 'Remember how we always said we'd travel the world one day?'

'Yes,' the right half of Tychicus' face lit with a smile. 'A wandering we will go,' he sung the childhood ditty in a faraway voice.

Pudens chuckled. 'I'm the able bodied one and I get to be stuck here while you go adventuring!'

'Ironic, is it not?' Paul added. 'But perhaps God has chosen Tychicus so that his power would be made perfect in his weakness.'

'It's as you say in the letter – God is able to do immeasurably more than we can ever ask or imagine, according to his power that is at work within us!' Tychicus grinned.

7. UNITING

Ephesians 4:1–16

*Be completely humble and gentle; be patient, bearing with
one another in love. Make every effort to keep the unity
of the Spirit through the bond of peace.*

Charlie lay on his back staring up at the ceiling. Jules lay beside him, playing with his hair. 'What you thinking?'

'About Dad.'

'I liked him,' Jules said eventually. 'I thought I wouldn't.'

'He was different,' Charlie sounded resentful.

'What d'you mean?'

'Why was he so …' Charlie searched for the word, ' … so nice? He's not normally like that with me.'

'Well you haven't really seen him for five years, other than the other day in the pub. Maybe he's realised a few things … maybe.'

Charlie swore and sat up, his feet dangling off the end of the bed. 'I wanted him to suffer today! I mean, I wanted him to squirm in his seat with us both there together.'

'Why? Is he homophobic?'

'Yeah!' Charlie exclaimed angrily. 'He was always trying to make me a "man". He never showed an interest in anything I was interested in. 'Cuz I didn't do what he wanted, he ignored me and focused on Josh. Josh this and Josh that,' he mimicked in a childish singsong voice.

Jules grinned, 'You're so attractive when you're angry.'

Charlie turned and scowled at him, but slowly a smile peeped through, despite his dark mood. 'I'm just so pissed off with him. I don't want him to be nice! I want to hate him! It's like he's hijacked what was coming to him. He doesn't deserve to have me as his son.'

Jules flicked his silky hair out of his eyes, 'I think he knows that ... that's what's making him so nice.'

Charlie looked surprised, 'You know you're awfully perceptive!'

Jules laughed and pulled him back down beside him, 'Let it go Chucker ... it's only screwing with your head.'

'I wish I could ... Maybe I just need to go and have it out with him ... you know, tell him how I feel ... maybe that would help?'

'Better out than in ... don't see what you've got to lose?'

'Mmmm.' Charlie returned his gaze to the ceiling thoughtfully.

Then they heard Chloe calling them down for a late lunch.

※   ※   ※

Mark almost ran the last corridor to James's room that afternoon. He burst through the door eager to tell him about his evening with Charlie, only to see several doctors and nurses crowded around the bed. 'What's wrong?' he gasped.

No one turned or replied. Mark came closer to the bed and leaned over one white-coated shoulder to try to see. He glimpsed James's pallid face. His eyes were closed. A nurse looked up and saw him, 'Excuse me, Sir, you shouldn't be in here.'

'Sorry,' Mark took a step back. 'He's my friend ... is he dying?'

'We're doing everything we can, Sir.' She came round and took him by the elbow, gently ushering him from the room. 'Please stay out here.' She left him in the hallway, staring through the chequered glass door.

For a time he stood transfixed and then it occurred to him that Marie might not know. How to contact her? He opened the door a little and asked, 'Has his wife been contacted?'

The same nurse looked up and nodded. With that he heard footsteps approaching, turned and saw Marie and the children coming towards him.

'What's happened?' she demanded.

'I don't know,' Mark replied. 'I've only just got here.'

'Can I go in?'

'Ask,' he said pushing the door ajar.

'Can we come in?' she put her head round the door.

'We're moving him to ICU, Mrs Martin,' the nurse replied. 'You can follow. Two of you will be able to sit with him at a time, once we've got him settled there.'

It seemed an interminable wait before Marie was allowed in to ICU with the eldest child. Mark sat out in the corridor on uncomfortable plastic seats with the other children. No one spoke.

After all the children had been in to see him, Marie came out again and beckoned to Mark. His heart sank as he saw his friend tubed and wired up to several machines. He felt awkward, as if he shouldn't be there in their possible last moments together. Marie saw and said, 'It's okay, Mark, I'm glad you're here. James would want it.'

Mark's throat constricted. He sat down and reached over to take one of James's limp hands in his. Marie leaned over James and said, 'Mark's here, darling,' as she stroked his cheek. There was no response.

Mark looked up at the heart monitor as it beeped methodically. He returned his gaze to the face, which had become so dear to him. 'James, I came to tell you about last night ... about Charlie and me ... we had such a great evening. He brought his boyfriend with him. He's nice ... Jules ... I liked him. I thought I'd want to strangle him, but I didn't,' he laughed at himself. 'I felt so much love for Charlie, and even for Jules. Feelings I don't think I've ever really had. Well ... maybe when he was a toddler ... but I ... I used to feel so embarrassed of him ... he was such a mummy's boy.' He looked up at Marie apologetically. She smiled a small, sad smile as she listened.

Mark returned his attention to James. This might be his last chance. He needed to say everything. It didn't matter if Marie heard, he told himself.

'It dawned on me last night that maybe I kept my distance from him because he reminded me of everything I was uncomfortable with in myself. I think I was actually jealous of his relationship with Chloe! I yearned for closeness with my mum but never had it,' he sighed, shaking his head.

'I hope you can hear me, because if it wasn't for your determination ... I don't think last night would have happened.' He paused to look at the heart monitor again. 'I still don't really understand what happened ... all I know is I'm saturated with love ... I can't describe it any other way ... thank you … thank you for coming back for me ….' His voice failed him and his shoulders shook as he rested his head on James's hand. The heart monitor flat-lined.

❊ ❊ ❊

Chloe came into My Sister's House for her night shift, to hear screamed obscenities coming from up the stairs. She dropped her bag and folders on her desk and ran in the direction of the noise, taking the stairs two at a time and arriving breathlessly on the top floor to see a cat fight in full flow. Anne, Gwen, Mo and Melanie were there trying to separate the girls who had each other by the hair.

'What on earth is going on?' she demanded, summoning all the authority she could in her voice. She lunged in, without any fear for herself, wedging her shoulder in between them. Mo followed suit, pushing hard, until the weight of the two of them forced the girls to separate, clawing, screaming and spitting.

A fingernail caught the mole on Chloe's face and blood spurted from it, making her yelp with pain. Mo sat on one girl while Anne had the other's arms locked behind her. Their hair obscured their faces in matted clumps as they both heaved and struggled.

'Calm down now!' shouted Mo. 'That's it – it's over!'

Chloe got to her feet holding her hand to her cheek, blood dripping through her fingers and splatting onto the carpet in fat, dark drops. Gwen returned from the bathroom with a wad of toilet paper, which Chloe gladly pressed on it. 'Now let me see your faces,' she ordered.

Slowly both girls revealed themselves. It was Charmaine and a girl called Jade, who had been a resident for several weeks.

'Right,' said Chloe. 'Charmaine, you come with me now. Anne, take her to the downstairs bathroom first and help her sort herself out, then we'll go to my office. Mo, take Jade in there. Don't let her out of your sight. Is anyone else bleeding?' she asked lifting away the tissue paper from her cheek to check if hers had subsided. The paper was almost saturated and the wound immediately poured a fresh surge down her face and chin. Gwen went to get more tissue paper.

When they'd settled in her office, Chloe said, still holding tissue to her cheek, 'Okay, Charmaine, what happened?'

The girl sullenly stared at the floor, flicking her long, red thumbnails against each other. 'Oh go on, Charmaine,' Anne urged, 'what have you got to lose?'

Charmaine lifted her eyes briefly and then returned them to the floor.

'Why were you fighting?' Chloe pressed.

'God, it's like being back at school,' Charmaine muttered.

'Go on,' Anne said, 'tell us. No one's going to judge you.'

'Really?' Charmaine sneered.

'Really,' Anne responded patiently.

Silence. Uncomfortable silence.

Anne broke it, 'Look Charmaine, you and I have a connection. I think I know how it is for you. We're not that different.'

'You have no idea about my life, so don't patronise me!'

'Okay,' Anne said calmly, 'let's see if I can get it right ... your parents screwed you up; they treated you like shit; beat you; controlled you; locked you up sometimes for days without food? Stop me if I'm wrong? School was your sanctuary until you hit puberty, then getting the boys' attention was *it* for you. You went from one abusive relationship to another; then it was older men; men with money ... until you decided you could make your own with the one lucrative currency you had to trade with. Am I right or am I right?'

Charmaine glared at her, arms folded tightly across her chest.

Chloe felt shocked at Anne's approach. It certainly was an unusual choice of tactics. She swallowed and waited.

'So what?' came the eventual hardened reply.

'So why were you fighting with Jade?' Anne wasn't letting it go.

'She was the one who grassed us into the police. It's her fault I'm in this place!' she said in disgust.

'Why did she do that?'

'Because she's a f – .'

'Yeah, yeah ... okay ... no need for that. Come on - why?'

'Jealousy? Envy? Ask her yourself!'

'I will, but I want to know your take on it,' Anne was as cool as a cucumber.

'We shared the same pimp. Can I help it if he preferred me to her? I was in – she was out.'

'Right,' Anne nodded, 'survival of the fittest?'

'Something like that,' Charmaine examined her nails coolly.

'So now you're both homeless and here. If you want to keep this roof over your heads, you're both going to have to get along, or you'll both be out. Do you understand?'

A cold stare was her reply.

'Do you understand?' Anne persisted.

'Sure ... I won't be staying long ... so she's welcome to your shitty place.'

Chloe could feel a strongly worded defence of My Sister's House clawing its way up her throat. How dare she! Who the hell did she think she was? She bit her lip and looked out the window at the twilight sky.

'Now I'm going to leave you with Chloe. She heads up our counselling service. If there're any issues you want to talk about, she's your woman. Okay?'

Neither Charmaine nor Chloe looked too enamoured with the idea, but Anne got up and without another word, left them to it.

'So,' Chloe said, mustering any scrap of human kindness she could find within herself, 'is there anything you'd like to talk about?'

Charmaine glared at her.

I couldn't care less if you don't want to talk ... I'll sit here quite happily in silence, Chloe thought.

Minutes ticked by. Then Charmaine seemed to relax a little. She changed position in her chair and studied Chloe's face, 'So you're a counsellor?'

'Yes.'

'You're a good-looking woman ... suppose you're happily married with two point three kids, a dog and a Range Rover?'

'Divorced, three kids, no dog and no Range Rover, and thanks for the compliment,' Chloe parried coolly.

'Ever do any modelling?'

'No,' Chloe suppressed a smile and dabbed her mole with the bloodied tissue.

'Oh I suppose that mole wouldn't have been acceptable. Sorry about that ... is it okay?'

'I don't know yet. I'll go to the mole clinic tomorrow and get it checked.' Bringing the subject back to Charmaine, Chloe said, 'You know, you're a good-looking woman too. Why didn't you go into modelling?'

'I tried it in my early teens, but got shafted a couple of times by agencies, so took to exotic dancing. Preferred being my own boss ... then this.'

Chloe frowned, 'Why this? Why lose your independence? Why not stick with dancing?'

'Oh the guy I was with lost his job and wasn't gonna get another one any time soon that paid the same money, so I went looking for more work. I like money, I like sex – I'm good – so why not – pays way more. I could earn over a grand a week doing both.'

'So what did your man think of that?'

'He threw me out.'

It felt is if a siren went off somewhere in the distant recesses of Chloe's brain. She struggled to isolate it and focus on it, but couldn't. 'So that's why you ended up living with your pimp?'

'Yeah ... shit happens,' she shrugged. 'So why did you become a counsellor?'

Why not? Maybe some disclosure will help her open up. 'I used to be a youth worker – lost my job and went back to university to study psychology. Then Grace and I set this place up.'

'Is that the chick-vic?'

'Yes,' Chloe smiled at the title.

'Why did you lose your youth worker job?'

Chloe laughed, 'I'm supposed to be the one asking the questions!'

'You want me to spill my guts while you hide behind a mask of smug middle-class self-satisfaction?'

'You're right,' Chloe uncrossed and re-crossed her legs. 'Well,' she looked at the floor and then up at Charmaine, 'I had an affair with the vicar of the church I worked for.'

Shock registered in Charmaine's eyes, 'You're *that* Chloe?'

'I knew the gossip chain worked well round here, but I didn't think I was that infamous!' Chloe mocked, 'Not after all this time anyway!' As she watched several emotions scuttle across Charmaine's face, the distant siren grew louder in her brain, until it drew up alongside her like an ambulance, lights flashing and siren wailing. Suddenly she knew. 'Oh my God!' she exclaimed. '*You're* Charmaine!'

❈ ❈ ❈

Grace sat at the table with the PCC secretary that evening, surveying the good people of the Church Council. How would they feel if she left St Stephen's for the job of Archdeacon? She hoped they would feel proud, but there was no telling.

Refurbishment plans had been agreed and the works were about to start. There was a buzz of excitement in the atmosphere. There was still money to be raised, but no one seemed overly worried. They were awaiting the results of two bids, which folk seemed quietly confident about. St Stephen's was a beautiful church and would continue to be for many years to come, so help them God.

'I'd like to start our meeting with the reading we'll be using this Sunday. It's taken from Ephesians *4: 1-16*. She cleared her throat and began to read. *'I urge you to live a life worthy of the calling you have received. Be completely humble and gentle; be patient, bearing with one another in love. Make every effort to keep the unity of the Spirit through the bond of peace. There is one body and one Spirit, just as you were called to one hope when you were called; one Lord, one faith, one baptism; one God and Father of all, who is over all and through all and in all. But to each one of us grace has been given as Christ apportioned it ... So Christ himself gave the apostles, the prophets, the evangelists, the pastors and teachers, to equip his people for works of service, so that the body of Christ may be built up until we all reach unity in the faith and in the knowledge of the Son of God and become mature, attaining to the whole measure of the fullness of Christ.*

Then we will no longer be infants, tossed back and forth by the waves, and blown here and there by every wind of teaching and by the cunning and craftiness of people in their deceitful scheming. Instead, speaking the truth in love, we will grow to become in every respect the mature body of him who is the head, that is, Christ. From him the whole body, joined and held together by every supporting ligament, grows and builds itself up in love, as each part does its work.'

Her mind flitted to the Morning Prayer where love had been so well administered to Marie by so many faithful St Stephen's servants. She looked down at the agenda before praying the collect of the day.

Preaching Team Report
Pastoral Care Team Report
Mission Action Team Report
My Sister's House Report

Refurbishment Report
Human Sexuality Paper Review

'... as we each seek to serve you and your people. Amen.'

A chorus of Amens followed by a rustling of papers and clearing of throats: Apologies, last PCC's minutes, and then into the preaching team report. Two new licensed Readers to add to the team of three – unanimous vote in favour. Both were present and glowed with pleasure after the forest of hands came down.

The pastoral care team, overseen by Val and Gwen, had doubled in size. The PCC agreed the listening training course that they had put together with Chloe's help. It would begin next month.

Anne reported on the recent activities of the Street Pastors Team, which came under the mission action team remit. There was a hum of encouragement as she told several moving stories. Grace followed this with her report on My Sister's House, which was no longer seen as the semi-detached-poor-relation-ministry-of-St-Stephens. More volunteers were needed and more CRB checks would have to be done by the two volunteer administrators. A discussion ensued about establishing a paid job-share administrator's post. The treasurer was hesitant about next year's budget, but wanted to encourage the PCC to go ahead with the idea, seeking to raise St Stephen's giving by 15 per cent, through a sermon series on giving. All were in favour.

The refurbishment report followed and all seemed well with that.

Finally came the human sexuality paper review. The congenial atmosphere changed. Lines were drawn, sides were taken, strong feelings were expressed, voices were raised. It was nearly nine o'clock. Grace stood up and called time on the debate. She closed by re-reading the Ephesians reading and then saying a simple prayer, 'Our Father, I pray you will help us to act justly, to love mercy and to walk humbly with you, our God. Amen.'

Silence hung for a moment as people collected their wits. She smiled as she surreptitiously watched those who had been in disagreement making the effort to speak to one another cordially as everyone put chairs and tables away. *Peace, peace, peace ...* she chanted her mantra.

When she got home, she threw her PCC folder down on her desk, went to the fridge and poured herself a glass of wine. She kicked off her low-heeled boots and went into the living room to find Peter and Zack watching a film. 'Hi, boys, what you watching?'

'New *Star Trek 2*,' Peter tore his eyes from the TV screen to briefly give her a smile.

'What's happening?' Grace asked as she threw herself down on the sofa beside Peter.

'Shhh!' Zack said.

'What's happening?' she whispered to Peter.

'Just watch it,' Peter said.

Grace tried to focus on the new Spock as he talked to the old Spock. 'Why are there two of him?' she asked knowing full well it would irritate them.

'Shhh!' they said in unison.

Grace giggled.

'Ha, ha!' Zack mocked scornfully.

The phone in the hall rang. Grace looked at her watch – nine thirty – it could only be an emergency at this time of night. She'd drummed it into her flock not to call after nine, unless it was life or death. She put her glass down and wearily pushed herself back on her feet.

'Hello? Reverend Grace Hutchinson speaking.'

'Hello, Grace ... it's me, Marie.'

'Hi, Marie, is everything all right?' she knew as she asked it, that it wasn't.

'It's James ... he died this afternoon,' Marie's voice was strangled.

'Oh, Marie, I'm so sorry! Were you with him?' turbulent emotions furrowed her brow.

'Yes ... yes I was ... so was Mark. The children all had a few moments with him too. He'd been moved to ICU ... He wasn't there for long.'

'Oh, Marie ... How are the kids?'

'Pretty broken up – I think they really thought he was going to get better.'

'Yes ...' Grace tugged a ringlet. 'Would you like me to come round now?'

'No ... I'm shattered. But maybe in the morning?'

'Yes, okay. Say ten o'clock?'

'Thank you. 'Night.'

"Night, Marie.' Grace replaced the phone in its cradle and stared at her reflection in the hall mirror. *It's over ... thank God ... he's gone ... oh shit ... poor kids ... poor Marie ... Wonder why Mark was there? ... How am I going to take his funeral? Oh God!*

When they went to bed, Grace snuggled up to Peter's back, wrapping her arms round him and quietly told him. He lay silent for a time. Then, 'Well I'm glad for you my love ... but also for him. He's free now, and hopefully enjoying the grace of God.'

'I didn't tell you what he said to me the other day ... he asked me to forgive him for what he'd done to me. He told me he'd been with Jesus when he was in his coma and that he'd met our daughter Rebecca – that she was beautiful and had hair like mine.'

Peter turned over, 'What?'

She repeated herself and then found she was crying uncontrollably. He took her in his arms, holding her tenderly as she cried out the cacophony of feeling she'd so carefully kept under lock and key.

❊   ❊   ❊

'Hi Grace, Julia here. I have Bishop Duncan on the line.'

'Hi, Julia, thanks,' she waited pensively while Julia put him through. She looked at the clock – half nine – *okay for time still ...*

'Hello, Grace,' the timbre of his voice soothed her instantly.

'Hello, Bishop Duncan, how are you?'

'I'm well, although the same cannot be said of Wendy.'

'Oh?'

'Haven't you heard?'

'No ... what?'

'She's got cancer ... liver cancer ... they've given her a few months to live,' he said it like he was reading a script for a play.

'Oh no!' exclaimed Grace, feeling overwhelmed. 'I'm so sorry ... when did you find out?'

'Last week. It's all come as quite a shock. She was losing weight and not eating much, but we all thought, you know, oh good, at last she's found a diet that works!' he laughed. 'When the pain started she wouldn't go see the doctor, putting it down to old age and poor bowel movement. We eventually convinced her to go to her GP and he did tests – they came back and – bang – we got the diagnosis and the life sentence all in one. To be frank, we're still in shock, I think.'

'I'm sure you are. Which hospital is she in?'

'She's not – she wants to stay at home for as long as possible – then it'll be the hospice.'

'Yes ... I see,' Grace said lamely.

'Anyway – that's not why I phoned,' he didn't hesitate, 'I phoned to say we have shortlisted you for interview with two others. I wanted to tell you myself!'

'Oh, thank you ...' Grace faltered at the exuberance in his voice. 'When's the interview date?'

'A week Wednesday – all day – starts at one o'clock – here.'

'Okay ... Julia could have informed me ... I'm sure you have a million and one things to be getting on with ... but thank you,' she felt confused.

'A bit of sunlight in an otherwise grim reality,' he said, allowing heaviness to creep into his voice for the first time.

A thought struck her and before she could chicken out, she said it. 'Have you been to see your spiritual director yet?'

His dry chuckle confirmed her suspicion, 'No ... not yet. But I know I need to go. Julia said the same thing to me the other day ... and so did Wendy. I thought I was doing rather well ... does the strain show through that much?'

Grace smiled, 'Not at all, Bishop Duncan. We're all just worried for you ...'

'Mmmm ... thank you Grace. I will have to give the old nun a ring. Well, I look forward to seeing you at interview. Bye for now.'

'Bye ...' she put the phone down and gazed at it. Her eyes slowly wandered up to her blue and gold icon and then across the wall to her Holman Hunt painting. 'What the hell is going on?' she asked.

She was just standing up and reaching for her bag when the doorbell went. When she opened it, there was Mark on her doorstep, 'Hello, Mark, this is a surprise!'

'Hi, Grace, can I come in?' his blue-green eyes searched hers eagerly.

'I'm just about to go and see Marie.'

'So you've heard?'

'Yes – Marie phoned me last night.'

'How was she?' he looked concerned.

'She was pretty exhausted ... she said you were there when he passed.'

'Yes ... that's what I'm here to talk to you about. Could I come in? It won't take long,' the pleading look in his eyes swayed her.

'Okay,' she opened the door wide and stepped aside, 'let me just call Marie and tell her I'm going to be late.'

She came into the living room after speaking to a relieved Marie, who had only just woken up and was not ready at all for Grace's visit. 'Would you like a coffee?'

'Yes, please,' Mark looked suddenly awkward. He followed her into the kitchen and while they waited for the kettle to boil he began telling her of what had happened to him in James's hospital room and the subsequent meeting with Charlie and Jules. His eyes swam as he finished by telling her about his last moments with James. Grace stood transfixed with the cafetiere in one hand and the coffee grounds in the other.

She had to boil the kettle again.

'So what do you make of it all?' Grace asked.

'I was hoping you could tell me?' Mark replied, cradling his coffee mug against his chest.

'Sounds like mercy at work,' she smiled slightly.

'What does that mean?'

'Oh nothing ... just, you know ... God doing his thing ....'

'You really think so?'

'I do.'

'It was amazing – I've never had an experience like it before. Has anything like that ever happened to you?'

'No – but it did to Trevor – you should go ask him about it.'

'I will! Hey I wondered what you thought of the possibility of maybe me seeing Chloe to tell her about all this ... I mean, would you consider facilitating a meeting between us?'

'Perhaps – shall I sound Chloe out first?'

'Yeah – that would be so helpful – thank you!'

Grace didn't feel too optimistic as to what Chloe's reaction would be, but she tried not to show her scepticism to Mark.

After he left, she came back to her desk and sat down, having forty minutes to kill before her re-arranged visit to Marie's.

She opened her story document and wondered how the story between Lila and Aaron was going to unfold ... and what on earth was going on in Anna's head? She thought of Jair and how different he was to James Martin ... and yet she had almost ... almost-sort-of prophesied his death by writing about Jair's. She marveled at the intuitiveness of the writing process ...And her own feelings about James ... were they the same as Lila's for Aaron? And what would Aaron do? Would he be affected by Paul's faithful prayers, shot into the ether from his prison in Rome, or would he continue on his mission to sabotage the Church. 'A house divided against itself cannot stand' she let the quote roll round inside her head ...

Despite the small amount of time left to her, she started to type.

Paul stood in his crowded room on the Lord's Day and began leading the morning time of prayer. 'Let us say together from Deuteronomy, from the prophet Zechariah and from the prophet Isaiah:

'The Lord our God is one Lord,' they said in unison.

'The Lord will be king over the whole earth. On that day there will be one Lord, and his name the only name.

'For to us a child is born, to us a son is given, and the government will be on his shoulders. And he will be called Wonderful Counsellor, Mighty God, Everlasting Father, Prince of Peace.

'A shoot will come up from the stump of Jesse; from his roots a Branch will bear fruit. The Spirit of the Lord will rest on him— the Spirit of wisdom and of understanding, the Spirit of counsel and of might, the Spirit of the knowledge and fear of the Lord— and he will delight in the fear of the Lord. He will not judge by what he sees with his eyes, or decide by what he hears with his ears; but with righteousness he will judge the needy, with justice he will give decisions for the poor of the earth. He will strike the earth with the rod of his mouth; with the breath of his lips he will slay the wicked. Righteousness will be his belt and faithfulness the sash around his waist. The wolf will live with the lamb, the leopard will lie down with the goat, the calf and the lion and the yearling together; and a little child will lead them. The cow will feed with the bear, their young will lie down together, and the lion will eat straw like the ox. The infant will play near the cobra's den, and the young child will put its hand into the viper's nest. They will neither harm nor destroy on all my holy mountain, for the earth will be filled with the knowledge of the Lord as the waters cover the sea.

'In the last days the mountain of the Lord's temple will be established as the highest of the mountains; it will be exalted above the hills, and all nations will stream to it. Many peoples will come and say, "Come, let us go up to the mountain of the Lord, to the temple of the God of Jacob. He will teach us his ways, so that we may walk in his paths." The law will go out from Zion, the word of the Lord from Jerusalem. He will judge between the nations and will settle disputes for many peoples. They will beat their swords into ploughshares and their spears into pruning hooks. Nation will not take up sword against nation, nor will they train for war anymore.'

The silence that followed the recitation was thick with emotion as each soul yearned for the day when these promises would come true. Slowly they all sat down, some on the floor, some on chairs and some on the bed. There was hardly any room for manoeuvring and the heat was sweltering.

Paul began to teach, 'In our Lord Jesus Christ this cosmic reconciliation has begun and it will be consummated in him. Alienation has been destroyed and reunification begun; the old division of humanity into Jew and Gentile has been overcome. Christ has begun to fill the universe with his reign of peace.'

A chorus of 'Amens' followed.

'We who are united with Christ,' he smiled at Tychicus and Pudens, 'have already begun to experience these things. The Church of Jew and Gentile is the place Jesus fills – the one heavenly temple – we are the place where cosmic powers see this reconciliation under way. And so we must strive to live in a way that reflects God's new creation of unity, harmony and peace.'

Paul paused looking around at his listeners, at Denas, Aristaralius, Onesimus, Mark, Justus and Epaphras – his faithful friends and fellow servants in the gospel. 'Dear brothers, we have gained a strong position in being united with our victorious Lord, but the battle is not over, even though the outcome is assured. These present days are evil – complete redemption lies ahead for us in the future, which is why we must never lose our hope.'

Another chorus of 'Amens' followed.

'We are the community whose lives and worship witness to the unity begun in our Lord. We are imbued with His presence – we are to be Christ bearers in this dark age.'

Paul turned to Tychicus and asked him to stand up, 'Our brother Tychicus is taking a letter with much of these thoughts expressed in it to the Churches in Asia – to Ephesus, Colosse, Magnesia, Tralles, Hierapolis and Laodicea. It would be good if we laid hands upon him and prayed for his safe travel and fruitful delivery of our message.'

'Excuse me, Father Paul,' a thin, dark youth stood to his feet.

They had found him, a runaway slave, starving in the streets of Rome. They had brought him to Paul and it didn't take long to restore him to health. He became a devoted disciple of Christ.

All eyes turned to him.

'Yes, Onesimus?' Paul asked.

'As you have been speaking I have had an overwhelming sense that I must go with Tychicus to help him in this endeavour. If you would write the letter to my master, Philemon, on my behalf as we have discussed, I will return to him and repay what I have taken from him with the rest of my life.'

Saddened, Paul very much wanted to keep the lad with him in Rome, but didn't want to do so against his owner's wishes. Paul nodded his old head, 'It is as you say Onesimus. I am loathe to lose you, but perhaps your master will forgive you and restore you to favour if I intercede for you. After all he owes me his life. I led him to Christ in Ephesus all those years ago and now he leads a Church in his home at Colosse.'

So Tychicus and Onesimus stood together next to Paul as the men all began to intercede.

'Let us bless them and send them on their way,' Paul said.

The heat and the buzzing of flies didn't deter them from their task and the two messengers were dripping with sweat by the time they were done.

They shared peace and broke bread together after this, solemnly remembering Jesus' death on the cross with thanksgiving. After that each one placed the food they had brought, wrapped in an assortment of cloths or pouches of leather. Paul's desk became a banquet table as they shared the meal together. Some men spilled out into the hallway and even out onto the street. In this way neighbours had joined them over the months that Paul had been imprisoned there. Many had believed the good news and become part of the humble beginnings of the Church in Rome.

❊ ❊ ❊

Tychicus was grateful for Onesimus's company. It had been a rough trip and he had suffered greatly with seasickness. Had Onesimus not been there, he doubted he would have made it. Timothy met them at Ephesus harbour with Ruth and Oni, as they would be their hosts for the duration of their visit.

So eager was Timothy to read Paul's letter, that no sooner had the travellers been settled in their accommodation, than he departed bearing the precious scroll away with him.

'Anna! Anna! I've got it! I've got Paul's letter!' Timothy shouted through the house. He heard her quick, light feet running towards him down the hallway from the kitchen. He was at his desk, set in one corner of the family room, spreading the scroll and carefully placing weights along its edges.

She wrapped an arm around his waist as she leaned in to look. 'Which is Luke's and which is Paul's hand writing?' she asked, kissing his cheek.

'I think the earlier part is Luke's – before he left to come here,' he ran a reverent finger along the lines of script, '"To the saints, the faithful in Jesus Christ . . ." Ah it warms my heart already!' he grinned like a boy with a new toy.

'I'll bring your food to you here, my love, so you can nourish yourself in every way. Shall I keep the children in the courtyard until bed time?'

'That would be wonderful! Just to have the time and space for a first read through ....'

'Of course,' she smiled. 'I will read it when they are all asleep.'

He nodded, already engrossed.

Later Anna, Mary and Lila sat together surrounded by as many candles as they could find to read Paul's letter. Mary's eyes were not good in the evenings, so Lila and Anna took turns to read aloud. Timothy sat across from them, his head tilted back on the couch, enjoying it all over again.

'"There is one body and one Spirit – just as you were called to one hope when you were called – one Lord, one faith, one baptism, one God and Father of all, who is over all and through all and in all." – I love that!' Anna said.

'Yes,' Timothy sighed.

She read on '"Then we will no longer be infants, tossed back and forth by the waves, and blown here and there by every wind of teaching and by the cunning and craftiness of men in their deceitful scheming. Instead speaking the truth in love, we will in all things grow up into him who is the Head, that is Christ. From him the whole body joined and held together by every supporting ligament, grows and builds itself up in love, as each part does its work."'

'Such wonderful imagery!' Mary said.

'I couldn't bear the thought of one of my little ones tossed about in the sea. The Lord must feel like that about us when we get deceived by false teaching.'

Timothy raised his head and looked at his wife, 'It must break his heart!' he agreed. 'How must he feel for Neo?'

'Pardon?' Anna asked.

Timothy realised his mistake ... she didn't know what he had done.

'What has happened to Neo that the Lord must be so distressed?'

Timothy sat forward, leaning his elbows on his knees, 'I didn't want to tell you at the time ... but perhaps I should have ... Forgive me,' he bowed his head slightly and then continued, 'When we went to visit Neo it was because he had circumcised himself.'

Anna was aghast. She looked at her mother and Mary, 'Why would anyone do that? How painful! No wonder he was so unwell!'

'We think he may have done it to please Aaron. We think Aaron has been subtly influencing him, and others, to obey Jewish law in order to please God.'

Anna's mouth hung open, 'Aaron wouldn't do that, surely? He has been baptised ... he is a great teacher of the scriptures.'

Timothy nodded, 'What you say is true, my love. But why is Aaron paying for all Neo's needs; why is he only inviting the Jewish members of the Church to his home; why does he hire a lecture hall and fill it with young men in order to hear Neo's testimony?' Timothy watched his dumbstruck wife as the conflict played out in her eyes. 'Neo went to Doctor Luke first, who deterred him from such action. They discussed the spiritual reasons why Neo felt the need. Luke thought he had convinced him that there was nothing else Neo need do to please God, other than to trust in his one and only Son. But he was wrong.'

'Oh ...' Anna said at last. She looked as if she would burst into tears.

Lila reached over and held her hand.

'The day I got so upset, they were talking about this very thing. I said exactly that – that we are not saved by anything we do ... but Aaron said I was speaking of things I didn't understand. Then he called me his dear child ... and I couldn't control my emotions ... I ... I don't know why?'

'It was so soon after Papa's death,' Lila soothed.

Timothy caught her eye as she said it, and Lila gave him an imperceptible shake of her head.

Mary added, 'We should never have held the Lord's Day celebration in your home so soon after the funeral. You were overwrought.'

'Yes ... yes I was ... I'm much better now, thanks to all of you, especially you Mary. But that still doesn't explain to me why I feel so strongly about that incident, why these terrible emotions boil up inside me?'

No one said anything. If anyone was to tell Anna the truth it must be Lila, and she was not going to, not then ... perhaps never.

Timothy questioned the wisdom of this, but wasn't going to challenge his mother-in-law. Instead he went to prayer, pleading that the Spirit of God would lead Lila in the way that she should go regarding the truth of her daughter's origins ... *speaking the truth in love,* he pondered Paul's words silently ... *so we will in all things grow up into him who is the Head, that is Christ.*

※   ※   ※

Aaron leaned over and whispered, 'Ten have followed your example so far.'

Neo looked at him in surprise, 'Last I heard it was five.'

'I have been to see all ten. You will notice that they are not here today.'

Neo looked around the Church gathering on the Lord's Day in Ruth and Oni's home. Sure enough as he counted those he discipled, ten were missing. 'Are they all healing well?' Neo asked, aware that it had been the prayers of Timothy and Luke, as well as the ointments they had administered, which had healed him.

'They are still in pain, but I'm sure they will heal as well as you have,' Aaron soothed.

'Did you pray healing prayers for them?'

Aaron looked bemused, 'No. They'll be fine.'

Timothy was calling the Church to order before the beginning of the service, 'We have received a letter from the Apostle Paul at last,' Timothy smiled broadly. 'I will read it aloud to you today, but be assured that we are making copies so that we can send it to every leader and smaller gatherings for closer scrutiny and reflection. It is a letter full of encouragement to keep unity in the Church between Jew and Gentile. This is an issue that has been very much on my heart of late.

'Let us pray first that the eyes of our understanding be opened, so that the same Spirit who inspired Paul to write this letter, be free to write it upon our hearts and minds.'

Everyone stood to pray, hands raised, eyes closed.

When they had seated themselves again, Timothy began to read to them. He stopped occasionally, pausing to let Paul's thoughts sink in.

'"... Therefore, remember that formerly you who are Gentiles by birth and called "uncircumcised" by those who call themselves "the circumcision" (which is done in the body by human hands)— remember that at that time you were separate from Christ, excluded from citizenship in Israel and foreigners to the covenants of the promise, without hope and without God in the world. But now in Christ Jesus you, who once were far away, have been brought near by the blood of Christ.

'For he himself is our peace, who has made the two groups one and has destroyed the barrier, the dividing wall of hostility, by setting aside in his flesh the law with its commands and regulations."'

Aaron rose to his feet, 'Excuse me brother Timothy, may I interrupt?' he didn't wait for permission, 'I'm sure I am not alone in feeling a growing sense of alarm on hearing this?' he looked round the gathering for support.

'What alarms you?' Timothy asked resting his hands patiently on the table on which he'd spread the scroll.

'Did I hear correctly that brother Paul says: the law with its commands and regulations has been set aside? This can't be right, surely?'

Timothy looked down at the letter and found the words, reading them out again, 'For he himself is our peace, who has made the two groups one and has destroyed the barrier, the dividing wall of hostility, by setting aside in his flesh the law with its commands and regulations.'

Aaron raised his voice, 'If I recall, Jesus himself said, and I quote: "Do not think that I have come to abolish the Law or the Prophets; I have not come to abolish them but to fulfil them. For truly I tell you, until heaven and earth disappear, not the smallest letter, not the least stroke of a pen, will by any means disappear from the Law until everything is accomplished. Therefore anyone who sets aside one of the least of these commands and teaches others accordingly will be called least in the kingdom of heaven, but whoever practices and teaches these commands will be called great in the kingdom of heaven. For I tell you that unless your righteousness surpasses that of the Pharisees and the teachers of the law, you will certainly not enter the kingdom of heaven." Am I not right?' Aaron looked around triumphantly.

'You are right,' Timothy agreed humbly, at which Aaron's expression changed to that of bemusement. 'So you agree that we must strive to surpass the righteousness even of the Pharisees, and the teachers of the Law,' he pressed the fingers of one hand to his chest, 'if we want to enter the kingdom of heaven?'

'But, Aaron, do you not see that Jesus is our righteousness?' Timothy leaned forward, 'He has surpassed yours or any other's righteousness. We put our trust in him – in his body upon the cross for us – bearing the law and our sins away – the sins of the whole world. He fulfils the whole of the Law for us. Do you not see?'

By then Neo had stood as had several others, 'Why have you hidden this teaching from us?' he asked forcefully.

Another young man near Neo angrily asked, 'Do you wish us Gentiles to be the least in the Kingdom of Heaven?'

'Why have we not been taught to keep the commands?' Neo's voice rose.

Soon the meeting dissolved into chaos, with factions arguing with each other. Timothy stepped back in dismay. He had lost control of the meeting and knew he wouldn't be able to get it back, not today.

He made his way towards Aaron and said, 'Come with me, we need to talk privately.' He pulled Aaron away from the young men and headed past arguing groups of people towards the courtyard door, which opened up onto the narrow cobbled street.

When they were alone he said, 'What are you trying to do, Aaron? Destroy the Church? You know as well as I that a house divided against itself cannot stand!'

Aaron's face was implacable, 'I seek the good of the Church – the highest good! Keeping all the commands, even to the smallest letter or the least stroke of a pen, will bring greatness in the Kingdom of Heaven. It's what Jesus himself taught – he was circumcised – as you and I are – why have we not encouraged the Gentile converts to obey all the Law?'

'Aaron – you have not understood the gift of grace that is freely given you. Gone are the days of relying upon ourselves to uphold the Law and a sacrificial system in the Temple to redeem us where we have failed to hit the mark. Jesus came to be our propitiation, to fulfil all the Law for us. Our job is to trust in his sacrifice. He is the perfect Lamb of God, who takes away the sin of the world.'

'I may no longer be able to offer sacrifices at the Temple in Jerusalem, but I cannot agree with setting aside the commandments! I do not want to be one who is "least in the kingdom of heaven!"'

'Aaron, if you persist in this attitude you will cause disunity in the Church and ultimately its fragmentation. Please don't do this. Please take a copy of Paul's letter and study it at your own leisure.'

'I will take a copy, but I can't promise that you will like my response to it.'

'I will pray for you as you study it. You are a good man, a wise man.'

Aaron looked surprised when he said this.

'You knew brother Paul and I hope you will have insight into his teachings. I know God has blessed you with great intellect and the powers of persuasion. I hope we will be able to work together for the good of the Church here in Ephesus.'

And if we can't, I will have to warn people against you – something I do not wish to do, Timothy thought.

※   ※   ※

Dismayed Anna sat watching the chaos unfold around her. As she watched Neo's face it occurred to her that a change had taken place in him. His happy, carefree approach to life seemed to have all but disappeared. In its place pride graced his features.

His joy has gone ... it used to be contagious ... People were drawn to him and the good news of what Jesus had done for him. Now he relies on what he has done for himself ... but why? He has received baptism, received the teachings of Jesus … so why was it not enough? Perhaps they have found a flaw in the gospel? Perhaps it isn't fully true? Perhaps salvation is from the Jews and always will be? Perhaps it is we who have been deceived?

She felt an internal earthquake crack through her soul. She turned to look at Ruth and Oni sitting near her and saw tears trickling down Ruth's cheeks.

Silence fell as Timothy and Aaron returned to the courtyard. They both waited until everyone was seated again and then Aaron spoke, 'Brother Timothy has given me a copy of the apostle Paul's letter to prayerfully read. I have agreed to suspend judgment until I am completely satisfied that I understand his message. So to those of you who are disturbed as I am, I ask you to be prayerful and watchful.'

'And to those whose hearts ache as mine does,' Timothy said, 'we too must prayerfully read Paul's letter and pursue unity. I think now would be a good time to share the peace together and break bread.'

Aaron looked strained, but nodded his head in agreement. He took Timothy's outstretched hand and clasped it firmly. 'The peace of the Lord be with you,' he said unsmilingly.

'And also with you,' Timothy held his gaze.

It was an awkward sharing of the peace, to say the least. It was only when Timothy began the ritual of breaking bread that a true peace began to descend upon the fragmented gathering. As he spoke of Jesus death on the cross and lifted the bread high and he tore it in two, Anna knew that order was being restored. The Prince of Peace had taken centre stage again. She glanced at Aaron's face to see how it was affecting him. She could not tell – his face was inscrutable.

✳ ✳ ✳

'Mama, could we pray together for Aaron?' Anna asked as they cut vegetables in the kitchen together.

Lila sighed and looked up from her work, 'Can you ask Mary, my love.'

'But why, Mama? You have always taught me to pray for all people.'

Lila didn't reply as she slowly continued to chop an onion.

'He needs our prayers most – he needs divine assistance to change his heart and mind.'

Again Lila said nothing. She pushed the segments of onion to one side and picked up another.

'Mama ... there's something you are not telling me, isn't there? What is it?' Anna leaned forward to try to make eye contact with her mother.

Lila sighed again and turned to face her daughter, 'Yes – I am keeping something from you – but it is for your own good. I know I should, but I cannot bring myself to pray for Aaron. God knows ...' her voice trailed away.

'Tell me, Mama,' Anna pleaded.

'I can't,' Lila said with tight lips. 'Please don't ask me again. Go and find Mary. Pray with her.'

At a loss, Anna put down her knife and obediently left the kitchen. She wandered out into the courtyard to find Mary. She was there with Sol, helping him with his reading. Anna sat down in the shade beside them, listening to her son's stumbling efforts. Mary was using a copy of Paul's letter for Sol's reading.

' ... speaking the truth in love ...' he read slowly, '... we will in all things grow up into him who is the Head, that is Christ. From him the whole body joined and held together by every supporting ligament, grows and builds itself up in love, as each part does its work.'

'Very good, Sol!' Mary said, 'Hasn't he come on so much in his reading, Anna?'

'Yes, you have, Sol ... that was excellent!' Anna agreed, stroking his hair.

'Can I go and play now?' the boy asked.

'Of course, but don't go far. Dinner will be ready soon. Nana is cooking it as we speak.'

Sol jumped eagerly to his feet and ran to the courtyard door. The boys in the street, whose laughter they had been able to hear for some time, cheered when they saw him.

Mary was rolling up the scroll carefully.

'Can I ask you something Mary?' Anna touched her on the arm.

'Of course,' the older woman smiled, staying her hand.

'Can we pray together for Aaron – that the eyes of his understanding would be opened – that he would grasp the gospel of grace?'

'Yes – yesterday's service sounded terrible. I'm glad I wasn't there. It's so sad to hear of disunity creeping into the Church.'

Anna looked pensive, 'Why won't Mama pray with me for Aaron? What is she hiding?'

Mary frowned, 'That is not for me to say, my love. You must trust her that she wants the best for you and that the best is what she is doing right now.'

Anna shrugged defeat, 'All right ... let's pray now ....'

And so they joined their voices, pouring out intercessions for Aaron's heart and mind. Despite her efforts Mary couldn't help but remember the night Aaron had their front door broken down and carried Anna into the night; she remembered the harrowing thud of the spear that nearly killed Jair; she remembered running from his house through Jerusalem's streets, Stephen carrying Jair's limp body; she remembered it was he who had enabled and approved Saul's persecution of the Church; she remembered washing and anointing Stephen's precious body – that body that should have been hers, but had been denied her. A bubble of grief rose within her soul – she began to weep.

'Is dinner ready?' Sol asked, breaking into the other dimension they had entered in prayer. They hadn't even heard him open the courtyard door or approach them. Anna opened her eyes as Mary dried hers with her headscarf.

'It must be ... can you go and call the others? Goodness, the baby must still be asleep!' Anna exclaimed getting up and running towards the nursery.

But when she lifted her baby, she could not wake her.

Lila and Mary came running from different directions on hearing the desolate scream that was to haunt them for a long time to come.

8. GIVING

Ephesians 4:17–5:14

*Be kind and compassionate to one another, forgiving each other ...
Be imitators of God as dearly loved children and live a life of love,
just as Christ loved us and gave himself up for us.*

Grace could hear the doorbell ring inside the house. She took several deep breaths and shifted her weight from one foot to the other. She watched Marie's petite figure approach through the marbled glass and held her breath.

'Hi, Grace, come on in,' Marie's voice was small and flat as she opened the door.

'Hi,' Grace said quietly as she stepped into the wide hallway. It reminded her of a Mediterranean villa with its clean lines and marble flooring. She'd purposely never been to their home – had never dreamed there would ever be a time when she would have to go there. Now she was walking through it looking at art and rugs and ornaments he would have chosen together with Marie. She felt like shrinking into herself, not wanting to leave a trace of herself there.

She sat gingerly on the edge of the kitchen chair as Marie made coffee. She didn't mention that she only drank green tea now. She accepted the steaming mug and waited for Marie to come and sit at the glass and stainless steel table with her. 'Did you sleep last night at all?'

'I think so ... it felt like being dragged through treacle when I came to this morning ... so I must have,' Marie stirred her drink slowly.

'What have the hospital said?'

'They want to do an autopsy. I think they want to study his brain. He'd laugh at that,' Marie could hardly raise a smile. Every word she spoke seemed to require huge effort.

'Have you made contact with a funeral director yet?'

'Yes – I rang them yesterday – straight away. They'll liaise with you and with the hospital and then inform me. It was one less thing I needed to think about once I'd called them. I hate the thought of waiting for an autopsy. I gave my consent, but I really didn't want to. I just want to get on with it. It feels like I've been waiting for long enough already!'

'Yes,' Grace raised her eyebrows ruefully. They both sipped their drinks thoughtfully. The butterflies in Grace's stomach were getting worse, rather than calming down. She shifted in her seat and curled a stray ringlet behind her ear. 'Perhaps you need the time to adjust to this new reality?'

Marie shrugged her tiny shoulders, 'It's all shit, isn't it? Trade one shitty reality for another.'

Grace smiled dryly, 'Yes ... Peter and I have often thought we'd like to write a book called *When Shit Happens*, but a title like that probably wouldn't sell well in the Christian market.'

Marie almost laughed. 'I like it. Could I contribute?'

'Certainly,' Grace sipped from her mug again. 'You're qualified!'

They drank in silence for a while, then Marie said, 'It's the children that upset me the most,' her eyes welled up. 'They are so bitterly disappointed with God. You should have heard how they prayed for James's recovery. What do I say to them now that God has failed them?'

Grace thought of several things to say in response, but knew that none of them were helpful right now. What she did say was, 'We can't shield them from the horrors of life, no matter how hard we try.'

'I shielded them from so much of the darker side of James's life ... but not from these last five nightmare years. I wish they'd been there when he told me about what he'd seen while in a coma. I've tried to pass it on to them ... but somehow as I hear it coming out of my mouth, it doesn't ring true. And I can see the look in their eyes. They don't believe me.'

Grace tried hard to disguise the alarm she felt, 'What did he tell you?'

'Oh that he'd seen Jesus and people he knew and how awe-inspiring and wonderful it had been for him; how he didn't want to come back here, but Jesus told him it would only be for a little while,' Marie furiously blinked tears away. 'Meanwhile I endured the interminable will-he-won't-he-make-it rollercoaster for five long years! Why? If God is good, why would he do that to me?' her voice was suddenly vital and sparking with anger.

Grace was at a loss. 'I don't know,' she breathed.

'Why don't you know? Someone like you should bloody know!' Marie burst into sobs. 'Oh I'm sorry – I didn't mean that – I'm so sorry Grace,' she covered her mouth with frail hands.

'Please don't be,' Grace came round to her and knelt beside her, wrapping an arm around her waist. 'I've had the exact same feelings and questions myself at times.'

Marie sobbed out the wave of rage and despair. Slowly it subsided. 'You know,' she said between sniffs, 'part of me is angry that he got to be with Jesus all that time, when he was such a bastard most of his life, and I was the good one who had to endure all the hell he put me through and those horrible years of limbo while he was in a coma. It's not fair.'

Grace smiled, 'No it's not.'

'I was raised a Catholic,' Marie sighed. 'We were taught that you could earn God's favour, that you ought to be good!'

'I know,' was all Grace could say. 'But we're called to goodness simply to display the family likeness, not to score points. Once James understood that, he changed, didn't he?'

'Yes he did,' Marie sighed. 'I could hardly believe it, yet I'd prayed for it all those years.'

Grace smiled, 'We don't always recognise the answers to our prayers when they come, do we?'

'I wondered whether James was doing penance while he was conscious and incarcerated in his immobile body? He didn't think so ... he said – "Why would I have to do that, when Jesus has paid for all my sins already?"'

'He really got it, didn't he?' the butterflies were finally beginning to calm down in her stomach.

'Better than me,' Marie fiddled with her wedding ring, 'and I'd been the Christian all my life!' She looked up at Grace, 'One of the things I've thought when I've been railing at God, is that when it feels so unfair I need to understand that it isn't all about me ... I need to get a handle on the bigger picture.'

'For you to be thinking like that already, Marie,' Grace replied amazed, 'says something to me about the quality of your character! Just keep going like that and you are going to be fine!'

'I think the Lord sent him back for Mark, at the right time, when Mark was ready,' Marie wiped her eye with her forefinger.

'Could be ... Mark told me what happened the other day in James's room. He's asked me to facilitate a meeting between him and Chloe so he can tell her about it.'

'Oh really?' Marie's eyebrows rose, crinkling her translucent skin.

Grace gripped Marie's hand and said, 'God doesn't waste anything, Marie, especially not our sorrows – they cost us far too much for him to waste them! Why don't we pray that he would spend them well for you; that he'd make every costly moment count; that he'd turn the tables on your sufferings, like he did with Jesus on the cross, turning the worst Satan could throw at him and using it for the greatest good?'

Marie was quiet for a while as she pondered this idea. 'I have never thought of suffering in that way before ... I always thought of it as a means of purification or character development – you know – like God allowed suffering to happen to us to make us holy – our cross that we have to bear.'

'There's some truth in that, but I don't think it's quite right. The only cross we have to bear is to deny ourselves and follow Jesus. I think God hates it when we suffer purely from living in a fallen world that isn't completely under his reign of peace yet. One day, when his Kingdom comes in full, there will be no more suffering. But for now, if we give him our troubles, he will bring good out of them ... somehow. He always wins, Marie, no matter what is thrown at us.'

'I don't know if I have the energy to pray right now Grace. Could you pray for me?'

'Of course,' said Grace and turned to prayer as best she could. She thought of Rebecca, with hair like hers, whom James had seen while he was in a coma. She wondered if James was with their daughter now and if they were talking about her ... the thought choked her, causing her to flounder in her prayers.

Marie squeezed her hand affectionately.

❈   ❈   ❈

'Oh God ... I'm not sure about this ... not sure at all,' Chloe said as she came into the vicarage. 'I feel sick!'

'What happened to your face?' Grace stared at the intrusive white dressing on her cheek.

'Oh, a cat-fight yesterday in My Sister's House,' she touched it carefully. 'Caught my mole on someone's nail. I've just come from the mole clinic. They're going to keep an eye on it.'

'You were in a cat fight?'

'No,' laughed Chloe, 'breaking one up!'

'Phew – for a minute there I was thinking I was gonna have to send you off to see your supervisor!' Grace chuckled. 'Who was fighting?'

'Jade and Charmaine – turns out they had the same pimp.'

Grace nodded understanding completely. 'Look, Chloe, if this is too much today just say so. You don't have to do it,' Grace said, touching her arm.

Chloe's brown eyes were troubled, 'I know ... but I think I should ... You'll never guess what happened yesterday.'

'What – more than a cat fight?' Grace asked curiously as they went into the kitchen. Chloe leaned up against the worktop and folded her arms. Grace noticed there was no muffin-top-belly between her folded arms and her jeans waistband. 'Hey – you've lost weight!'

'Yeah – nervous energy and that green tea you recommended.'

'Wow ... you must be pleased?' she asked as she boiled the kettle and got two mugs out.

'Mmmm ...' Chloe replied distractedly.

'So tell me what happened?'

'Well, I had Charmaine for a one-to-one after the fight, and ... well ... it turns out she is Mark's Charmaine!'

'What?' exclaimed Grace, spilling hot water all over the worktop.

'Yes – I think she realised before I did.'

'Oh babe, what did you do?' Grace said appalled.

'Well – we ended our meeting right away – that's for sure!'

'I bet!' then a thought struck her, 'Is she still a resident or has she done a runner?'

'She's still there – I checked this morning – I was on night duty. I told Mel to keep an eye on her. Mel knew before either of us. She'd met her once years ago, but Charmaine didn't recognise her.'

'What a mess!'

'I know!' Chloe shook her silky head. 'It's made me think there's more to this praying mercy, than meets the eye. Should come with a government health warning!'

Grace laughed dryly, thinking about her earlier meeting with Marie. She wiped the counter and then mixed their green teas. As she handed Chloe her mug she said, 'Are you sure now's the right time to do this – after yesterday's shock?'

'In for a penny – in for a pound,' Chloe shrugged matter-of-factly. 'Still feel sick though.'

'I'm sure you do. He'll be here soon ... I just thought it would be good for you to come earlier, to prepare yourself and calm down.'

'Good thought,' Chloe smiled pensively. 'You're a good friend Grace. Not just to me.'

'I don't know about that – haven't seen him for years – but I have to admit it was good to see him the other day.'

'What does he look like?' Chloe looked up through a curtain of hair that had fallen forward.

'The same ... he really does have the most beautiful eyes!'

'Yeah ...' Chloe's tone held sadness in it. She shook her head, 'But it's too late for all that now ....'

Grace sipped her tea and said nothing. The doorbell went. 'That'll be him.'

She squeezed Chloe's arm as she passed her to answer the door. 'Hi, Mark,' Chloe could hear Grace injecting energy into her voice.

Chloe waited pensively as they exchanged a few pleasantries in the hallway and then made their way towards the kitchen. She realised she was holding her breath.

'Hello, Chloe,' Mark said on seeing her.

'Hello,' Chloe breathed.

He was wearing a white linen shirt, open at the collar, and a pair of faded jeans with tan suede dessert boots. Chloe knew he'd thought about what to wear, just as she had. She was wearing her favourite colour – sea green. The top was a wrap-around, accentuating her figure and her jeans were black. She'd always held that a woman could never have enough black jeans or trousers – they were so slimming.

'Well …' said Grace, 'Do you want to sit in here or in the living room?' Can I get you a drink Mark?'

'Coffee please,' he said. 'In here's good,' he looked enquiringly at Chloe.

How can he be so calm? She thought. *I'm a nervous wreck!* But in her best counsellor voice she said, 'Yes, here is fine.'

They sat round the table with its fresh yellow and white check tablecloth and bowl of yellow rosebuds in the centre. 'So,' Grace began. 'Would you like to begin Mark, seeing as you asked for this meeting?'

'Okay … thanks Grace,' he said and smiled at her. Chloe noticed that the muscles round his mouth quivered. He was more nervous than she'd realised. That was oddly comforting.

'Firstly – thank you for agreeing to see me. It was a long shot – I really didn't think you would,' he looked cautiously at Chloe.

'I nearly didn't,' she said softly.

'May I ask what made you change your mind?' he asked, leaning forward slightly.

'You may – something that happened yesterday.'

'Can you tell me what?'

'No … but go on,' Chloe's voice hardened.

'Well, I wanted to tell you about what's been happening in my life and how it's changing things with the kids.'

Chloe folded her arms and waited, not helping him in the slightest. Mark looked to Grace, who gave him an encouraging nod.

So Mark began at the beginning, when he'd lost his job. He didn't embellish his story, but told it straight as he remembered it. As he talked Chloe's expression softened. Grace watched her friend, wondering if the disillusionment was too deeply rooted in her for this meeting to have any effect on their present non-existent relationship. It occurred to Grace that his was a prodigal son story, but that Chloe's part was the older brother's as was Marie's earlier: such different perspectives on the same events.

When he got to his experience in James's hospital room and subsequent evening with Charlie and Jules, Chloe was visibly moved.

She loves Charlie so much. Any kindness towards him will go a long way. Grace smiled thinking of her own love for Zack, and how fierce it could be.

'Have you seen or heard from Charlie since?' Chloe asked.

'Jules has been texting. We're going to meet up again before they go back to uni. They were telling me about the house move. Sounds great. Virginia Water is a nice location.'

Chloe nodded, 'It makes sense. No point me rattling around in that big old house now that Mel is moving out with Rose and Josh is moving in with his girlfriend. Soon Charlie and Jules will want their own place too ... so I thought with your financial troubles, it made sense to downsize and move now, so I don't need to rely on your contribution as much.'

'I will keep giving you what we agreed,' Mark protested.

'I know you want to, but in these uncertain times, you don't know if you'll ever get a job at the level you were at before.'

Mark smiled gratefully, 'Thank you for thinking of me – I don't deserve it.'

'No, you don't,' Chloe agreed coolly.

'None of us do,' Grace interrupted. Chloe looked at her as if to say *shut up!* 'Sorry,' Grace added, squeezing her eyes shut and opening one to check to see if she was forgiven.

Chloe wasn't looking at her, but out of the window. 'You know, I woke up one morning a while ago with your name and the word *mercy* in my head. I think it must have been around the time you lost your job.'

'Did you know I had?' he asked.

'Yes – I think I'd got your email telling me. I'd not been to church for years or read the Bible or prayed or anything like that since our divorce. Had just given up on the whole idea of God altogether. But when that happened I couldn't get it out of my mind. Not knowing what the word *mercy* really meant, I went and looked it up. Well it sent me on a journey ... back to faith ... back to prayer ... praying mercy for you.' She turned and looked at him candidly.

Mark was stunned, 'What does mercy mean?' he asked eventually.

Chloe deferred to Grace with a look. Grace answered, 'It means to be able to step into another's shoes and feel with their feelings and think with their thoughts. It was what God did when he sent Jesus to become one of us.'

Excited Mark said, 'Maybe that's what happened to me in James's room? The only way I've been able to describe it has been that I've been saturated with love ever since. When I met Charlie and Jules – I really thought I'd want to strangle Jules, for one thing, but I didn't. Instead I was overcome with real affection for them both, but a burning love for Charlie – like I had when he was first born. I suppose I was filled with mercy for him?' he looked to Chloe at this.

She was blinking hard.

'I've realised that he's so like me ...' Mark smiled. 'I think he reminded me of all my own inadequacies whenever I was near him,' he sighed and ran his fingers through his hair. Grace watched Chloe watching Mark, and smiled to herself. 'I've got a lot of making up to do,' he dropped his hands on the table looking resolute.

'Thanks for meeting with me and listening to me, Chloe. It means a lot. Especially hearing a bit about your journey and the part you've played in praying for me. I couldn't even have dreamed of that!'

'Nor could I,' Chloe laughed ruefully.

'Well, I'd better go ... I've wasted enough of your time, I'm sure.' He stood up. The women got to their feet too. There was no way round the awkwardness of the moment. 'Thanks ... bye,' he said uncertainly, 'I'll see myself out.'

'Okay, Mark. Bye,' said Grace shoving her hands deep into her jeans pockets.

'Bye,' Chloe said lamely.

When he'd gone, they both flopped back into their seats. 'God, I'm exhausted!' Chloe exclaimed.

'Me too!' Grace leaned back, rocking on the two back legs of her chair.

'Do you think I should have told him about Charmaine?'

'I don't know – it's up to you what you tell him – I thought you did great! Are you glad you decided to see him?'

'Yes ... yes I am,' Chloe looked mildly surprised. 'Thanks Grace – thanks for helping make this happen.'

❊   ❊   ❊

It was Peter who woke her up the morning of interview for the job of Archdeacon. He beat the alarm clock by fifteen minutes, enough time for what he had in mind.

'I like that kind of wake up call,' Grace stretched luxuriously still encircled by his arms afterwards.

'Mmmm ... that was my way of saying all the best,' he kissed her between her breasts.

'With an afterglow like this, I'm bound to get the job,' she grinned.

He chuckled, 'Or they may actually decide that you're too hot to be an Archdeacon.'

She rolled over to get out of bed. Peter kissed her all the way down her back to the dimples above her cheeks. She turned round, 'Oh don't ... you're just making me want to stay for more and I've got to get up!'

'No can do, not for a while anyway ... maybe to celebrate later tonight, if you get it?'

'If I get it ... and if I don't,' she grinned wickedly.

'If you insist,' he put his hands behind his head and watched her walk across the room. 'You really do have the best ass!' he laughed.

'Well, thank you,' she said sticking it out at him before going into the en-suite for a shower.

She arrived half an hour early at the Bishop's house. She debated whether to wait in the car or go in. Deciding on the latter she got out and crunched across the gravel to the front door. Wendy opened it, 'Oh hello, Wendy! I didn't expect to see you,' Grace couldn't hide her concerned surprise.

'Hello Grace, how lovely to see you,' Wendy smiled as she opened the door wide. 'Julia has just had to pop out to get milk and sugar – we'd run out of both!'

Grace detected several disturbing emotions both in Wendy's face and voice, which she could not put her finger on. She put them down to pain control and came past her into the hallway, 'I thought you would be in bed?'

'Bed?' Wendy snorted, 'not me, not if I can help it!'

'I must say you're looking incredibly well,' Grace felt foolish as she said it, thinking how ridiculous Wendy would think it was to dwell on appearances when faced with her own mortality.

But Wendy looked pleased, 'Thank you Grace, that means a lot coming from the most beautiful female priest in the Diocese.'

Grace's cheeks flushed, 'Oh please, Wendy!' Grace felt utterly lost.

'Well, I know that's what Duncan thinks anyway,' she said in a stage whisper, 'but don't tell him I told you so,' Wendy had moved down the hall towards the Bishop's study by this time, so Grace followed helplessly behind her, trying to think of something to say in return.

'Ah Duncan, there you are – look who has arrived early?' Wendy said as the Bishop opened his door to them.

'Grace!' his face lit up. 'Good to see you,' he stepped towards her and kissed her on the cheek. 'Can you put the kettle on, dear?' he said to Wendy.

Grace was amazed that he was treating her as if there was nothing wrong with her. 'Of course, Duncan, but we'll have to wait for Julia to return with the milk.'

'Oh, Grace drinks green tea too,' Bishop Duncan smiled, 'so no need.'

'Shall I just bring in two mugs and a pot of hot water?'

'Yes dear, that would be wonderful.' He pushed his office door open and beckoned Grace to enter.

Feeling hugely uncomfortable with the dynamics between husband and wife, Grace obeyed uncertainly, catching the scent of his aftershave as she passed him. He closed the door behind them and sighed, 'So are you all set for today?' he looked keenly at her.

'As much as I can be,' Grace sat down. 'How are you? I can't believe Wendy is up and about like this?'

'Oh, she's an activist – always has been and will be up until the minute the Good Lord takes her. We're like chalk and cheese you know – many's the time I've wished I never married, but had followed my true calling to be a monk,' he sighed and came to sit next to Grace.

'Bishop Duncan!' alarmed, Grace looked him in the eyes. 'Why are you talking like this – at this time – and to me, of all people?'

A tormented look filled his soft grey eyes. 'I'm not very good with sickness and death and all that sort of thing,' he waved a beautiful hand dismissively.

'I don't believe you!' Grace said sharply. 'Have you been to see your spiritual director?'

'No,' he said sheepishly. 'I've had too much to do, with going back and forth to the hospital on top of my busy schedule.'

'Are you seriously telling me you haven't got Julia to cancel a whole load of things for you?'

He looked perturbed. 'That's what I mean about not being good around sickness and death. I just want to keep busy.'

214

Grace studied the face that caused so much conflict for her. 'Does Wendy understand that? I'm sure she's feeling hurt by your lack of attentiveness.' Grace could hardly believe she was talking to him like this.

'Oh Grace ... if you only knew,' he took hold of her hand.

'Bishop Duncan,' Grace tried to pull it away.

'Don't, Grace, please ... I need you,' he leaned in pulling her towards him at the same time. She was so stunned that she didn't resist. Then his lips were on hers, pressing tentatively at first and then more insistently. Feeling the pleasure she'd always wondered about stab her with arousal, a cacophony of emotions exploded in her brain. As the first erotic wave passed, sanity returned and she began to struggle to unlock her mouth from his, but it was too late. Wendy had opened the door silently and was standing watching them.

'Wendy!' Bishop Duncan jumped to his feet.

Appalled, Grace sat paralyzed in her chair.

'Here's your hot water and mugs,' Wendy said pragmatically. 'I'm assuming you have your tin of green tea here, dear?'

'Yes ... um . . .yes ...Wendy ... I ...' Bishop Duncan stammered.

Grace finally found her will power and stood up, 'I am so sorry Wendy ... I feel so ashamed ... I shouldn't have ... I ... I was ....'

'It's quite all right, dear,' Wendy said mildly. 'I did warn you, didn't I? Now if you've got everything you need I will retire to my room. Julia should be back any minute now,' she said turning and walked out of the office as soundlessly as she had walked in. Bishop Duncan followed her, turned at the door and said, 'Stay here, Grace ... I'm so sorry ... please forgive me ... I'm not myself ... I ....' His face was a picture of despair. He turned and left.

Grace's knees buckled. *How can I go through this interview now? I'll have to make my excuses and go. I can't believe it! What am I going to say to Peter? Oh God, oh God, oh God ...* her thoughts swirled round and round.

She heard Julia's firm steps down the hallway and then she was standing in the study doorway. 'Hello, Grace – are you all right? You look like you've seen a ghost! Where's Bishop Duncan?'

'I'm fine – he's just talking to Wendy,' Grace heard herself say.

The doorbell went. 'Ah that'll be the other candidates, no doubt,' Julia said jovially. 'Here we go!' she winked at Grace. 'My money's on you,' she threw over her shoulder as she headed for the front door, 'so stop worrying!'

She heard male voices conversing with Julia and then heard Bishop Duncan's footsteps coming down the wide staircase. An image of a rabbit caught in a trap appeared in her mind's eye. Her thoughts were in chaos as she watched Bishop Duncan come into the room again. 'It's okay Grace ... it was my fault entirely ... I hope you can forgive me ... I hope you can focus enough now to get on with the day ahead of us?'

Grace raised her eyebrows, 'Well ... I think I should leave.'

'And discount yourself from this process? No!' he said adamantly.

Three clergy came into the office as he finished speaking. He turned, becoming the perfect Bishop and host again, welcoming them and enquiring after their health and families. Grace got unsteadily to her feet and shook hands with them in turn. It was surreal, to say the least.

She heard Julia greeting members of the interview panel and leading them to an adjoining room. She made polite conversation with the other candidates as they drank their coffees and nibbled their shortbread biscuits.

She didn't know how she got through the day, and couldn't remember whole chunks of it. She drove home in a blur, apprehension growing in the pit of her stomach as she approached home, uncertain as to whether she should tell Peter, and if so, what to say? She tried several versions of events in her head, only to shake it at each. What would be the point of him knowing? It was a stupid mistake ... an accident brought on by the trauma Bishop Duncan was going through. But what excuse did she have? None! She knew Peter would ask her why she allowed it – why she had let him do it. It would hurt him too much – he didn't need to know.

She heard a text message come in on her phone as she pulled into the drive. It was from Peter, asking how the day had gone and saying he was sorry but he was going to be home late, as something urgent and last minute had come up at work. She texted back to say the day had gone well and that she'd keep dinner warm for him.

She sat and stared out the windscreen at nothing in particular. Returning from school, Zack found her like that. He knocked on her window, making her jump. 'Hi, Mum – you okay?'

They went into the house together, Grace deflecting furiously, asking him about his day. *God, he would hate me if he knew ...* The thought upset her so much that she had to go to the bathroom to cry, pulling herself together and then coming back to the kitchen to make dinner.

'Mum – what's wrong? You're not yourself at all tonight,' Zack pressed as they ate together.

'I had an interview for the job of Archdeacon today,' she replied truthfully. 'It's rather preoccupying my mind, that's all love. They said they'd let us know their decision later this evening.'

'But you look like you've been crying?' Zack persisted.

'Do I?' she asked hoping he would leave it at that. 'Do you want some Chunky Monkey ice cream?' she asked standing up and moving to the fridge to distract him.

It worked. 'Yes please! Can never have enough Chunky Monkey!' he grinned.

They'd cleared the kitchen and filled the dishwasher when the phone went. Grace went to her office and sat at her desk before picking up the receiver. 'Hello, Reverend Grace Hutchinson here.'

'Hello Grace, this is Stuart Frank. We met earlier today.'

'Oh hello, Stuart,' her heart pounded against her ribs.

'I'm ringing on behalf of the panel to thank you for attending the interview and for all your input. We thought it was a most invaluable day.'

'Thank you – yes I enjoyed meeting the other candidates immensely. I wouldn't have wanted to be in any member of the panel's shoes – you faced a tough choice today,' Grace forced a smile.

'Yes ... yes we did,' Stuart seemed to draw breath.

In the silence, which seemed interminable to Grace, she wondered what excuse Bishop Duncan had given for not making this call.

'I am sad to say that you weren't selected for the job of Archdeacon,' Stuart's disembodied voice echoed in her ear.

Of course I wasn't! How could I even think I might be, after what happened today! Stupid woman - she berated herself viciously. 'Well, thank you for letting me know so quickly, Stuart. It would have been a great privilege and honour to serve in that capacity, but I look forward to finding out who you did appoint so that I might keep them in my prayers. They were all brilliant candidates.' She felt like such a fraud.

'Yes,' agreed Stuart.

'Thank you, Stuart – goodbye,' she said lamely.

'One moment please, Grace. I haven't finished yet. I have some more news for you.'

'Oh?' she sat forward, feeling panic grip her chest. *They know what happened – Bishop Duncan must have told them – they want me to hand in my orders!*

'Bishop Duncan ....' At the sound of the name Grace dropped the phone, a wave of nausea rising up her torso. She could hear Stuart's voice in the distance, as if it were coming, not from the receiver on her lap, but from a very long way away.

'Hello ... hello, Grace – are you still there? Can you hear me?' Stuart's voice insisted.

Grace shook her head, swallowed hard, telling herself to grow a pair and face whatever was coming to her. She picked up the receiver again. 'Sorry, Stuart, I didn't hear what you said,' she steeled herself for the inevitable.

'Bishop Duncan has decided to take early retirement. A very wise decision, I think we all agree, given Wendy's condition.'

'Oh ...?' Grace replied.

'So it is my great pleasure to invite you for interview with the Crown Nomination Committee for the role of Bishop.'

※ ※ ※

Long after Peter was asleep, Grace lay awake.

He'd been over the moon for her at the turn of events. 'You do realise I'll have to be the tart at any Bishops and Tarts party we go to?' he'd laughed, hugging her tightly.

'Or I could go as both,' she'd said, her irony lost on him.

Eventually she got up, slipped her dressing gown on and went down to her study. She opened her laptop and went to her story document, wondering whether Lila would tell Anna the truth about Aaron or not? *What she doesn't know, won't hurt her,* she said to herself, thinking of what she was hiding from Peter and what she was hiding from Marie. But then the argument kicked off in her head.

To try and thrash it out she began to type ....

Anna stood gazing up at the statue of Artemis, standing proudly displaying her many breasts on the platform in front of the entrance to the temple. The virginal mother goddess of all living things was adorned with the signs of the Zodiac around her neck, symbolizing her unsurpassed cosmic power over astrological fate. Her skirt was decorated with fierce animals, symbolic of her power to deliver from all fear.

Usually Anna hurried past the temple as quickly as she could, if she had to pass it at all. Trying to restore some semblance of normality to her life, she'd dutifully gone to the harbour fish market that day. The rank smell from the basket on her hip would usually have sped her on her way home. However today she was oblivious to it, as well as to the heat and the flies.

What if she is real? The thought crept up on Anna unbidden, unchecked, as she studied the goddess. Since she'd found her baby, lifeless and cold, her thoughts had been chaotic, unfamiliar, unboundaried and terrifying. When she asked Timothy how he knew if God was good any more, he reminded her to think of Jesus, because *he* had said, 'If you have seen me, you have seen the Father.'

He had begun a morning ritual of helping her face the day by reading her a story of Jesus that the Apostle John had written – his work in progress – his Gospel. She would sit, rocking ever so slightly, on their bed, not really hearing him. He prayed for her and wept with her over their loss, but try as she might she was not able to take hold of the lifeline he continually threw towards her. She was like one tossed about in a sea of grief, each wave that submerged her, more cruel than the last. She had no idea how to view the world around her any more. Which way was up and which way was down, she did not know. The turbulence of maternal loss raged on in her body, mind and soul, bashing her relentlessly against the rocks of her empty arms.

The other children suffered as she withdrew more and more into herself. Their care fell increasingly to Lila and Mary, as Anna spent endless hours sitting in the nursery or beside the grave.

If you are real, she prayed looking up at the goddess, *take care of her for me, nurse her at your breasts, hold her in your outstretched arms*. She

219

began to weep. She dropped the basket of fish on the ground and crumpled beside it, unaware of the stares she was attracting from passers-by.

A young priestess, no more than fourteen years old, approached her, her bare feet silent on the marble steps. She knelt down beside her. Anna looked up through the blur of tears into an oval face, not dissimilar to her own. Her lips were painted red, but other than that she wore no other make-up. She had a serene demeanour, as if she knew herself to be among the elite of humanity. She seemed to embody the spirit of the goddess: virginal and sacred yet paradoxically motherly. Encircling her small waist was a belt of solid silver bees, causing the fine, white linen robe she wore to press against her flesh, revealing the soft, raised nipples of her developing breasts.

'Can I help you?' she asked compassionately. Anna, mesmerised by her lips, gazed at them in a daze. 'Are you overcome by the heat? Did you faint?' the girl asked gently.

'My baby ... I lost my baby,' Anna said, her voice catching like a rag on the thorns of her pain.

The priestess seemed to instantly intuit the depth of Anna's loss.

'Come,' she said, 'come with me. You are in the right place. Artemis will help you.' Carefully she helped Anna to her feet and walked her up the warm steps onto the shaded, cooler marble of the inner court. 'Sit here. You will feel better presently as the goddess ministers to you.'

They sat together on a marble bench and watched people go by. Some were worshippers coming in with their offerings and going out carrying amulets or tiny silver shrines; some were there on business, doing their banking; others were there seeking sacred sexual intercourse with a priestess, her virginity divinely perpetuated through her year of service in the temple.

This was all forbidden territory to Anna, yet sitting there, like Eve, she began to wonder why it had been forbidden. 'My name is Aurelia,' the priestess said, her red lips forming beautiful shapes around her name.

'Are you a priestess – a Mellissai?' Anna asked, curiosity distracting her from her grief.

'Yes. Do you know what it means?'

'I think it means "bee" in Greek, doesn't it?' Anna asked, uncertain of her grasp of the language.

'That's right – the bee is the symbol of chastity – asexual reproduction – the goddess's symbol. You've seen it on any common coin, haven't you?'

'Yes – but – please don't be offended – how is she chaste? Do you not practice prostitution here as part of worship?'

The young face was shocked, 'Oh no – it is not prostitution. It is sacred intercourse portraying Artemis's divine propagation of life.'

'And you do this?' Anna asked.

'My year of service is nearly at an end – yes – that has been part of my duties,' she nodded her beautiful head. 'Our Megabyzos, the chief high priest, has overseen my ministry well. I will be sad to leave him.'

'Did he show you how to have sacred sex?' Anna asked incredulously.

The girl laughed. 'Oh no – he is a eunuch. He only instructed me and watched over me. How do you not know these things?' Aurelia studied her strange charge with a raised eyebrow.

'I am Jewish ... a follower of the Messiah Jesus Christ.'

'I have heard of you people. Aren't you cannibals?'

It was Anna's turn to look shocked, 'No! We remember our saviour's death on the cross for us by drinking wine and breaking bread together. They are symbols of his body and blood, just as your bees are symbols,' she pointed at Aurelia's belt.

'Oh I see,' smiled the girl uncertainly. 'Have you come here today to find comfort, which your own religion has not afforded you?' Aurelia asked perceptively.

'I ... I ... don't know why I am here,' Anna whispered.

'Would you like to lie down? Come rest your head in my lap and I will sing to you,' said the priestess simply.

Anna was so struck by her youthful beauty, composure and her certainty that she did lie down. Aurelia began to sing in a high, soft voice. She sang of divine mother love. Anna could not remember hearing anything so beautiful or so comforting. She closed her eyes and let the tears flow.

※　※　※

'Where have you been?' Timothy asked, 'I have been going out of my mind with worry!'

'I met a friend – Aurelia – you do not know her – we lost track of time talking. Sorry, Timothy,' she ended her half-truth abruptly.

'My love, you must tell me where you are going and be sure to be back at the time you say you will be,' he squeezed her arm gently. 'This is a big city and not everyone here is a person of peace.'

'I know – I've said I'm sorry – but I'm back now – I'm safe,' she smiled but it did not reach her eyes.

Timothy studied her for a moment and looked like he was about to comment further, but thought better of it, in his usual quiet way. Relieved, Anna went to the nursery to sing the song she had learnt from Aurelia.

※　※　※

Concern for the ten young men who had circumcised themselves had driven Aaron to seek the help of a local Jewish sorcerer. Aaron liked to think of him more as a seer, but whatever his title, he usually delivered what was sought. Aaron couldn't understand why their wounds had not healed as quickly as Neo's, and fearful that he would lose influence, he had turned to the old man. In Jerusalem he would never have associated with such people, but since living in Ephesus, a centre of magic, his eyes had been opened to the possibilities of power and persuasion that this esoteric aspect of Judaism held for him in so superstitious a culture.

He watched and listened carefully as the old man prepared the tiny scrolls with the powerful words written upon them. He helped him roll and slide them into the silver, cylindrical amulets that the men would tie around their wounded part. He paid the full price and then some, and set out on his mission to bring healing.

The effects were instantaneous and very pleasing. Aaron's subtle influence grew as a result. He decided to take lessons with the old man in the Jewish art of exorcism and spell casting. He no longer wanted to pay someone else to do it; he wanted to understand how to manipulate the spirit world himself, just as he had the political world. His love of knowledge drove his fascination for the subject, making him an excellent pupil. People began to seek him out, before calling the elders of the Church to anoint the sick with oil and pray for them.

Timothy became of aware of what was happening when he discovered an amulet while visiting one of the sick in their home. When he asked where they had got it, they were evasive. When he asked them to destroy it so that he might anoint them in the name of the Lord and pray for them, they refused, saying they had received it from a Church member and they wouldn't say whom.

On the Lord's Day, Timothy taught from Paul's letter:

'So I tell you this, and insist on it in the Lord, that you must no longer live as the Gentiles do, in the futility of their thinking. They are darkened in their understanding and separated from the life of God because of the ignorance that is in them due to the hardening of their hearts. Having lost all sensitivity, they have given themselves over to sensuality so as to indulge in every kind of impurity, and they are full of greed. That, however, is not the way of life you learned when you heard about Christ and were taught in him in accordance with the truth that is in Jesus. You were taught, with regard to your former way of life, to put off your old self, which is being corrupted by its deceitful desires; to be made new in the attitude of your minds; and to put on the new self, created to be like God in true righteousness and holiness.'

❋ ❋ ❋

Aaron had heard of Anna's loss, and it had affected him in a strange way. He had never had much paternal feeling for any of his children or grandchildren, but somehow Anna was different. The death of her child, although he cared little for her remaining children, had felt personal to him. Eager to offer his condolences he made sure he sat as near to her as he could during the sacred service. When it was over and they were sharing the meal together, he made his way to her side.

'Shalom, Anna,' he smiled tenderly.

When she looked up into the warmth in his eyes, her own immediately welled with tears. She couldn't speak. Not wanting to draw attention, Aaron whispered, 'Meet me in the street,' and walked casually through the crowded courtyard towards the outer door. She watched him go, wiping the tears away furtively. When she thought she had waited a decent amount of time, she got up, went in the opposite direction, skirted around the edge of the courtyard and then out through the door. She was sure that no one had noticed.

She didn't understand why her heart was hammering its way out of her chest, or why she was risking her reputation as one of the Church leaders, but she was past caring. She stood, holding the iron door hoop firmly closed behind her, so she would know if anyone was trying to follow. Aaron was leaning his back against the wall. He turned when she appeared, concern all over his face.

'Anna – I did not wish you the embarrassment of coming undone in public. I only wanted to say that I feel your loss as if it were my own. I am so sorry.'

The tears flowed freely down her cheeks. 'I am so lost Aaron,' was all she said.

'I know dear heart, I know,' he reached over and wiped her cheek with his thumb. A look of confusion clouded her eyes. 'Oh no sweet ... it is not like that ... I feel for you as a father does for a daughter ... not as a lover ... truly,' he fished out a silk cloth from inside his cloak and handed it to her.

She took it and buried her face in it, sobbing uncontrollably.

'Anna, my dear child ... I have waited long to say this ... but I think perhaps now is the time ....' He took a deep breath and then said, 'Anna, I am your father.'

She lifted her head mid-sob, shock making her hiccup.

'Yes,' he nodded his head slowly, 'that is why you and I have this bond, why I am sure you have feelings for me that you do not understand.'

She hiccupped several times more, her mouth hanging open. 'But Jair?'

'He was not your blood father, although he cared for you deeply and I cannot fault him in his raising of you. You are a credit to him.'

'How ...?' she asked her eyebrows pulling at her eyes in disbelief.

'Your mother and I were lovers for a time. I'm not proud of it. Jair was one of my dearest friends. I am sorry for my part in deceiving him. But we couldn't help it ....' He was watching her carefully as he spoke. 'When it finally came to an end, as affairs do,' he shrugged nonchalantly, 'your mother did not see fit to tell me she was pregnant with you. She had got what she wanted from me, but would live as if the life growing in her had come from Jair.' He saw the next question in her eyes. 'Yes – he knew. He took your mother back and you as his own. I will always be grateful to him for that.'

Anna had become very calm. Her tears had ceased and she was folding and unfolding the silk cloth between her fingers. 'When did you find out?'

He sighed and stroked his beard, 'I guessed when I met your mother with you one day in Jerusalem. You looked so like me – your eyes – well – they are mine, without a doubt – I knew then. Your mother realised and tried to hide the truth from me. And that was when I came to get you ....'

'When,' her head lifted and her eyes bored into his.

'After I discovered the truth I made my plans and came to get you. But by then the bond was too deep between Jair and you. He and your mother and Mary stole you back from me.' He looked forlorn. 'When I arrived in Ephesus and realised who you were I could not believe my good fortune. You are part of the reason I joined the Church. I was happy just to be near you.'

'Why have you not told me this before?' she asked, defended, suspicious, distrusting.

'I wanted to after Jair's death. Remember when I called you "my dear child"?' The jigsaw puzzle pieces were falling into place. Anna nodded as her chin wobbled. 'But when I heard of the death of your child ... of my grandchild,' he pressed, his hand to his chest, 'I felt it deeply. Jair is not here to comfort you any more so I resolved that now was the time to tell you.'

'Oh,' she exhaled, bursting into a fresh flood of tears. He reached over and drew her to him, cradling her in his arms and stroking her hair because her headscarf had fallen. She clung to him, sobs wracking her body.

When she had calmed down, she pulled back but stayed within the circle of his arms. Looking up into his face she said, 'I think I've known all along ... I just didn't know what it was that I knew.'

'Yes,' he said softly. Then, 'What will you do now?' He let her go and stepped back a little.

'I will confront my mother. I have known she has been keeping something from me ... now I understand why.'

'Well, you know where I am if you need me – any time, night or day, dear heart,' he reached out and cupped her chin in his hand affectionately. 'It is so good to speak like this at last.'

'Thank you,' she said simply, turning and going back through the door, leaving Aaron to exult in the street by himself.

❈ ❈ ❈

Anna waited until the evening, when all the children were in bed and the chores of the day were done. For the first time in days she felt energised and joined her mother and Mary in bath and bedtime with the children. She did not speak to her mother. The children responded with excessive hugs and kisses, glad that their mother was not so distant.

As the women made their way to the lounge, tired after their long day's work, Anna said, 'Could I have a word with you, Mama?'

'Certainly,' Lila replied, 'In your bedchamber?'

'Yes please.'

When Lila had shut the door behind her Anna turned from the window. 'You might want to sit down for this,' she indicated the bed.

Lila came and sat down, sensing now that something was terribly wrong.

'I know!' Anna said, her voice held tightly under control.

Lila looked aghast and clutched at her stomach.

'Yes – Aaron is my father!' her eyes sparked.

'Only by blood,' Lila blurted as tears tripped her.

'Why didn't you tell me? Didn't you think I had a right to know? How dare you keep this from me all these years! I cannot believe you would be so utterly deceptive!'

Lila wept into her hands, a mixture of relief and guilt and grief pouring through her fingers. 'Many times we thought of telling you, but the time never seemed right ... but he loved you ... Jair loved you as his own ... he was a true father to you ... in ways that Aaron could never be!'

'How dare you presume that!' Anna's voice had risen dangerously.

'You don't know what he's like Anna ... you have no idea ... I have tried to protect you from him ... and now I have failed,' she wailed.

Hearing them, Timothy came into the room, 'What's going on?' he asked.

'She knows,' Lila cried, 'Aaron told her.'

'Did you know?' Anna asked her husband in horror.

'I've known for some time, yes,' he said gently. 'You look so alike ... it is hard not to see it,' he came and sat beside Lila on the bed and put a comforting arm around her.

'And you never thought to tell me?' Anna demanded.

'I did – but it was your mother's to tell – I could not break her confidence.'

'I don't believe it! The ones closest to me – my husband and my mother – have deceived me?' Anna was close to hysteria.

Mary came into the room at this point, 'And you knew all along too ....' Anna pointed a shaking finger at her.

'I was there when he kidnapped you and when he nearly killed Jair!' Mary's voice was strong and commanding.

'Kidnapped? You mean he came to get me, to be with me – the daughter you never told him about? How could you?'

'You don't know him,' Lila cried, 'you don't understand!'

'Oh I understand all right,' Anna retorted.

'Anna,' Mary cried, 'listen to me! Aaron funded the first persecution of the Church. He approved the stoning of my fiancé, Stephen. He even tried to have Paul killed! You cannot trust this man, no matter if he is your father!'

Anna stared at each of them, her mind whirling. 'I'm not listening to you – to any of you! You are all liars and deceivers! How can it be that I get to this stage of my life only to find that everything I have believed in has been a sham – a ... a ... mockery? Well if you think I'm going to stay here and carry on the happy families game you've all been playing, you are very much mistaken!' Her chest was heaving, her eyes wild.

'You are overwrought, Anna,' Timothy stood up and reached out towards her.

'Don't touch me,' she said, shrinking from him. 'One more thing before you all get out of this room – does Joshua know?'

'No,' Lila whispered.

'So I have at least one family member who is true,' Anna breathed deeply.

'That is so unfair,' Lila looked up at her daughter, wondering where the girl she had raised had gone.

Anna glared at her, 'I want you to leave now – all of you – leave!' she shouted.

As soon as they'd gone she packed a bag, climbed through her window to avoid any more confrontation, and made her way to Aaron's house in the gathering dusk. He was overjoyed when he opened the door to her. The same could not be said for Leah, his wife.

9. HOMING

Ephesians 5:5–6:9

Make the most of every opportunity, because the days are evil ...
understand what the Lord's will is ... be filled with the Holy Spirit ...
Submit to one another out of reverence for Christ.

Mark knelt awkwardly at the rail. The church keys Grace had given him lay
on the worn velvet kneeler beside him. He looked up at the dark wooden
crucifix standing on the altar between two large silver candlesticks. His
eyes were drawn beyond it to the reserved sacrament in its glass case
with its flickering candle above. Everything was unfamiliar to him. His past
Church experience was middle-of-the-road evangelical. He almost got up
to go, thinking he'd over-romanticised the notion he'd had that morning of
coming to sacred ground to make his peace with God.

But something made him stay. The silence slowly settled him. He tried
closing his eyes for a while but got distracted by his thoughts. He opened
them again and focused on the candle, which symbolised the constant
presence of God.

*Are you here? Are you real or just a psychological construct – the opium of
the masses? I guess even if you're not real, living as if you are is a good way to
live. Faith, hope, love ... kindness, mercy, forgiveness ... all that good stuff. But that
would mean I'm just talking to myself now ...*

He waited, straining to sense a response. The candle flickered. The
silence wrapped more closely around him. Tentatively he continued, *I'm
scared that if I come back to you again, it won't be sustainable – like last time.
You know what I'm like – if you made me ... if you're there.*

I'd like to do better this time – be a better dad – a better man. Help me ... please ... If I could stay saturated with love, that would be so great ... maybe I'd make better choices ... I'd be able to resist temptation. I'm sorry for hurting Chloe ... why do we hurt the ones we love? I'm sorry for using Charmaine ... I know she was using me too ... but still ... I know it doesn't make what I did right. Help her. Help Chloe ... if you're there ....

His right knee began to hurt. He shifted his weight. He felt a slight gust of air on his cheek and immediately his nervous system tingled and the hair rose on the back of his neck. *Is that you?* he asked, closing his eyes and concentrating hard. He had the overwhelming feeling he was no longer alone. His heart rate accelerated. *God, I want to live for you ... do your will ... show me how ... fill me with your Spirit so I can do it.*

He became aware of a fragrance ... a very familiar fragrance. His eyes flew open and he turned around. There she was sitting just behind him on the first pew, her eyes closed and her head tilted slightly forward so that her hair obscured half of her face. 'Chloe?' he said incredulously.

She lifted her head. 'I thought it was you,' she smiled.

Mark laughed. 'You scared me! First I felt a breeze and then I had this unmistakable feeling I wasn't alone ... I really thought I was having a religious experience!'

'Nope ... just me,' she tucked her hair behind her ear.

'So what are you doing here during the day?' he asked getting up and coming to sit near her on the pew.

'I could ask you the same question,' she replied.

He looked embarrassed. 'I thought I'd make it formal – the thing that happened in the hospital with James the other day – I wanted to officially make my peace. Somehow I felt it had to be in a church – you know – on sacred ground.'

She nodded, 'That's good.'

'So why are *you* here?' he asked again.

She laughed dryly. 'I don't really know. I was on my way in to My Sister's House, when I just had this urge to come in here. I didn't even know if it would be open ... but it was ... and there you were ... I recognised you right away, but didn't want to disturb you.'

'Huh!' Mark looked at the floor then up at her face. 'I didn't ask you before, but what happened to your face?'

'Oh, I broke up a fight between two girls in the house. I caught my mole on someone's nails.'

'That must have hurt?' he grimaced.

'Yeah it did. I have to go to the Mole Clinic every day this week so they can keep an eye on it. I'm sure it'll be fine though,' she raised a hand and touched the dressing.

'You really must get some creatures in there,' his upper lip curled derisively.

Chloe looked at him wondering how he could be so judgemental, *Yeah – creatures like the woman you left me for!* She ranted in her head. *You weren't so judgmental back then, were you?* But she heard herself say, 'They're no different than you or I – they've just had a shitty hand of cards dealt them and are trying to make the most of what they've got. Sure some have made bad choices – but most of them have been at the mercy of someone else's bad choices – usually someone ruthlessly selfish and cruel.'

'Sorry ... you're right. I shouldn't have said that. Look at me! I'm a bit of a creature myself!'

Chloe smiled at him, wondering at the coincidence of their meeting in this place. 'At least you seem to be finding your way home ....'

He looked at her oddly, 'I don't suppose ... no ... never mind.'

'What?' Chloe asked.

'Well ... would you want to maybe have a drink with me later ... or something?'

She suddenly felt panicked. *Not again ... I can't do this again ... trust him only to be disappointed ... no ... I can't ...* she realised she hadn't said anything and was just staring at him. *Say something!* She yelled at herself. But she still didn't speak. A phrase came into her head, *'You don't have to earn forgiveness, but you do have to earn trust'.*

She took a deep breath and said, 'I don't know Mark. I ... I know it's weird that we met here today, and it's great about what's happening to you, but I've got to look after myself ... you know?'

He smiled bitterly, 'Once bitten, twice shy?'

'Something like that ... but it would be thrice shy, wouldn't it?'

She saw the shame in his eyes and regretted saying it.

✳   ✳   ✳

'Hi, Mel,' Chloe kissed her daughter in My Sister's House.

'Hi, Mum, you okay? You look a bit pale.'

'I felt prompted to go into the church just now ... and guess who was there? Your Dad!'

'What was he doing there?' Mel asked, surprised.

'Looked like he was praying,' Chloe raised her eyebrows incredulously.

'Well ... that's ... something!'

They both started to laugh at the same time.

'How strange,' Mel mused.

'Yeah! Anyway,' Chloe shrugged, trying to collect her wits. 'what's been happening here?'

'If you mean Charmaine – she's still here. She wants to see you.'

'Does she now? What if I don't want to see her?'

'It's your call ....'

'I'll think about it. Has Grace been in today?'

'Yes – she's upstairs with Gwen right now.'

'Right ... do you want a coffee?'

'Oh, yes please, thought you'd never ask!'

Chloe went into the kitchen and gazed out the window at the back garden as she waited for the kettle to boil. She heard footsteps on the stairs and lifted out two more mugs for Grace and Gwen. 'Coffee?' she called.

'Hot water for me,' Grace replied.

'Oh yes – you only drink green tea now, don't you?'

Grace came into the kitchen, 'Yep,' she said, tucking her shirt into her jeans.

'I couldn't give up coffee altogether. Don't know how you've done that?'

'I don't miss it,' Grace shrugged. 'Right ... I've just been with Charmaine. She says she wants to see you. What do you think?'

'Yeah – Mel said – I don't know, Grace.'

'I could facilitate?'

'Mmmm ....'

'Think about it.'

Chloe poured boiling water into one of the mugs and then the rest into a cafetiere. She watched the coffee granules swirl around before she slowly plunged. *What good would it serve? It would just churn up a whole load of stuff that's better left undisturbed.* She pushed the plunger hard, with some satisfaction, until all the grounds were trapped at the bottom.

✻   ✻   ✻

Mark anxiously checked the time again. It was nearly 7.30 p.m. He leaned down and looked into the oven – everything looked fine. His reflection came into focus on the glass oven door. He saw the anxiety in his expression, 'Catch a grip!' he said to himself, forcing a grin. 'Relax, it's going to be a good evening.'

The doorbell rang.

'Hi lads, come on in,' he said opening the door.

Jules followed Charlie, bottle of wine in hand. 'Thanks for having us,' Jules said.

'It's great you could come before you go back to uni,' Mark took the wine. 'Nice!' he smiled approvingly at the label.

'We like it, don't we?' Jules said.

Charlie turned from appraising the apartment to look at Jules and then his father. 'Yes – we do. It's a smooth one,' his expression was strained.

'Make yourselves at home – can I get you a beer or would you like some wine now?'

'I'll have a beer, thanks,' Charlie said awkwardly. 'Jules only drinks wine.'

'Okay – go on into the living room – I'll be in, in a sec.'

'So how's your day been?' Mark asked as he brought the drinks in.

'Fine,' Charlie replied tightly.

Jules leaned back on the sofa, trying hard to look relaxed, 'How about you?'

'I saw Mum today,' Mark replied too quickly, looking past Jules to Charlie, pathetically wanting his approval.

'Oh?' Charlie was surprised out of his guardedness.

'Yeah,' Mark grinned. 'I went into Grace's church to um ... to ... oh doesn't matter ... I had something I wanted to do there ... anyway ... and then your mum came in. Bit of a weird coincidence, but it was nice. We sat and talked for a while.'

'Did she know you were going to be there?' Charlie asked.

'Don't think so.'

'Bet she wouldn't have gone in if she had!'

'Charlie!' Jules exclaimed.

'I can't help it! I don't want to do this! This happy families bullshit – like nothing's happened – like we're just supposed to forget the past?' Charlie exploded.

'Charlie!' Jules said again in a despairing voice, 'We've not been here five minutes and already you've lost it!'

'It's okay Jules – it's okay Charlie – I'd far rather you be real than pretend anything. If you've got stuff you want to say to me, then say it. I know I've let you down. I know how angry you are ... and you have every right to be,' Mark leaned forward hoping Charlie would look him in the eye.

Instead he was glaring at the blank TV screen. There was a long silence in which Jules flicked his hair three times, glancing back and forth nervously between father and son. Then Charlie was on his feet, hands balled into fists at his sides. 'All my life I've wanted you to acknowledge me, to make time for me, to be interested in me ... and only now you decide to oblige? And you think I'm going to lap it up and be grateful?'

Mark looked up into the raging blue-green eyes, so like his own. 'No Charlie – not grateful – I don't want that – I just want a chance to make amends – to get to know you and make the most of the time we've got left.'

'What if I'm not interested? How does that feel?' Charlie's knuckles whitened.

'I wouldn't blame you.'

Charlie suddenly looked lost, his anger seeping away like a wave on sand. Jules reached out and took hold of one of his fists. 'Come and sit down Charlie, come on,' he urged. Charlie looked down at him and let him pull him back to the sofa. He sat there looking miserable, while Mark watched them, helpless to know what to do next.

It was Jules who broke the silence eventually. 'Well, this is fun,' he quipped. Charlie glanced sidelong at him and then at his dad.

'Look – none of us have done anything like this before,' Mark said. 'We're making it up as we go along ... let's just promise each other that whatever happens we'll try to be honest. I want a real relationship with you, Charlie. I never knew my dad ... could never know him ... I don't want that for you. Please don't say it's too late.'

Charlie looked at him properly, 'Well you're not going to like a lot of what I've got to say, but if you want honesty – you've got it! And if you can take it, maybe, just maybe we can start building some sort of relationship.'

'Okay … good … um … well is there anything you want to say now?'

'Yes. I want to know if you knew what I was before I did?'

Mark looked at Jules and then back at his son. He sighed, 'Probably … I don't think it was conscious … but, yeah, I probably did. What I do remember is how you were so close to Mum – you never seemed to want me – I kind of felt redundant.' He paused, searching for what he wanted to say. 'I think I was a bit jealous.' He saw the surprise on Charlie's face and hurried on to explain, 'I think I was jealous because I'd always wanted to be close to my mum, but never was – she was so depressed and withdrawn after Dad died. I felt like an orphan. Watching the way you were with Mum heightened my sense of loss and the unfairness of it all,' he looked at his hands and then at Charlie. 'I'm so sorry I was so immature – that I wasn't able to rise above it and be a father to you.'

Charlie looked bewildered. This was obviously not what he had expected to hear.

'God, I wish I could have a conversation like this with my dad!' Jules grinned at Mark.

'Me too,' Mark smiled back. 'Charlie – it's taken losing the love of my life, my career, my income and my self-respect to bring me to my senses. Apart from living on the streets, I don't think I could have got much lower.'

'The love of your life? Do you mean Charmaine?' the revulsion in Charlie's voice was undisguised.

'No,' laughed Mark, 'not Charmaine! Your mother has always been the love of my life.'

'So why did you leave her – leave us – for that – that girl?'

'I don't know … because I was an idiot! Because I knew I wasn't good enough for your mum.'

The look in Charlie's eyes said, 'Yeah – you're not!'

'Thanks for not agreeing out loud!' Mark smiled wryly.

A very faint smile skimmed Charlie's lips.

'Oh shit! The lamb!' Mark jumped to his feet as they all became aware of the acrid smell coming from the kitchen.

Dear Grace,

I cannot begin to express to you how sorry I am for the strain I put you under on that significant interview day. My behaviour was inexcusable. I hope you will find it in your heart to eventually forgive me.

As you know, I have taken early retirement. Losing self-control in the way I did, caused me to realise how badly Wendy's illness and prognosis has affected me. In a way, I am grateful. I hope that doesn't sound too strange?

I hope you will accept the call to interview for my job. As you know, I think you will make a fantastic bishop.

We are going to the Wye Valley, to the cottage we own there. It's where we got engaged. Wendy has wanted to go there for some time now. It's a short drive to Bristol and the University Hospital if she does suddenly deteriorate and need help.

Please be assured of my prayerful support as you go through the process ahead of you.

Yours always,

Duncan

Grace lifted the letter to her nose. It smelt of lavender and leather. She smiled. She pulled a piece of paper out of her printer, pushing her laptop out of the way and picking up her pen.

Dear +Duncan

Thank you for your letter.

There is nothing to forgive.

I have accepted the invitation to interview. I can't quite believe it is happening! Peter said he'd have to go as a tart to any Bishops and Tarts parties, and I said I could go as both! I thought that might make you smile.

Please know that you and Wendy are in my thoughts and prayers as you go through this very difficult and painful time.

Yours truly,

Grace

She pulled her perfume bottle out of her handbag and sprayed the letter with her scent. She put it in an envelope, addressed and stamped it and went to post it straight away.

As she was returning from the post box, her mobile phone rang. It was Chloe.

'You better get over here now!'

'Why? What's happening?' Grace quickened her pace.

'Charmaine is ....' The phone went dead.

'Chloe? Chloe?' Grace started to run.

She burst into My Sister's House, shouting, 'Chloe? Where are you?' Coming into the office she saw Charmaine had Chloe pinned up against the wall, with Anne desperately wrestling to trying to break the girl's grip around Chloe's neck.

'Charmaine, stop it! What are you doing? Have you gone completely mad? Let her go right now! Right now!' Grace yelled.

It was enough to distract Charmaine, giving Anne the chance to break her stranglehold. Both she and Grace had Charmaine on the floor in a second, while Chloe gasped for air and staggered to the kitchen.

'Calm down, Charmaine! Calm down!' Grace instructed as she held the girl's hands behind her back. 'You do not want the police involved, do you? So pull yourself together, or I swear I will call them.'

'Okay, okay!' Charmaine finally capitulated.

'God, you're strong!' Anne gasped.

'Now are you going to behave if I let you go?' Grace demanded.

'Yes,' Charmaine said into the carpet.

'If you make one wrong move – I'm calling the police, do you hear? And that'll be it for you! So I'm letting go now. I want you to sit up slowly – no fast moves.'

'Yeah, yeah.' Charmaine sat up, pushing her long blonde hair back off her face.

'Right – sit over there,' Grace pointed to a chair on the far side of Mel's desk. Charmaine obeyed.

'So what the hell was that all about?' Anne asked, sitting beside her, blocking her in.

Grace meanwhile went into the kitchen after Chloe. 'You okay?' she came and put her arm around her shoulders.

'Yes ... just about.'

'What happened?'

'She just went for me ... she came in saying she wanted to talk to me. I said I didn't want to listen to her. I phoned you, and she went for me ... that was it!'

'Ooh ... you're going to have bruising!' Grace traced where Charmaine's hands had been round Chloe's throat.

'That's the least of my worries,' Chloe turned the tap on and poured herself a glass of water.

'Do you want to go out the back way?' Grace asked.

Chloe looked at her and thought for a moment, 'No,' she said finally, 'Now you're here ... I might as well hear what she's got to say.'

'You sure?'

'Yeah – I think she just saw red when I said I wasn't going to listen to her.'

'Well ... I don't know how wise this is ... if there's even a hint of her kicking off again, I want you to run for the door. You sit at Gwen's desk – it's closest to the hallway.'

'Okay,' Chloe said, finishing her drink and rubbing her neck again.

They came back into the office together to find Charmaine crying on Anne's shoulder.

They exchanged bemused looks as they took their seats. Charmaine heard them come in and sat up, wrapping shreds of dignity around herself as she wiped her face with the backs of her hands. Grace handed her a box of tissues from her desk to mop up the smeared mascara.

Chloe was the one to break the silence. 'So what did you want to say to me?'

With the make-up gone, Charmaine looked almost innocent. Crying had left her vulnerable. She looked like a child.

Gazing at Chloe she said, 'I was trying to do you a favour – trying to be nice to you and you wouldn't let me – you wouldn't listen! It was like you were throwing anything good I had to offer back in my face ... like my best wasn't good enough!'

Surprised Chloe said, 'And you thought going for my throat would make me listen?'

'No,' Charmaine swore, 'I just got mad.'

'Yes – yes you did,' Chloe agreed sarcastically.

Charmaine couldn't help smiling. 'I've always had a temper. Your Mark hated it.'

Chloe shifted in her seat uncomfortably, 'He's not mine.'

'That's what I wanted to tell you – he is yours – he always will be. He never loved me. It was just sex.'

A red rash crept up Chloe's already mottled neck. She pursed her lips.

'I thought you should know. That's all.'

Grace watched Chloe heroically struggle to overcome a variety of emotions. She found herself praying in tongues for her, leaning forward and willing her to shine in this most bizarre of all circumstances.

Chloe's eyes brimmed with tears as she asked, 'Why did you settle for that Charmaine?'

It was the girl's turn to look surprised. 'Settle for what? Just sex? What do you care?' she retorted.

A tear spilled over and down Chloe's cheek. 'I shouldn't care – you're the reason my whole world was destroyed. It's been five hard years for my kids and me. I shouldn't give a shit about you ... but yet here I am wondering why such a beautiful girl like you would settle for just sex and not hold out for love as well.'

Charmaine shrugged, as if refusing to bear the weight of responsibility Chloe was throwing her way. 'What is love anyway?'

The tears were falling down Chloe's face by this time. Grace realised as she watched that something more was going on. Her praying intensified. She looked over at Anne and saw that something similar was happening in her. Her eyes were glistening as her lips moved in silent prayer.

'Would you really like to know what love is?' Chloe asked, brushing the tears away.

'Why are you crying? You're not crying for yourself … are you? Are you crying for me?' Charmaine looked indignant.

Chloe didn't answer – she just held her gaze. Grace was forcibly struck by the love that was pouring through Chloe. She could see the effect it was having on Charmaine. The girl was wrestling fiercely to keep her defences up, but was losing the battle. Grace marveled at the miracle she was witnessing – it wasn't humanly possible.

Charmaine buckled, curling in on herself. Her hands went around her head, pulling it down to her knees, which rose to meet it. She toppled off the chair and onto the floor at Anne's feet, letting out an anguished wail. Anne got down beside her, as the two other women drew near, praying all the time.

They ministered love to Charmaine like that for over an hour. They didn't stop praying until she stopped crying and her whole body relaxed. When she finally opened her eyes and looked up at them in bewilderment, she asked, 'What was that?'

'The love of God,' said Chloe.

※ ※ ※

Grace was so nervous that she couldn't seem to get her collar into her clergy shirt. She stood at the vestry mirror wondering how the stupid thing had suddenly got too big for the slots it normally slid into around her neck. She could feel perspiration breaking out on her forehead and under her arms. She wanted to scream with frustration. The Church Warden came in to pray with her, and finally the collar submitted and slid in.

'Would you pray?' Grace asked. The Warden was a little taken aback, unused to taking the lead, but nodded and committed the funeral service, the bereaved family and friends into God's hands. He finally prayed for peace and clarity of thought for Grace. She held out her hands, desperate for those things, but felt no different.

'Right – here we go,' she said pragmatically. The Warden went ahead into the church and down the aisle to wait with her for the coffin to arrive. As Grace came behind him, she caught Peter's eye. He and Zack were sitting in the front row on the far side of the church. Their presence comforted her. As she passed Marie and the children on the other side of

240

the central isle, she gently touched her on the arm and they exchanged a little smile.

Chloe sat a few rows behind the family, with Mel and the staff and trustees of My Sister's House. Charlie and Jules had come too, and sat behind Chloe, with Josh and his girlfriend in support of Chloe. There were also people Grace didn't know – business types in expensive suits and even some doctors from the hospital. Her eyes scanned them and moved on to Omar and his entire family, sitting near the back, with many other Street Pastors. Grace smiled at Anne among them, and was amazed to see Charmaine there beside her. She came and stood next to Mark who was waiting at the door to bear James's body in. 'You okay?' she whispered.

'Not really ... Do you know Charmaine – my ex – is here?'

'Yes.'

'If Chloe and the kids realise – they will freak out!

'It's going to be okay,' Grace whispered sounding more confident than she felt. She squeezed his hand as they watched the hearse, full of red roses, pull up. As Mark shouldered the coffin with the other men, Grace took a deep breath, focusing herself to lead them in with the Anglican funeral sentences. In a loud voice she began to read as she walked:

'I am the resurrection and the life, says the Lord: he that believes in me, though he were dead, yet shall he live: and whoever lives and believes in me shall never die.

I know that my Redeemer lives and that he shall stand on the last day upon the earth. And though this body decays, yet shall I see God.

We brought nothing into this world, and it is certain we can carry nothing out. The Lord gave, and the Lord has taken away; blessed be the Name of the Lord.

Man that is born of a woman has but a short time to live, and is full of misery. He comes up, and is cut down, like a flower; his life is fleeting as if he were a shadow.

In the midst of life we are in death: of whom may we seek for comfort, but from you, O Lord?

I heard a voice from heaven, saying to me, Write: From now on blessed are the dead which die in the Lord: even so says the Spirit: for they rest from their labours.'

She was acting a part in a play, she thought. Relieved she introduced two of James's business colleagues and his eldest son to do readings. Then Anne, Omar and Mark stood to speak in turn.

Anne and Omar talked of their experiences with him as a Street Pastor; how they had both volunteered for the work because of him; how terribly the assault on his life had affected them; how tragic a waste the last five years he had spent in a coma had been; how deeply impacted they were by his return to consciousness; how he had told them, with his one-finger-typing, of the things he'd seen while asleep; and how confidently they believed he was now with his Lord in glory.

Mark's speech was different. He came to the microphone, clearing his throat nervously. 'I really only got to know James recently in hospital,' he began. 'I had met him another lifetime ago – shortly after he must have become a Christian. He offered me help with something I was struggling with – something we both struggled with. But I foolishly refused it.

'This led to the utter destruction of my life as I knew it. I cannot tell you how many times I have wished over the years that I had taken hold of the hand of friendship he offered me back then,' Mark sighed, shaking his head.

'But, as many of you will know, James was a determined kind of guy,' a ripple of laughter went through the congregation. 'It's probably what made him so good at business, along with many other characteristics and attributes.

'Anyway ... he hung in there ... in a coma for five years, waiting for the time when I would be ready to accept his help.

'I lost my job in the city and ended up finding work as a porter in the local hospital. God, it was hard donning that uniform every day!' he shook his head. 'But it was then, as a porter, that I met James again and my real friendship with him began. Maybe I had to be humbled first before I could receive the love letter he'd become?

'Anyway ... he told me that Jesus had sent him back for a little while ... for me, to help me come home,' Mark's voice cracked with emotion. He cleared his throat. 'I didn't believe him at first ... I didn't want to,' he looked around the congregation. 'But I had hit rock bottom, and he was there for me, as trapped in his body as I was in my self-inflicted circumstances.'

Mark looked at Marie and smiled. 'Just before he died, he told Marie that angels were in his room, waiting to usher the Kingdom in. She thought he meant that they'd come to take him. But they hadn't – they'd come for me. When I visited him that day something very strange happened. I was overcome with what I can only describe as the most wonderful experience of being loved I have ever known.'

You could hear a pin drop, the congregation was absolutely riveted. 'I cried like a baby, then laughed for ... oh I don't know how long! I had no idea of the passing of time. In fact it was two hours later before I was able to get up and walk out of James's hospital room.'

Mark paused. Then, 'James died shortly after that. I never got to speak with him again. I guess he'd completed his mission and was glad to go. He's free now.' Mark's smile lit up his entire face. 'And if I know him, he's up there climbing waterfalls like Bear Grylls.'

Another ripple of laughter went through the church.

'Well, thanks to you James, my life has changed,' he looked at the coffin then up to the vaulted ceiling of the church. 'I've come home ... home to God ... to my true self as His son. If it weren't for you, I don't think I would ever have found my way back again – I was so lost. So thank you for the sacrifices you made.' He turned to Marie and said, 'And thank you Marie. None of us understands the big picture – the grand scheme of things – we just have to walk obediently, with enough light for our part of the jigsaw. You did that so faithfully. You are an amazing woman and I want you to know that you have a friend in me for life. I will never be able to repay the debt I owe to you and James, but I'm damn well looking forward to trying.'

Grace rose as Mark went back to his seat. She walked to the altar and silently prepared the elements of the Eucharist. She was glad of the ritual. It gave everyone time to process what they'd heard and to open themselves up to the possibility of the Presence of God.

After she broke the bread she looked out across the sea of faces, 'Some of you may not be comfortable with receiving communion. Perhaps you never have before or you don't know what you believe about God, or His Son Jesus. Please come forward with your service sheet and I will know to simply pray a blessing upon you. Please don't count yourselves out, please make the most of this opportunity.

'However, if there are any here today, who like Mark, would like to "come home", as he put it so aptly, then I invite you to receive this bread and this wine. The Lord is here by His Holy Spirit. We cannot apprehend

Him with these eyes. But we can with our hearts, with this intuitive organ, that knows we were born for more than this. Come home sons. Come home daughters,' she smiled, elated in her role as priest.

'So draw near with faith,' she stretched her arms out wide, 'receive the body of our Lord Jesus Christ, which He gave for you and His blood, which He shed for you. Eat and drink in remembrance that He died for you, and feed on Him in your hearts, by faith.'

The sides-people stood at the end of each isle, ushering people forward. Not one person stayed in their seat.

Grace prayed: *Let me be hidden in you, in your goodness. Cover me, my failures, my weaknesses, my wrongdoing. Use me for your glory Lord. Pour through me so they encounter you, not me.*

Marie prayed: *Make his life count. Make my sufferings count. Don't waste any of them. Feed your lambs, call them by name and help them hear your voice.*

Tell James I love him. Tell him I'm proud of him and that I can't wait to see him again and be held by him, to run with him and see him laugh.

Chloe prayed: *He'd have to earn it ... I can't just trust him because of this. I've heard him be eloquent in church before ... I couldn't let his unguarded weaknesses hurt me again. Please make your power perfect in him. Please heal me more, so that I could at least begin thinking about it.*

He is so gorgeous ... why can't he be an ugly, old boot?

Is he really mine?

There's no one else for me, I'm sure of that.

Mark prayed: *Father, please replace the years that have been wasted. Thank you that you promised to give me what I don't deserve. I can hardly believe that you would, but if James was sure about it, I can be too. Show me how to win Chloe ... if she will let me. Help Charlie forgive me ... help us love each other. And Charmaine ... why is she here? I suppose you love her too. I'm so sorry I used her and that I didn't help her discover who she really is or what she's really worth. Please help her find you too and herself.*

Charmaine prayed: *God, I need a drink! This is freaking me out! Did all that really happen? All that stuff Mark said? He's such a bullshitter – I know what he's like. Or maybe I just know one side of him. Maybe there is more to him? Well, if you're there God, if you don't mind broken things, take me. I've never felt love like this before … that's for sure. It's better than any high I've ever had.*

Charlie prayed: *Don't know if you want me … or Jules … I've heard you don't … but Grace doesn't seem to be saying that. I like the God she worships … I'm not sure if you're the same in other churches? Anyway … if you can accept Dad, you can accept anyone! Help me want to forgive him … part of me does already … but I'm still not sure he's for real. We'll see ….*

As they received communion the song 'Grace' by U2 played over the sound system. The last line lingered in the air, *'Grace makes beauty out of ugly things.'*

✖   ✖   ✖

Later that night Grace sat at her desk gazing at James's funeral service sheet. She had done it … and done it well. She felt pleased and smiled to herself. She said a prayer for Marie and the children and was about to shut her computer and join Peter in bed, when Lila and her children came strongly to mind. She went to her writing document and read what she'd last written. As ever she could not resist the temptation to slip into that other world.

✹   ✹   ✹

'Mama, I believe the Lord is calling me to return to Jerusalem.'

'What?' Lila asked in a shocked voice.

'Yes … I keep dreaming I am in the Temple praying. I have shared my visions with Luke and he agrees with me that he thinks it is the Lord. He is on his way back to Paul in Rome, but I must go home – back to Israel.'

'Joshua, my son,' Lila dropped her voice almost to a whisper. 'Jerusalem is being destroyed from within and without. War has broken out and terrible things have happened – things that are unspeakable! You cannot go there. It would be madness!'

'I have come to you to ask you to pray, along with Mary and

Timothy. I do not wish to go – for I have heard the stories just as you have. With all my heart I wish to stay here with you and Timothy and work to bring Anna back. But the only safe place is to be in God's hands. You have taught me that. I do not want to disobey – to step out of his protective hands. So please seek the Lord with me – see if this is of him or not.'

A long forgotten childhood memory suddenly came to Lila's mind. That terrible day in the Temple courts with Grandma – the day she had died! A sudden rush of grief overwhelmed her. The old man – her Grandma's friend – what was his name? Simeon – that's right. He had taken a baby in his arms, just after he had been dedicated at the altar. The young mother had watched as first Simeon and then her Grandma prophesied over the child. *'This child is destined to cause the falling and rising of many in Israel, and to be a sign that is spoken against, so that the thoughts of many hearts will be revealed. And a sword will pierce your own soul too.'*

She now knew for certain that the baby had been Jesus. Mary, his mother, had confirmed the story. The prophecy was about him. But it was the last line, which echoed through every fibre of her being now as she looked at her beautiful son's face. *'A sword will piece your soul too.'*

It was too much. She had lost her daughter and now was being asked to give up her son? *No!* she cried internally. *How can you ask this of me?*

Joshua saw the struggle in her eyes, 'I will wait for you to hear from the Lord, Mama. Please promise me you will seek him?'

She nodded her head reluctantly. She had modelled a life of obedience to him. What else could she do?

❊ ❊ ❊

More and more people had been gathering to the meetings Aaron held in his home. He had grown financially wealthy through payments for his cures and exorcisms. His power and influence had woven their way throughout the Church. Not only did he have a strong following among Neo's friends and acquaintances, but since

Anna had come to live with him, word had spread, and many of the young women had joined them also, not all with pious motives it must be said, but some with the hope of catching a husband.

Timothy, Lila, Mary and the other Church leaders could only watch, fast and pray as disunity spread through the Church in Ephesus. This added to the distress Timothy felt over the death of their baby and the effect it had had on Anna. He wrote of what had transpired to Paul, asking for help.

Anna refused point blank to see Timothy or her mother. Aaron made sure she was guarded at all times, even on her frequent visits to Aurelia at the Temple of Artemis. No one could get near her. Mary commented that he had successfully kidnapped her a second time. It broke Lila's heart.

In his old age, Aaron had become fixated with Anna. His mind was not as sharp as it once had been and his involvement in magic had blurred many of his boundaries. He was greatly influenced by his daughter. Many an evening they would sit together and discuss new ideas late into the night. Their thinking grew around Judaism, combining the teachings of Artemis with the teachings of the Old Testament and the new spiritual insights Aaron was discovering.

'I think Eve is much more important than we have realised,' Anna said one evening. 'She was the seeker of knowledge, wasn't she?'

'Yes,' Aaron agreed, 'You identify with her, don't you? You know what it is like to have been deceived by those you loved and trusted. Perhaps now your mission in life is to seek the real truth and to reject much of what you have grown up with?'

'One of the ideas I've had is around the whole creation story,' Anna said.

'Tell me,' Aaron smiled indulgently.

'I think Eve should be seen as the "illuminator" of mankind because she was the first to receive "true knowledge" from the Serpent who was the revealer of truth. I'm beginning to believe that maybe Eve enlightened Adam, and being the mother of all, was the progenitor of the human race. I wonder if Adam was Eve's son rather than her husband?'

'That would tie in with the goddess cult beliefs you've been learning about. Artemis bringing forth children without male involvement,' Aaron stroked his beard as he explored her idea intellectually.

'I also wonder whether physical matter is actually evil and that only the world of the spirit is good?' Anna ventured further. 'Do you think perhaps God made a mistake in creating the material universe and therefore he calls us to focus only on the spiritual?'

'What an interesting idea,' Aaron mused.

It wasn't long before Anna's ideas got a wider audience at Aaron's gatherings.

Timothy eventually received a reply from Paul, who encouraged him to confront the problem of false doctrines head on. He told him to forbid certain people, even if it was his wife, from peddling false teachings in the Church and to admonish others to turn away from myths and endless genealogies. He told him to oppose those who spoke falsely of the living God, to warn people about what he called doctrines of demons and stupid, senseless controversies, and have nothing to do with old wives' tales such as the corrupted story of Adam and Eve. He urged Timothy to use the Scriptures as an antidote for sound teaching, reproof, correction, and training in righteousness.

So Timothy called a gathering of the citywide Church. He and the other Church leaders fasted that week, praying fervently that Aaron and Anna would attend with their growing following. They prayed in particular for Anna that she would realise how deeply she had been deceived. They booked the lecture hall of Tyrannus, where Paul had first brought the gospel to Ephesus and prayer-walked around it, asking for the same authority that he had had.

When everyone was gathered, Timothy stood to read from Paul's letter. He was feeling faint from lack of food, but energised in his spirit. It had been so long since he had seen Anna that he could not tear his eyes from her beautiful face. He fought to control his emotions, for when she met his gaze, her eyes were cold and hard.

Lila sat near Timothy with Mary on one side of her and Priscilla and Aquilla on the other side. They did not cease praying in tongues throughout the entire gathering. Lila looked at Anna twice, but it was too painful for her. She noticed how frail Aaron looked, yet even so he struck fear in her.

Oh Lord, how has it come to this? How could you let him take her from us again? Please Lord, open the eyes of her heart ... she is a grown woman now. I cannot rescue her. She needs to come back to Timothy and the children of her own volition.

Timothy started reading out Paul's letter. 'Paul, an apostle of Christ Jesus by the command of God, our Saviour and of Christ Jesus our hope.'

He read Paul's opening warnings against false teachers of the Law, making a point of looking at Aaron several times. He read about the grace Paul had received even though he was the worst of sinners and about those who had shipwrecked their faith. Again he paused and looked at Aaron.

He came to the section for instructions on gatherings for worship and read, 'In this present situation I am not allowing a woman to teach or to claim to be the author or the originator of man, but she must be in agreement with the Scriptures and with sound teaching in the Church. For it was Adam who was first created, and then Eve. Eve was not the "illuminator," and carrier of new revelation. And it was not Adam who was deceived, but the woman being deceived, who fell into transgression.'

Timothy fixed his gaze on Anna, pleading with her to listen and repent. Before he could go on Lila was on her feet, 'Anna, my love,' she cried, 'please listen – in your grief you have given the devil a foothold. Please come back to us. Your children need you. They miss you terribly. We all do. Please, Anna ... your mind has been confused by sorrow. Darkness like a flood has poured into your thinking ... please ...' she broke off, unable to speak any more for crying. Mary held her as she collapsed into her arms.

Ripples of concern broke out among the people. Timothy waited for a moment until he had regained his composure and then called the meeting to order to continue reading the letter.

He eventually came to the final charge, 'Timothy, guard what has been entrusted to your care. Turn away from godless chatter and the opposing ideas of what is falsely called knowledge, which some have professed and in so doing have wandered from the faith. Grace be with you.'

Timothy raised his head and scanned the crowded lecture hall. His eyes settled upon Anna again. 'We will get copies of Paul's letter out to all of you as quickly as possible. Please be prayerful as you consider the things Paul has said. Please remember that we are being built into the living temple in which God makes his home. Please flee from what is evil, cling to what is good.' He raised his hand for the final blessing, invoking the grace of God to fall upon the Church and enable them to hold to the truth of the Gospel of Christ.

Afterwards through the milling crowd, Lila saw Anna approaching her. Her heart soared, 'Oh Anna!' she cried, only for the sound to die in her throat. The cold, hard look was still in her daughter's eyes.

'Where is Joshua? Why is he not here?' she asked abruptly.

Lila gazed at her in dismay, 'He has gone.'

'Where?' Anna demanded, 'Back to Rome – to Paul? Why did no one inform me?'

'We cannot inform you of anything – Aaron has you so well guarded and I suppose you have not received any of my messages that I have sent?'

'What messages?' Anna frowned. 'You're just saying that to make me doubt my father.'

Lila winced. 'No – I have written to you every few days since you left. I have delivered each one to Aaron's door. He must have kept them from you.'

Anna looked momentarily uncertain, then rallied. 'So when did my brother go to Rome? He is the only one among you that I trust. I wish to speak to him about these things,' she gestured in Timothy's direction who was carefully rolling up Paul's letter.

'He has not gone to Rome, my love,' Lila said quietly, 'he has gone back to Jerusalem, to intercede in the Temple during Passover.'

Lila watched the colour drain from her daughter's face. Her lips parted in shock. 'Jerusalem? But it is not safe – there is no hope for it. Why did you let him go?' she cried.

'He believed the Lord was calling him. I could not stop him.'

'When did he go?'

'Two days ago.'

With that Anna turned and walked away. Lila watched her as a sword cruelly twisted in her soul.

※ ※ ※

Timothy woke in a pool of sweat, his breathing ragged, his heart pounding. He lay still trying to remember where he was. As he came into full consciousness, wiping his brow with the back of his hand, relieved that it had only been a dream. He got up and began pacing the room, thinking through the details of it.

He'd been in a boat, a storm surging round him. He'd been leaning out the bow shouting her name. Yes ... Anna ... shouting Anna's name. Ahead, barely visible through the spray and waves, another boat bobbed at the mercy of the elements. She was in it ... but where was she going? Could she hear him shouting?

He left his room and went down the corridor to Lila's bedchamber. He knocked softly on her door, and as if she too had been awake she opened it almost instantly. 'I had a dream ... about Anna,' he said.

'I haven't been able to sleep too, thinking about her and praying,' Lila responded. 'Come in. What was the dream?'

Timothy told her and she agreed that it sounded like it could be some kind of premonition. 'What shall we do?' she asked.

'I'm going to Aaron's house – he will know where she is going.'

'I'll come with you,' Lila said. Timothy knew not to argue with his mother-in-law and respectfully waited out in the hallway for her to get ready.

When she emerged she said, 'Maybe she has followed Joshua to Israel?'

'I wondered that myself,' Timothy replied as they made their way through the dark streets of Ephesus. When they reached Aaron's house, Timothy knocked firmly on the polished wooden door. Eventually a servant girl came and opened it to them.

'Oh I'm so glad you're here – how did you know?' she asked.

'Know what?' Timothy enquired cautiously.

'Aaron is dying – I thought that was why you are here?'

'Dying? But we only saw him this morning at the lecture hall,' Lila said, then she remembered how frail he had looked.

'Follow me,' said the girl, leading with a lamp through the wide hallways and arches of Aaron's beautiful home. They came to his bedchamber and on entering saw him lying on his bed with his wife, Leah attending him. His breathing was shallow and his skin slick with fever sweat. Timothy came and knelt by his head, while Lila remained at the foot of the bed. He took his head in his hands and called his name. But Aaron did not respond.

'When did this start?' Timothy asked Leah.

'When the girl left,' Leah replied dully. 'He loved her more than any of the children I bore him. He was obsessed with her. When she left it was as if the life went from him.'

Timothy studied her face, 'Do you know where she went?' he asked softly.

'No,' she replied. 'I don't know and I don't care.'

Lila felt the woman's bitterness like the cut of a switch on the palms of her hands. She flinched but held her tongue.

Timothy slapped Aaron softly several times on both cheeks, calling his name. Slowly his eyes slid open, looking at them vacantly at first. Then as they focused on Lila at the end of the bed, a faint smile graced his lips. 'So eager,' he whispered.

Lila felt the heat flush up her neck.

'Where is Anna?' Timothy asked in a loud, clear voice.

'So beautiful ... like her mother,' Aaron sighed, his eyes rolling in his head.

Timothy held Aaron's face between his hands and asked again, 'Where has Anna gone?'

'Home ... gone back home,' he struggled for breath.

'When did she go?' Timothy demanded.

'Before sunset,' Leah informed them. 'She took one of our
manservants with her.'

Timothy dropped Aaron's head back onto the pillow and started
to stand up, but Aaron's hand reached out and caught his sleeve,
'Pray for me ... full of sin ... pray ...' he gasped.

Each person present thought of the wrongs this man had done
them and knew the time had come to forgive. No one struggled
more than Lila.

Timothy looked down on him and thought of Paul – one of the
worst of sinners. What if he had never been forgiven? He wrestled
with his own desire for justice, relinquishing it eventually to the
One in whom he knew justice and mercy would meet. He placed
his hand on Aaron's head and said, 'You are forgiven in the name
of Jesus, who died to carry all your sin upon himself, so you might
enter into eternal life. I forgive you your sins against me, against the
Church and against my wife and children. Go in peace,' he made the
sign of the cross on his forehead.

Lila whispered, 'Go meet your Maker.'

Leah said nothing aloud.

Aaron lay inert, his breathing growing shallower and shallower,
until finally it stopped.

Silence hung between them. Then Timothy committed his soul
into the Lord's keeping. He stood up and came to stand next to Lila
who gazed down on Aaron's body. It looked less and less like him
as the moments passed.

You woke me,' she said to him silently, *'made me come alive – you
gave me Anna – and you brought me to Jesus' feet.*

You deceived me and disillusioned me.

But because you did, I was able to value true love.

You stole Anna from us.

*You endorsed Stephen's death and funded Saul's persecution of the
Church before he changed his name to Paul.*

Yet God has used everything you fashioned against us to prosper us.

You were a tool in His hands.

*And yet again you tried to destroy the Church here from the inside –
through disunity and through taking advantage of Anna in her grief.*

Yet still you will not prevail. The Church will be cleansed of false teaching and will unite in our love for Christ.

Anna WILL come back to her senses and we WILL find her.

Truly the Lord is in control even of you, the most skilful of politicians, the craftiest of schemers.

She closed her eyes, *Goodbye Aaron. May the Lord have mercy on your soul.*

Sensing she had finished doing business with God, Timothy gently took her arm and led her to the door as Leah and the servant girl began their preparations for burial.

They made their way back home in urgent silence, each pre-occupied with their own thoughts.

❋ ❋ ❋

'Nothing you can say will deter me,' Lila said.

Timothy frowned. He knew how stubborn she could be, 'But what about the children?' he asked.

'Mary will look after them, won't you, Mary?' Lila fixed her friend with a fierce look.

'Yes – I'm sure Priscilla and Ruth will help me. We'll be fine – you go!' Mary shooed them with her hands.

'But, Lila ... it will be dangerous and the trip itself is arduous enough. Please think sensibly about this. Let me go and bring them back to you,' Timothy pleaded.

Lila shook her head, 'No, Timothy. I am coming with you and that is the end of the matter.'

And so it was that they boarded a ship bound for Israel in the breaking dawn.

❋ ❋ ❋

The last time Lila had been in Israel was just as the troubles were brewing in Jerusalem. Yearning for solid ground, she gazed at Caesarea's coastline as their ship approached and wondered what awaited them.

Like everyone else, she had heard the news of the greed of the Roman governors, which had driven many of the Judaean aristocracy to join forces with the religious rebellion. She knew that Aaron had departed shortly after, leaving behind him everything he had worked so hard for. Some of his aristocratic friends, such as the historian Josephus, had chosen to defect to Rome rather than join the rebellion, whereas his choice had been, like theirs, a new life in Ephesus.

The rebels, who were left, were a mix of religious Jews and bandits, exploiting the decline of Nero's reign and the chaos that followed his suicide. They wanted to expel the Romans and establish an independent Jewish state, based round the Temple. But, as Aaron had expected, the Jewish revolt immediately started to implode, with bloody in-fighting and gang-warfare.

While Lila and Jair had made their new life in Ephesus, three emperors followed Nero in quick succession and when Vespasian finally emerged as emperor and dispatched his son, Titus, to take control of Jerusalem, the city was divided between three warlords.

Lila had heard how these warlords fought against each other in the Temple courts, causing them to be awash with blood. She'd heard how they had plundered the city, ransacking the richer neighbourhoods and turning the city into a brothel and torture chamber all at once – while still keeping it functioning as a shrine.

How she would find Joshua and Anna in an unrecognisable Jerusalem, she did not know. How could they possibly be safe and alive amidst such madness?

She knew that despite all of this, many pilgrims from around the Mediterranean would still have arrived in April for the Passover. Her son was one of them, with her daughter in hot pursuit. Jerusalem's population would be swollen to hundreds of thousands of people. She prayed they would be guided through the chaos.

Lila thought of Anna arriving there before them. She wondered what her next move had been. Would she have sought out Junia's help, in the same way as they were about to? As the ship docked, she prayed fervently that she had.

10. STANDING

Ephesians 6:10–24

*Therefore put on the full armour of God, so that when the day
of evil comes, you may be able to stand your ground,
and after you have done everything, to stand.*

Women had never been ordained priests in St Paul's Cathedral, let alone Bishops. Bishop Duncan, the Suffragan Bishop of the episcopal area, had ordained Grace to the priesthood in St Matt's Church. Her ordination to the diaconate had been a far more moving event in St Paul's Cathedral. She had felt short-changed that she'd been barred from the Cathedral for her priesting, by nature of her sex (although no one would ever openly admit that this was the true reason).

But finally the times had changed, and here she was. She had to pinch herself to make sure it was really happening. The atmosphere was electric as the congregation waited to consecrate their first woman bishop in the Diocese of London. The press had clamoured outside for photos and sound bites. She was glad to be past them and inside the hushed, vaulted, awe inspiring sacred space. She took a deep breath and calmed herself, wanting to savour every moment.

The organ struck its first dramatic note and the congregation stood to sing with the choir. The procession began, leading Grace to her destiny of deeper self-sacrifice. *Why have they barred women from this for so long? We're so good at self-sacrifice!* She smiled to herself as she walked, kicking her purple robe before her with each step.

She thought of Lila and Mary and all the women she'd studied in the

New Testament who had given their lives for the cause of the Gospel. She smiled again at the foolish arguments around Junia, whom Paul described as being outstanding among the apostles.

As she drew near the central dais she pictured Henry Moore's sculpture of 'Mother and Child', hidden from view in the north choir isle. She'd gone to see the seven-foot high sculpture in beautiful Italian marble many times. She thought of Jesus' mother, Mary, living out her days in Ephesus with the apostle John, helping him write his Gospel.

Her eye caught Zack's as she came level with the front row. He winked at her. She smiled. Peter's gaze overwhelmed her — the pride and pleasure she saw there choked her. She cleared her throat and blinked hard as she took in her mother's elegant pale yellow hat sweeping down to one side of her immaculate head. When their eyes met she saw the conflict in her mother: pleasure in her girl, but embarrassment too; delighting in her strong identity, yet still wanting male affirmation for her; fearful of those who would certainly reject her because of her role, yet proud of her achievement.

She'll always be conflicted, Grace thought. *I've done everything I can ... I just have to stand in my identity and hope I will help her find hers.*

The hymn ended. The liturgy began. Archbishop Justin said, 'Blessed be God, Father, Son and Holy Spirit.'

The congregation responded, 'Blessed be his kingdom, now and forever. Amen.' The collective sound echoed through the huge marbled space, sending tingles down Grace's spine.

After the introduction the Bishop of London presented her to Archbishop Justin. Beside him she felt small, an unusual experience for her. His huge frame and deep voice somehow comforted her. He made her think of the apostle Peter and how, when he'd raised Tabitha from the dead, he'd restored Mary to her right mind. *Give me a sound mind, O God,* she prayed.

After the readings Bishop Duncan slowly climbed the steps to the lectern to speak. Grace was among the few who knew he had come from Wendy's hospital bedside especially for this occasion. She felt deeply grateful to Wendy for sending him to be with her on this day. They held each other's gaze for a split-second before he began, and in that moment she knew she would always love him.

'You have given yourself whole-heartedly to Christ and His Church,' he said, 'serving His people as a deacon and priest — teaching the Scriptures and pastoring with that disarming directness — a directness, which speaks the truth in love, with a wonderful sense of humour.

'You have demonstrated your love for God in your hard work, as a parish priest and in your charitable work. Your vision to see My Sister's Houses spring up in every diocese is ambitious, but it has already begun to be realised. You are a champion of women and of those who are oppressed and we look forward to how you will continue to proclaim God's favour towards them in this new ministry, which is being bestowed upon you.

'So today, it is our privilege to pray for you, as the Lord Jesus calls you to a deeper life of grace, calls you to consecrate yourself to Him, His Church and His world, and to be His living love letter to all whom you meet.'

His grey eyes rested on her. Gone was the urgent neediness, the lust, the selfishness and confusion. Instead they were clear pools of love and affection. Knowing she would never look into them again, Grace held his gaze, taking a mental snapshot and tucking it away in her heart.

As all the bishops laid their hands upon her to consecrate her, tears sprang to her eyes and trickled down her face. *Why am I crying? I didn't even want to be a bishop ... I'm not ambitious ... it doesn't mean that much to me ...* But from deep within her heart came the response: *This is who you really are and have always been. You just didn't know it.*

Joy overwhelmed her.

Archbishop Justin prayed, 'Send down the Holy Spirit on Grace for the office and work of a bishop in your Church.'

The 'Amen,' reverberated around her like cannon fire.

❋ ❋ ❋

The after-party went on into the night. The girls from My Sister's House really let their hair down. Grace laughed until her sides ached. It was 2.30 a.m. when the taxi dropped them home.

'I'll be up in a minute,' Grace said to Peter as he climbed the stairs with Zack.

'Yeah, right!' Peter grinned. 'I know you – you're going to start writing or something.'

'Maybe ... just want to savour the day.'

'Okay Bishette – night-night,' he blew her a kiss.

She smiled as she shook her head, walking to her study. When she got there, she closed the door behind her, got down on her knees and laid her forehead on the floor. *Thank you, thank you, thank you,* she prayed. She stayed like that for a while. When she got up, she saw stars and had to quickly sit down. It took a moment for her vision to clear, but when it did she opened her laptop and went to the last bit of Ephesians and to her story.

The armour of God – the struggle against evil – the call to stand and after you've done everything to keep standing – to keep fearlessly making the Gospel known ...Ah, Lord, thank you for helping me so far. Help me now.

She thought of the Church in Ephesus – recovering from disunity and deception; of Lila and Timothy pursuing their loved ones, against all the odds; of Mary – not knowing if she would ever see hers again; of Joshua – praying in the Temple as the Romans surrounded Jerusalem; of Anna – out of her mind with grief, deceived and disillusioned – risking her life to find her brother, the only one she still trusted.

She wanted to finish her story along with this chapter of her life. She knew she would soon no longer have the luxury of free time in which to write. Her new role would demand all her focus, energy and time. She sighed as she sat down at her desk.

AD 70

If the apostle was surprised to see Anna that morning, she did not show it. Instead she eagerly asked for news of her mother. Anna was not very forthcoming and it became quite clear to Junia that there was something terribly wrong with her. She watched her carefully as she listened to her explain her plan to go to Jerusalem and bring Joshua back. It did not take long for Junia to discern Anna's despair, grief and confusion. It reminded her much of her own mother's grief after Phillip had died. She gave her a donkey and cart and sent her on her way, despite her misgivings.

Anna and the manservant arrived in Jerusalem in the afternoon. She knew exactly where to find her brother, so without resting, left the servant with the donkey and cart amongst the crowds at the foot of the Golden Gate steps.

When she reached the top she stopped to catch her breath and surveyed the city and the surrounding countryside. It was only then that she saw the dust cloud on every side. As she strained to see, she realised that a vast army was approaching. The watchmen in the watchtowers began shouting and soon men were running to the walls to get a better look at what was about to befall them.

The Romans closed in around the walled city straddling its two craggy mountains. It was only as they encircled the city that the Jewish rebel warlords stopped their in-fighting. They met together that evening to unite their 21,000 warriors to face their enemy together.

Urgently Anna ran through the Golden Gate, the Outer Court, through the Beautiful Gate and into the Court of the Women. She reached the entrance to the Court of Israel (of men), pulled her shawl further down round her face and, because of the chaos around her, dared to step into the domain that had been forbidden to her all her life. No one challenged her or even seemed to notice. She began calling Joshua's name as she looked for him, eventually finding him kneeling, lost in prayer, between the altar and the steps that went up to the Holy Place.

She took him by the shoulders and shook him, 'Joshua!' she shouted.

His eyes flew open as he returned to the present. He gazed up at her in a daze, 'Anna? Are you really here? Are you a vision?' he asked.

'I'm as real as that army out there,' she shouted and pointed.

'Oh it's so good to see you,' her brother said in a rush, jumping to his feet and hugging her tightly. 'What army?' he asked as he drew back to look at her.

'The Romans are surrounding Jerusalem as we speak,' she said, her heart pounding.

He looked about, listening to the sounds of men preparing for war. 'As I thought,' he sighed, his eyes returning to her face. 'How did you get here? Didn't you know how dangerous it would be?'

'If you knew how dangerous it would be, why did you come?' she demanded angrily. 'I had to see you,' she pulled back from him and held his dear face in her hands. 'You're the only one I trust. I had to find you,' she cried.

'Sweet Anna – you have suffered so greatly – I hope following me here won't bring more suffering,' he looked around at the ominous preparations for war.

'Oh Joshua, we are not safe.'

'Don't be afraid, sweet sister. We are in the Lord's hands. There is no safer place.'

She gazed at him longing to be able to believe like that again, but she knew she couldn't.

❊ ❊ ❊

When their ship docked Lila and Timothy went straight to Junia for assistance. On hearing their story of recent events she nodded her head, 'She did come to me. I could see she was very disturbed – not herself at all. I did not let her know it because I didn't want to frighten her with too much challenge. I gave her a donkey and cart. She must be there by now.'

'Can you get us a horse?' Timothy asked.

'Won't you stay here and rest? You look exhausted. You probably won't make it to the city in time before they close the gates for the night,' Junia's concern was real.

'No – we must get there tonight. If we had a good horse, I know we could make it. Can you help us?'

Andronicus and Junia bought them a horse. It wasn't long before they were saddling the beautiful, glossy creature. 'We will return it with interest,' Lila promised as she climbed up behind Timothy.

'No – it is a gift Lila, shalom!' Junia cried as they galloped away.

It wasn't until they were in sight of the city that they saw ahead of them the ranks of Roman legionaries. Appalled, they both began praying that somehow they would be able to pass them without being seen or stopped. When they reached a craggy pass, they saw a gap between the ranks, and under the cover of dusk they somehow made it through without being noticed. They continued praying fervently the whole way, expecting at any moment to hear the zinging sound of arrows behind them.

They reached the city walls just as the gates were being closed. They left the horse with the gatekeeper, hoping what they paid him was enough money to keep the animal alive. Walking through Jerusalem's darkened streets there was little sense of safety. They reached the Golden Gate steps and passed an old man with a donkey and cart. Timothy turned and asked him who he was waiting for, but the man was evasive. Timothy came back down a few steps and said, 'Is the name of your mistress Anna and have you come from Ephesus?'

He saw his answer immediately in the old man's eyes. 'I am her husband and I have come to bring her home. I hope that you will cooperate with me so that we may speed our return to safety?'

The servant nodded earnestly and swore his loyalty to Timothy.

Timothy turned and took the steps two at a time, overtaking Lila and leaving her to follow behind. He was gasping for breath by the time he reached the top.

The Temple Guard did not challenge them.

It took a while but they eventually found Anna and Joshua in Solomon's colonnade, wrapped in shawls, sleeping side by side on the warm marble floor.

Exuberant at seeing his wife's face again, Timothy leaned his back against a huge column and slowly slid to the floor in relief. Lila dropped to her knees bowing her head until it rested on the ground, giving thanks, then lay down next to them. Timothy watched over them through the night.

As dawn stroked the sky, Anna stirred, opening her eyes. Her gaze fell on Timothy.

In that precognisant moment, he saw the old Anna looking at him with tender love and affection. But then her conscious mind took over and she sat up abruptly, 'What? ... How? ... How did you find me? When did you get here? The Romans? How did you get through?'

He smiled and slowly slid closer to her. Not too close so as not to frighten her, but close enough to talk quietly with her. 'I had a dream telling me you had left Ephesus on a ship,' he said softly. 'I went to Aaron's house and found you had gone. He was dying. Before he passed he told me that you had come here.'

'Dying? My father?' Anna looked incredulous.

'Yes – he asked us to pray with him ....'

'Us?' Anna asked in a far-a-way voice.

'Your mother and I,' he gestured to Lila's body on the other side of Joshua. Anna's eyes widened further. 'We made our peace with him. We enabled him to go gently to God.'

'Oh ....' Anna said in a small voice, her eyes round and unblinking. Slowly the tears filled them and spilled over their rims and down her smooth cheeks.

'Dear heart – I'm so sorry – you have been through so much. I can't believe you came all this way! You are amazing!' Timothy's own eyes welled with tears. 'When did you last eat?' he asked.

'I don't know,' she replied absently, 'yesterday morning?'

He pulled out a leather pouch from his side and opened it. He gave her some bread and figs. As they ate slowly watching the sunrise, Joshua woke up. He rolled over and stretched, hitting Lila in the face with an outstretched hand. Surprised he jerked his head round to see who it was. Lila raised her head with a huge grin on her face.

'Mama!' he exclaimed. 'What are you doing here?'

'Wild horses couldn't have kept me from my children!' she declared.

'It's true,' Timothy nodded and laughed. 'You know what she's like.'

'But it's such a long journey and it's so dangerous ... you should have stayed in Ephesus,' Joshua wrapped an arm around his mother's neck.

'What point is there in me being safe when my children are not?' she asked gazing into Anna's eyes over Joshua's shoulder.

'Oh, Mama,' Anna whispered biting her lip.

'Now we can all intercede together for our people and this great city,' Joshua said as he sat up and took a sticky fig from his brother-in-law's outstretched hand.

'I was hoping we could get out as quickly as possible and back to Ephesus,' Timothy replied with some feeling.

'I don't think we will be able to – the city is completely surrounded,' said Anna.

※　※　※

Anna was right. They had defied Rome for almost five years from the heights of their fortified city. But the Jews had not reckoned on Titus's ambition and persistence. Not only did he command a vast army, but also siege engines and catapults, which overcame the outer wall within fifteen days. He led a thousand legionaries into the maze of Jerusalem's markets and stormed the second wall. The rebels pushed them back, but the Romans retook the wall immediately. Then Titus paraded his army in all its glory before Jerusalem.

As they watched from the wall, Anna whispered, 'How long will this go on?'

'I see no sign of the warlords surrendering,' Timothy replied, his arm protectively around her shoulders. 'They are defiant, no matter how much the people suffer. I fear it is going to be a battle to the bitter end.'

Lila looked at her daughter's profile. She thought of her grandchildren far away in Ephesus with Mary. She wondered if Anna's maternal feelings had begun to stir again. Surely the numbness and detachment of grief must pass soon? But still Anna did not speak of them or refer to life before she'd discovered Aaron was her father. She was still diffident towards Lila, although she seemed to have softened towards Timothy. She only truly came alive when she was talking with her brother.

It was late June when Joshua finally challenged her. They were watching the Romans as they completed the wall they had been building around the city.

'There is no hope for us now,' Anna said dully. 'We shall starve to death here.'

'No, sister, we shall not. You will return to your children and grow old in safety.'

'How can you be so certain?' Anna turned her harrowed eyes upon him.

'I don't know – I just am,' he smiled.

'I wish I could believe as you do, Shua. My faith has gone ... died ....'

'No, Anna, it is just resting. It has endured the death of our father, the devastating loss of your child and the revelation concerning Aaron. Just like a farmer leaves a field to lie fallow for a time ... so it is with your faith. The Lord is the author and finisher of it, and he will restore you in His good time.'

Anna gazed out past the Roman wall, blinking back tears. 'But I don't know if I want it back. Everything I believed was a lie.'

'Like what?' Joshua asked, knowing the answer full well.

'Like Jair was *my* father; like God would protect and bless my children; like my mother was not an adulteress nor I a bastard!' she said bitterly.

Joshua said nothing. He watched two legionaries lift a huge stone and place it carefully on the nearly completed wall. 'And what of Jesus?' he asked simply.

When she looked at him, he saw the anguish and conflict in her eyes. She didn't speak, but turned and left him. As he watched her go, he realized how painfully thin she had become and his heart ached for her.

When the Romans completed their wall, Titus stormed the Antonia Fortress and razed it to the ground, except for one tower where he set up his command post. By mid-summer the city's food reserves were almost gone.

Joshua became ill. Lila stayed with him, leaving the hunt for food to fall on Anna and Timothy's shoulders. They had run out of money long ago. Daily Lila prayed they would be guided and most days they found something, but occasionally by the time night fell they had eaten nothing.

Hunger stalked Jerusalem's streets. Armed gangs prowled for food. Locked doors suggesting hidden provisions were broken down and the rebels drove stakes up their victims' rectums to force them to reveal their stores of grain. Neighbour denounced neighbour as hoarders and traitors. The young wandered the streets with swollen bellies. Famine devoured whole families, leaving their corpses with dry eyes and open mouths. The streets were heaped with dead bodies, despite Jewish burial laws. Soon the rebels were probing and dissecting the dead for gold, crumbs of bread or seeds. They were reduced to eating leather, hay and even cow-dung.

Finally Titus declared that preserving the Temple had become too costly. One night at the end of July he ordered that the huge silver plated Temple doors be burned. That night the fire, spread by the molten silver, engulfed the Temple so that all the wooden windows and doors, tapestries and curtains caught alight.

Anna woke, choking on acrid smoke. She looked about her and saw that the Holy of Holies was on fire. She covered her mouth with her headscarf and shook the others awake.

'Shua! Wake up! Wake up!' she pleaded. So depleted was he by illness, he did not stir. Lila lifted his head into her arms and covered his mouth and nose with her shawl.

As Anna watched, a wave of love swept through her. Mother and daughter reconciled as their eyes met. In that moment Lila knew that she had been forgiven for her past and for hiding the truth from her daughter. A tear carved a pale path down her blackened face. Anna crawled over to her and kissed her cheek.

Timothy looked on in wonder at the answer to his prayers. Anna crawled round Joshua and curled up against Timothy. He stroked her head and whispered, 'We are in the Lord's hands, my love.' They huddled among those both living and dead who were barricaded in the Inner Court. They could do nothing but helplessly watch in horror as the fire consumed all that had been holy to their people.

The fighting raged around them amongst the flames. Over a thousand rebels stood on the steps of the altar to fight. In the end most of their throats were cut by the blood- drunk Romans as though it were a mass human sacrifice. Ten thousand died that night in the Temple courts. Unable to move and totally desensitised, Lila, Anna and Timothy watched as legionaries gleefully trampled corpses in their triumph and plundered the Temple treasury before setting fire to the rest of the complex.

As the next day dawned, the Romans searched among the dead for the living, taking them prisoner. Encumbered by an unconscious Joshua, Lila, Anna and Timothy could not run. They were dragged out and bound roughly together to await their fate. Those who had the power and opportunity to do so broke through the Roman lines and into the city. Titus sent the cavalry after them to finish them off.

In utter dismay they watched as the Romans carried their eagles onto the Holy Mount, sacrificed to their gods and hailed Titus as their great commander-in-chief. All the Temple priests were executed, as it seemed fitting to Titus that the priests perish with their Temple.

'He was so sure we would be saved,' Anna whispered to her mother, her head resting on her shoulder. 'I'm glad he is not conscious to see this. I hope he dies before they feed us to the lions.'

Lila's head rolled towards her daughters. She kissed the top of it weakly, 'Fix your eyes on Jesus, Anna. He is the author and finisher of our faith. For the joy set before him, he endured the cross, scorning its shame and sat down at the right hand of God. Consider him, so that you will not grow weary and lose heart, my love.'

On hearing this, a wan smile broke out on Timothy's face. He was slumped against the wall on the other side of Anna. 'Spoken like a true daughter of Abraham,' he said in a cracked voice.

Jesus ... Anna prayed, *help us to endure, help us to stand firm until the end.* She found herself spilling over into her prayer language, which she had not used for a long, long time.

Within her skin and bones she felt a shift occur. It reminded her of the time she had fallen and banged her head as a child. The world had spun and moved like the ocean. She had been violently sick. When her vision finally cleared and the spinning stopped, it had been a huge relief. That's how she felt now ... just like that ... all of a sudden. She looked at her mother, 'Thank you Mama ... that is just what I needed to hear.'

Lila returned her gaze, wordlessly pouring out all the love she could upon her.

'At least now as prisoners, we will be fed and watered,' Timothy said hopefully.

※　※　※

A few rebels still survived in the labyrinthine tunnels under Jerusalem. They took control of the Upper City to the west. It took Titus another month to conquer the rest of Jerusalem. When it fell the legionaries poured into the streets and massacred indiscriminately and burned every house. At night the killing stopped, but the fire raged on in the streets. Then Titus ordered the plundering of the Lower City, pushing the remaining warlords back to Herod's Palace. In mid-August the Romans stormed it. John of Gishala finally surrendered and then Simon ben Giora emerged in a white robe from a tunnel under the Temple. He was assigned a starring role in Titus' Triumph in Rome.

Josephus, who had been recording Titus' victory over Jerusalem, was given permission to search through the prisoners in the Temple courtyards. As he looked for family and friends, Anna caught his eye. He took her chin in his hand and turned her face this way and that, in the searing sunshine. 'Who is your father?' he asked.

With what little strength she had left, she lifted her chin away from his grasp and gave him Aaron's full name.

A look of grief mixed with guilt filled his eyes at the name of his friend. 'You have his eyes,' he said. 'I will ask Titus to release you and your family.' He could no longer meet her gaze. 'Wait here. It won't be long now.' He turned and gave instructions to the legionary who attended him.

Emaciated, weak and traumatised, they were given safe passage to Caesarea on a donkey-drawn cart. When they reached Junia's door it was Lila who knocked. 'Lila? Oh, dear Lord!' Junia exclaimed taking her into her arms. 'Is it really you? I thought you were dead! How did you survive?' she said looking over her shoulder to the others in the cart. 'Is that Joshua?' she asked in disbelief at the shrunken body wrapped in a shawl.

'Yes, it is … he's alive, but only just,' Timothy said as he climbed down out of the cart and carefully lifted Joshua into his arms.

'Come – come in!' Junia ushered them into her courtyard. She began calling urgently for Andronicus.

※　※　※

'Come with us,' Lila urged.

'But the Lord has called us to Israel,' Junia replied.

'But is He still calling you here?' Lila persisted.

Junia looked dubious, 'With the Roman conquest we have been wondering and praying.'

'There is much to do in Ephesus.'

'There is always much to do everywhere,' Junia countered.

Lila smiled.

Then Anna said, 'You need to know that I played a part in developing false teaching in the Church. We have much to do on our return to put this right, especially where the women are concerned. We could do with your apostolic leadership.'

Junia studied Anna's thin face, 'Well let's see, shall we. You can't sail until you are all strong enough, so perhaps the Lord will have shown us what to do by the time you are ready. I know my other sisters are eager to be with Mama again. We have talked many times about us all moving together to Ephesus, but something has always held us back.'

※　※　※

Mary's eyesight had deteriorated over the last year. As news had filtered through of the terrible atrocities being committed in Israel, she had spent many a tear-drenched night in prayer for her daughters, for Lila and for the others. The uncertainty of waiting daily for news had been intolerable, but she had borne it well for the sake of Anna's children.

The Church had rallied to them, led by Ruth, Oni, Priscilla and Aquilla. A day had not gone by when a kindness of one sort or nother hadn't come their way: a meal cooked; the children taken on an outing; flowers left at their door.

Mary had come to love many in the Ephesian Church like they were her own flesh and blood. But it didn't stop the deep pain of loss in her soul.

She had just finished baking bread one morning, when a messenger arrived with a letter from Caesarea. She struggled to undo the outer casing as her hands were trembling terribly. Excitedly she called Sol, who came running from the courtyard where he had been playing with the younger children. 'Read this for me,' she asked handing the scroll to him.

He took it obediently and spread it on the kitchen table. 'It's from Junia, your daughter.'

Mary clutched the side of the table, her knuckles whitening. 'What does she say?' her voice was barely audible.

Dear Mama,

I am writing with good news.

After many months of hearing nothing but stories of disaster from Jerusalem, Lila, Anna, Timothy and Joshua arrived safely at our door.

They were all shades of their former selves, especially Joshua, but we have been nursing them back to health. The Church in Caesarea has been so generous in their outpourings of love towards them. You and Papa would be very proud!

They are all well enough to travel now so we will be setting sail for Ephesus in two days' time. It will be a three-day journey.

We hope you will meet us at the harbour.

We are all so eager to be with you.

Anna asks especially that you tell the children she loves them and cannot wait to be with them again.

At this last sentence Sol's voice broke and his face crumpled.

'Oh, Sol,' Mary moved round the table and took him into her arms.

※　※　※

Having given them up for dead, Mary and the children wept and laughed and sang all the way through the city's streets, to the harbour. They watched as the ship came in, Sol describing to Mary everything he could see. 'I see Grandma and look, there's Mama and Papa – look! Papa!' he shouted and waved furiously, unable to contain himself.

Mary squinted, shading her eyes, hoping to catch her first glimpse of them. Who else was with them? Was Junia? 'Is anyone else with them?' she asked.

'I don't know,' Sol replied distractedly.

'Oh, I wish I could see!' Mary said in exasperation.

When they finally disembarked the children were in a frenzy of excitement. Timothy ushered Anna first over the gangplank. She knelt down on the harbour side as her children gathered round her. Tentative at first and then suddenly they engulfed her in joyful, tearful embrace.

Lila and Joshua followed, 'Oh, Mary, it is so good to see you again. I thought I never would,' Lila cried, hugging her friend.

'I know, neither did I!' Mary laughed. 'Did anyone else come with you?' she asked, looking over her friend's shoulder hopefully. 'It's only that Junia said "we" in her letter.'

With a twinkle in her eye, Lila drew Mary towards the gangplank, 'Since you ask, yes ....'

And with that all four of Mary's daughters appeared. It was clear that they had practiced this surprise many times on their journey.

'Junia? Is it really you?' Mary cried, blinking and squinting up at her eldest daughter.

'Yes, Mama – and look who else has come.'

※　※　※

Titus decided to raze Jerusalem to the ground, just as Jesus had predicted. Toppling Herod the Great's awesome monument was a feat of engineering in itself, but the rubble and wreckage was successfully dumped in the valley between the Temple and the Upper City. Only the Western Wall survived.

When he had completed that, Titus began his victory tour, starting in Caesarea Philippi, where he watched thousands of Jewish prisoners fight each other or fight wild animals to the death. A few days later he saw 2,500 killed in the circus at Caesarea Maritima and yet more in Beirut before returning to Rome to complete his Triumph.

With the destruction of the Temple, Christians all over the known world began to believe that the Jews had lost the favour of God. They developed a replacement theology, believing that Christians were now the rightful heirs to the Jewish heritage.

Ironically five hundred years later Muhammad founded his new religion based on Jewish traditions, praying towards Jerusalem and revering the Jewish prophets. He too saw the destruction of the Temple as proof that God had withdrawn his blessing from the Jews and bestowed it on Islam.

Two thousand years later Jews, Christians and Muslims all still look to Jerusalem for the final Biblical prophecies to be fulfilled:

'In the last days the mountain of the Lord's temple will be established as the highest of the mountains; it will be exalted above the hills, and all nations will stream to it. Many peoples will come and say, "Come, let us go up to the mountain of the Lord, to the temple of the God of Jacob. He will teach us his ways, so that we may walk in his paths."

'The law will go out from Zion, the word of the Lord from Jerusalem. He will judge between the nations and will settle disputes for many peoples. They will beat their swords into ploughshares and their spears into pruning hooks. Nation will not take up sword against nation, nor will they train for war anymore.

As we watch and wait, praying for the peace of Jerusalem, pray that more and more people of all faiths or none will be able to say, "Blessed is he who comes in the name of the Lord."

Then we will see him again – the Prince of Peace – coming to establish his kingdom on the earth. Then there will be no more crying, or sorrow or death, for he will wipe every tear from our eyes.'